**"When you stand in front of the fire,
I can see your body through your nightdress."**

"Good," Rebecca said. "Then look at me. It is what you want to do, is it not?"

"Becca . . . please. Go back to bed. Perhaps we can talk tomorrow."

Rebecca inhaled deeply.

"I should like it if you made love to me."

His hand still shading his eyes, Connor gave a short laugh.

"And how on earth would you know that, wee Becca?"

She struggled to keep her voice even. "Perhaps it makes you feel less afraid to treat me as a child, but I know for certain you do not see me as one."

Afraid. He looked at her then, helplessly. The firelight illuminated her through her nightdress, the heart-stopping curve of her breasts and hips, the long shadows of her legs. Something caught in his throat.

"You do not know who I am . . ." he faltered.

"Connor, I know you are something more than you claim to be. You are Irish one moment and as English as Wellington the next . . . but it matters little. I think I know the man you are, perhaps better than anyone."

She moved away from the hearth and stood next to him. His arms, as if of their own accord, reached up for her . . .

Please turn to the back of this book for a preview of Julie Anne Long's next novel, *To Love a Thief*, available April 2005.

PR

THE Runaway Duke

JULIE ANNE LONG

WARNER
FOREVER

NEW YORK   BOSTON

Copyright © 2004 by Julie Anne Long
Excerpt from *To Love a Thief* copyright © 2004 by Julie Anne Long

Warner Forever is a registered trademark of Warner Books, Inc.

Cover design by Diane Luger
Cover illustration by Alan Ayers
Hand lettering by David Gatti
Book design by Giorgetta Bell McRee

Warner Books

Time Warner Book Group
1271 Avenue of the Americas
New York, NY 10020
Visit our Web site at www.twbookmark.com.

Printed in the United States of America

First Paperback Printing: August 2004

10 9 8 7 6 5 4 3 2 1

*To Daveed, dear friend, witty malcontent,
fellow survivor of the corporate trenches—you cheered me
on from the very beginning, and look what happened!*

Acknowledgements

Throughout this process I benefited from the astounding generosity and support of so many people . . . my undying gratitude goes to Elizabeth Pomada, agent extraordinaire, who believed in me and found such a wonderful home for my novel; to Beth de Guzman and Melanie Murray at Warner, for their heady enthusiasm for *The Runaway Duke*—and Melanie, I can't thank you enough for your patience, guidance, and humor. I'm so glad you're my editor! And a special thank you to Diane Luger and Mimi Bark at Warner, too, for my beautiful cover. I feel blessed to be a Warner author.

And then there are the folks who kept me sane throughout:

Thanks to Lisa Martin, best bud, sister (at heart) and master craftswoman—what on *earth* would I do without you, Lis? To David George, for loving the story from the very beginning, which pretty much guaranteed I'd finish writing it; to Ken Mierow, for graciously allowing his brain to be ruthlessly picked and for always, *always* knowing the right thing to say; to Doreen DeSalvo, for her humor and stellar feedback and friendship—I'm so glad *The Runaway Duke* brought you into my life, Doreen! To Steve Czerniak, for his ever-cheerful blunt appraisal, support and laughter—you're a true pal, Esteban. To my sis Karen Crist and to Melisa Phillips, for endless encouragement and endless listening. And to Chris . . . just because.

And to everyone else out there who ever said something kind or positive or supportive: I'm living proof that your words made a difference. I hope you know who you are, and my deep appreciation goes to all of you, too.

Prologue

~

June 1815

He was dreaming, or he was awake; he couldn't be certain anymore. Smoke and gunpowder scorched his lungs. His musket, slippery with sweat where his fist clutched it, was hotter than his lungs, and nearly slipped his grip as he fumbled to reload. His legs and arms had gone numb from exhaustion, and the sounds raging around him—screams of horses and men, the clash of metal, the thud of boots, the boom of cannons—pulsed, collided, fused into one sound. From somewhere within that one sound an echo of hideous pain howled, distinct, relentless.

"Son? Can you hear me, son?"

Someone grabbed him by his hair, grown long during the endless weeks of marching, and yanked his head back; he looked into the cold glinting eyes of his father, who threw him to the ground and kicked him in the ribs. And when he curled his arms around his knees to protect himself, his father kicked him again, and again, and then pulled him to his feet, because it infuriated his father when he could not see in his son's eyes the pain he was inflicting. And then his father let him go, and when he looked up again, still fumbling to load his gun, he saw Roddy Campbell take a musket ball in the gut; saw the blood fountaining from him, saw Roddy flying backward to lie like so many others on the field, no longer a laughing Irishman who occasionally cheated at cards and always missed his mother, but a pile of rags and bones and meat.

"Tell us your name, lad," *came the voice again, a sound disconnected from the wall of raging noise, soft but excruciating and unwelcome, because it wanted to drag him closer to the surface, where the pain was.*

"I don't think he can hear you, Doctor. I was able to give him some of the bark water, but the fever seems to have him now."

"Roddy," *he gasped.* "Roddy." *It seemed important to tell the voice about Roddy. Someone should know, someone should acknowledge his fall.*

"What did he say just then?"

"I believe we have our answer. He said 'Roddy.' "

The doctor dropped his head to his chest with a deep sigh, then quickly lifted it again. Gestures of resignation and loss were indulgences here. He could afford them only sparingly.

"If this is Roddy Campbell, then the lad with his chest blown in must be young Blackburn. First name Roarke, according to Pierce, then a half-dozen other names, like any proper nobleman. Dunbrooke's heir. We've lost the future Duke of Dunbrooke here tonight."

"Oh," said the woman, a sigh. They turned to look at the body of the young man whose face they had just covered. Awe of the aristocracy had been bred into the English bone for centuries, and even now, surrounded by the blood and misery of Waterloo, they mourned more than perhaps they ought to for the dead young man, simply because he was the eldest son of a very wealthy duke.

"Word has it that he enraged the duke by serving at all, let alone in the infantry," the doctor said. "Bloody rash young fool. Send a messenger to Colonel Pierce—he personally saw these two lads loaded onto the hospital cart. He was fond of Dunbrooke. The rest of their regiment is dead on the field."

"Does the duke have any other sons?"

"One other. Word is the younger son's a bit of a rake-hell."

"I'll pray for young Roarke Blackburn's soul, then, may he rest in peace. Do you think Campbell will live?"

"If he survives this fever, yes, he will live, or at least it won't be his leg that kills him. Give him some more of the Peruvian bark water when he'll take it. The ball missed the bone, so he'll likely keep his leg. Lucky chap, unlike his friend."

His fever broke the next day and the searing pain in his leg became all too real evidence that he was alive. He opened his eyes to the shy, kind smile of the woman kneeling next to him—was this her house? It was a farmhouse, and bodies of soldiers—dead, dying, struggling to live— lined the floors, and the stench of suffering thickened the air. The woman offered him some water and called him "Roddy." And as he had decided somewhere in his fitful sleep that his life thus far had been nothing but battles and that if he lived he would never do battle again, he saw this as a sign from God. He thanked God for the innate resourcefulness that allowed him to recognize an opportunity when it reared before him. He silently thanked his father for the cool control he had at his command, a control that had been forged from violence and manipulation. He thanked Wellington, who cared little what his men wore on their backs as long as they fought well and bravely, for no one would be able to identify him from his uniform. And he thanked Roddy Campbell for the temporary loan of his name, and was certain that Campbell would have been thoroughly amused.

In the chaos of Waterloo's aftermath, it was easy to become someone else. When he was able to limp out of the makeshift battlefield hospital and away from the horrors wrought by Napoleon and his own countrymen, Roarke Blackburn, now known as Roddy Campbell, boarded a ship for England and disappeared into the English countryside, to a life empty of everything but the freedom to choose what came next. At the first pub he encountered, he offered a final silent prayer of gratitude and a toast to his unlucky friend, then retired Roddy Campbell's name. He had decided to use two of his own names; since he had so many to choose from, it seemed the right thing to do.

Roarke Blackburn is dead, *he thought with a smile, and toasted himself.* Long live Connor Riordan.

June 1816

"Jenkins—I mean, Riordan—may I beg a favor of you, m'boy?"

Connor stifled a smile and looked up from the saddle he was polishing. Imagine Sir Henry Tremaine "begging a favor" of his head groom. But Sir Henry was like that: kind and respectful, if absentminded—occasionally Sir Henry called him Jenkins, who was the gardener, and he called the gardener Riordan. Connor merely considered the extra layer of anonymity afforded by Sir Henry's forgetfulness an added benefit of his employment. They'd met in a country pub a week or so before—Sir Henry had mistaken Connor for an Irish laborer, which was precisely what Connor intended to be mistaken for—and they had begun talking about horses, a comfortable, manly topic. At last, filled with bonhomie and ale, impressed with Connor's extensive equine knowledge, Sir Henry had impulsively offered him a job. *Why not?* Connor had thought. He knew horses; he had been wandering aimlessly for nearly a year. Some structure to his day, a kind employer, a small but sufficient wage . . . it had seemed like the perfect way to bide his time until he knew what he intended to do for the rest of his life.

"A favor, sir? But of course. How can I be of assistance to ye?"

"Well, 'tis my daughter, you see . . ."

"Your daughter, sir?"

"My youngest. Rebecca. She's in a tree. Something to do with a hound."

It seemed that Daisy, a big old brown hound Connor had met just a day ago, had died in her sleep during the night. Shredded with grief, Rebecca had taken to the largest apple tree in the orchard shortly after breakfast. Suppertime was growing nigh, and she showed no signs of desiring to set foot on the ground ever again, regardless of the shouted coaxing that her mama and papa had done from below.

"I'm not as spry as I once was, Riordan, and I wondered

if you'd mind going up after her? She's a stubborn little thing, and a bit of a hoyden at times, but very dear in her way."

Connor had a soft spot for stubborn hoydens. "I'll have a go at it, sir."

He followed Sir Henry to the tree, an impressive tree to be sure; it sprang up out of the ground like an immense gnarled hand. He scaled it and found a pale, redheaded twig of a girl, all long limbs, fierce expression, and tear-streaked cheeks, huddled on a thick branch.

"Who are *you*?" she demanded imperiously, sniffling, when his dark head came into view.

"I'm Connor Riordan, m'lady. I work with your da's horses in the stables. I understand you are Rebecca. Pleased to make your acquaintance."

"Oh! Pleased to make your acquaintance, Mr. Riordan." Connor smiled; her startled imperiousness had given way to politeness, as though she was loath to make anyone feel unwelcome. "You're not English, are you?"

"No, m'lady. Irish as St. Patrick."

Rebecca nodded, studying him curiously now.

" 'Tis a sad thing about Daisy, eh, lass? She was a fine hound. I liked her very much."

"You met her?" Rebecca asked, half hopeful, half suspicious. Her eyes began to tear again.

"Oh, yes, I had the pleasure of making her acquaintance yesterday. She had very kind eyes, a lot of gray around her muzzle, and a particularly nice smile for a dog. She looked a bit tired, but happy to meet me."

Rebecca began blinking rapidly, because the tears were coming again, but she laughed a little, too. "Her back legs hurt her, and she couldn't see very well anymore, and she had more gray fur than brown on her face. I think you are right—she *was* very tired. But she was my best friend, and I will miss her very much."

"Oh, you are a lucky lass then, if you were her best friend. Daisy was very lucky, too, to have you for a friend. And she's lucky to have folks who miss her. I wish I could have known her better."

Rebecca nodded somberly, reflecting on this philosophy.

"What do you think Daisy is doing now?" she asked in a near whisper, as if fearing the answer.

"Oh, she's most definitely in heaven, Rebecca, chasing her tail, and maybe some rabbits, too, and every now and then she catches one. But they have an agreement, she and the rabbits—it's just a game of tag, no eating allowed. She has the hind legs of a pup. She'll have scraps from God's dinner table every night."

Rebecca laughed again, then swiped the back of her hand across her eyes. She looked a little relieved at his answer.

"The vicar isn't certain whether animals go to heaven," Rebecca mused. "But I thought that Daisy might."

"I will tell you a secret, Miss Tremaine: vicars do not always know the answers to the big questions. But do not tell the vicar that I told you that."

Rebecca nodded. "I believe you are right. Our vicar doesn't seem to like it when I ask questions, but I cannot help it. There's so much that wants questioning."

"I'll wager you ask *excellent* questions," Connor said with a grin.

Rebecca nodded somberly, as if this went without saying.

"Did you know your da bought a new horse today? A young Arabian colt, name of Maharajah. A big gray fellow. I think we all need to make him feel welcome. Would you like to meet him?"

After a moment of reflection, Rebecca nodded, and Connor held out his arms, an eyebrow cocked.

"I can get down on my own," she said with an indignant sniffle.

"I know, lass, but you're tired, aye? Everyone will think I'm a hero if they see me helping you down, and I'd like to impress your da, seeing as how I'm new here. What do you say? Will you help me out?"

Rebecca smiled, mulling this over. And at last, she gave in and trustingly hooked her hands around Connor's neck.

And so Connor shinnied down the tree with one arm wrapped protectively around the gangly little girl. She seemed to weigh barely anything at all.

Chapter One

❦

May 1820

A word, Rebecca."

Lady Tremaine stood on the stairs with a lit candle in hand, a sleeping cap pulled down over her graying curls. She was a short woman who had gone very round in her middle years, and her night robe was flamboyantly ruffled. The overall effect was usually endearing; tonight, however, it was simply terrifying. Above all those ruffles Lady Tremaine's mouth was a grim line, and her eyes were shining with unspilled tears.

"To bed with you, Lorelei. Come with me, Rebecca."

Rebecca, in her incriminating black clothing, followed her mother to the sitting room, her heart a frozen fist in her chest.

Her mother did not sit down, or invite Rebecca to sit. She merely turned to speak.

"Clearly I have failed you, Rebecca."

"Mama—" Rebecca began, pleading, but her mother raised her hand abruptly.

"No, it is quite clear that I have failed you. I think it can be fairly said that you are perhaps a special case, but it remains a mother's duty to give her daughter the skills she needs to fulfill her obligation in life. And I have tried—"

Here Lady Tremaine's voice broke, and one tear slipped from her eye. Rebecca watched, transfixed in dread, as the candlelight lit its path down her mother's cheek. She had seen exasperation on her mother's face before—many times before, truth be told—and frustration and anger, too, all a result of something she had done or failed to do. But she had never before made her mother cry.

"I have tried," Lady Tremaine continued, her composure regained, "to teach you modesty. And honesty. And gentleness. I have tried to demonstrate by my own actions the proper way to behave. I have tried to ensure that you could lay claim to at least a few ladylike refinements, such as the pianoforte or embroidery. And I have not undertaken this in order to punish you, Rebecca, though I am quite sure you have thought otherwise, but to protect you: a woman is nothing without a husband. For the sake of your future happiness and security, for the sake of your place in society, for the sake of your honor, I have attempted to teach you these things, so that when the time came you would be a suitable wife deserving of a suitable husband."

"Mama—" Rebecca tried again, a hoarse whisper. Lady Tremaine shook her head in warning. The tears were falling swiftly and silently now, and her voice had gone thick.

"And though you have a good heart, Rebecca, you have willfully resisted all of my teachings, which has caused me no end of distress. I am convinced that it is only through an accident of fate that you have not brought great shame down upon us. At this very moment, you can be certain that your father is securing your engagement to Lord Edelston. Your honor and the honor of your family will thus be protected, and Lorelei's prospects will not be threatened. You may count yourself fortunate that instead of becoming a social pariah and a burden on your family, you will become the wife of a baron. You may go to your room now. We will talk further in the morning."

An hour earlier . . .

It had been almost disappointingly easy to leave her bedroom just before midnight, creep down the stairs, tiptoe out through the kitchen, and dash across the back garden lawn to crouch behind the tall hedge near the fountain. Obviously, it had never occurred to her parents that one of their daughters might ever be tempted to do such a thing; they had retired hours earlier, and were no doubt already sleeping the sleep of the blissfully unaware. All the servants were safely in their beds and snoring, too; her own maid Letty, as usual, slept as though she'd been clubbed in the head. The entire estate seemed to be dreaming, dogs and horses included. Rebecca was satisfied that no one had witnessed her furtive excursion.

Her exultation at having successfully arrived at the fountain ebbed a bit, however, when she discovered that it was colder than she had anticipated. Although she had, quite cleverly, she thought, donned a pair of black gloves and a dark wool cloak and tucked her treacherously bright hair into a dark furry hat before she left the house, the chill was beginning to penetrate every last bit of her protective covering.

To distract herself, she exhaled extravagantly and admired the white cloud her breath made. There had been a very interesting article on vapor and condensation in one of her father's scientific journals, and Rebecca had been happily engrossed in it this afternoon in the library until her mother herded her into the solarium, where she was forced to poke at the pianoforte for the rest of the afternoon.

The midnight trap she had planned for her sister had promised to more than make up for the torture of pianoforte practice, but the midnight chill, as much as she hated to admit it, was proving daunting. She hoped her sister Lorelei would hurry up and appear and fall into the arms of Anthony, Lord Edelston, who, no doubt, was creeping across the lawn to the fountain at this very moment. Rebecca planned to leap out from behind the hedge with a hearty "ah-HA!" and thus buy freedom from future extortion by her sister.

It was quite by accident that Rebecca had overheard the exchange between the tall, golden-haired Lord Edelston and her fair sister, Lorelei, who, by the age of eighteen, had done her duty to her relieved parents by growing into precisely the sort of pristine beauty the ambitious name "Lorelei" implied. Lorelei was very nearly unnerving, with her silver-blond hair, pale blossom of a mouth, and enormous crystalline blue eyes fringed with the most unfair dark lashes. Rebecca's own lashes were a sort of pale chestnut, which she supposed matched her hair well enough and did nothing to detract from her own handsome gray-green eyes, but they simply lacked the drama of

Lorelei's. Rebecca sometimes feared her entire face lacked drama, which seemed to her a gross—or perhaps merciful—misrepresentation of what actually went on in her mind and heart.

Whereas Lorelei had inherited her mother's smooth refined oval of a face, Rebecca had inherited her bones from some more rugged ancestor: her cheekbones soared, her mouth was wide and plush, her nose was straight and strong and resolute, and her firm little chin had a dimple in it, for heaven's sake, exactly the size of the tip of her forefinger. When one considered them side by side, one could see that Lorelei and Rebecca were sisters, but Lorelei's hair seemed like something spun from silk and moonlight, while Rebecca's hair was merely numerous shades of red and rambunctiously curly to boot.

"Titian," her mother described it, optimistically; "That unfortunate red" is what Lorelei called it when they were sniping at each other, which was rather frequently.

Rebecca did not dislike her older sister, and Lorelei did not dislike Rebecca. They were, in fact, very fond of each other. But Rebecca was widely loved by the servants and the neighbors, partially because she was everything Lorelei was not: she laughed loudly and easily, she was curious, she read far more than a decently bred girl ought to read, she galloped her horse hard (astride, no less) and came home happily sweaty. She was affectionate and kind and immensely opinionated about things she should really know nothing about, but then Sir Henry Tremaine *was* a trifle careless about where he left his scientific journals.

She was, naturally, the bane of her mother's existence and affectionately tolerated by her father, who had taught her to shoot on a whim and then basically left her to her own devices, as she could never *really* be the boy he had always wanted. Both of her parents secretly despaired of finding a husband for Rebecca, let alone one with a title.

Lorelei, on the other hand, was typically regarded with the sort of nervous reverence her kind of beauty always inspired, and although she secretly reveled in the awe, she found herself increasingly unable to step out of her regal reserve. She had begun to regard her own beauty as something sacred that had been entrusted unto her safekeeping, and thus she felt obliged to treat herself with somber respect at all times. Lorelei was fully expected to make a spectacular titled marriage, and her mother never tired of pointing this out.

Consequently the Tremaine sisters were jealous of each other, which manifested in an ongoing exchange of blackmail threats that rarely reached their parents' ears, although the possibility was always tantalizingly present. Yesterday afternoon Lorelei had threatened to tell Sir Henry, their father, that Rebecca had been poring over the anatomy book he purposely kept on a very high shelf in the library. This was a serious threat, indeed, as the book had been forbidden to Rebecca, and punishment would no doubt be severe—she might even be deprived of her horse for a fortnight. And doubtless the book would then be spirited away forever, safe from Rebecca's voracious hunger for knowledge, and Rebecca would never learn the complete story of how blood circulates through the veins (it was much, *much* too late to protect her from the story of how babies were made).

In a sense, it was all her father's fault. Upon retirement, Sir Henry had indulged his long-denied interest in science and medicine by subscribing to any journal that could be had on the subjects. Rebecca had happened upon the journals one day in the library and waded into them cautiously, keeping a wary eye out for her mother.

She had never been more enthralled by anything in her life.

Shockingly matter-of-fact debates regarding whether musket balls should be left in wounds if they could not be retrieved easily, the best methods of amputation, the uses of mercury, words like "laudable pus" and "trepanning"—the journals were both appallingly, titillatingly gory and strangely reassuring. Human beings were subject to a staggering array of illnesses and disasters, but the fact that learned men could discusses such things in dispassionate detail made human frailty seem less mystical and frightening and more a matter of course, of philosophy, essential to the pattern of life itself. Whenever Rebecca encountered a word or the name of a body part with which she was unfamiliar, she referred to her father's anatomy book, and thus inadvertently gave herself a very unorthodox education.

As a consequence, Rebecca nursed a secret desire—or rather a semisecret desire—to be a doctor. She had broached the subject once at the breakfast table, and in light of the spasm of pain that had crossed her mother's face and the condescending bark of laughter it had surprised from her father, she had thought it best not to bring it up again. However, the desire remained, and had only increased in poignancy, as is the habit of all secret desires. Thus, this newest threat of Lorelei's required momentous ammunition by way of counteraction, and she had prayed hard for the appropriate solution.

Rebecca's prayers had been answered in an almost comically swift fashion. Anthony, Baron Edelston, who was staying with the nearby family of Squire Denslowe, had effortlessly and instantly fascinated all the young women in the area simply by behaving toward them the way every young rake in London behaved: politely resigned to boredom, ever-so-slightly tragic and languid, a slight hint of danger glinting in his eyes as he lingered a little too long over the hand of some lucky maiden. Rebecca thought he was handsome but somewhat repulsive. Why on earth anyone found his air of boredom and tragedy captivating was beyond her ken.

However, Lorelei was poised on the brink of her first London season and had yet to meet a man like Edelston. Her careful reserve soon proved no match for Edelston's cultivated indifference. Edelston, indeed, behaved as though Lorelei's sort was as common as the dandelions that sprinkled the garden lawn, and Lorelei found herself actually exerting herself in an attempt to charm.

As exertion was unfamiliar territory for Lorelei, she was in over her head rather rapidly. One moment Edelston was coolly surveying the room full of overly cheerful provincials over the top of Lorelei's moonlight-colored head; in the next moment, he had dropped his voice to a fierce murmur, suggesting a tryst in the back garden at midnight the following night. Rebecca, surreptitiously moving through the room, heard her sister murmur a shocking acquiescence.

Because it would be ever so much more satisfying—and much more potent an arrow in her blackmail quiver—to actually catch her sister in the outrageous act of meeting a young man at midnight, Rebecca had decided to precede the pair to the garden. If the two of them didn't appear soon, however, Rebecca decided she would return the way she came, as catching a chill was becoming a real threat. She clapped her mittened hands together to warm them and gazed up at the stars sprinkling the sky, picking out constellations to pass the time.

Sir Henry Tremaine had rheumatism in his left knee. It had made itself at home there after a hunting accident a few years ago, and every now and again, particularly on chilly nights, it plagued him mercilessly. It was plaguing him tonight, and he had lain awake long enough. Careful not to disturb his sleeping wife, he slid out of bed, slipped into his robe, and lit a candle to light his way to the library, which was where he kept the brandy. From experience, he knew that a quickly bolted glass would muffle the pain long enough to allow him to sleep.

But halfway down the stairs, Sir Henry caught a glimpse of a pale head of hair and a swirl of dark skirts. Astonishingly, Lorelei appeared to be exiting the house through the kitchen. At *midnight*. In seeming deference to his shock, his throbbing knee went quiet. Sir Henry decided the brandy could wait. He stealthily followed his daughter outside.

Tom Jenkins, the Tremaines' gardener, was arriving home from The White Sow, the best place in the village for a glass of comfort and a relaxing chat with a large-busted barmaid, when he saw a dark figure dart across the back lawn. It was tall enough to be a man, and as he had only consumed two pints this evening—Tom liked his ale well enough, but he liked his job better—Tom was certain his eyes were not playing tricks on him. Thinking quickly, he armed himself with a spade from the toolshed, and cautiously glided across the frost-stiffened lawn toward the fountain, where the shadowy figure had disappeared.

Rebecca was deeply disappointed. It appeared that she had risked a great deal for naught, because no one had yet appeared near the fountain. She sighed and straightened her back, then stepped out from behind the hedge to return to the house.

Right into a pair of masculine arms.

"There you are, my sweet. I feared you had changed your mind," said Lord Edelston in the same fierce murmur he had used to entice Lorelei here to begin with. Before Rebecca could register this astonishing turn of events, Edelston lowered his mouth to hers, slid his hands down to cup her bottom, and flicked his tongue at the corners of her mouth.

Rebecca was paralyzed by a number of conflicting realizations, including the fact that, for all intents and purposes, she was being ravished for the first time in her life and it wasn't entirely unpleasant, even if the loathsome Edelston was doing the ravishing. The curious part of her wanted to see what would happen next. The rational part of her was infuriated and frightened indeed. Her hands hovered in the vicinity of Edelston's shoulders, undecided as to whether they should rest there and settle in for a while or shove him away.

The decision was taken out of her hands by a feminine scream, a masculine roar, and a dull thumping sound.

Rebecca leaped away from Edelston and turned slowly, her eyes squeezed shut. After a moment, because there seemed no other choice, really, she opened them.

There, frozen as if in a tableau, stood Lorelei with her

hands clamped over her mouth, and Tom the gardener brandishing a spade. This was quite bad enough. But when Rebecca looked down and saw her father struggling to his feet, having apparently been felled by a spade blow to the thighs, she understood that she was doomed.

All three of them wore identical expressions of horror.

Sir Henry Tremaine gently divested Tom the gardener of his spade and tucked it meaningfully in the crook of his arm, the blade of it riding over his shoulder. It looked at home there; Sir Henry was an old soldier, after all, knighted in the service of His Majesty King George III, and skilled in the art of wreaking damage with musket, bayonet, and undoubtedly all similarly shaped objects.

"Take your sister inside, Lorelei," Sir Henry said. He watched the girls scurry into the house, and then motioned with his chin for Edelston to walk in front of him. Edelston, wisely, obeyed. They followed the girls into the house and paraded past an aghast Lady Tremaine, resplendent in her ruffled night robe, to the library.

Sir Henry installed Edelston in a chair and then settled himself comfortably behind his desk. For a long silent moment, they regarded each other across the glossy expanse of oak.

"Would you like a drink, sir?" Sir Henry asked, finally.

Edelston, pale and stricken, had not yet regained the use of his voice, and so he simply nodded, trying not to appear too grateful.

Shaking his head pityingly, Sir Henry pushed a glass of brandy across the desk to Edelston.

Edelston toyed with the idea of asking for something

stronger, but refrained. He curled his hand around the glass of brandy and held on to it for dear life.

"You do know," Sir Henry began slowly, "that you now have a fiancée."

Edelston swallowed hard. It was all working out rather too neatly, and as the shock of discovery abated, relief and elated triumph nearly sent him dancing out of his chair. It was all he could do to control his expression. He struggled to arrange his facial features into the blend of humility, rebellion, and reluctant honor that he thought appropriate to the situation, and wished he had a mirror so he could review the result.

"Drink your brandy, son," Sir Henry said. "You look as though you may lose your dinner."

Edelston dutifully took a large gulp.

As for the fact that he had managed to compromise the wrong girl—well, it was a bit of a disappointment, Edelston thought, but young women did wear long gowns, and they had been known to trip on them at the tops of staircases and tumble to their deaths. And if the cinch of a saddle came loose while a young woman was out riding and she took a deadly spill as a result—well, sadly, these things did happen. Edelston was fairly certain he would not find his rustic wife an encumbrance for long.

The marriage settlements, however, would be welcome indeed. More than welcome. They were desperately, quickly needed. One unusual and rather ingenious source of income was all that stood between him and the devastation of his mounting gaming debts. However, a decent-sized settlement—and Edelston knew that Sir Henry Tremaine had been quite fortunate in his investments, and that the Tremaine girls were endowed quite well—would resolve this issue once and for all. Edelston would obtain a disposable, anonymous, and well-to-do bride, the sort that was rather unavailable in London, he would settle his debts, and he would resume living his life precisely as he liked to live it.

"I will do my duty by your daughter, sir," Edelston said humbly. "I appeal to your memories of yourself as a young man, when confronted by a girl whose charms surpass—"

"Please spare me the pretty speeches, Edelston," Sir Henry interrupted politely. "You may hope to win a swift exit from this library through a show of capitulation, but let me remind you that your host, Captain Denslowe, is a crack shot. If you attempt to leave the neighborhood before the wedding, you will undoubtedly suffer an unfortunate accident."

"Threats, sir, are hardly necessary," Edelston protested. "Your daughter . . . er . . ."

"Rebecca," Sir Henry supplied wryly.

"Yes, Rebecca . . . your daughter Rebecca is a lovely girl, and I shall be honored to take her to wife."

"Indeed." Again wryly. "Return Wednesday noon, Edelston. We will discuss the marriage settlements. Rebecca is heiress to a nice home in Collingwell, and I am not displeased that she will be the wife of a baron. You are dismissed, sir."

Sir Henry, satisfied that he had protected his daughter's honor and the honor of his family, watched as the handsome Lord Edelston squared his shoulders and took leave of the library.

Chapter Two

❧

Connor Riordan, Sir Henry Tremaine's head groom, was brushing Maharajah's pewter coat with long strokes while Rebecca observed him morosely from atop the door of an empty stall. Her heels thumped the sides of the door in an agitated fashion while she viciously gnawed a straw.

"They are going to make me *marry* him, Connor! Apparently, I am 'ruined.' I am to consider myself fortunate to be accepted by Edelston, they say."

Connor's hands stilled on the horse's neck for the briefest of moments as he registered this stunning bit of information, then he resumed combing. Maharajah's neck would soon be shining like a mirror.

"Well, Becca, the lad did have his hands firmly planted on your bum, did he not? Many a lass would happily consider that a proposal of marriage." He hid his grin behind the convenient arc of the Arabian's neck.

"Oh, please do not tease me! This is serious!"

Connor of course knew the sordid details of her midnight jaunt. Tom Jenkins had shared it with all of the Tremaines' servants, enjoying a brief celebrity. As a result, all the servants and gentry within five miles had more than likely heard the tale by now, which no doubt had evolved and acquired a few more juicy details in the retelling.

"You believe me, don't you, Connor? Because I cannot make anyone else believe me. I only meant to catch Lorelei with him. Truly. Edelston is so . . . oh, he is awful. Pompous, dull—"

"I believe you, Becca, if only because I know your taste in adventure runs more toward target shooting than to grappling at midnight with randy young lords."

Rebecca frowned as though Connor's assessment of her range of inclinations displeased her.

"It wasn't altogether unpleasant, you know," she said crossly, in a lowered voice. "And what kind of word is 'grappling' for a groom, anyway?"

It was a childish attempt to startle him, but Connor merely cocked an eyebrow and quirked one corner of his mouth, and Rebecca looked properly abashed.

"Promise me you will no' be sharin' your impression of the event with anyone else but me, eh, wee Becca? You may cause your da to spit out his brandy, and with you for a daughter, he needs every drop."

Rebecca laughed. "Perhaps I should take to the big apple tree until everyone abandons this . . . *preposterous* idea of a wedding."

"The branch would likely crack under your weight now, great girl that you are. Why would you want to ruin a perfectly good tree as well as your reputation?"

Rebecca laughed again. Connor loved to watch her face when she laughed. Her eyes went bright then nearly vanished with mirth, and she always tossed her head back, showing her smooth white throat and most of her teeth. There was nothing dainty at all about her laugh.

In truth, Connor enjoyed watching Rebecca's face in repose, too. It seemed a magical thing, the way the strong lines and soft curves and hollows of her face had evolved from the face of the child she had been just a few years before. Her hair had darkened, too, and the pale reds and golds of her baby curls were now entwined with deeper russets and coppers and chestnuts. Connor thought Rebecca's hair was marvelous.

"The puzzling thing, Connor, is why Edelston is so very willing to marry me."

Connor carefully considered his response. He knew, as did all the servants for miles and probably half the *ton* knew, why the handsome Anthony, Baron Edelston, was so willing to marry the daughter of a country squire.

"Well, perhaps Lord Edelston has a sense of honor after all, and simply desires to do his duty by you since he was . . . overcome by your charms."

Rebecca snorted. But her face did brighten somewhat at the suggestion. "Perhaps then I can admire him just a little. Honor and duty are at least admirable traits, and he seems to have so few others to choose from."

"Do you consider honor and duty very important traits in a man, then?" For some reason, it suddenly seemed vital to know Rebecca's thoughts on the matter.

"But of course. Do you think otherwise?"

Connor paused. "Duty is not my area of expertise, wee Becca."

Rebecca frowned. "But—"

"There may be another reason Lord Edelston is happy to marry you." Possibly it would be more cruel than helpful to further illuminate Edelston's character for her, seeing as how she must wed the man regardless. But perhaps in the spirit of truth . . . surely he had no other motive than that for telling her . . . surely not a *selfish* one . . .

"What would that be, Connor?"

" 'Tis expensive to be a baron."

"Ah." She looked deflated. "He has need of the money I will bring to the marriage, you mean, to maintain his properties."

"And for seasons in London, and fine clothes, and horses and servants and carriages." *And gambling debts*, Connor thought. *And mistresses*.

Rebecca was quiet for a moment, pensive. "Still, in a way, marrying me will help him fulfill his duty to his title, is that not so?" she suggested weakly.

Connor gazed at her wonderingly. In typical Rebecca fashion, she was trying to find the good in a situation that could at best be described as hellish.

"Perhaps," he said softly.

Rebecca sighed.

"May I help you brush Rajah?"

"You'll smell of horse, and lunch just an hour away." Connor handed her a currycomb, knowing it wouldn't matter.

"Horse is the best smell in the world," Rebecca said dreamily.

She stepped to the other side of Maharajah's neck and began combing him, her technique nearly as accomplished as Connor's. They worked together in companionable silence for a moment, and then Connor paused to push a hand through his hair, which had fallen over one eye. Connor routinely grew his great mop of wavy dark hair to his collar before enlisting the help of Mrs. Hackette, the housekeeper, in shearing it away nearly to his scalp. Unvanquished, it always returned to full bloom rather quickly, and more often than not, a forelock of black hair curved jauntily down over one of his brows.

Rebecca giggled.

"And what amuses you, wee Becca?"

"It's just that . . . well, you've always rather reminded me of a horse, Connor. But not Rajah. Sultan." She gestured to the big, black, silky-eyed Andalusian awaiting his turn under the brush two stalls down.

"Aye? Would that be because of my enormous muscular haunches?"

She giggled again. "You are as lean as a hound, Connor."

"A *hound*?"

"With rather broader shoulders, perhaps."

"But I thought I resembled a horse. Am I a menagerie, then?"

"No! But you *do* resemble Sultan. It's your forelock."

Connor pushed his hand through his hair again, self-consciously this time, as though expecting to find pointed ears sprouting up through it.

"Yes, your forelock, and your eyes, too, I think," Rebecca continued. "Except you've gold specks in *your* eyes. Like . . . like coins at the bottom of a wishing well. You can see them when you turn into the light."

The matter-of-fact lyricism of her scrutiny was both flattering and utterly disconcerting. Odd to think that Rebecca was as familiar with the details of his face as he was with hers.

"Coins, wee Becca?" Connor turned to look again at

Sultan; the horse gazed back at him with eyes as dark and soft as turned earth. There *was* a resemblance—at least from the eyes up. Thankfully, the rest of Connor's face— the lean, angular jaw, high-planed cheekbones, and firm full mouth—resembled no one except his brother, and his father, and his father's father, and so on back to the year 1600 or so.

"Yes. Gold coins. They make you look rather mysterious and wise."

Connor's mouth quirked again as he moved his brush over Maharajah's haunches. His face, absurdly, was growing warm. "What a shame it is, then, that I am neither. Now, who does Maharajah resemble? Your mama? Lorelei?"

Rebecca giggled and stopped brushing to plant a kiss on Maharajah's soft gray nose.

"What now, are we throwing ourselves at man and beast both, these days, Miss Tremaine? Best be careful, or they'll have you and Maharajah in front of the vicar before I can say Finn MacCool."

Rebecca laughed, delighted with the image. "I'd much rather be Mrs. Maharajah than . . . than . . ."

She stopped suddenly, as though she could not bear to finish the sentence, and the laughter left her voice.

"Connor . . . do you think I should practice the pianoforte? Isn't that what . . . well, *wives* . . . are supposed to do? I already know about the . . . the . . . well, *you* know. Other marriage things. From Papa's book."

Connor went still. She had always been able to do this, had done this to him since she was twelve years old. She'd say something so utterly . . . *Rebecca* . . . something so simultaneously shocking, insightful, hilarious, and heart-breaking that he never quite knew how to react, and so, in defense, and to buy time for a response, he'd learned to be quiet for a moment and to school his face to stillness. A cocked eyebrow would do in a pinch, on occasion. Not now, though.

Rebecca ceased combing, too, and they stood together in silence. Without banter to shield him, the chill, mundane horror of the fate that awaited the young woman in front of him seeped into his bones. Connor would not, could not, picture what marriage to a dissolute lordling would do to the remarkable Rebecca Tremaine. He felt the noose of the consequences as surely as if it were being tightened around his own throat.

"No. I do not think you should practice the pianoforte," he said finally, inadequately. His voice had gone strangely husky.

"I am so sorry, Becca, I am, truly. This folly is all my doing," Lorelei said, wringing her hands. Her eyes, however, were glued to the mirror. Rebecca had become accustomed to speaking to her lovely sister in this fashion, perched on the bed behind her while Lorelei sat at her vanity, gazing with meditative fascination at her own reflection.

"Bah, Lor, it is not your doing. We are both to blame. But whatever were you thinking? The garden? At midnight? With *Edelston*? Mama and Papa are saving you for a duke, at least."

"I was *not* thinking. And therein lies the problem. Edelston had quite fogged my brain. Let us blame Edelston, then. He is not a gentleman. He is *loathsome*."

"*Loathsome*," Rebecca agreed vigorously.

There was a silence.

"But handsome," Lorelei added, a trifle reluctantly.

"*Very* handsome," Rebecca confirmed, after a moment.

"Becca?"

"Hmmm . . . ?" Rebecca, freshly filled with lunch and feeling a little sleepy from it, was now sprawled on the bed.

"Your shoes. You've just come from the stable."

Rebecca scooted forward obligingly so that her sullied feet could dangle off the edge of Lorelei's counterpane.

"What . . . what was it like?" Lorelei asked tentatively.

Rebecca thought a moment. "It was very . . . *interesting*," she said, finally, imbuing the last word with rich layers of nuance and innuendo that it mostly did not deserve. Lorelei gasped and covered her mouth with her hands, and they giggled together wickedly. It was fun to make Lorelei giggle, especially since she had so lately embraced what she considered ladylike reserve.

"Everyone thinks you came out to the garden to rescue me," Rebecca mused.

"I know. I cannot disabuse them of that notion."

"Good heavens! Do not try! I am sorry I had to tell Mama and Papa the truth, as it is. I was in a panic, you see."

"Oh, but, Becca!" Lorelei moaned. "It *is* my fault! If only it were not my responsibility to marry a duke or an earl, I would offer myself up to Edelston in your place." Lorelei eyed the glorious reflection that had made such a noble sacrifice impossible.

"Oh, nonsense, Lorelei," Rebecca sighed. "Mama was right. Something scandalous was bound to happen to me sooner or later, and we both know it. I enjoy so many things that Mama does not approve of that I cannot keep track anymore of what is considered right and what is considered not the 'done thing.' My reputation was bound to become hopelessly tarnished without my knowing it. I cannot help it, really."

There was a short silence while the two sisters contemplated the odd, inescapable truth of this statement.

"Lorelei, do you agree that it is my duty to marry Edelston? Mama said it was a question of honor. My honor. And your honor. Our family's honor."

"I cannot say, Rebecca." She sounded as helpless as Rebecca felt. "I suppose it is. Mama and Papa seem to think so."

Rebecca nodded once, grimly, as though this was what she had expected to hear.

"Mama has invited a modiste to visit this afternoon," Lorelei ventured. "She wants your dress ready in less than a fortnight so we can have the wedding the day before we leave for my London season."

Rebecca shot straight up, all the color drained from her cheeks. "A *fortnight*?" she squeaked.

"Only think, Becca!" Lorelei seemed to cheer a little. "I can be your attendant, and we can have the most marvelous enormous cake, and your dress will be of white satin all sewn with beads, although perhaps we don't have time for beads, but maybe we could use silver tissue instead . . ." She trailed off, noticing the look of incredulous horror on Rebecca's face.

"Beads?" Rebecca squeaked. "Cake? A *fortnight*? Two *weeks*?"

She threw herself off the bed and knelt near the startled Lorelei's feet.

"I do not want to marry him, Lorelei. I do not want to be a wife."

"Ever?" Lorelei asked, astonished.

"I want to be a doctor," Rebecca said miserably.

The words had never sounded so pathetic and naive to her before. Rebecca was just beginning to realize that the longings of the daughters of English country squires were considered as consequential as a cloud of breath on a cold day. Vapor and condensation, indeed.

"Oh, Becca." Lorelei turned away from her burdensome reflection to take her sister's hands in her own. "It seems so terribly wrong, even if it *is* your duty. But what can we do?"

"That's just it. What *can* we do?" Rebecca tried to keep the words light for Lorelei's sake, but her voice had gone thin with despair.

And after a moment, because they both knew the answer to the question was *absolutely nothing*, Lorelei carefully knelt down, mindful of not crushing her dress, and pulled her sister into a hug.

As threatened, the modiste arrived that afternoon and unfurled a length of pearly satin in the upstairs parlor, spreading it across a chair so Rebecca could see how it reflected the light from the window. Conscious of the sharp eyes of her mother, Rebecca obediently ran her fingers over it and tried not to flinch in revulsion.

It looks like a shroud, she thought, and the now-familiar sensation of a giant hand closing around her throat returned. Rebecca imagined herself suffocating under the folds of that white satin, and her heart began to hammer. She swayed, and tiny black dots danced before her eyes. For the first time in her life, Rebecca nearly fainted, all thanks to a bloody bolt of satin.

The modiste and Lady Tremaine misinterpreted her pale cheeks and the swaying and were utterly charmed.

"It is fitting for a young bride to be excited, *non?*" said the modiste as the two women lowered Rebecca into the satin-draped chair with motherly clucks. "It will be all right, *ma chérie*. After the wedding night, you will see." She gave Rebecca a particularly French wink.

Lady Tremaine gave the modiste a brief reproving frown and waved a lavender pomander under Rebecca's nose.

But when her mother wasn't looking, Rebecca returned the modiste's wink. The modiste looked startled. *Let her wonder*, Rebecca thought.

Stripped to her underclothes, Rebecca submitted to being draped and pinned for the rest of the afternoon. She felt strangely removed from the proceedings, as though she had vacated her body and was watching a group of strangers from a polite distance. *This is not really happening*, she told herself. *It simply cannot be happening.*

But when she saw herself in the mirror swathed in creamy satin, her mother and the modiste standing behind her beaming in pride, Rebecca finally understood, without a doubt, that it was.

Chapter Three

❧

Connor was rubbing away at the scuffs on Sir Henry's favorite saddle when the tack room suddenly darkened.

He glanced up from his work to find Rebecca hovering almost hesitantly in the doorway, blocking the sunlight. He was immediately suspicious; "hesitant" was not a word one typically associated with Rebecca Tremaine. She was wearing the pale pink riding habit he knew she despised—the color had been her mother's choice. Secretly, however, it was one of his favorites; the pink seemed to collaborate with the multitude of reds in her hair to do wonderful rosy things to her complexion.

And then he glanced down and saw that she had a very good reason to be hesitant.

"Wee Becca, where on earth did ye get a musket?"

"It's Papa's. From the war."

"And does he know ye've taken it out?" Silly question. It was hardly as though Sir Henry Tremaine would hand a musket to his youngest daughter with his blessings: *Go shoot something, m'dear.* Though Sir Henry had taught Rebecca to shoot with pistols, he had stopped short of bringing out the larger firearms, perhaps remembering just in time that she was in fact a girl.

"Papa is away in St. Eccles today. And he didn't lock it up or hide it."

"Well, he doesna lock ye into your room at night, either, does he, and just look at the trouble *that* wee bit of oversight has caused." Connor shook his head ruefully. "Your poor, trusting da. Wee Becca, a man is entitled to believe his muskets are safe from his daughters."

"Connor, I'd like to shoot a musket at least once in my life before I am married and can no longer do anything at all."

To Rebecca, *anything at all* no doubt meant galloping a horse astride at breakneck speed or firing pistols at apples or laughing too loudly or reading and quoting from controversial books or . . .

Or simply being Rebecca. He felt again that strange sense of strangulation on her behalf; his throat tightened. He massaged his neck absently, then swiveled to resume rubbing vigorously at the saddle, as though he could somehow erase the events of the past few days.

He turned to her again after a moment. "Well, and I suppose ye'd like me to teach ye?"

"Well . . . you were a soldier, were you not?"

"Aye. I was a soldier."

"I've brought a picnic." She lifted her other arm; a basket dangled from it.

"Oh, well, in *that* case." He rolled his eyes.

"Do women in America shoot muskets, Connor?"

He smiled at the shameless appeal to his favorite topic of conversation: America. A place he longed to visit, and one day planned to call home. Rebecca had always been a rapt audience for his musings about America.

"No doubt American women shoot all manner of things with muskets, wee Becca. Wild beasts, Indians, their husbands. But *you*," he reminded her, "are English."

Rebecca held both the musket and the picnic basket up before her, mutely beseeching.

She would go whether he accompanied her or not, of that Connor was certain; she'd probably find a book about how to load muskets, or some such nonsense, and attempt it herself. He sighed. Suddenly he wanted nothing more than to teach Lord Edelston's future wife how to fire a musket.

"Have ye powder and shot?"

"In the basket."

"May I see the musket, please?"

Wordlessly, she handed it to him. Just as Connor had suspected, it was in pristine condition. Sir Henry cleaned his guns for the same reason other men read books or whittled wood: because he found it soothing.

"All right, then," Connor told her. "We'll go out to the wood."

Rebecca gave a cheerful little hop.

Rebecca's mare danced and frisked so much as they rode out to the wood edging the Tremaines' property that Rebecca struggled to keep her seat.

"Ye didna come riding yesterday afternoon, wee Becca. Pepper is happy to be out with you."

He sympathized with Pepper. By the time the sun had fallen yesterday, Connor had realized he measured his own days by Rebecca's visits to the stable. *And this will be what it is like when she is married,* he had thought. *This . . . absence. This silence.*

"I *could* not come riding, as I was being fitted for a shroud," Rebecca said darkly.

"Well, and isn't that clever, to plan your wedding and funeral both at once."

"I was being fitted for a *wedding dress*, Connor. Oh, and it will be quite lovely, too," she said bitterly. "Trimmed in silver ribbon, as we've no time for beads."

Connor opened his mouth to reply, but the image of Rebecca gleaming in pale satin and silver, her bright hair perhaps coiled and tamed beneath a circlet on her head, defeated his stock of glib responses. Rebecca, being led from the church by Lord Edelston, who no doubt at this moment was simply counting the hours before he could return to the gaming tables and spend his bride's money . . .

Connor cleared his throat. "It sounds like a fine gown indeed, wee Becca."

Rebecca snorted. "Well, no doubt you will see for yourself in two weeks' time, as all the servants are invited to our . . . *celebration.*"

Two weeks. Connor rode in heavy silence for a time, taunted by disquieting images: Rebecca in her wedding gown, on Edelston's arm, in Edelston's bed, her face, usually so glowing and animated, instead taut with misery . . .

In Edelston's bed? But she was still just a girl, wasn't she?

And yet, in less than a fortnight, she would be someone's *wife.*

Connor shook himself out of his bleak reverie and pulled his horse to a halt. They had reached the edge of the wood lining Sir Henry Tremaine's property, out of earshot of the house and a safe distance from anyone or anything that might accidentally be blown to bits by an errant musket ball.

"See that large rock, wee Becca? We'll put our apples on it, and use them for targets."

Rebecca dismounted eagerly, leaving Pepper to nip at short grass. She poked about in the picnic basket for an apple, and then carefully arranged it on the rock and almost skipped back to where Connor stood.

"All right, wee Becca. Do I need to give a speech about how ye'll blow your own sweet head off unless ye're very careful?"

"Father gave me that speech before he taught me to fire a pistol, Connor."

"Very well. Watch closely."

Connor hefted the musket in his hand, then peeked into Rebecca's basket. Bread and cheese and cold fowl and apples and a water flask and . . . two paper cartridges containing powder and balls. He smiled to himself. A very unorthodox picnic.

It had been years since he had performed this very drill, but it was still as innate to him as breathing; he often lived it again in his sleep. Crisply, he tore the cartridge with his teeth and took the ball in his mouth, shook a bit of powder into the pan and closed it, rammed the remaining powder, the ball, and the empty paper cartridge down the barrel, and pulled the cock all the way back. And then he lifted the musket to his shoulder.

All in less than a minute.

Rebecca gave a gratifying little gasp of awe.

"And will we be pretending the target is Lord Edelston, wee Becca?" Connor had drawn a bead on the apple.

"Oh, no, he's much too handsome to shoot."

Connor lowered the musket, feeling an unusual fit of pique welling up.

"So the lordling is handsome now, is he?"

"I never said he wasn't *handsome*, Connor. For heaven's sake, just look at the man. You've seen him, have you not? A veritable Adonis."

"An *Adonis*?"

"Yes. A frightfully dim Adonis, I'm afraid. The first time I met him, when asked whether he thought women should serve in the army—"

"Oh, now, why'd you go and ask him a question like that, wee Becca?" Connor sounded pained. "A question calculated to fluster any man?"

"It would not fluster *you*."

"Aye, but *I* am accustomed to you, wee Becca. And that, I assure ye, didna happen in one day."

She made a face at him.

"Well, and what did Lord Edelston say when you asked him such a question?"

"He said . . . he said: 'Well, you see, war is a messy business. One can get hurt. I am not even certain *men* should serve in the army.' "

A delighted smile spread slowly across Connor's face.

"*Did* he now? Is that what he said, truly?"

"He was not jesting, Connor."

"Which is what makes it so delightful, of course."

"As I said: *dim*. What do *you* think, Connor? Should women serve in the army?"

"Well, if you must know, it's my thought that they already do, wee Becca, though they do not collect a soldier's wage. They tend the sick and wounded. They take care of homes and land and children while they wait for the men to come home. They suffer just as much as the soldiers, in different ways."

"I *knew* you would understand."

"Aye, I am like that," Connor said with mock solemnity. "Very understanding. Now, shall I shoot the apple?"

"Yes, please, Connor. Perhaps we can pretend the apple is . . . the regrettable circumstance of my engagement."

Connor pretended the apple was Lord Edelston.

A deafening roar later, the apple was in smithereens, and smoke puffed around them. Rebecca coughed and clapped delightedly. Connor gave a bow, lowering the musket to the ground.

"My turn please, Connor!"

She scurried through the smoke to place another apple on the rock, and then held her arms out for the musket.

Connor talked her through the loading steps: "Aye, very good, tear the cartridge with your teeth and take the ball in your mouth, but dinna swallow it; no, dinna laugh, or ye *will* swallow it; close the pan now, good girl, just like that—all right, *now* spit the ball into your hand and load it and the powder and—good, good—now cock it."

Rebecca leveled the musket at the apple, her finger on the trigger; Connor rested his hands on her shoulders briefly to give her form a gentle adjustment. And then he stood behind her, just shy of touching her.

"Fire, wee Becca," he said softly.

She pulled the trigger.

The shock of the firing launched her back a step into Connor. His arms went around her; his senses briefly took in firm female and the scent of something sweet and heady; her hair, perhaps, or the nape of her neck. He exhaled slowly, loath to relinquish the scent of her, and pushed her gently upright again.

They waited for the smoke to clear before ascertaining that the apple had indeed been blown to Kingdom Come.

"Well done, wee Becca. Wellington would have been proud."

"Thank you, Connor. But I suppose that's all the shooting we can do. I could only find the two cartridges." Her face was a study in regret.

He smiled crookedly. Rebecca was a vision, all long thick eyelashes and pink riding habit, her lips powder-blackened where she'd bitten the cartridge. Unconsciously, he reached out his thumb to rub the powder from her mouth.

The silky, generous give of her lip beneath his thumb shocked him. He froze, staring down at her for a moment, bewildered. He had reached out to rub Rebecca clean, and he had instead touched what felt very much like . . . like a *woman.*

A woman who would be someone's wife in a mere fortnight.

He pictured Edelston forcing his rake's mouth down upon that tender pink mouth . . . and he no longer found a shred of amusement in the image. He was rigid with disbelief that someone who was so much *less* than Rebecca would soon be solely entitled to her, to *all* of her, her soft lips and strong young body, for the rest of his born days.

Connor dropped his hand. "You've . . . powder . . . " He motioned to his own mouth.

"Oh!" She laughed. "You, too."

*　　*　　*

Rebecca fought valiantly to stifle a yawn, but the yawn was winning. Abruptly she bent to bury her face in one of her father's prized damask roses, and the unfortunate rose took the yawn full force. Edelston, absorbed as he was in his own conversation—he was nattering on about wine, or something; she'd lost track as well as interest long ago—strolled on without her, and never noticed her quick pause. She caught up with him with one long stride before he turned toward her again. He did that periodically, Rebecca had noticed—turned his face toward her in order to maintain the pretense of including her in the conversation. Much like a weather vane in a spring breeze.

Papa had insisted Edelston come to call on her and take her for strolls, just as though he'd been courting her for ages, as though he hadn't compromised her in this very same garden only a few nights before. So now she was trapped here with him, and it was a glorious clear day and Pepper remained in her stall again with no one to ride her. For the first ten minutes or so of her stroll with Edelston, she had diverted herself by admiring, in a very objective way, his handsome features. His gold hair lay in lovely tidy spirals all over his head, and he had very fine bold blue eyes—a bit small, perhaps, but effective when considered along with his Greek statue cheekbones and his elegant, piquantly tilted nose. His lower lip dipped in a sultry curve.

It was truly a pity he was so excruciatingly dull.

Edelston did one of his head turns then, and Rebecca, startled in the midst of her thoughts of boredom, made her eyes go wide and bright and interested.

Perhaps too wide and bright and interested.

Edelston slowed his stride. "And what thoughts do you have on the subject of wine, Miss Tremaine?" he asked, sounding peeved. "Do you agree with me that the Bordeaux region supplies the best grapes?"

"Thoughts?" Rebecca replied sweetly. "You wish me to have thoughts, my lord? You seem to have so many of your own, I hesitate to burden you with mine."

Edelston narrowed his eyes and stopped midstride to look her over thoroughly.

Oh, dear, Rebecca thought.

A great galloping rustic, Edelston had thought when he'd first met Rebecca Tremaine, but then again, any woman compared to the fair Lorelei was likely to suffer a similar description.

But as he followed the line of Rebecca's body with his eyes, he could see she was slim and sweetly curved, a fact that was apparent despite the fact that nearly every inch of her was covered in an unpresuming gray printed cotton. He discreetly considered her rounded bosom, and found himself nostalgic for the deeper necklines popular a few years ago. Her clear gray-green eyes, a very singular shade, regarded him coolly through her chestnut lashes, and a lock of red-gold hair, which she seemed to have rather a lot of, had escaped from its confines and was fluttering about her mouth. Edelston remembered pressing his lips against those plush lips. Of course, his intent at the time had been to compromise and thus snare a different girl entirely.

She's really rather lovely. Very lovely. For some reason, the realization irritated him. And the chit was actually *bored*. He was unaccustomed to being considered anything other than fascinating. When one had a godlike profile and golden hair one was fascinating by default; everyone knew this was virtually nature's law.

"What shall we talk about instead, Miss Tremaine? Shall we talk about gowns? Shall we talk about the best way to serve a roast of beef?"

"If you'd like me to join the conversation, sir, perhaps we can talk about circulatory problems." The words were innocent enough, but her eyes were glinting strangely, and her left brow had lifted in the faintest hint of challenge.

"Circulatory prob—what on earth are you running on about?"

"It seems that many diseases of middle age can be traced to circulatory problems." She appeared to be warming to her subject.

Edelston forced himself not to splutter.

"Miss Tremaine?"

"Yes, Lord Edelston?"

"Did you enjoy my kiss the other evening?" This he asked in the patented low fierce murmur that never failed to render innocent young ladies weak with fascination. It was a desperate ploy, designed to knock the unnaturally poised Miss Rebecca Tremaine off her mark.

"Oh? Was that a kiss, Lord Edelston? I have very little experience in these things, you see, and so I could not be certain." Again, the innocent tone, the glinting eyes, the upraised brow.

Edelston gaped at her in astonishment until he realized he was gaping and clapped his mouth shut.

"Perhaps I should demonstrate it for you again, Miss Tremaine."

"Perhaps you should behave like a gentleman, Lord Edelston."

"If I were a gentleman, Miss Tremaine, we would not at the moment be engaged to be married."

Rebecca paused as though conceding the truth of this to herself and contemplated Edelston warily. "Perhaps you can demonstrate it again on our wedding day," she said finally. An effort at diplomacy.

Edelston was lost amid the strangest exchange of words with a woman he had ever experienced, and his cool detachment and godlike profile were proving of no use whatsoever. His composure utterly deserted him, and he floundered for a way, any way, to vanquish the alien creature that stood before him.

"I hope you are aware, Miss Tremaine, that when we are married I shall be your lord and master—by *law*. I shall forbid you to discuss circulatory problems. I shall kiss you whenever I wish. I shall beat you whenever I wish. I am beginning to suspect that I may wish to beat you rather frequently."

"I suppose you could *try*, sir."

"And how do you propose to stop me?"

A moment later Edelston was on his back in the dust on the garden path, the breath knocked out of his lungs.

"Your friend Robbie Denslowe taught me to do that. Hook one foot behind your opponent's knees and down he goes. The trick, however, is to take your opponent by surprise." Rebecca's gray-green eyes laughed down at him.

Edelston stayed on his back for a moment, staring up at that plush laughing mouth. And then something happened. The bottom seemed to drop out of his world, and yet he felt weightless, buoyant. The colors in his field of vision sharpened to a supernatural brilliance, and as he gazed up at Rebecca, transfixed, he could have sworn, as he blinked, that a nimbus of gold light outlined her head.

Edelston, for the first time in his life completely confused, out of his depth with a woman and stripped of all his defenses, could perhaps be forgiven for what he did next: he fell madly in love with Rebecca Tremaine.

Chapter Four

∽

*H*e's writing poetry to me, now, Connor. I cannot bear it.
And I'm expected to walk about with him every *day*."

Rebecca spoke across Sultan's back while Connor in-
dustriously applied the currycomb to Sultan's flank.

"Poetry?" Connor repeated, amused.

"Yes, very bad poetry, as a matter of fact. He rhymed
'rose' with 'nose,' of all things."

"What did he have to say about your nose?" Connor
was curious despite himself.

"That is beside the point, Connor," Rebecca said, exasperated. "Edelston is a boor."

"The man is merely besotted, wee Becca. The besotted
are frequently boors or figures of amusement, or both."

"Besotted? With *me*?" Rebecca was bemused. "No one
has ever been besotted with me before. Hmph. Besotted,
you say? How could that be?"

"Aye, woman, *besotted*." Connor sounded a little exasperated himself. "You told me you knocked the laddie into
the dirt and then laughed at him. Could anything be more
irresistible?"

Rebecca giggled. "Still, I don't believe anyone has ever been besotted with me before. It's rather novel."

"What about Robbie Denslowe?"

"But he was a boy. Edelston is a man. A *baron*," Rebecca added unnecessarily.

Connor felt another unusual fit of pique welling up. "Will you wed the lordling simply so that you may have poetry about your nose every day?"

"Good heavens, what a thought!" Rebecca looked shocked. "It's just that it's a novel experience. I suppose it's flattering," she added rather wistfully. "I have never seen myself as particularly special in anyone else's eyes."

"Trust me, wee Becca. You are special indeed."

Connor kept his voice sarcastic and his face averted, so that she would laugh and not be startled by the vehement sincerity of his expression.

"Oh, Connor. I'm not sure which version of Edelston I prefer—the rude, pompous boor or the fawning, poetry-spouting boor. And he still has not grasped the art of including me in conversation. So I listen to his monologues interspersed with poetry, and every now and then, just to keep from going mad with boredom, I ask him a difficult question."

"No doubt he appreciates the challenge, wee Becca," Connor observed wryly.

"It *is* somewhat amusing to watch him flail about when I do it. Sometimes he becomes overbearingly gallant— during our last stroll in the garden, just to change the subject, he said he would happily face Napoleon Bonaparte with a drawn sword to defend me."

"Ah. We should all have such gallant defenders."

"But other times . . . well . . . he . . . "

Something in her voice made Connor look up alertly. "What is it, wee Becca?"

"Well, truthfully, it was only the one time, and perhaps it meant nothing, which is why I did not mention it before . . ."

"*What* was 'only the one time,' Rebecca?"

She took a deep breath. "Edelston said it would be his right *by law* to beat me once I was his wife. And that he suspected he may wish to beat me rather frequently." Her eyes were wide and hopeful and slightly abashed, as if she hoped Connor would find this amusing but feared he would not.

A red haze drifted over Connor's eyes. His breath nearly stopped.

"I beg your pardon, wee Becca." He measured each word out with great care; his voice shook almost imperceptibly. "Did you say Edelston threatened to *beat* you?"

"Well, you see . . . it was just the once. Doubtless it was because he did not want to discuss circulatory problems. He *did* also threaten to kiss me frequently."

Connor was silent for a very long time. In his mind, he was neatly and slowly rending Edelston limb from limb, savoring the lordling's screams.

"You don't suppose he . . . he actually would? Beat me, that is?"

Connor's breaths still came short and shallow; it was a struggle to speak under the weight of his rage. "Only a very weak man would threaten to beat a woman, wee Becca. Was he perhaps jesting?"

"I'm not sure Edelston knows how to jest, Connor. He takes himself very seriously. I *do* rather deliberately provoke him. Perhaps if I never spoke of circulatory problems, or the army, or . . ." She trailed off.

". . . or anything else, for that matter," Connor completed for her curtly. "Perhaps if you never spoke at all."

Suddenly Sultan tossed his great black head and switched his tail, perhaps sensing the tension in the man leaning against him. Connor murmured to the horse soothingly, apologizing. And the act of soothing the animal soothed Connor a little, too.

"I do believe you would best him in any contest, regardless, wee Becca." A weak attempt at levity.

"Oh, of course." Rebecca shrugged. Connor smiled a little.

"And who *wouldn't* want to discuss circulatory problems?"

"My point precisely," Rebecca agreed sadly.

There was another dismal little silence. Funny, but there had never been any dismal little silences between the two of them before Edelston had appeared.

"Connor?" And now Rebecca's voice was shaking, too.

"Yes, wee Becca?"

"I have tried and tried. For Papa's sake, for everyone's sake. I honestly have. But I think . . . I mean, I don't think . . ."

He waited.

"Connor, I cannot marry him."

Two pairs of eyes, gold-shot brown and clear gray-green, met and locked, in silence, for the space of perhaps a dozen heartbeats.

"Well, then, wee Rebecca," Connor said at last, moving the comb across the horse's flanks as though his next words were a comment on the weather and not the pivot on which her future would turn, "you shall *not* marry him."

Oh, you bloody, bloody, bloody great fool. " 'Then,' " Connor said, mimicking himself out loud to himself rather nastily, " 'you shall *not* marry him.' Dear God in heaven."

Connor sat morosely at the table in his quarters, the bottle of whiskey he preserved for only the most serious occasions standing at attention next to his right hand. He tipped it into his glass for the third time this evening and held it up to the light, eyeing it with grave tenderness.

"To hanging by the neck until dead," he said, the whiskey coaxing his native morbid humor out of him, and tossed it back.

Connor did not have a plan. Thanks to an impulse this afternoon, he now had exactly eight days to decide and plan how to whisk a gently bred seventeen-year-old girl away from a dreadful impending marriage. Most likely the whisking would have to happen in the dead of night and involve the theft of a horse or two. *Now there's something to look forward to,* he thought, *an evening filled with activity, each activity a hanging offense. A noble way to cap my checkered career.*

There was, however, no question that he would do it. For somewhere during his second glass of whiskey Connor had admitted to himself that Rebecca was very likely the reason he had stayed with the Tremaines at all.

For five years, Connor's life had been peaceful and relatively uneventful here on this remote country estate.

But from the moment he had retrieved her from the apple tree, Connor had felt somehow responsible for Rebecca. He recognized in her a kindred spirit; he knew that the reach of her soul far exceeded the confines of her circumstances, and she ricocheted more or less happily off the walls of those confines on a daily basis. Rebecca never deliberately set out to displease her mother or startle her father with her predilections, but she was nearly helpless not to. To be female and possessed of a hungry mind in 1820 England was to be cursed, indeed, Connor thought, and he had often quietly sympathized with Rebecca while wondering what on earth would become of her.

The main difference between Connor's upbringing and Rebecca's, however, was that the magnitude of Connor's destiny had been pounded into him from the moment he could walk. His father had defined a template for his life, and any digression from this template was simply not tolerated; indeed, it was viciously punished. With every breath he took, it seemed, he drew in the cold, leaden immensity of responsibility. His old life had been a hand that pressed against his chest, limiting his motion, his thoughts, his spirit.

How ironic, and fitting, somehow, that a war would be the doorway to his freedom. Connor had walked away from his life at the very first opportunity, and though guilt occasionally played faintly in his mind like a half-remembered tune, he never really felt regret; in fact, each time he thought about it, he relived the rush of gratitude he had felt the day he had finally managed to slip the shackle of his birthright. Only one element of his old life had followed him into the new: Melbers, the dear, reliable, discreet old Blackburn family solicitor, sent him a small but welcome sum at the same time each year. It was Melbers's own quiet way of protesting the brutality of the old duke. That sum should have, in fact, arrived at the end of last month. Perhaps Melbers had been preoccupied this year.

Connor had found peace and equilibrium of a sort with the Tremaines, and for this he was grateful, too. But he was twenty-nine years old now, and he felt as though he was biding his time, though for what he knew not.

Rebecca, as a woman, would never be able to simply walk away from her life. And Connor cursed the indulgence of her parents, the father who treated her with benign neglect and the mother who clucked and fussed and badgered but who had never managed to instill in Rebecca a true sense of the . . . *smallness* . . . of her future.

But perhaps Rebecca would be a different person if they had.

Funny, but he had always half suspected that Rebecca Tremaine would someday mean the end of his peace of mind, she of the astonishing vocabulary, courtesy of her father's scientific journals ("Oh! My gluteus maximus!" she had exclaimed one day, after a long ride on Pepper) and embarrassing questions ("Can puppies have more than one father? Because I saw Bonnie underneath both Bruno and Glider"). He had long ago vowed never to fight another battle, but for Rebecca's sake, he surveyed his own raw memories tonight, looking for something useful, because it appeared as though another battle was going to begin, after all.

He examined the elements of his past the way he would examine a chessboard, each piece potentially useful if maneuvered with skill. And little by little, an idea, a strategy, began to take shape. He rolled the idea around in his mind for a bit, tasting it the way he'd been savoring his fine whiskey, and thought, yes, of course, it could work, it *must* work . . .

Once accomplished, it would be off to America and a new life for Connor Riordan, the life he knew he had only been postponing here with the Tremaines.

Finally, satisfied, Connor tipped the bottle again, held his fourth and final glass of whiskey up to the fire, and toasted himself.

"To my brilliant plan," he said wryly, and tossed the whiskey back.

Edelston's feet had grown wings; he had not walked upon solid ground for more than a week. A laughing, green-eyed, red-haired angel-devil had liberated him of the need to eat or drink or speak to other mortals, and all he needed now was the divine pleasure of her company and a few sheets of foolscap for his poetry. *Rebecca. Rebecca. Rebecca.* It was really a pity she didn't have a more rhymable name, but this was a surmountable obstacle, as she could be compared so easily to so many other things . . . *flowers . . . showers . . . bowers . . . hours . . . spring . . . suffering . . . inspiring . . .* it was heavenly.

Ever since that day in the garden, Rebecca had excited him peculiarly. Perhaps it was the light in her eyes when she asked her horrible startling questions, or the thrum of something he couldn't quite identify that ran through her words when she spoke to him. It made him feel strangely unsure of himself for perhaps the first time ever, and it was an intriguing sensation. At the very least, it was an alternative to boredom. It seemed a distant, desperate memory now, his plan to rid himself of her once they were wed. Now he could not imagine ever relinquishing this maddeningly intriguing female. Fortunately, she would be his wife in a mere week.

He needed a piece of foolscap for something other than poetry, though: a brief letter that would put an end to one ongoing, regrettable circumstance, one that had proved profitable and serendipitous for him; indeed, one that had kept him afloat financially lo these many months.

From nervous habit, Edelston moved over to the wardrobe and opened the door. He reached in and felt about in the inner pocket of his overcoat, and when a reassuringly solid lump met his questing fingers, he sighed with relief. The lump was the subject of his special arrangement: it meant he was guaranteed at least one consistent source of income. The marriage settlements offered by Sir Henry Tremaine, however, had rendered this special arrangement unnecessary, and in light of the . . . er . . . warm relationship Edelston had once shared with the party involved, he felt that concluding the circumstances would be the honorable thing to do. Edelston had recently discovered honor, and he found the concept very compatible with the notion of true love.

An apology and a polite invitation to meet to conclude business was all that seemed necessary. Strange to think that another female face and body had at one time caused him fits of longing. And yet the memory seemed trivial in light of the vast celestial emotions he felt for Miss Tremaine. He wrote the letter; he posted it; he returned to his rhymes.

"Did you know, Connor, that I am a *'creature divine, with eyes so fine, any fool would vastly prefer them to wine'*?"

"Ah. So Edelston's poetry is . . . improving?" Connor was rubbing oil into a saddle.

"Difficult to say, isn't it? However, I *can* tell you what isn't improving: my *mood.* Yesterday he read the poem about my fine eyes to me aloud, and then do you know what he said to me?"

"I am all ears."

"He said: 'You are never so appealing as when you are listening, Rebecca.' "

Connor nearly choked on a burst of startled laughter. "Oh, I think I may miss Edelston when we've gone, wee Becca."

"But now do you see, Connor? If I suffer through too much more of Edelston I may expire or go mad with boredom." She lowered her voice. "When are we leaving?"

"In four days, wee Becca—two days before the wedding," Connor answered. "I will give you more instructions one day prior to our departure."

"Why won't you tell me everything *now*?"

"Because, wee Becca, I think it is all you can do now to maintain a secret, and if I gave you a head full of instructions and still more secrets to keep, I think your face would betray your thoughts to everyone who saw you."

"Don't you trust me?" She sounded wounded.

"If I didna trust you absolutely, we would not be having this conversation," Connor said firmly. " 'Tis a compliment I'm giving you, wee Becca. A talent for playacting is not an admirable skill in a female. I do not wish to burden you with the need to become an actress."

"But what if I were a spy?" Rebecca said dreamily. "In service to my country? Then I would need to know playacting, would I not?"

Connor rolled his eyes. "You are not a spy, you shall never be a spy, and I have a few questions for you. Are you listening?"

"Yes," Rebecca said obediently, which fooled Connor not at all. He gave her a quick mock-warning frown, and she grinned in return, but stayed quiet.

Connor spent a few moments brushing Sultan's hindquarters before he spoke again.

"After we leave," Connor said slowly, "there is a possibility that you may never see your family again. Not a certainty, but a possibility. You may never again live the comfortable and carefree life you live here. Have you truly given thought to this?"

Rebecca gazed somewhere over his shoulder for a moment, as though looking toward the future he described and assessing, and then met his eyes frankly.

"I have weighed the possible consequences, Connor. My life is not really carefree, is it, nor so comfortable, if I am essentially to be imprisoned by marriage to a man I neither like nor love? It would be slow death by strangulation, and I like to think that my family, if ever I could make them understand, would prefer that I leave. I would rather have risk and freedom. I have made my choice."

Connor nodded, satisfied; he had needed to hear her say it aloud.

"Are we going to America?" Rebecca asked suddenly.

Connor stared at her thoughtfully, with some surprise, for a long moment.

"Perhaps," he said finally.

"Because . . . you have mentioned America so many times, and I know they need doctors in America. Perhaps the need will be such that they will not be prejudiced against female doctors," Rebecca said shyly.

"Perhaps," Connor said again, and smiled, to soften his change of subject. "Now, tomorrow, bring a picnic hamper out to the stables. Pack in it just one gown and an extra pair of boots. You will have two such picnics, this week, wee Becca. Keep in mind, however, when you are choosing gowns and shifts and cloaks and what have you that we must travel light."

Rebecca's heart began to hammer.

"The wedding is Sunday," she said.

"A pity we shall not be there for it, eh, wee Becca?"

"Lady Montgomery—"

"Yes, dear, that was very fine, very fine indeed," Gillian, Lady Montgomery said absently.

Her young pupil beamed, encouraged, and bent to her trumpet again. The resulting blats and squeals were meant to be "Greensleeves," and someday, Lady Montgomery thought distantly, perhaps they would actually sound like "Greensleeves." This particular pupil, the daughter of a rich and eccentric Scottish landowner named Honeywell, showed no real aptitude for anything, but she made up for it by throwing herself into everything she undertook with a great deal of enthusiasm. Lady Montgomery believed in rewarding enthusiasm. Nothing worthwhile is ever accomplished, she thought, without enthusiasm.

She held a letter that had been delivered to her earlier. It was addressed to her in a hand that seemed vaguely familiar, and while her pupil practiced, she thought she would read it. Lady Montgomery had always been able to do a number of things at once; listening critically to a trumpet pupil while absorbing the contents of a letter posed no real challenge.

She fumbled in her apron pocket for her spectacles, and pushed them up to sit snugly on her nose.

Dear Aunt, she read while Miss Honeywell blatted away. Dear *Aunt!* Who on earth—

> *I pray you continue in good health. If I did not have a good deal of faith in your remarkable constitution and a very pressing reason to make myself known, I would not risk startling you with this letter. However, at the moment, I have both. The Aunt Gillian Montgomery I remember would be pleased, and even amused, I think, rather than distraught to hear from me, and would find it in her heart to forgive me when I appear in person to tell my whole story.*
>
> *I am alive and well, Aunt, not killed in battle as previously assumed. I am sound of mind and sound of body. And though I hardly dare hope you will receive me, I write to beg a favor: I bring a friend, a young woman, who wishes to escape a hateful impending marriage. Her mind will delight you, I am certain of it, and I think in her you will find an eager pupil and kindred soul. When you meet her, I know you will not think my action rash; rather, I think you will believe as I do: that I have done the right and only thing that could have been done under these circumstances.*
>
> *I apologize if this places a burden on your conscience, but I beg of you, do not mention this letter to anyone. I do not intend to take up my title or proper-*

ties, or to displace Richard from his current role. I will deliver my friend into your safekeeping and then depart the continent. You may expect us in Scotland before the end of June. I remain your Loving Nephew,

Roarke

She read the letter twice, first to understand the content, then merely to savor it, and then Gillian Montgomery slowly lowered the letter to her lap.

Well, then. The young scoundrel was alive. Memories began flapping about in her mind, haphazardly, like sleeping bats disturbed by a blast of sunlight.

Roarke had been her sister Elise's eldest son, and Lady Montgomery had always blamed the old duke for his death. But now she smiled to herself: *Ah, your son, he pulled one over on you, you vicious old sod,* she thought. *He lives.* And thanks to you, he does not want his legacy. He does not even seem to know that his brother no longer lives. Perhaps I can change his mind. But perhaps the best revenge would be to help Roarke live the life he wants to live, rather than the one you tried to force upon him.

On the whole, Lady Montgomery found revenge amusing. Her school for girls was revenge of a sort; her conservative Scottish husband had died and left her with piles and piles of money. A good Protestant, he would have been aghast to find Miss Honeywell playing trumpet in his parlor.

I will see what I can do for Roarke and for his young friend, Lady Montgomery thought. And her heart leaped at the thought.

* * *

There is a possibility you may never see your family again.

Connor's words rang in Rebecca's head as she left the stable. She'd meant what she'd said to him; she *had* weighed the possible consequences of leaving. She did truly believe it was the right thing to do.

But that didn't mean it would be an easy thing to do.

On the way back to the house, she'd made another decision, and it, too, was a risky one. But again, Rebecca felt it was the right thing to do. She wanted to say good-bye to Lorelei; in a way, she felt she could not leave until she had Lorelei's approval and understanding, for it was possible her disappearance would affect her beautiful sister's future.

She found Lorelei in her bedroom, her bed covered in a spill of colors and fabrics, silks both muted and brilliant, glossy satins, fine laces and gauzes: her wardrobe for the London season. Lorelei was standing over all of it, a look of disbelieving rapture on her face.

"Lorelei—"

"Oh! Rebecca! You startled me! I was just planning my ensembles. What do you think? Do you like the lavender silk with the pink slippers, or perhaps with the darker—"

"Lorelei."

This time, Lorelei noticed the note of quiet urgency in Rebecca's voice. She looked up in surprise.

"I have something to tell you," Rebecca began carefully.

"Rebecca, are you unwell? Shall I call Mama?"

"Good God, no! It's . . . Lorelei . . . please just listen. If there was a way I could . . . avoid marrying Lord Edelston . . . would you approve?"

Lorelei looked uneasy. "Well . . . it is not for me to approve or disapprove, Becca, but . . ." Lorelei took a deep breath. "I care more for your happiness than I do for my honor, if that is your question," she finished staunchly.

The words throbbed in the air between them.

Rebecca took a deep breath. "Lorelei, I do not intend to wed Lord Edelston."

"But when—how—the wedding is *Sunday!*"

"I intend to . . . *miss* the wedding."

Rebecca stared meaningfully into Lorelei's crystalline blue eyes, willing her to take her meaning.

And after a moment, Lorelei did take her meaning. "I have some money, Rebecca," she said slowly. "You may have it. But, oh, Rebecca, *please* be careful."

Lorelei lifted the lid of her jewelry box and extracted a pound note.

"A wager I won from Susannah Carson. She thought her nephew would be a boy. I guessed otherwise. Her new niece was born last week."

"Wagers? Trysts? Whatever shall we do with you, Lorelei Tremaine?" Rebecca teased. "I do not believe the vicar would consider these events stops on the path to righteousness."

Lorelei placed the pound note in Rebecca's hand with a squeeze and an intent, imploring look. They shared a moment of awkward silence.

"I didn't come for money, Lorelei."

"I know. But you will need it."

Rebecca smiled slightly. "I just wanted you to know that I . . . I will miss you."

Tears began to well up in Lorelei's eyes. "Oh, Rebecca! 'Tis all my fault! If only—"

"For heaven's sake, Lorelei," Rebecca teased again. "I thought we decided to blame Edelston."

"But . . . when I marry an earl . . . Becca, I want you to be there."

"I want to be there, too, Lor." Oh, *wonderful*, now *she* was going to cry, too. "You will not tell Mama or—"

"Never. Perhaps it is *their* fault."

Rebecca was not inclined to disagree with her at the moment. "I just wanted to tell you that I know what I am doing, and that I will be very safe."

"When will you—?"

Rebecca shook her head. "Better that you don't know, I think. Mama and Papa will winkle it out of you somehow, and see you as an accomplice. Try to be happy for me, Lorelei. I can promise you I will be happier away from Edelston than with him."

"All right." Lorelei's voice was soft and sad.

"And take care of Pepper for me."

"All right."

"And . . ." But Rebecca could no longer speak for tears, and there really wasn't much left to say, anyhow. She kissed her sister's smooth white cheek and dashed out of her room.

Rebecca scanned the top shelf of the library bookcase for her father's infamous *Caldwell's Book of Anatomy*, meaning to take a farewell look at all the lovely gory line drawings and arcane words before she was forced to abandon the book forever. Her face was fierce with concentration, and as she searched, in vain, her foot tapped out an irritated little rhythm. Rebecca's whole body habitually participated in whatever mood she happened to be in.

It was the eve of her departure. For the last few days, she had tried, in her mind and in her heart, to bid farewell to the things she loved, the garden and apple tree and the horses and dogs, to Mama and Papa and Lorelei, who *would* insist on gazing at her forlornly. Fortunately, her parents seemed oblivious.

But all of the things she loved had already taken on a new and distant and even slightly sinister cast; each seemed a bar, however benign, of the genteel prison she had recently learned she occupied. Perhaps she would ache for them later.

Her irritation at the moment, in truth, was directed at Connor, and it had been growing in magnitude all morning. Although it never crossed Rebecca's mind to doubt whether Connor would indeed successfully spirit her away from Tremaine House and the nightmare of her impending nuptials—Connor was, after all, preternaturally competent—she was a trifle irked that he hadn't allowed her to participate in the planning of her own escape. Rebecca had made the decision to leave impulsively, but she had also reconsidered her decision later, at length and with a good deal of gravity, and had stuck by it with admirable maturity. Connor, she thought, should have been impressed by her coolheadedness and made her a full partner in his scheme. Instead, he was behaving much like her father or even Edelston would: utterly confident she would mindlessly do exactly as she was told. Connor, of all people, should know better, she thought.

She longed for an opportunity to demonstrate her own resourcefulness. As she rotated about in order to scan the opposite bookcase, her eyes lighted on the heavy service-able gray overcoat draped over the back of the library chair. Papa's overcoat, she thought idly.

Inspiration struck.

Glancing stealthily toward the library doorway, Rebecca plunged a hand into the left outside pocket of the coat. Quite empty. Undaunted, she transferred her hand to the right outside pocket and rummaged about. Nothing.

Finally, she gingerly lifted the coat from the back of the chair and felt for an inner pocket. When her hand moved over a lump that made a promising rustling noise, her heart began beating in wild triumph. *Money!* She could contribute money to their journey, if nothing else. She slipped her fingers into the slash of a pocket . . . and pulled out a one-pound note. Very anticlimactic. Rebecca sighed. She had been hoping for a much higher denomination.

But there was something else in the pocket as well. Something cool and smooth and heavier than a coin. She closed her fingers over it and drew it out.

It was a gold locket, a simple gleaming oval attached to a long gossamer chain that pooled in her palm, tickling it. She stared at it in blank astonishment. What on earth was Papa doing with a piece of woman's jewelry?

Rebecca ran her thumb along the edge of the locket, and gasped when it sprang open.

Inside was a miniature portrait of a stunning woman, her face alight with the certainty of her own beauty, her intelligence apparent in the imperious, amused cant of her blue eyes and uptilted chin. Her hair, gathered into a complex arrangement of curls, was a lustrous black, and her full rosy mouth turned down a bit at the corners in one of those frowns that seemed more like a smile. A peacock feather arced over the top of her head. Rebecca stared at the portrait, confused and mesmerized, as if she could will it to make sense by simply staring.

She froze at the sound of footsteps in the hallway. The efficient measured clicking of heels on marble belonged to Gilroy, who, no doubt, wanted to check the library for empty brandy glasses and refill her father's decanter. Rebecca frantically stuffed the pound note and the locket into her pocket, smoothed her damp palms against her apron, squared her shoulders, and moved toward the library exit as casually as her pounding heart and guilty conscience would allow.

"Oh, hello, Miss Rebecca." Gilroy looked a trifle startled. He threw a swift glance over his shoulder, then lowered his voice to a whisper. "He's hidden the book, you know."

"So I *gathered*, Gilroy," Rebecca said, more crossly than necessary. Belatedly remembering her manners, she nodded briskly, moved past the confused butler, and nearly dashed down the hallway.

Gilroy stared after her. "And here I was hoping Miss Rebecca's dear self would rub off on that young lordship Edelston, and not t'other way 'round," he said sadly to himself as he collected the brandy glasses.

Chapter Five

❦

The first light of dawn always seems to obscure more than it illuminates, Connor thought with some satisfaction. On this morning of all mornings, this worked beautifully in his favor. He circled the sturdy gray horse standing between the shafts of the cart and ran his fingers under the leather strap on his back one more time, checking the fit of the harness.

It was serendipity, plain and simple, Connor decided, that Sir Henry Tremaine had decided to combine one of Connor's routine trips to the village for supplies with a visit to a squire in South Greeley to inspect a mare for sale at a shockingly reasonable sum.

Naturally, Connor had thought this trip was a capital idea.

The rest of his plan lined up in his mind's eye: a dear friend, a woman, who had gladly done him a favor. A town called Sheep's Haven, far enough off the coach road to throw any pursuers off their trail. A well-hidden hunting box on an estate that had once been both purgatory and paradise for a young boy. And his aunt, his mother's sister, who ran a school for girls in Scotland—their final destination.

And then it would be off to his new life in America, the life he had only been postponing here with the Tremaines.

With any luck the connection between his trip to South Greeley and Rebecca's disappearance would not be made for a day or so if at all, allowing them a precious day of relative anonymity on the road. And Connor would not be expected to return from South Greeley for at least a week. By then, Sir Henry and Lady Tremaine and Lorelei would be in London, for he doubted even a missing daughter would cause Lady Tremaine to postpone Lorelei's London season.

Harness inspection completed, Connor bent to pick up the lunch basket that Mrs. Hackette, the housekeeper, had packed for him. He moved to the back of the cart and lifted the canvas to tuck the basket in with the sacks of feed already there.

"Don't move. Don't speak. Breathe as little as necessary," he hissed under the canvas, then lowered it again.

The cart heaved and squeaked as Connor hoisted himself aboard. Then with a snap of the reins, the gray trotted briskly out of the stable yard.

Edelston was watching a fat bee hovering above one of the fluffy damask roses that lined the front garden of Tremaine House. He gifted it with a dreamily benevolent smile. *I am as the bee*, he thought, *and my sweet Rebecca is as the rose. The bee seeks to drink the nectar from the fragrant petals of the rose, and the . . .*

He interrupted himself midthought and shifted on the stone bench, turning his thoughts to a more immediate concern, one that had very little to do with propriety and much to do with his recently discovered sense of honor. In light of the hastiness of the proceedings, he had invited but one guest to the wedding, and the clattering of hooves in the courtyard announced that she had arrived, in a carriage bearing the Dunbrooke arms. Edelston stood, hat doffed, and watched as Cordelia Blackburn, Duchess of Dunbrooke, was helped from her carriage by a brace of eager Tremaine footmen.

She was wearing some restrained confection of a hat, straw with a bit of blue feather fluttering from it. He smiled. It was almost cruel, the way Cordelia always skillfully highlighted her extraordinary features with a tassel here, a bit of lace there. It was one of her weapons, and not the least of them by far. Edelston watched as Cordelia gave some instructions to her maidservant and the dark, bent little manservant who always seemed to hover near her. Finally the clutch of servants dispersed into the house, staggering under trunks.

Then she turned and saw Edelston waiting for her in the front garden, just as they had agreed, and moved toward him.

Cordelia did not so much walk as *shimmer,* her movement a seeming product of the meeting of sunshine and air. Her face bloomed like a lily atop the delicate stem of her neck, and one gleaming blue-black curl caressed the slope of her cheekbone, as deliberate as the final note of a symphony. But just like everything else about Cordelia, Edelston knew her ethereal air was an illusion. Cordelia Blackburn could clamp her silky thighs around a man's waist like a vise, and he had more than once heard her howl like a banshee in the throes of . . .

He was beginning to feel warm.

"Tony," she said in that song of a voice, and extended a hand encased in blue kid.

Edelston grasped her proffered fingers and bent over them.

"Cordelia. You are . . . a vision. You steal my breath, as always."

She laughed, a sound like tiny bells spilling out onto the lawn.

"I see your silver tongue has not been tarnished by your prolonged stay in the damp country air, Tony. Once again I am at its mercy."

Cordelia did not appear to be at the mercy of anyone at all, Edelston noted. She cast her eyes up at him from beneath the brim of her snug little straw hat. Those eyes were another of her weapons: a limpid sapphire encircled by a rim of midnight blue, enormous with just the hint of a tilt to them. The expression in them rarely changed. There was always some degree of ironic amusement, cool detachment, or subtle challenge reflected there. Edelston had once considered this the height of sophistication, her control of every situation a breathtaking thing. Now he found he preferred unpredictability, specifically the unpredictability of a particular redhead.

"I have indeed been spared tarnish, Cordelia. But do you perhaps detect a . . . patina of happiness?"

"A patina of happiness," Cordelia repeated slowly, incredulously, as she withdrew her fingers from his. "Oh, dear."

"Yes, it's true, Cordelia," Edelston said solemnly as he led her to the bench and sat down at her side, "I am in love. For the first time in my life."

It had apparently never occurred to Edelston that some-one whose name he had more than once shouted in the throes of passion might wince upon hearing such a confession. But if Cordelia was wounded she did not show it; her eyes merely widened and the amused glint in them glittered more brightly.

"Ah, I see," she said. "You are in love. That would certainly explain the purple speech. Are you perhaps in love with your bride-to-be? This Tremaine girl, this—?"

"Rebecca," Edelston said dreamily, because he could not say her name in any other way.

"Rebecca. And is she in love with you?"

Edelston was startled by the question. He had been so busy being in love with Rebecca that he had failed to notice whether or not Rebecca was in love with him.

"We shall be husband and wife soon. It hardly matters, does it?"

"Oh, *hardly*," Cordelia agreed. Edelston missed the note of irony in her voice; he was buffered thickly by infatuation. "And what will you do with a wife once you are married?"

"Why . . ." he said, and stopped. Here was another issue he had failed to consider. He had a vague image in his mind of Rebecca embroidering pillows in the parlor of his country estate while he went about his life in London.

"Why, I shall be happy, of course."

"Why, of *course*. And this marriage will allow you to conclude our . . . financial arrangement?" Cordelia prompted delicately.

"Ah, yes," Edelston said, reddening. "Cordelia, I regret the necessity of, er . . . taking advantage of your generosity—"

One of Cordelia's feathery black brows shot nearly to her hairline at these words, and the corner of her mouth lifted skeptically, but she nodded, encouraging Edelston to continue.

"—and I am happy to say that I no longer have need of your funds. Sir Henry Tremaine has been quite generous with the marriage settlements."

"It shall be forgiven and forgotten, Tony," she assured him.

Although Edelston had been vigorously blackmailing her for some time now, Cordelia was not lying about forgiving him. She had begrudgingly appreciated the brash desperation that had prompted Edelston to blackmail her. After all, Tony was a fellow opportunist. One did what one must to survive in the world, and if ever Cordelia had a credo of her own, that was it. Not that the whole episode hadn't made her angry and resentful indeed; but now that it was nearing its end, she was finding harsh emotions quite a waste of energy. In general, Tony amused her.

"Forgiven and forgotten, that is, once the article of jewelry in question has been restored to me." She laid her blue-kid encased hand briefly on Edelston's upper thigh for emphasis. Her eyes widened again at what her hand encountered.

"Missed me, have you, Tony?" she murmured. Her hand lifted slowly.

"Guh . . . er . . ." Edelston reddened, staring for a moment like a startled doe into her amused, knowing blue eyes. Then he collected his wits and reached into the inner pocket of his coat for the locket.

The pocket was empty.

His fingers thrashed about in the pocket's recesses. It was truly empty. Excruciatingly, resoundingly empty.

"It was here, I swear, I never remove it from here, it *must* be here, my pound note is missing, too," he muttered insanely.

Cordelia froze, and then turned slowly and fixed Edelston with a long blue stare, which terrified him. Edelston had been on the receiving end of this particular utter absence of expression several times before, and each time it frightened him in a way he didn't fully understand. It was as though Cordelia had left her body completely, leaving behind a stranger comprised of indifference so absolute she seemed capable of anything.

He patted at his other pockets in an agitated fashion and made a show of glancing around at the ground near the bench, but he knew it was useless. For as long as it had been in his possession, he had kept the locket in his inner overcoat pocket.

He finally stopped searching and squeezed his eyes shut in disbelief. It was gone.

Cordelia and Edelston lifted their heads from their respective torments when they heard the crunch of footsteps in front of them. It was Gilroy the footman, looking reddened and mussed and nearly as agitated as Edelston.

"I'm sorry to disturb you, Lord Edelston, Your Grace, but have you seen Miss Rebecca at all today, Lord Edelston?"

Edelston frowned. "No, Gilroy. I thought she was dressing for luncheon."

"She seems to be . . . well, sir . . ."

"What is it, Gilroy?" Edelston's voice had gone weak with dread.

Gilroy capitulated with a sigh. " 'Twould seem that Miss Rebecca is missing, Lord Edelston. And Sir Henry would like to see you in the house at once. If you would, sir."

Edelston's ears began to ring. He found he lacked the breath to stand up.

"Come, Tony, let's go see what this is about, shall we?" Cordelia said sweetly. She looped her arm through his and nearly pulled him off the bench. Side by side, they followed Gilroy into the house.

From the back of a horse, the road leading away from Rebecca's father's estate had always seemed a civilized thing. The cart, however, revealed otherwise; it lurched over countless bumps and pebbles and ruts with a sadistic thoroughness. Before long, Rebecca was convinced that by the time they reached the village her bones would be jellied inside her skin and her teeth would be rattling around inside her mouth like dice.

And Connor's admonishment not to breathe had proved unnecessary. Breathing had ceased being an attractive pastime once she realized that whatever had occupied the cart before her—dead cattle? rotten turnips?—had generously left behind its essence.

In the cart, she measured the passing of time by the increasing warmth of the sun seeping through the canvas that covered her. Mercifully, after about what Rebecca estimated to be hours and hours, Connor pulled the gray to a halt. The cart lurched and squeaked as he swung down from it, and she heard his boots crunch toward her.

"Rebecca?" he whispered.

"Who else? The Duke of Wellington?" she said crossly,

and the canvas lifted from her head to reveal Connor's white teeth shining down at her like a bright crescent moon.

"Bit of a bumpy ride, eh, wee Becca? It's smoother up top, but seeing as how we're spiriting you away, I thought it wisest you should ride like cargo."

She never could stay cross with Connor. She smiled back at him. "Where are we?"

"Come," he said, and extended his hand. She gripped it; his hand was warm and rough, dark hair curled at his wrist. With a start she realized she had probably not held his hand since she was twelve years old. The sensation was both new and strangely eternal, and she felt a peculiar impulse to examine it the way she would any newfound treasure. But Connor gave a pull, and Rebecca's protesting bones and muscles were soon in an upright position on the ground in back of the cart.

In front of them was a little cottage, clean but weather-worn, and a woman stood in the doorway. The woman ran a hand through her dark hair, which was pulled back and fastened into one long braid that trailed over her shoulder, and then rubbed her hands down the front of her apron.

"Ye caught me at me chores, Connor Riordan," the woman said in a mock scold.

"Aye, my timing is always excellent, eh, Janet luv? This is the friend I told you about. Miss Rebecca, Miss Janet Gilhooly."

Janet and Rebecca took the measure of each other. Janet had fair skin and large dark eyes set beneath stern straight eyebrows and a wide, generous mouth bracketed by faint grooves. She was very pretty, and older, Rebecca decided, easily thirty or so. Her dress was a clean but faded gray, like the outside of her cottage.

" 'Tis jus' like ye not to run off wi' an ugly lass," Janet said at last to Connor, who burst out laughing and had to be heartily shushed by Janet.

"Come inside, the two of ye, for ye haven't a minute to spare. You can hire a coach going north in St. Eccles, but best ye get there before the sun is too low in the sky. We'll get yer clothes and a cuppa and then off wi' ye." Janet stood aside and made sweeping motions with her hand to usher them into the cottage.

Rebecca felt suddenly shy and very young in the face of Janet's brisk competence and wondered how on earth Connor knew her.

"Connor first," Janet said. She pointed to a stack of clothing folded neatly upon the table in her main room. "Use me bedchamber to dress, Connor. I'll put the kettle on."

Rebecca stood awkwardly in the center of the main room watching the back of Janet as she whisked cups and saucers down from a shelf.

"Sit, Rebecca," Janet commanded, and pulled a chair out from the table. Rebecca, grateful to be given anything at all to do, did as she was told.

"Now, lass," Janet said kindly and matter-of-factly, "dinna bother to be shy. 'Tis glad I am to be helpin' ye. I gave my youth to a brute of a man because me family said I should, but every breath I took I was sorry for it. We was married for ten years. He died under the hooves of a mule and dead drunk he was at the time, and it's been a hard but better life since. He left me wi' no children, but the house is mine, the mule and the chickens are mine, this little bit of land is mine, and nobody owns me. Life is hard for women, Miss Rebecca, as you'll learn, and we are rarely free, but if we are offered freedom I say it is worth the price."

As if to demonstrate the price, Janet stretched her hands out in front of her and smiled upon them; they were gnarled and rough, laced with scars, the nails ground short. They were twenty years older than her face.

Dumbfounded and drunk on the first dose of adult honesty she'd ever heard except from the mouth of Connor Riordan, Rebecca stared, half in envy, half in revulsion, at those hands, hands that could plow and bake and sew and carry and suffer and decide. It was heady. Just as she'd suspected, life was messy and fascinating and had very little to do with everything she'd lived up until today. Suddenly she wanted to know every bit of it, and her fatigue dropped away.

"Edelston said he suspected he might wish to beat me rather frequently. But he *is* writing poetry to me. And he is a baron," Rebecca began guiltily. For some reason she wanted this woman's absolution. She wanted to hear Janet's thoughts on shucking a marriage and an ostensibly very comfortable life for one of near reckless uncertainty.

"Prisons can be made of velvet," Janet said with a dismissive snort. She was already convinced of Edelston's lack of worth. "If ye're lucky, love and respect can grow in a marriage, but a man rarely sees the need in that, ye ken? If he can do what he likes, what need has he to learn to love his wife? He can go about his business, gaming and womanizing and whatnot, pleasing himself. His wife is his property and broodmare." She stopped to see if Rebecca was blushing and laughed to notice she was not.

"I know what a broodmare is," Rebecca confirmed firmly.

"I hear tell there *is* such a thing as love, though, Miss Rebecca," Janet said, "and God willing, love will find ye someday and ye will be able to keep it without too dear a cost."

Rebecca nodded. She thought of Mama and Papa. Not a grand love story, that one. More a story of tolerance and practicality. Rebecca suspected she was destined for something altogether different, something she was by no means able to define yet.

"And where exactly would Connor be takin' ye?" Janet asked her.

"I . . . I don't know yet. He would not tell me."

Janet's eyes went troubled for a brief moment. Rebecca blushed, because her answer sounded hopelessly naive even to her own ears. "Away" had seemed a sufficient destination not more than a day ago.

"Rebecca, Connor is a rare man, but no man alive deserves that sort of trust."

"And are you filling wee Becca's ears with your usual revolutionary talk, Janet?" Connor said, emerging from her room.

The women gawked at him. Gone were his grimy rolled shirtsleeves and work trousers, the scuffed boots, the uniform of a groom. In their place were close-fitting fawn-colored trousers, a coat of fine dark brown wool open over a waistcoat striped in deep gold and cream, and an almost-new pair of boots, polished to a glow. A conservatively tied silk cravat, whiter than summer clouds, billowed beneath his chin. In one hand he held a pair of brown kid gloves; in the other a round, flat-crowned hat.

"Ye look like a bloody lord, ye do," Janet drawled, but her eyes had gone soft.

"Thanks to your skill with procurement, Janet," Connor said, his own eyes soft.

"Ah, but I did it wi' yer coin. I canna take credit for it all," Janet replied, and Connor laughed.

Rebecca was flabbergasted by the change in Connor. He looked more at home in the fine clothes than Maharajah did in his own skin, his long elegant body almost insolently regal as he stood holding the hat between both hands. The stripe in his waistcoat picked out the gold flecks in his eyes and set them dancing; the soft folds of the cravat emphasized the bold lines of his jaw and cheekbones. It was faintly disturbing, because although Rebecca knew the clothes were meant to disguise him, in some strange way they seemed to reveal him instead.

"Wee Becca, from this point on I shall be known as Mr. Jonathan Hazelton, Esquire, a solicitor, and you shall be my shy and very, *very* quiet nephew . . . Ned. Aye, I think Ned would suit you."

"I'm to dress like a boy?" Rebecca's interest was piqued. Connor had known this portion of the escapade would appeal to her.

"Yes, for the duration of the coach trip, ye shall be a boy. Now be a good lass and follow Janet into her bedchamber to get dressed up."

In a few minutes, Janet had divested Rebecca of her gown and shift and had helped her into a pair of light-colored trousers (a bit too large, but this worked in their favor as it muffled the unmistakably feminine curve of her hips), and a loose white shirt. Janet clucked worriedly over the healthy size of Rebecca's bosom, but once Rebecca had slipped into the overlarge coat that had been acquired for her, she decided the whole ensemble provided adequate camouflage.

"But now we must do something wi' yer hair," Janet said musingly. "Connor, will ye bring me sewing basket, please?"

Connor, aka Mr. Hazelton, Esq., appeared obligingly in the doorway a moment later with the basket.

Janet fished about until she found her scissors and then seized a hunk of Rebecca's hair.

Both Connor and Rebecca let out dismayed squeaks.

Janet let the scissors fall to her side. "Oh, fer heaven's sake, the two of ye, we canna let her out the door like this. The lass has more hair than will fit into a cap. It will tumble out if she so much as sneezes."

"A little of it, then?" Rebecca said bravely.

"Three inches or so," Janet said speculatively. "We can stuff most of it up into your cap that way, then club the rest and tuck it in your shirt collar and pray no one looks too close at ye."

Rebecca nodded stoically and closed her eyes. *Snick, snick, snick.* A soft rain of wavy gold and red and copper fell to the floor at her feet. Janet swept the shorn hair into the corner and then deftly bundled the rest of Rebecca's hair under the cap.

"Ye'll do. Now let's 'ave our tea and then off wi' ye both."

She ushered Rebecca out of the room in front of her and followed close behind. Connor lingered a moment in the room. When Janet and Rebecca were safely in the kitchen, he bent to select a copper curl from the small soft heap of swept-up hair and tucked it into the inside pocket of his coat.

"My thanks for the offer of tea, Janet, but I think we must be on our way," Connor said when he was once again in the kitchen.

Janet did not reply; she went very still and stared up into Connor's face, smiling faintly and sadly. He met her gaze for a moment, then tore his eyes from her.

"Come now," he said, motioning for Rebecca to precede him out of the door of the cottage. "You're a young man, wee Ned. I canna be assisting a great lad such as yourself into the cart. You must do it yourself."

Rebecca made a face at Connor to illustrate how weak a challenge this presented to her. Somewhat reluctantly, she left the warmth of Janet's kitchen, Connor and Janet close behind her.

"Good-bye and good luck to ye, Miss Rebecca. I hope the future brings ye naught but kindness," Janet said.

"Good luck to you, too, Janet. I cannot thank you enough for your help and your words of encouragement. I shall never forget it." Something that felt dangerously like the beginnings of tears began to prick at her eyes.

"Oh, now, boys don't cry," Janet scolded. "Into the cart ye go." Janet gave her a quick squeeze and a kiss on the cheek and an impertinent pat on the bottom.

Rebecca swung herself into the cart, marveling at the nearly sinful freedom the trousers afforded. No wonder men behaved as though they owned the world.

She turned to watch for Connor. To her astonishment, she saw him take both of Janet's hands in his own and kiss each one lingeringly, with what looked remarkably like tenderness. Janet put her hands briefly on either side of

Connor's face, then dropped them back to her sides, and Connor took his leave of her.

The militarily efficient Sir Henry had assembled the servants, Lorelei, and Lady Tremaine in the parlor. Edelston's first impression of the scene was of pale faces taut with a sense of impending tragedy. A movement caught his eye; Lady Tremaine was cruelly twisting a handkerchief between her two plump white hands.

"Ah, Lord Edelston," Sir Henry began, "please have a seat. We were just discussing . . ." He stopped when he noticed Cordelia standing behind Edelston. Sir Henry regarded her unblinkingly for one rattled moment before arranging his features into something resembling a gracious welcoming expression. "And, Your Grace, what an honor and a pleasure. No doubt you are exhausted from your evening's travel. Molly will show you to your room and see to your needs."

Hearing her name, a tiny dark-haired maid snapped to attention in the corner of the room and, at a loss as to what to do next, dropped a curtsy. All the other servants, startled into motion by Molly's sudden movement, began dipping and bending, too, although not one of them was entirely certain what sort of etiquette a duchess required, never having been in the presence of one.

"Oh, thank you so much, Sir Henry, but I'm not tired at all." Cordelia remained rooted to the spot.

Sir Henry silently eyed the exquisite creature in front of him. Part of him wanted to bellow, "Begone, woman!" The other part of him, the pragmatic, bred-in-the-bone part, was aware that where there were duchesses, there were bound to be dukes and various other lofty titles, some of whom might be in need of a wife named Lorelei. He glanced at his own wife, who was giving him an imploring look that he was finding difficult to interpret. Did it mean, "Pacify the duchess, for God's sake?" or did it mean, "Get rid of her while we deal with this mess?"

Meanwhile, Edelston's nerves were twanging dangerously, and he feared they would snap at any moment if the matter at hand was not addressed promptly. He was quite certain that Cordelia would happily fence Sir Henry into the ground with verbal obtuseness if it took all evening, and he needed to put a stop to it. He cleared his throat. All heads swiveled toward him.

"The duchess is a dear family friend, and as such, my happiness is of great concern to her. Her discretion may be taken for granted."

The statement rang by itself in the parlor for a moment. The problem of what to do with the duchess solved for him, Sir Henry ignored the lengthy formalities of introductions all around and leaped immediately to the business at hand.

"I would like everyone to tell me when they last saw Rebecca. She did not appear at breakfast, and she was not in her room when Lorelei looked in on her. Furthermore, we have already determined that her horse is in the stable, that she is not in the apple tree, and that she does not appear to be in the house or taking the air anywhere on the grounds. I think Letty may have something to share with us. Letty?"

"Sir, I sleep very soundly, sir," Letty began hesitantly.

"And snores like a warthog, she does," muttered Tom the gardener.

"Rebecca was gone when you awoke?" Sir Henry prompted impatiently.

"Y-y-es, sir. I thought she was out riding, see, sir. But then I noticed that some of her . . . well, some of her things are missing, sir. Clothing things."

Sir Henry pursed his lips. "Gilroy?"

"I did not see Miss Rebecca today, sir, but I saw her twice yesterday. When yourself and Lord Edelston had gone to look at the greenhouse, sir, I took the opportunity to fetch the empty brandy glasses from the library. Miss Rebecca was in the library when I entered it. She exited in rather a hurry, which I thought was a bit odd, seeing as how Miss Rebecca always liked to pass a word or two. And then I saw her when I attended the family at dinner."

At these words, a roaring started up in Edelston's ears, and he saw Sir Henry's lips moving, and Gilroy's lips moving in response, but he observed the tableau as though he were underwater. The greenhouse. The library. Yesterday. Of course.

Yesterday, Edelston had been intercepted by Sir Henry in the front garden before Gilroy could divest him of his overcoat. Sir Henry had offered him brandy in the library while they concluded their discussions of the marriage settlements and, warmed to gruff cordiality after several glasses, Edelston had finally shucked his overcoat over the back of a chair and went tromping off with Sir Henry to the greenhouse to see more bloody roses. These Tremaines were simply mad for bloody roses.

It was becoming clear that his bride-to-be had robbed him while he was looking at the bloody roses with Sir Henry. Edelston felt as though he'd been run through with a pitchfork.

*　　*　　*

Cordelia was watching the greening of Edelston's face with grave fascination.

"Tell me, Sir Henry," she said suddenly, "does Rebecca have any money of her own?"

Sir Henry glanced from Edelston to Cordelia, and their respective expressions must have been eloquent, for Sir Henry held a hand up, a silent instruction to Cordelia to hold her thought.

"Thank you for your time. You may go," Sir Henry told his household staff. "If at any point during the next week or so I hear word of this conversation from anyone that was not present in this room, I will dismiss each and every one of you without references."

Sir Henry, the servants knew, though fair and kind and occasionally vague, did not make idle threats. In fact, he did not make threats at all. They began filing out of the room, silent as ghosts. As an afterthought, Molly curtsied in the general direction of the Duchess of Dunbrooke again, which triggered another epidemic of bobbing and bending and a few collisions among the household staff as they attempted to leave the room.

"Oh, hold one moment," Sir Henry commanded. The servants halted midstep. "Where is Jenkins? Not *you*, Jenkins," he said when Tom Jenkins the gardener stepped forward. "I mean *Riordan*. Connor Riordan. My groom. I would ask him about Rebecca, too, as she does spend much of her time in the stables."

Tom Jenkins cleared his throat before replying. "Riordan was off to South Greeley this morning, sir, to see about an Arabian mare and to fetch some supplies for the stables. He will be gone for the week."

"Oh, yes, yes of course." Sir Henry's grim face brightened ever so slightly. "Now there's something to look forward to. A bonnie new mare. A good lad, that Riordan."

The servants remained motionless, watching Sir Henry carefully.

Noticing, he frowned a little. "Thank you. You may go."

More dipping and bending in the direction of the duchess ensued and the group finally exited the room, much to the relief of Mrs. Hackette the housekeeper, who had not the knees for curtsies.

"My apologies for interrupting you, Your Grace. May we revisit your question?" Sir Henry asked.

"I wondered if Rebecca had any money of her own with which she could hire a coach or a room."

"She has one pound," Lorelei blurted.

Sir Henry stared at Lorelei for a moment, and then sighed a long-suffering sigh. "Where, pray tell, did Rebecca get a pound?"

"I . . . I gave it to her. I won a wager with Susannah Carson," Lorelei stammered, perhaps realizing belatedly that she had just stumbled down a disastrous conversational path.

Lady Tremaine began weeping quietly.

Cordelia eyed Lorelei (a beautiful girl, but so very . . . incomplete, as of yet) with interest. These Tremaine chits were proving to be entertaining, indeed.

Sir Henry drew in a long breath and let it out slowly again. "I cannot recall ever encouraging you to indulge in wagers, Lorelei, but we shall address that issue later. It seems as though your headstrong sister has run off. And since you saw fit to help finance her cause, may I assume that you knew of her intentions ahead of time and might even have an inkling of her whereabouts?"

"No, Papa, I swear to you I do not know!" Lorelei blurted. "All I know is she would not have run off if it were not for *him*."

She fairly spat the word and pointed a delicate white finger straight at a shocked Edelston. Lorelei, who tried never to demonstrate extreme facial expressions lest lines begin to encroach upon her flawless countenance, was glowering like a gargoyle.

"But why did you give her money if you did not know she intended to run off?" Sir Henry sounded almost amused, as though he was certain Lorelei would be sobbing out a confession in mere moments.

"Rebecca said only that she could not marry him, and I inferred her meaning, so I gave her my money. She said nothing more after that. She did not need to. We *are* sisters, you know." Lorelei glared at Sir Henry defiantly.

Nonplussed, Sir Henry gawked at Lorelei as if she had suddenly stripped away her face like a mask to reveal Napoleon Bonaparte sitting in his parlor. Cordelia had the distinct impression that she was witnessing Lorelei Tremaine's first ever rebellion.

Fortunately, an interlude of quiet weeping and handkerchief twisting seemed to have prepared Lady Tremaine to step into the breach.

"Lord Edelston, Your Grace, please forgive the uproar. Lorelei is merely a trifle overwrought. We are leaving for London for her first season in a few days, you know, and I'm sure you can recall, Duchess, what a vibrant—and *important*—time this is in a young woman's life."

Cordelia could recall nothing of the sort, since she

herself had taken a rather unconventional route to becoming a duchess, but she curved her lips in a sympathetic smile, anyhow. Being a strategist at heart, however, she did fully comprehend the significance behind Lady Tremaine's emphasis of the word "important." Important, because Lorelei's face was most certainly her fortune, and it would be a pity indeed to waste it on any chap not of the noblest blood. And important, because Lorelei's worth on the marriage market would be severely compromised if word got out that her sister had disappeared into the countryside like a Gypsy. Well-bred young girls did not typically do such things. The Tremaines most certainly did not want the ballrooms of the *ton* to buzz with vicious skepticism about their ability to breed proper young wives for titled gentlemen.

"And, Lord Edelston," Lady Tremaine continued, "I am certain that Rebecca is merely indulging in a case of prewedding nerves, and that she will turn up shortly, safe and sound and ready to be wed. I know you've learned by now that she is a young woman of strong and sudden inclinations. It is part of Rebecca's unique charm. And I know she has grown quite fond of you."

She smiled winningly at Edelston, encouraging him to agree with her, and Edelston offered up a sickly grin in return.

Sir Henry shot his wife a look of gratitude.

Cordelia continued astutely and discreetly assessing the expressions on the faces in the room with one objective in mind: how to get the locket back with little or no attention called to the search. For she was certain she had correctly interpreted Edelston's expression: his resourceful bride had robbed him. It could hardly be a coincidence that Edelston's pound note, the locket, and Rebecca Tremaine had disappeared all at once. The troublesome Miss Rebecca Tremaine could vanish into the ether, for all Cordelia cared, but she would not allow the locket to fall into hands other than her own. It would, quite simply, ruin her life.

She could see that Edelston was still floundering about in a soup of mixed emotions; he would be of no use to her. She spoke again.

"Since the grounds have been thoroughly searched and Rebecca has not been located, and her horse has not been taken out of its stall, I believe we need to consider that she had some assistance in leaving. Do you think perhaps this Connor Riordan—he is a member of your household staff?"

"My groom?" Sir Henry was puzzled.

"—yes, this Riordan who left for South Greeley this morning—do you think perhaps he could have helped her? He seems to be the only one besides Rebecca to leave the grounds."

"Never!" Sir Henry spluttered. "He's a good, honorable Irish lad, Riordan is. Best man I've ever had on the job. A wonder with the horses and a friend to Rebecca. More likely my hoyden of a daughter stowed aboard his cart, if that is the case."

At the mention of Rebecca stowing away in a cart, Lady Tremaine went as white as the handkerchief in her nervous hands. Cordelia hurried over to her side and took her hand.

"Please do not fret, Lady Tremaine, Sir Henry. Perhaps I can ease your minds. I have at my disposal . . . *contacts* . . . who can help us quickly and discreetly find Miss Rebecca. We all know that it is *essential* that you accompany your wife and Lorelei to London, Sir Henry, to chaperone them during this special time of Lorelei's life. Lord

Edelston and I would be honored if you left the matter of Rebecca in our hands. We shall all meet in London shortly, and Lord Edelston will have his bride. And I am fairly certain that I can arrange for Lorelei to be admitted to Almack's."

Lady Tremaine gasped. "Oh, Your Grace, you are too kind, too good a friend! To have come upon us in such a state and to gift us with such generosity!"

"It is nothing at all. Rebecca is merely young. We will find her, and a splendid husband for Lorelei, as well."

Lorelei gave up glowering for a more abstracted air. Cordelia could almost hear Lorelei's thoughts: *Almack's! Imagine!*

"And have you a place to stay in London?" Cordelia asked, half dreading the answer.

"My husband's cousin, Lady Kirkham, owns a town-house in Grosvenor Square. She is quite elderly and has retired to the country, and allows us to use the house as we please. Sir Henry will inherit, of course, upon the unfortunate occasion of Lady Kirkham's demise." If Lady Tremaine had attempted to keep the pride from her voice, she had failed miserably.

Cordelia was indescribably relieved that she would not have to extend her own hospitality to the Tremaines. "How fortunate for you! Grosvenor Square is a very fine address. Now, if I may ask to be escorted to my room? I find that I *do* wish to rest before dinner," Cordelia said.

Molly was summoned by a pull of the bell. When they arrived at the threshold of her assigned chamber, Cordelia turned to the little maid. "Find my footman, Hutchins, and send him to me," she snapped. "Immediately." She entered the room and closed the door in Molly's cowed face.

Chapter Six

࿐

$\mathcal{A}$ mail coach teeming with trunks and travelers hurtled out of the yard of St. Eccles's small coaching inn just as Connor turned their cart into it. Rebecca clamped her hand over her cap; the wind created by the passing coach nearly yanked it from her head.

"Well, we missed that one, Ned," Connor shouted to Rebecca over the clatter of hooves. "Or rather, it just barely missed *us*."

Connor pulled the gray horse to a halt and swept the yard with his eyes. They had just witnessed the departure of the coach he had intended to take. And according to the schedule he'd obtained a week ago, the next mail coach wouldn't arrive for another hour or so.

"Oh, no! Connor! Look, it's—" Rebecca ducked her head.

Katie Denslowe, Robbie's sister, was bustling across the yard. Three tiny youngsters scurried behind her like ducklings, colliding with each other, and the air rang with their shrill little voices. Katie had married and moved away years ago, and now appeared to be home for a visit. Which meant a member of the Denslowe family, all of whom had known Rebecca since her birth, would be along any minute to fetch Katie and her brood.

"Off to an auspicious start," Connor muttered. It was now painfully clear that they could not afford to linger in the yard of the St. Eccles Inn. "And in the future, wee Becca, when ye see someone ye know, kindly do not call out '*Oh, no!*' unless ye want very much to be discovered."

"Oh, *all* right, your majesty," Rebecca muttered.

Connor smiled at her. "And keep your head down, Ned. Remember you are shy."

They stepped down from the cart and pulled down their packs while Connor scanned the yard for other conveyances. They simply could not take their cart and horse to Scotland, unless they wanted a ten-day journey. He would be leaving them in the care of the inn's stables.

"Beggin' yer pardon, guv, but ye've the look of someone who's off t' London. And I'm yer man, if that be true."

Connor looked down at the speaker, who resembled nothing so much as a small, round, cheerful toad. The man's wide smile revealed a gap where his two front teeth had once been, and a single button strained to hold his coat closed.

"Sorry to disappoint you, Mr. . . ."

"Sharp. Chester Sharp, sir. I've an empty hack. Took a certain Miss Mackie this far from London."

"I am Mr. Jonathan Hazelton, Mr. Sharp. How much to Scotland?" Connor thought he'd come straight to the point.

"Oh, I canna take ye all the way to Scotland, guv. I've a London hack. I can take ye for part of the trip, if ye've the blunt."

"Eight shillings," Connor said. "Each. To take myself

and my nephew as far as Sheep's Haven." He motioned to Rebecca in the cart. She nodded politely to Mr. Sharp, her eyes lowered.

"*Sheep's* Haven? But ain't that off the coach road?"

"It is." Connor regarded Chester Sharp levelly.

Chester Sharp suddenly looked intrigued. "And would that be the point, guv?"

"Will you take us, Mr. Sharp?"

"Yerself and yer"—Sharp looked at Rebecca—"nephew, eh?" Sharp for some reason sounded amused. "Hmmm . . . ten shillings each and 'tis done."

Ten shillings each? Good Lord. The annual payment from Melbers had unfortunately never arrived, and ten shillings would go a long way toward depleting their coffers.

"I've one other passenger, guv, but I'll be leaving 'im in a town no' an hour's ride from 'ere. An' then ye'll 'ave the coach to yerselves." Sharp gestured to a large man standing placidly next to a trunk. "Mr. Grunwald, 'e's no' much of a talker, from wha' I can tell."

Mr. Grunwald was definitely an eater, however, from what Connor could tell.

"Can we depart right away, Mr. Sharp?"

"I'd hoped to fill my coach first."

"I would think Mr. Grunwald fills your coach admirably."

Chester Sharp burst into laughter. "Oh, ye've the right of it, guv! All right. Another shilling, and we'll be off, then." Chester Sharp strolled off to help Mr. Grunwald with his trunks.

Connor turned to Rebecca. "Ned, we'll ride with Mr. Sharp."

"A moment ago, you almost sounded English, Connor."

Connor's mouth twitched. "Thank you, wee Ned."

"And we are going to Scotland?" Her voice was obediently soft, but it was simply pulsating with curiosity.

He hesitated. Of course she'd heard his conversation with Chester Sharp. Where was the harm in telling her just a little of the truth? "Aye. I've . . . I've an aunt there, ye see . . ."

Rebecca glanced up, and her huge gray-green eyes glowed delightedly at him for an instant from beneath her boy's cap like a shy wild creature peering from a cave. Then she obediently looked down again. It was silly, but Connor immediately felt bereft. It occurred to him that looking at length into Rebecca's clear eyes was a luxury he'd always taken for granted.

"Scotland will do." She sounded pleased with him, as though he'd at last mastered a difficult feat. He was oddly touched.

" 'Tis an adventure, Ned," he said softly. "And ye're a brave lad."

Rebecca smiled and shrugged, as though this went without saying.

Dinner at the Tremaine household that evening featured a fish, beef, pudding, wine, and tortured silences served alongside stilted words. Lorelei listlessly pushed her food about the plate, Sir Henry was quietly thunderous, Lady Tremaine wore a strange, stiff smile all the more gruesome for not reaching her eyes, and Edelston, despite being seated across from Lorelei and next to Cordelia and treated to a display of fetchingly candlelit display of white neck and bosom, persisted in behaving like a man in torment.

Cordelia and Lady Tremaine did what was expected of them and invented wooden conversation. Cordelia's coach was complimented; Lady Tremaine's candelabra was complimented. Dresses and manners and puddings were complimented. But as if in tacit agreement, no one said the word "Rebecca," as if the issue, having been discussed earlier, had been neatly disposed of forever.

Cordelia encountered Edelston in the hall later in the evening as the Tremaine household made ready to retire. She stopped in front of him, the flame from the candle in her hand casting their faces in amber.

"Ah, Tony, it seems we are in a bit of a predicament, yes?"

Edelston nodded slowly, as though the motion were painful. "Rebecca has the locket, you know. I'm fairly certain of it."

"So I gathered from your expression in the parlor today." Cordelia smiled wryly. "I now understand how you managed to acquire your extraordinary amount of debt. You *really* must work on your game face. No matter: I have taken the liberty of sending Hutchins with some instructions for a few acquaintances of mine who have experience with . . . locating missing objects. They know they will be paid handsomely for the return of the locket, so I trust if Rebecca is on the road to South Greeley or heading north in a hired coach, they will find it."

"What of Rebecca?" Edelston asked, aghast. "Who are these acquaintances?"

"Oh, for heaven's sake, they are too well paid to even consider touching the girl, and I did not tell them to retrieve *her*. I simply asked them to determine which direction she was traveling. You might consider letting her go her merry way, Tony. She clearly does not want to be wed to you. We can find a new heiress for you—one who is considerably more rich and less slippery—and we'll leave Rebecca to her adventure. No doubt she is spreading her legs for her father's groom as we speak." She smiled and rested her hand on his arm, because Tony had always liked a ribald joke, especially when delivered from exquisite lips.

Edelston gently removed Cordelia's hand from his arm. "No, you are wrong there," he said slowly. "She would not spread her legs for a groom, Cordelia. She is not you."

Cordelia's palm flew up and cracked against his cheek. The sound echoed in the hallway.

"I am a *duchess*," she hissed. "I have sacrificed much and worked longer and harder than you have at anything in your short and worthless life, Tony. I endured two years of marriage to a debauched aristocrat. I *belong* here, and I will not allow anyone to take this life away from me, and that means I will do anything necessary to get that locket back. You *will* treat me with respect, Tony. How dare you treat my life with such callous disregard? How *dare* you?"

Edelston cradled his face in his hands for a moment, as if to blot out the sight of Cordelia's anger, then lowered them again with a deep sigh. "Please forgive me, Cordelia. I am a perfect ass. I know not what possessed me. You have always been a friend to me, and I will do what I can to help us both. It's just . . . Cordelia, I know you find this amusing and difficult to believe, but I *am* in love."

Cordelia stared at him, and her delicate brows dove in confusion.

"I am in love," Edelston repeated despairingly.

"But why?" Cordelia found herself asking, her voice uncertain. "Why this girl?"

"Do you know when you visit Brighton, how you can smell the sea long before you see it? The salt in the breeze?" He hesitated, searching for the right words. "It's like that. Rebecca is the salt in the breeze. She makes me aware that I am . . . somewhat less than I could be. She is so completely herself, she makes me want to become . . . someone else. Forgive me, I cannot explain it adequately."

It was enough for Cordelia. She skillfully schooled her face, as usual, to hide what she felt, which this time was a penetrating and unexpected hurt. Cordelia had never been able to indulge in the luxury of being herself in her entire life.

"You are a few weeks shy of debtor's prison, Tony. This is perhaps not the most appropriate time to grow a soul."

Edelston's head snapped up. He glared at her, and Cordelia found that she preferred anger to the blank misery that had been in his face all evening.

"Let us not quarrel." She placed a conciliatory hand, tentatively, on his arm again. He did not shake it off. "All will be well, you will see. And only think: the season is upon us. A twirl about a ballroom or two in the *ton* will take your mind off your troubles a bit."

Edelston nodded reluctantly. "Perhaps," he said grandly. "But perhaps I will look for Rebecca instead. Good night, Cordelia."

He left her standing in the hallway.

Chapter Seven

❧

Out the coach window, soft, low green hills butted up against a brilliant blue sky. Rebecca, having been instructed to talk only when absolutely necessary, obliged Connor by remaining silent and feasting her eyes on the unfurling countryside. Her thoughts had been roiling since they had left Janet's cottage.

On the seat across from her, Connor seemed to doze, his hat brim tipped nearly to his brow. Mr. Grunwald was not merely dozing but sleeping with an admirably reckless abandon, his chubby limbs outflung, his mouth moistly agape. Sounds roughly similar to a rusty saw being dragged across a boulder came from him at intervals.

Rebecca wanted to engrave every bit of her journey on her soul, but soon the scene outdoors began to swim before her avid eyes, the blue and the green of the colors outside blurring together, and the sounds of Mr. Grunwald grew more and more faint . . .

When she awoke from a deep and dreamless sleep, it was dark inside the carriage and Mr. Grunwald was conspicuously absent. Apparently Rebecca had slept through one entire coach stop. Connor was awake and gazing at her.

"Was Janet your lover?" Rebecca asked. She had been dying to ask this very question from the moment they left Janet's house.

Connor sat bolt upright.

"Dear God, wee Becca, can ye not wake like a normal person? Take a little time to yawn and stretch and remember where ye are, that sort of thing?"

"You kissed her. I saw you."

"Aye, that would be because I didna attempt to hide it."

"Why will you not answer my question?" Rebecca persisted.

"Are you sure it is a doctor you want to be, wee Becca? Because I think perhaps you will make a fine lawyer."

Rebecca fixed him with an intent gaze. "I am merely asking a question. You have never been afraid of answering my questions before."

"*Afraid?*" Connor was indignant.

Rebecca continued staring at him, a keen and stubborn stare, and Connor could feel the heat from her pale eyes from across the carriage. He knew that stare. She would not relent.

"Aye, she was my lover," he sighed finally. "But mostly she was my friend, ye ken? I shall miss her." Connor watched Rebecca carefully for a reaction.

Rebecca kept her eyes even with Connor's a moment longer, then turned her head toward the window to watch the night fly by. "Mine!" she had wanted to scream, like a child, when Janet had placed her hands on Connor's face. And in Rebecca's mind, Connor *had* been hers, all her life, almost like a toy; she had never felt as though she had to share him with someone else. She had enjoyed his company whenever she wished it, had brought him little gifts of flowers and stones and once even a handkerchief with his initials stitched into it (perhaps her greatest needlework achievement) as a Christmas gift. She had shared her most controversial thoughts with him, and he had received them with wisdom and humor.

But it had never occurred to her to imagine that he led a life between her visits with him.

Rebecca knew the world as defined by the confines of Tremaine House, and she was familiar with a vast esoteric world of science and physiology as revealed by her father's scientific journals, and she knew history and politics from the newspapers. But gazing out the coach window, she had the depressing sense that the vast blackness she looked out on represented the chasm between what she knew and what she did not yet understand, the extraordinary complexities presented by the ordinary. She felt very young, and very selfish, and suddenly ill equipped to be on the adventure to which she was now committed.

"I am sorry, Connor," she said, finally, softly.

"Sorry?" he repeated, confused. He had been watching her face; even in the half-light of the carriage he could sense the tick of her mind. He had always enjoyed anticipating what she would eventually say. His favorite thing about Rebecca, however, was that she managed nearly every time to surprise him.

"I am sorry . . . if you are leaving her to help me. Do you . . . do you love her?" These last words were nearly inaudible.

"I care for her, Rebecca, but it is not love in the way you imagine love to be. We are two adults who are free to take solace in each other's company, and we have done just that, and that is all. Janet is a strong woman, and will not pine long for me."

Rebecca quietly mulled this over, head toward the window again.

"I have not thanked you for helping me leave," she whispered at last. Beneath the ridiculous boy's cap she wore, Rebecca's face was stricken. She gazed down at her lap.

Impulsively, Connor moved across the coach to sit next to her. He hooked a finger under her chin to lift her eyes to his.

"I wouldna be here if I didna choose to be, wee Becca. In fact, I do very little that I do not choose to do. It has something to do with a vow I took long ago. I can think of no place I'd rather be at the moment. It's an adventure, aye?"

She smiled weakly at him.

"Aye?" Connor asked again, and gripping her chin, moved her face in an affirmative nodding motion.

Rebecca laughed and swatted at his hand. He captured her swatting hand in his for a moment, and then, startled by an awareness of the softness of her skin, he slowly, reluctantly, let it go again. Rebecca smiled at him, and when a cloud momentarily moved away from the full moon, shadows made valleys of her cheekbones and her dimples.

She will not thank me, Connor thought, *when I leave her.*

A gunshot exploded the stillness outside the coach.

The coach lurched to a halt, the horses whinnying and rearing in their harnesses in protest, and Rebecca and Connor were nearly thrown from their seats. Rebecca gasped;

Connor threw an arm across her to prevent her from tumbling to the floor.

"Highwaymen. Do not move and do not make a sound," Connor hissed. Rebecca stared at him, then nodded quickly, silently, in comprehension. He gave her a quick smile, rueful and tender, and released her shoulders. *Brave wee Becca*. Even though her eyes were wide with fear, he knew it would kill her not to comment on the proceedings.

Connor tossed his hat on to the coach seat, then reached into his boot. Rebecca reared back in astonishment when he pulled a darkly gleaming pistol out of it. He heard her draw in a sharp breath, as though to speak; he turned to her quickly and shook his head roughly, once, a finger over his lips, then crouched near the door of the carriage.

"No 'arm will come to ye, guv, if you do as ye're told," a voice was saying to the coachman. "Our business is with yer passengers, like. Jus' set yer musket down and keep yer 'ands up where we can see 'em, there's a good lad."

The voice raised to make itself heard by the occupants of the coach.

"Step ou' o' the coach, 'ands up, now." Deep and raspy, cockney, very sure of itself.

Connor could see them through the window, just barely, two mounted men, black kerchiefs tied across their faces just below their eyes, each holding a pistol. He gauged the distance between the coach and the first man at about six feet; the second man was slightly behind him to the left. He made his decision.

He could hear Rebecca's swift breathing; he glanced back one more time at her, a silent attempt at reassurance. The whites of her eyes were bright in the darkness of the coach; her hands gripped the edge of the seat. She offered him a weak smile, and his heart gave a strange lurch. *Good girl.* He turned away from her and lifted the latch of the coach door achingly slowly, soundlessly. Then, tugging the sleeve of his coat over his hand to partially cover his pistol, Connor raised his arms over his head and tucked the fingers of both hands into the shallow ledge between the top of the door frame and the ceiling of the coach. Using his knee, he gave the coach door a nudge, and it creaked open cooperatively.

The highwaymen saw a gentleman, arms raised, knees bent, framed in the doorway of the coach.

"We're lookin' fer a bit of jewelry, guv. A locket. Jus' 'and it over, and we'll be on our way," the closest highwayman said, his pistol pointed to a spot in the center of Connor's chest. "Oh, an' any other jewelry and blunt ye've got, we'll take that, too. We could be in a shootin' mood any second now, so step lively, guv. First yerself, then the lady."

Connor swung out from the coach and with devastating speed and aim kicked the closest highwayman's pistol from his hand, knocking him off balance in his saddle. The highwayman's mount reared and shrieked and dumped its cursing cargo to the ground, then launched itself into a gallop and disappeared from view. The other highwayman, unable to steady his aim from the back of his own nervously dancing horse, got off a wild shot at Connor, and Connor, ready for him, took aim for the man's gun hand. He missed the hand—boot pistols were damned capricious weapons, and he accounted himself lucky the bloody thing had fired at all—but the highwayman clapped a hand to his shoulder, wobbled in the saddle, then slid beneath his horse and lay still.

His horse, evidently affronted by all the noise and the highwayman's graceless dismount, pranced delicately over him and fled at a dead run in the same general direction as the other horse.

Silence of a sort descended, and a cloud obligingly moved away from the full moon again.

The first highwayman began to stir from his supine position. Connor swiftly tossed aside his fired pistol and pulled its mate from his other boot, then strode over to the highwayman and placed his boot on the man's wrist. He yanked away the black kerchief and pointed his pistol into his face.

"Now," Connor drawled in a voice so glacially, glitteringly English and aristocratic it could have cut a pane of glass, "you will tell me who sent you."

It was a question that had plagued Connor the moment the highwayman had stated the gender of his companion. *First yourself, then the lady.* A lucky guess perhaps, but Connor was not inclined to believe in luck. Highwaymen had become scarce on well-traveled coach roads, and the fact that these two had intercepted a pair of runaways seemed less a coincidence than an intent. He knew Sir Henry Tremaine would never send highwaymen in search of his daughter, and yet . . . someone else might have. Edelston? And what was this about a locket?

"No one sent us, guv. Now let me go, there's a good lad, I'll be on my way, like, and we can forget we met."

Connor increased his weight on the man's wrist, and the man groaned.

"I have heard it said that wrist bones make a very singular and delightful crunching noise when broken," Connor said. "Shall we find out?"

"*No no no no no . . .*" the man moaned.

"Tell me who sent you," Connor snapped.

"'Er Grace," the man gasped. "It was 'Er Grace. Dinna know 'er name, like, jus' we do a little business fer 'er now and again. She sends 'er man to us, 'Utchins, 'e's called."

"Her Grace," Connor repeated. He was astounded, though his voice revealed nothing of the sort. A duchess had sent the highwaymen? Then again, the proprietress of the Velvet Glove, a brothel near the West Indian docks in London, was known as the Abbess. Lofty titles did not necessarily indicate lofty positions.

"What does she want?"

"She wants the locket. And to know which way the girl is 'eaded in the coach."

The girl? The tiny hairs on the back of Connor's neck rose.

"Well, now. It is a shame you will be disappointing *Her Grace* this evening. I haven't a locket, and I haven't a girl. Why did you stop *our* coach?"

"Jus' lucky, I guess," the highwayman said cheekily. Connor ground his boot a little more emphatically into the man's wrist. "*Ow ow ow ow ow.* All right, guv! We stopped yer coach because we was told to stop all coaches going north."

Connor eased off his wrist. "Do you have any more weapons?"

"Wha—huh?" The change in topic seemed to bewilder the highwayman.

"Do I need to force you to strip naked here at pistol point so I can ascertain whether you have any more weapons, or will you tell me where to find them on your person?"

"Belt," the highwayman muttered. Connor kept his pistol to the man's ear and parted the man's coat to find a long knife sheathed in his belt. Connor pulled it and dropped it a few feet away.

"Thank you. Where can I find Her Grace?"

"She finds *us*. Or 'Utchins does, that is. She's a fancy London sort, is me guess. We, me and Edgar, we likes it 'ere in the country, though. Less competition, you sees."

The unfortunate Edgar began to stir and mutter.

"Don't worry, guv, I've got 'im," Chester Sharp said cheerily from atop the coach. He had taken a flask from his coat pocket and had been swigging at it while watching the proceedings with fascinated glee. By way of assistance, he was pointing his musket at Edgar.

"My thanks," Connor acknowledged the coachman. To the highwayman he said, "I do not believe you have given me your name, *sir*."

The highwayman scowled. Connor applied a little more weight to his wrist.

"*Ow ow ow ow ow ow ow*," the highwayman said. "Me name's John."

"Of *course* it is," Connor mocked. "The two of you, *John*, best move on to London, because I will make very certain you will not work these roads again. But before you go, I will just take this"—he picked up the man's knife and pistol—"and this, and your friend's pistol, as well." He walked over to where Edgar's pistol had been flung. Edgar had regained his breath and was attempting to sit upright, his hand still pressed to his shoulder. Connor hesitated a moment, struggling with his conscience.

"Did the ball go in?" he asked Edgar finally.

"Just a graze, guv. Ye're not *that* good a shot."

Connor nodded and knelt next to him and tugged Edgar's kerchief from his face and took a quizzical look. The pale pinched visage rang no bells of recognition. "I'll need your other weapons, too."

"Left boot," Edgar muttered. Pistol pointed at Edgar's temple, Connor gingerly dipped a hand into the man's boot and retrieved a small pistol.

"See to your friend," Connor said to John. "Oh, and London is in that direction." He waved his hand vaguely off to the southeast. "Enjoy your walk. You may start now."

John the highwayman gave Connor one last glare, then hauled himself to his feet. Silently he helped Edgar stand, and the two limped off into the night.

Connor exhaled deeply. He noticed then that he was trembling slightly.

"Would you like a pistol?" Connor asked the coachman. "I seem to have several."

"I should like a pistol," came a voice from inside the coach.

Rebecca's face appeared in the doorway. Even from where he stood, Connor could tell her eyes were dancing with excitement.

"That was certainly a sight!" Sharp piped up enthusiastically. "Never seen anythin' to match! Right useful for a lord, ye are."

"What did you say?" Connor asked sharply.

"About ye bein' useful, milord? I meant no offense —"

"Why did you call me a lord?" Connor demanded.

"Because for the past half hour or so you have sounded just like the bloody Duke of Marlborough." Rebecca was nearly bubbling with excitement. "Not a single 'wee' to be heard. Where on earth did you learn to speak like that?"

"Beggin' yer pardon, yer lordship, er, sir, I mean, but you could be the bloody King of England with a voice like that," the coachman agreed.

"Our king is a bloated sot. Kindly do not compare me to him. Ned, get back in the coach, now. Don't say 'bloody.' And ye shall not have a pistol."

"Oh, give the lass a pistol," Sharp said supportively. "Ye never know when a lady might need to shoot a highway bugger."

"Lad," Connor corrected sternly. "Ned is a *lad*, and the *lad* does not need a pistol."

"Whatever ye say, yer *lordship*," Chester Sharp said cheekily. "Not fer the likes o' me to comment on the goings-on o' the quality. Go ahead and toss me up a pistol, guv. We'll be in Sheep's Haven right soon, though why ye'd want to stop there instead of a proper coaching inn . . ."

Connor tossed up Edgar's pistol to the coachman and boarded the coach once more.

He reached for Rebecca at once and gripped her by both shoulders with something akin to a shake. "Are you all right?"

Rebecca stared at him, her eyes wide and wondering, and her hands fluttered up as though she meant to touch him. But she dropped them into her lap again instead.

"I am perfectly sound, Connor," she said gently. "I had no time to be afraid, you see, as I was in awe. How did you learn to do . . . to do . . . *that?*" She made a sweeping gesture with her hand meant to encompass the enormity of what had just happened.

Connor released her along with the breath he had been holding and sat back hard against the wall of the coach. Rebecca rubbed at her arm where his fingers had been.

He was quiet for a moment, his shoulders heaving with deep breaths. Finally, he gave her a crooked grin.

"I wasna certain I could do it until I did do it, wee Becca, and that is a fact."

"But . . . you shoot as though you have been practicing all your life at Manton's," she said, baffled. "It was extraordinary. *And* you have a very fine pistol. A gentleman's pistol."

"I learned to shoot in the army," Connor said abruptly. "And how do you know about Manton's, of all things?"

"Robbie Denslowe told me about Manton's, and I'll thank you not to change the subject."

Connor smiled. Most women would be weeping or swooning in hysteria by now; trust Rebecca to launch into an interrogation. "Did you learn how to speak like a lord in the army, as well?"

"Perhaps," Connor said airily. The whole speaking-like-a-lord nonsense was making him nervous indeed. He had been completely unaware that he was doing it. His adopted Irish accent had become so second nature to him that he occasionally even *dreamed* with an Irish accent. But an unvarnished Connor Riordan, a Connor Riordan who had not existed since Waterloo, had vanquished the highwaymen tonight. The realization left him disoriented, but peculiarly buoyant, as well.

A subject change was definitely in order, he decided.

"For your information, Miss Tremaine, the highwaymen did *not* stage this encounter for your entertainment. I assure you, they wouldna have hesitated to gut me and have their way with you, given the opportunity. A little more dismay on your part would be more than appropriate."

"I am sorry, Connor." Rebecca feigned contrition. "I have always had difficulty doing the appropriate thing. I shall endeavor to utter little shrieks of fright next time."

Connor gave a snort of amusement.

"From where I sat," Rebecca added, "it appeared you were enjoying yourself."

Connor merely snorted again.

"There is one thing that troubles me a bit, though, Connor," Rebecca continued, hesitantly.

More than one thing was troubling Connor at the moment, particularly the nagging sensation that the highwaymen had indeed been in search of the two of them. "And what would that be, wee Becca?"

"Do you recall the highwayman mentioning a locket?"

Connor made a little sound indicating that he was fairly certain he would not like what she said next.

"Well, there is something I forgot to tell you in all the excitement of leaving. I wanted so much to help with the preparations of this journey, you see, and as you would not allow me to do so . . ." She trailed off defensively.

"Finish your sentence, Rebecca."

"Well, I looked in Papa's overcoat before I left . . . and I found . . ."

She paused, her hands fumbling a bit at the back of her neck. Connor watched in apprehension as she slowly drew something up out of her shirt.

". . . this."

In her palm was a gold locket.

Chapter Eight

❦

The Thorny Rose Tavern's battered sign creaked forlornly on its chains in the breeze; a murmur of voices came from within. And then the tavern door swung open, releasing a wedge of lamplight. A lone man staggered out at a lean, spun about twice like a wheel off a cart, and collapsed in a heap.

"Ye sure this is the place, guv?" the coachman called down dubiously.

Connor was thankful Chester Sharp had dispensed with the "yer lordship" appellation for the time being. A "yer lordship" within earshot of any of the Thorny Rose's customers would very likely get him robbed and knifed before morning.

"This is indeed the place. Thank you for your services, Mr. Sharp."

"Say nothing of it. Never 'ad a more entertainin' evenin' in me life, and that's a fact. I'll see to the stablin' of yer new mounts, if ye'd like."

The coach had come upon the two horses belonging to the highwaymen walking along the road together, saddled but still riderless, for all the world as if they were headed for the Thorny Rose Tavern in Sheep's Haven themselves. They had peacefully allowed themselves to be tethered to the back of the coach. Connor was encouraged by this little bit of happenstance; he was running out of money, and having mounts for the last leg of the journey would save coach fare into Scotland.

"That would be helpful, Mr. Sharp, thank you." Connor grasped Chester Sharp's hand in thanks, and when Sharp pulled his hand away it was filled with coins.

Chester eyed the coins in astonishment. "Ye certain of this, guv?" he said weakly. "It's no' like I took ye to London and back, is it now? Just a bi' off the coach road."

"I'm sure. We may meet again, and I want ye to think of me kindly."

"Many thanks, yer *lordship*," Sharp said, although he did muster the judgment to lower his voice. "And dinna worry, guv, I'm no teller of tales." He gave Connor an exaggerated wink and strode off in the direction of the stables.

Connor stood still for a moment and inhaled deeply, and was almost sorry that he did. Sheep's Haven was on the outskirts of Dunbrooke land, and the night air was saturated with his past: the sweet grass of meadowlands, the earthy smell of sheep, the sharp green scent of the oaks and aspens. His heart lurched. Purgatory and paradise. Dread and joy. Every good memory of his life at Keighley Park was paired with an equally dark one.

But I escaped. He would never be proud of the way he had done it, but he felt anew the triumph and relief of it. And if some small part of him yearned toward Keighley Park, it was the least part of him; it was the small boy in him who still longed for something that had never been and never could be. Soon he would be a world away, on another continent, and his past would never touch him again.

"Are you quite certain you will not let me have a pistol?"

Connor gave a start. He had not heard Rebecca disembarking from the coach.

Rebecca correctly interpreted his startled expression. "Trousers are a wonderful invention," she said cheerfully. "One can climb up into carts and step down out of coaches with no assistance whatsoever. It is no wonder men keep them for themselves. Now, may I have a pistol, please?"

Although Connor knew that Rebecca could shoot an apple from a fence post at fifty paces, shooting a highwayman in the dark presented a bit more of a challenge. Something about the events of the evening, however, had prompted Connor to change his mind about giving Rebecca one of his new pistols. If anything happened to him, he would feel better knowing that Rebecca would at least have a slim chance of shooting someone.

"Wee Ned, if I give you a pistol, do ye promise not to shoot me or yourself?"

Rebecca held out her hand, knowing she had won, and he handed her one of the pistols. She tucked it expertly into one of her boots, which made him smile.

"A tavern?" she whispered excitedly. "We shall be staying in a tavern? I have never been in a tavern. What happens in a tavern?"

"Hush, wee Ned. Please remember that you are shy." He handed her the pack containing her belongings and, shouldering his own pack, pushed open the Thorny Rose Tavern's door.

They were immediately engulfed by heat and haze and a dank smell that exhaled from the timbers of the place, the smell of decades of spilled ale and sweat and smoke. Rebecca had started coughing. Connor turned to look at her; her eyes were tearing.

"Your cravat, Ned. Tip your nose into your cravat," he murmured. "Stay close."

The main room featured a begrimed assortment of customers, a few with a right nasty look to them, a few others who were probably just laborers in for a pint and a chat. A pair of men fitting the "right nasty" description seemed to be eyeing them with a specific sort of malice. Then again, malice was the native expression of a particular sort of man. Perhaps it meant nothing.

A bulky man with a head as smooth and shiny as a porcelain teacup hurried toward them, wiping his hands on his apron. His shrewd little eyes flicked over Connor and Rebecca, assessing. "And what can I do for you gentlemen this evening?"

"A room, if you would, good sir, for myself and my nephew. For the evening. And oats for our horses." Connor's accent, though quite English, was a mere wan cousin to the glittering weapon he had used on the highwaymen.

Connor held out a coin and watched the proprietor's face brighten and relax. So many members of the quality took service on account and never paid, Connor knew.

"Upstairs and to the right, gents. Ye be needin' any supper, a pint? Annie will see to ye."

Annie was already seeing to Rebecca.

"Wot's yer name, lad? Care fer some company this evenin', fine lad like yerself?"

Rebecca looked up to see who was purring into her ear and found herself eye level with an enormous quivering white bosom scarcely contained by its bodice.

"Ah—" She was about to deliver a polite refusal and was considering the accent and timbre she should employ when she felt Connor's hand on her elbow.

"Thank you, sir. We'll be down for supper after we get a bit of the dust off. Come, Ned," he said gruffly. He steered Rebecca none too gently up the stairs.

Once they reached their room, Connor shut the door behind them and immediately lit a candle.

"The locket," he demanded.

Rebecca handed it to him. He examined the plain, gleaming surface of it, turning it over in his hand. And then, as Rebecca had instructed, he ran his thumb along the edge to spring it open. His whole body went still.

"Connor?" Rebecca was alarmed.

Connor remained silent, motionless. He stared down at the locket.

"Connor?" Rebecca repeated, her heart suddenly racing. She touched his arm.

"There's an inscription, wee Becca," Connor said, finally, his voice hoarse. "Perhaps ye didna see it before."

Rebecca stood at his elbow as he read it aloud.

"*To my dearest love Roarke Blackburn from Marianne Bell, on the occasion of my Lady Macbeth, 1813.*"

"Marianne Bell," Rebecca repeated. She was back in familiar territory—feeling young and uncertain, with a dark, anxious pull in the pit of her stomach that she had begun to recognize as jealousy. "She is very beautiful," she said softly, hesitantly. "Do you know who she might be?"

Connor cleared his throat. "Aye, I know of her. She was an . . . actress. In London."

"Oh," Rebecca breathed. She had caught the hesitation in Connor's voice; *actress* in this instance meant very nearly the same thing as *whore*, she was certain. She absorbed this astonishing bit of information.

Connor moved slowly over to the bed and sat down at the edge of it. He continued gazing down at the locket, cupping it gingerly, as though it might wake and bite him if he made a sudden move.

"Ye found this in your da's overcoat pocket, wee Becca?"

"I took it from the pocket of a coat in the library. Quite by accident," she said hurriedly, when she saw amazement flicker across Connor's face. "Gilroy interrupted me suddenly, and I had no choice but to . . . well, to stuff it in my apron pocket."

"What, pray tell, were you looking for in the pocket of a gentleman's overcoat, wee Becca?"

His eyebrows were raised and he was wearing an expression of encouragement, as though he had all the faith in the world that she would issue a plausible excuse for stealing a locket.

"Money," she mumbled after a moment.

"Ah."

"You see, as I said, I had none of my own, and I so wanted to help . . ."

"Will you promise me, wee Becca, that in the future ye'll trust me when I say I shall take care of things, and not go thieving in the pockets of random overcoats?"

"I promise," she muttered.

"So ye found this in your da's coat pocket, Rebecca? For I think such a thing would more likely belong to Edelston."

"But it is addressed to Roarke Blackburn. Who is Roarke Blackburn, do you suppose? Her . . . lover?" Rebecca said daringly.

Connor's mouth quirked at the corner. "Oh, now, wee Becca, and it's wise in the ways of the world ye are, is it?" He returned his gaze to the locket. "Aye, wee Becca, he was her lover, I'm very nearly sure of it. But how did the locket get in the pocket of your da's coat? Or Edelston's coat?"

Rebecca sat down carefully on the bed next to Connor. Such a thing —a young unchaperoned daughter of a country squire sitting on a bed next to a groom—would have caused her mother to die a thousand deaths. But Rebecca wanted to look at the portrait in the locket again to see how she felt about it after having seen the expression it had caused on Connor's face. She peered just as Connor absently ran a finger over the inscription—and they both leaped back in surprise when the inscription panel popped open.

To reveal a miniature of Marianne Bell, sprawled on her back, one white arm flung over her head, quite naked.

Rebecca stared. She had seen drawings of naked people before in the anatomy book in her father's library, but never like this, never any that were clearly labeled with the name of the naked person in question. Marianne had been lovingly and explicitly rendered in rich ivory and cream with dabs of soft pink for her mouth and nipples and a sinuous stroke of black for her hair, which fell across her shoulder and trailed across one breast. There was a mere shadow of color at the V in her legs. The artist had clearly taken pleasure in his work.

"Oh, my," Rebecca whispered.

Connor abruptly stood up. "I am going downstairs for a pint of ale, wee Becca. I shall bring supper up."

He dropped the locket on the bed and walked out the door.

Rebecca immediately snatched the locket up again and continued staring. Naturally she had never been encouraged to gaze at length at her own naked self in a mirror, but she had tracked her own development with a furtive glance here and there, taking an objective sort of pleasure in the interesting new curves of her body. She had never dreamed, however, that a naked female body could be celebrated in the way Marianne Bell seemed to be celebrating her own. Nor had she realized that a naked female body could cause a man, who had served in the army and had recently single-handedly vanquished two armed highwaymen, to drop a locket like a hot coal and bolt from the room.

Rebecca stared at the door thoughtfully. If Connor was having a pint, he would be gone for a while. And she was seized with a sudden overwhelming desire to perform an experiment.

Keeping her eyes pinned to the door of the room, she carefully withdrew her newly acquired pistol from her boot and then yanked the boots off. Then came the coat and the trousers, and then the shirt, her fingers fumbling with all the little buttons, until at last she stood nude and covered in goose flesh in the midst of her heaped-up clothing.

She approached the bed and stretched her nude length

artfully (she hoped) across it. The counterpane was scratchy on her bare backside, a peculiar but not altogether disagreeable sensation. She pulled her hair down over one shoulder, lifted her arm up over her head, and rotated her hips ever so slightly, then stared up at the ceiling with what she hoped was an abstracted, clever, inviting expression, an expression of womanly knowing, the expression, she hoped, that Marianne Bell was wearing in the miniature painting.

She very much wanted to feel whatever it was that Marianne Bell had felt when she posed for the painting; she wanted to see if arranging herself just so would make her more knowing, more worldly, more womanly, more adult. She imagined Connor's eyes on her body, imagined his expression when he took in the soft white curves of her, and wondered if he would bolt from the room, or . . .

She waited for the new feelings. Her bottom began to itch. She reached down to scratch it.

And then, out of the corner of her eye, she saw the doorknob turning.

With a shriek, she flung herself off the bed and landed with a thud amid her clothing.

Connor stood in the doorway with two steaming bowls of stew in his hand.

There was a moment of silence.

"Rebecca?" Connor finally said cautiously.

"You are certainly back soon," Rebecca called from the other side of the bed, her voice both a bit miffed and muffled. "You . . . gave me a fright. I thought I would . . . I was . . . taking a nap."

"I see," Connor said, though he thought the fright part

unlikely, in light of the fact that the young woman in question had actually been entertained by an encounter with two highwaymen. He listened with great interest to the scrabbling and rustling taking place on the other side of the bed.

"And did ye break any bones when ye fell?" he asked politely.

"Only a few," Rebecca retorted. She straightened her spine in an obvious attempt to reclaim her dignity.

But as she did, Connor caught disconcerting glimpses of soft white skin through the gaps of her unevenly buttoned shirt. He overcompensated by immediately casting his gaze up to the ceiling until she was standing in front of him once again.

"Are ye hungry, wee Becca?" He decided not to ask any further questions about what she had been doing.

It had been a long time since they had polished off the last of Mrs. Hackette's picnic basket. Connor claimed the rickety chair the inn had thoughtfully provided.

Rebecca scanned the room as though deciding upon the best place to devour her dinner, absently tugging the boy's cap from her head as she did. She shook her hair from its tether, and Connor watched as the candlelight played the tangled coppers and golds and russets like the world's softest symphony. He thought of all the kinds of light there were in the world, all the kinds of light that could possibly dance across Rebecca's hair, and felt a brief stab of happiness.

Rebecca finally decided to settle on the bed, and held her hands out for her bowl of stew and bread.

"Why do you think the highwaymen want our locket?"

Rebecca asked between bites. She had refastened it around her neck.

"A mystery, wee Becca." Connor was concentrating on his own plate.

"Perhaps it was taken from her lover and her lover wants it back," Rebecca mused.

"Aye, that could well be true," Connor said, taking pains to sound noncommittal. He loved the way she pinkened ever so slightly over the word "lover." He found himself pleased that she was bold enough to include it in her vocabulary but modest enough to be a trifle shocked at herself for using it.

"Roarke Blackburn," Rebecca said dreamily. "It is a very romantic name, don't you think, Connor? He sounds as though he could be a pirate."

Connor nearly choked on his mouthful of stew. "Oh, aye, a very romantic name," he agreed.

"Connor, I did not know that you could read."

Oh, but the girl was astute. This was faintly treacherous territory; very few grooms could read, and Connor had read the bloody locket inscription aloud. He looked up from cleaning his plate.

"Aye," he said carefully. "I can read. My da insisted I learn." This much was true, at least.

"What was your father like?" Rebecca asked.

Connor looked up from his plate for a moment and stared at her. Her plate was shiny from the rigorous mopping she'd given it, and her eyes, those eyes the color of the sea at dawn, were fixed on him with a sleepy, gentle curiosity. There was a dark spot at the corner of her mouth that he assumed was stew. He pointed to the corner of his own mouth, and Rebecca took the hint, her pink tongue darting out to take care of the last of her dinner.

"You've a need to ask questions, wee Becca, now that your belly is full?"

"Aye," she said, mimicking him. Connor laughed. Because she deserved whatever version of honesty he could offer her, he tiptoed out over the quicksand of his past, and gave her a careful answer.

"My father was an angry man, wee Becca. Angry and proud."

"He must have been very unhappy, then, if he was angry."

This brought Connor up short. He had never once thought to question his father's happiness. He still sometimes woke at night from dreams of his father's blows, his skin tingling, his heart racing from the shock of it. It was part of him now, in his blood, in his soul, the humiliation that came from knowing that someone had the right to do this to him merely because he was blood, the despair that came with knowing that his only defense was a pathetic sort of endurance and his own stubborn pride, the Dunbrooke pride. Speaking out of turn, taking his horse out without permission, arguing with his brother, a less than perfectly completed lesson—anything, everything could bring down his father's wrath. His brother, Richard, had not been spared. And his mother, who gave her life giving birth to Richard one year after Connor was born, had not been there to witness it, or temper it.

What a bitter thing life must have been for his father, for his rage to be so easily shaken loose. Had his father seen his duties to his family, his title, his lands, his country, as chains, and fought them blindly? Had an inward turning of grief over the death of his wife festered into anger? Connor would never know. His father was dead.

"Aye, I think ye've the right of it, Rebecca," he said softly. "I think my father was an unhappy man. But I only knew fear of him. I left home as soon as I was able."

Something was stirring in him, though; a bud of comprehension that could very well bloom into forgiveness if left unchecked. *But then who will I be?* he thought. He pushed the feeling away; it was too much all at once.

"What did you do then?" she asked softly.

"I found it very soothing to shoot at the French," he answered wryly. "I was wounded. I've a grand scar," he added, surrendering to a less than noble impulse to impress her.

Rebecca's mouth made an "O" of awe and morbid fascination just as he'd suspected it would. She scooted to the edge of the bed and peered intently as he pulled off his boot, rolled up his trouser leg, and peeled off his stocking. And there it was, a hard shiny path of gouged and raised white skin where the musket ball had plowed his calf.

Rebecca stared at the scar, which seemed to glow hotly still. And then, because curiosity had always been her compass, her eyes moved up the length of his calf. It was magnificently hairy and the line of it had a very unexpected and almost brutal beauty, curving as it did down to his long white foot, tufted with a few more dark hairs. She traced it with her eyes and then found herself oddly restless; her eyes felt thwarted at the interruption in the view his rolled pant leg presented, for the implication was that there were other parts of Connor that were equally magnificently hairy and intriguingly formed. She wanted to see them.

Realizing that she had been quiet for a very long time, Rebecca finally forced herself to lift her eyes up to Connor's face, and she cursed her fair skin, for she knew her cheeks were flaming.

Connor was watching her, his dark eyes nearly black, his expression unreadable. Rebecca's senses were crowded; she found she could not speak. At last, Connor drew in a long breath, then rolled his trouser leg down, still watching her.

"We've need of sleep, wee Ned, as we will be leaving at dawn. You take the bed, and I'll take the floor." The words were light, but Connor's voice betrayed a bit of a strain.

Rebecca nodded, realizing a protest from her would result in a conversation about propriety that would have seemed like so much banter a few days ago, but which now seemed strangely fraught with shadowy implications.

"How will you stay warm?"

"Oh, and are ye forgetting so soon I was a soldier, wee Becca? The ground is as feather down to the likes of us, and the air is as a blanket of wool." This, of course, was not at all true, but it made Rebecca giggle, and the peculiar tension in the room sifted away.

"You may use my cloak for a pillow," she said magnanimously.

"Thank you, my fine lady. But I shall use my own cloak for a pillow, and we've a blanket or two among our supplies. Now please go to sleep, and kindly do not leap off the bed in the middle of the night in fright, for I've no wish to be crushed."

Rebecca had never before slept in a pair of trousers and a long shirt and thought yearningly of the soft cotton nightdress she had included among her things, but since Connor seemed to think nothing of sleeping in his own clothes, she decided she would do the same. She wriggled under the counterpane, which though coarse seemed clean enough, punched the pillow to soften it a bit, and settled down to sleep.

She sincerely doubted she would actually sleep.

A drone of voices came up through the floorboards of their room. Not the voices of Mama or Papa or servants, but of a crowd of rough-looking men laughing and arguing over tankards of ale. Every now and then she could even hear the clink of glasses, or the crash of a chair tipping. Good God. She was in a *tavern*. In a place called Sheep's Haven. A mischievous little smile curved her lips. Lorelei would simply be *appalled*—

She might never have a chance to tell Lorelei about it at all.

A swift pang of longing for home, for Lorelei and Mama and Papa, stopped her breath for a moment. The Tremaines' neighbor, Bessie Hardsmith, was a grandmother many times over, and she had never set foot outside of St. Eccles. Rebecca almost understood; once upon a time, Tremaine House had felt like a universe to her.

How small her world would have been if she had stayed.

If not for Connor, she would have spent the remaining nights of her life lying in a marriage bed next to the loathsome Anthony Edelston. With the blessings of her parents.

Rebecca lay very still so she could listen to the sound of Connor breathing on the floor next to her, and the sound filled her with gratitude and an immeasurable, piercing tenderness. She pictured him as a lad, bullied and afraid of his father, and the thought that anyone could treat him with something other than thoughtful affection curled her hands into fists. She forced her hands open and took a deep breath; she had lately come to understand injustice and tricks of fate, and how they could turn you into someone else completely, maybe even turn you into the person you were meant to be.

Rebecca gingerly moved to the edge of the bed and stared down at him through slitted eyes. With a new avid absorption she watched his chest move with his breathing, his lashes trembling on his cheeks, noticed the short coarse beard beginning to shadow his normally smooth jaw. Janet Gilhooly had put her hands on Connor's face, had touched him freely, as though it had been her right to do so, as though she had done that very thing dozens of times. Janet Gilhooly had probably put her hands on the rest of him, too—not only his beautifully hairy calves, but the rest of what lay underneath Connor's clothes. And though the very idea of it made Rebecca want to growl like a savage dog, she was peculiarly grateful to Janet Gilhooly, too. She was grateful to anyone who had given comfort to Connor Riordan.

For Connor was here with *her* now. By choice.

And as she looked down at Connor, she longed to touch him, too.

Once wrapped in a blanket and settled on the floor, Connor was quickly reminded of just how comfortable sleeping on a completely unyielding surface really was. Sleep would come slowly, and his muscles would complain about it in the morning.

Good God, why now, when he was poised to leave his

past completely behind, did it return in the form of a *locket*, of all things? At last, he let his thoughts slide to the place he had held them back from all night, and that was Marianne Bell.

More than anything, Connor thought, Marianne Bell had been an *achievement*. Out of boredom and perversity one night, a lifetime ago, it seemed, he had visited a seedy little East End theater called The Sweet Apple, far from the more refined entertainments offered by the *ton*. It was not the sort of place that one typically found the *heir* to any-thing; *riffraff* was in fact a diplomatic way to describe the audience.

But that's where he had first seen Marianne.

The part had required little more of her than walking on and off the stage, but something about the way she moved caught his eye. When he finally caught a glimpse of her face, the totality of her beauty had been very nearly over-whelming. At first Roarke could only withstand it by let-ting his eyes dart from one of her features to the next, from a delicate black brow to the full perfection of her bottom lip to the daunting blue of her eyes. He had wanted to im-merse himself in it, to somehow own it.

He had returned to the theater night after night. He sent expensive gifts to her and plied his charm insistently; Mar-ianne Bell politely demurred again and again. But in the end, there was no denying that Connor was the heir to the wealthiest duke in all of England; as such, there was very little he wanted that he could not have, and this extended to Marianne, as well. Ultimately, naturally, she capitulated.

He set her up in discreet lodgings, gave her a generous allowance, and set about enjoying the woman he had won. She was a careful creature; cool, proud, and watchful, with a wit that occasionally surprised him. Making love to her had proved to be a quick immersion in physical splendor— he had not been her first, but he had cause to give thanks for the tutelage his predecessors had clearly given her. But the experience always left him feeling strangely dissatisfied, perhaps because her true essence remained as intangible as a breeze; he could feel something in her retreat the moment he rolled away from her. He could every now and then surprise a genuine laugh from her, and once or twice he thought he caught something in her eye, something raw, yearning, wounded, but whatever it was had vanished so quickly he had decided he must have been imagining it.

On the occasion of my Lady Macbeth, the locket said. And he remembered, with a twinge, the night he'd left her for good.

He had come to her filled with a barely suppressed rage, for he had come to her from his father.

"When are you going to do your duty and get a proper wife, Roarke? It's time to stop pissing my money away on your whore and get down to the business of breeding an heir," his father had said as he departed the London townhouse.

He had long since learned to meet his father's goading with a show of impassiveness, and had even come to appreciate, in a sense, the great reservoir of resentment that resulted. He had discovered that he could channel it with grim precision into shooting at targets, picturing his father's face in the bulls-eye, and learning to fight, picturing his father's face on his opponent. Consequently, he was accounted an excellent shot and a skilled and almost deadly pugilist. But he was tired that evening, and had drunk a little more than usual the night before. And perhaps it was because he was still young, and had not yet calcified into the sort of cold, bitter man who could equal his father in a contest of control and measured vitriol. But the words were out of his mouth before he could reconsider them.

"Get a wife?" he drawled. "So I can get her with child and watch her die in childbirth, the way you killed my mother?"

The fist connected before he could duck. It surprised him; his father had not hit him since he had gone off to Oxford, and usually he used the flat of his hand, not his fist. The blow knocked him down, and his father had then driven a contemptuous foot, over and over again, into ribs.

Connor, who could happily strike anybody in the name of pugilism, could not bring himself to strike his own father. And so he had struggled to his feet, gathered his coat and hat, and calmly and silently exited the townhouse. He had gone to Marianne, but his thoughts had been fixed on retaliation, on his long-suppressed burning need for retaliation, the perfect, most appropriate sort of retaliation, and not the luscious semidressed female standing before him.

She had asked him, he recalled, if he minded whether she played Lady Macbeth at the Sweet Apple Theater.

"The theater manager thought he would try something new," she told him. "He is hoping to attract a different crowd, perhaps friends of yours with blunt to spend."

"Macbeth is hardly *something new*," Roarke had murmured, bemused. "Will there be naughty dances during the soliloquies?" Naughty dances were a specialty of the Sweet Apple Theater.

"Roarke, I am quite serious. He would like me to play the role of Lady Macbeth. Do you mind?"

At the time, he had thought perhaps he should object—

he wasn't terribly keen on his mistress spending a good deal of time before the public, let alone becoming a potential laughingstock—but he hadn't the strength to withstand her disappointment if he objected. A night or two earlier it might have seemed a far more pressing concern, and might have warranted a heated discussion, but his thoughts were loath to budge from the events of earlier this evening, from retaliation. And so he had given her permission to play Lady Macbeth.

He had joined the army the next day. He had not seen Marianne Bell since.

Yes, Marianne had been an achievement, a challenge, an enigma, but never truly a person to him, Connor admitted to himself, and he felt shame. She had never been able to touch the core of him, and whether it was something about her that failed to reach him or something about the young man he was at the time that could not be reached, it remained true. It enabled him to leave her with little thought and little regret, and he had thought of her rarely over the years.

The locket shamed him, the simplicity of it; she had most likely paid for it, and the portraits inside—and oh, how the image of her stretched nude along the chaise would have warmed those long weeks with Wellington— with the money she had earned for herself on the stage, not the allowance he had given her. Her "dearest love" she had called him. He knew what that must have cost her careful pride. He now understood how gravely he must have hurt her.

Even so, he would most likely need to trade the locket for supplies before they continued on their journey. Connor had very little money left.

Oh, you're a fine one, a hero, he told himself mockingly. It was still a mystery how the locket had come to be in the pocket of an overcoat in the Tremaines' house, but in a way, it seemed inevitable it would find its way to him. He had tried to run from his past, but it was now clear that he had only succeeded in damming it. The moment he made a move away from the static peace he had achieved in the stables of Sir Henry Tremaine, his past had come rushing back at him in a torrent, in fragments. For reckoning, he supposed.

He knew why he resisted telling Rebecca who he really was and where they were going: he was afraid she would think less of him for leaving his duties behind. Rebecca truly did think of him as a hero; when he looked into her eyes, he *was* a hero. And he never wanted disappointment to darken her face. But he still wanted nothing of it, not the immense burden of centuries of grandeur that came with the title, not the money and the ludicrous and unjust power it gave to those who had it, not the enormous houses decorated in cold gilt and marble, not the suffocatingly superficial company of what passed for society in London. None of it. He wanted to learn himself from the ground up, he wanted to make his own way, and he wanted to do it in America.

Eyes shut, he lengthened the space between his breaths so he could listen to Rebecca breathing. How she caught at him, with her eyes that saw everything and understood without judging, with the light that seemed to come off her, with the effortless blooming loveliness that robbed him of speech. He wanted to warm his hands over her, breathe her in. He would revisit any part of his past for Rebecca, he realized. *I will do it so that she can decide for herself where life will take her.*

What bloody nonsense, you great fool. At last, he forced himself to look at the truth beneath the truth. *You're taking Rebecca away because you cannot bear the thought of her belonging to someone else.*

Just then, Rebecca's cool fingertips landed softly on his face.

Connor's heart leaped into his throat.

For a moment Rebecca's fingers merely rested against him, a tentative delicate pressure. His heart began to jump. *What was this?* With a monumental effort, he continued breathing slowly and steadily, in and out. Did she believe he was asleep?

Or did she know that he was not?

With one finger, Rebecca slowly followed the line of his jaw, a touch soft as a breath, barely a touch at all. A tiny, sensual benediction.

Connor's breathing grew unsteady. Tension gathered in him, drawn ever more taut by the progress of her finger. *What should I do?*

Her finger rounded the curve of his chin, paused, hesitating. If he turned his head just a little, only a little, her fingers would fall against his lips . . .

God help him, he knew what he *wanted* to do.

Rebecca took her hand away.

He nearly groaned aloud. *Thank God.* He lay as still as possible, breathing deeply and slowly. His heart was beating so hard the blood rang in his ears.

Finally, an eternity later, the cadence of Rebecca's breathing told him she was asleep.

It was curiosity, nothing more, he told himself. *It was*

Rebecca being . . . Rebecca. But his body remained tense, awakened to an astounding, and not entirely welcome, realization. Connor threw an arm over his eyes, as if he could smother his roiling thoughts; he silently counted up to one hundred, and then back down again.

But still the feel of her touch, the scorching delicacy of it, lingered, as though he'd been branded by the light of a star.

Chapter Nine

❦

The gold brocade chair with the gilded legs was so ornate it seemed less furniture than jewelry, and normally it hurt Cordelia's eyes just to look at it. She preferred it the other way around; she favored simple yet elegant furniture upholstered in colors that set off her own vivid coloring, furniture as a *setting* for a jewel. But this particular chair had reportedly once supported the bum of Louis XIV himself. Cordelia had fetched it from the Dunbrooke country estate specifically for the London townhouse for this very reason. It was emblematic of her place in life, a talisman; sitting in it stabilized her sense of entitlement whenever it grew shaky.

There had once been a set of such chairs. Her late husband, a man so handsome he could stop conversation by entering a room, a man in possession of one of the oldest titles and grandest fortunes in all of England, had mistaken the other one for a chamber pot one drunken night and sprinkled it thoroughly. A servant had subsequently whisked it away. She knew not its fate.

In exchange for enduring marriage to Richard Blackburn, a man who began drinking shortly after breakfast and enjoyed giving and receiving spankings, Cordelia Blackburn, Duchess of Dunbrooke, had become the most influential woman in polite London society. The soothing aristocratic gleam of her bearing helped offset her disquieting beauty, both of which, it was universally assumed, were the result of some ancient and extinct royal bloodline, most likely French. As the Duchess of Dunbrooke, she entertained frequently and exquisitely, and presided over her functions with grace and wit tempered with demure self-deprecation, earning the protective regard of the women in her circle and ensuring that none of them feared for their husbands. In truth, Cordelia knew she could smite any of the husbands in the *ton* with one precisely aimed glance from beneath her dark lashes. Husband smiting presented so little challenge that Cordelia indulged in it on only the dullest of evenings.

All in all, as the wife of the Duke of Dunbrooke, Cordelia had created a life for herself that was as artful, complex, and mathematically constructed as any Bach composition.

The end of her marriage had come sooner than she had thought possible: her husband's throat was slit by a footpad a scant two years after his own father died. Thanks to Hutchins, impediments to her happiness had a way of conveniently disappearing. A wan expression, a softly muttered, "I wish Richard were dead," and soon, interestingly enough, her wish had come true. She thought it wisest not to question this phenomenon; after all, the end result was a more comfortable, and perhaps safer, life for her.

Cordelia was left with the extraordinary Dunbrooke fortune, for Richard had no heirs, not even any distant cousins. There was a dearth of children in this particular generation of Blackburns.

She had been in love, truly in love, just once, and that folly was, ironically, the source of her current aggravation, thanks to Anthony Edelston. But she still could not muster any significant degree of rancor toward Edelston, and—in a number of subtle ways—she had made it clear to Hutchins that despite the blackmail, she preferred Edelston alive for the time being. Although at first glance he seemed no different from any spoiled lordling of the *ton*, Cordelia knew that Tony was perhaps more of a rogue than any of them, but also possessed a rare, pronounced, and reluctant streak of decency. True, Edelson had rifled her jewelry box and helped himself to the locket while she slept off the effects of wine and lovemaking. But he had also kept a secret so delicious that in and of itself it could have become his sole form of currency, a secret the *ton* would have gnawed and sucked the marrow from for years.

Which was that Cordelia Blackburn was perhaps the most gloriously perfect fraud ever to breach London society.

The cup and saucer she was holding began to rattle in her hands. She placed them carefully on the spindly table next to her, lest she ruin yet another Louis XIV chair, and folded her hands together in her lap, burying them in the soft, expensive folds of her gown.

A tap sounded at the drawing-room door.

"Enter, please," she said.

Hutchins paused in the doorway and, as usual, made a deep low bow to Cordelia. Her face softened at the sight of him. Her face was, in fact, probably the only face in the world that would ever soften at the sight of Hutchins. It wasn't that he was grotesque; he was short and a trifle bent, but that described a goodly portion of the London population. It had something to do with his eyes. They were enormous and stygian dark and set deep into his skull, and something about them, something bleak and implacable and infinitely still, suggested a pair of freshly dug graves. They gave one shudders, and Hutchins appeared to know this; when required to be in the presence of The Quality for any length of time, he kept his head deferentially lowered. He seemed to move in his own personal twilight, which afforded him a sort of invisibility that his mistress found very useful.

Hutchins seemed to be at least peripherally acquainted with every cutthroat, card cheat, and all-purpose reprobate within a fifty-mile radius of London. Cordelia knew nothing and preferred to know nothing of the specifics of his past; she only knew that he had a weakness for the theater and a gift for strategy, two qualities that had beautifully complemented Cordelia's own gifts and ambitions for many years now. For reasons known only to him, Hutchins had decided long ago that Cordelia was worth serving. For fifteen years he had treated her like an empress.

"Your Grace, I come to make my report."

His hands were empty. The locket had not been retrieved, then. She lifted her cup again and took a long sip of tea, hoping it would steady her nerves.

"Please do take a seat, Hutchins," Cordelia said. Normally she would not invite any of her servants to sit, but she knew Hutchins's hip pained him on damp days, which was nearly every day in London.

"Thank you, Your Grace." Hutchins gingerly settled himself on a plump rose-colored satin chair. "Our . . . assistants on the road to South Greeley encountered no coaches, Your Grace. Our other assistants, however, had an unusual encounter with the passenger of a hackney coach on the road north of St. Eccles."

"Oh?" Cordelia asked. "What transpired?"

"Our assistants did as asked—stopped the coach and requested the locket from the passengers—but apparently a lord of some kind, and I quote, 'a bleedin' gentry madman,' shot one of them, not badly, but drew blood. Divested them of their weapons. Frightened off their horses. Knocked them on their arses."

"Knocked them on their arses?" Cordelia repeated. "Another quote, I presume, Hutchins?"

"Indeed, Your Grace."

"The story sounds rather apocryphal, Hutchins. Just one man did this to two armed men? What on earth would a lord be doing riding in a hackney coach? And was there no sign of a girl?"

"They said the man—tall fellow, dark-haired—spoke like an English nobleman and was a frightfully good shot. He made short work of them, madam. Came swinging out of the coach kicking and shooting and what have you, they tell me. I took the liberty of compensating them for the loss of their horses, Your Grace. We may need their services in the future."

Cordelia nodded, distracted. "In short, they did not find an Irishman or a redheaded girl in the coach."

"They did not actually *see* a girl, Your Grace, and the madman denied that a girl was aboard the coach. But one of our assistants—Edgar, he's called—swore that when the madman offered one of our assistants' pistols to the coachman, he heard a young girl's voice say, curiously enough: 'I should like a pistol.' "

Cordelia went still. For some reason, from what she knew of her, this sounded like precisely the sort of thing Rebecca Tremaine would say. Suddenly she was certain this story, at least in part, was true.

"You said the coach was continuing north?" Cordelia asked.

"Yes, Your Grace. Perhaps farther on toward Scotland. It is difficult to say."

"Hutchins, will you arrange for our assistants to track this 'madman'? Rebecca Tremaine has not been located anywhere near the vicinity of her own home, and something about this story piques my interest."

"Consider it done, Your Grace."

"Thank you."

"Your new solicitor is waiting in the parlor. Shall I send him up, or will you go down to meet him?"

Cordelia sighed. Very inconveniently, the Dunbrooke family solicitor, an ancient but gratifyingly consistent chap named Melbers who had been with the family for more than thirty years, had died in his library chair about a month ago. On the recommendation of Viscount Grayson, Cordelia had engaged a Mr. Matthew Green, and Mr. Green had requested time to familiarize himself with the accounting of the Blackburn family and the Dunbrooke Estate before he made his report to Cordelia, who had completely forgotten their appointment.

"Do send him up, won't you, Hutchins, and ask the maid for more tea?"

"Certainly. And, Your Grace?"

Cordelia looked up.

THE RUNAWAY DUKE   139

"We will find the locket," Hutchins said softly. Cordelia gave him a swift, bleak smile, then nodded crisply. He nodded in return and backed out the door.

A moment later the maid entered bearing a tray of tea, followed closely by Mr. Matthew Green. He looked as solicitors ought: grayish, thin, bespectacled, competent but not self-important, respectful but not obsequious.

"Take a seat, Mr. Green. I trust you found everything in order?" Cordelia said, and set about pouring tea for the two of them.

"Yes, Your Grace. I knew Melbers well, and he was the best of his trade, if I may take the liberty of saying so."

Cordelia smiled politely. She was the Duchess of Dunbrooke, for heaven's sake, she thought to herself. Of course she would have employed the best solicitor that could be found.

"However, I did find one small irregularity that you may be able to assist me with," Mr. Green continued. "It is an expense that has occurred at intervals of once a year for the past five years. The name associated with the expense does not belong to any of your employees, and I thought perhaps it might represent"—and here he lowered his voice apologetically —"a gaming debt. But the payment occurs at precisely the same time each year. And it is recorded in a separate book."

Cordelia twisted her mouth wryly. She found it difficult to believe that Richard could have been lucid enough or honorable enough to pension off a mistress, but one never knew.

"What is the name in the book, Mr. Green?" she asked.

"The name is Connor Riordan, Your Grace."

Cordelia promptly dropped her teacup, splashing, perhaps inevitably, the Louis XIV chair.

Mr. Green leaped to his feet, flustered. "Your Grace! Shall I call your maid?"

"Oh, do forgive me, Mr. Green." To her horror, her voice emerged as a flutelike squeak. She cleared her throat to steady it before attempting speech again. "I fear I am very tired and somewhat clumsy as a result. May we meet again another day?"

Mr. Green, who seemed a bit overwhelmed by her sudden distress, muttered an agreement and fled from the room.

Cordelia's mind reeled with possibilities.

She waited until she could hear her butler ushering Green from the house, then bolted for the office once kept by the old duke. It was a musty room, unused since the elder duke had died, and Cordelia had planned to burn everything in it and turn it into another sitting room. She muttered a short, rare prayer of thanks that she had not yet gotten around to it.

Frantically, she pulled open the old duke's desk drawers, rifling through musty papers, glancing at them, tossing them aside, working until perspiration made the bodice of her gown cling damply to her body, until tendrils of hair shook loose, not entirely sure what she was looking for, and then . . .

The draft of the duke's first will. The will he made before his eldest son died at Waterloo.

"To my eldest son, Roarke Edward Connor Riordan Blackburn . . ."

She sank to her knees. He had been given all those bloody names, and she had only ever known the first and the last of them. At one time, no two words had ever been more beloved to Cordelia. Now, no two words were more dangerous.

Colonel William Pierce was having difficulty remembering precisely why he'd purchased a subscription to Almack's. There were card games and dancing in progress; a competent orchestra was playing a tasteful quadrille, and fresh young women in softly glowing colors glided about the floor in the arms of men, quite a few of whom were not at all fresh. But this was the way of their world; only a fortune, not beauty or youth, was required if a gentleman wanted a well-bred young wife. Matrons resplendent in turbans and plumes and conspicuous jewels lined the walls, watching the dancers with practiced, appraising eyes; wagers and barbs were traded behind strategically wielded fans.

Pierce was feeling a bit awkward and removed; he was not in search of a wife just yet, his own having died a short two years ago, and the gaming did not tempt him. Nor did any of the feminine faces about him. Pretty ornaments, they seemed; all the eyes and smiles appeared uniformly bright, but none of them seemed illuminated by any specific quality of character. Pierce considered that perhaps he was being unfair and then promptly forgave himself if this was the case. His thoughts drifted longingly to his country estate, where the hunting had been particularly fine this year, and to his young son, Nicholas, who had stayed behind with his tutor when Major-General Munson had persuaded Pierce to have a go at the London season. Pierce was beginning to restlessly rationalize a quick bolt out the door, maybe a trot over to White's for a relaxing drink and a peek at a newspaper, when he spotted Sir Henry Tremaine.

This was a pleasant and entirely unexpected surprise. Sir Henry also looked as though he were merely tolerating the evening, and doing a poor of job of it at that. Knowing that the only thing that could possibly entice Tremaine away from his comfortable estate was a daughter in need of a husband, Pierce searched the faces of Sir Henry's little group.

He was astounded to see the Duchess of Dunbrooke among them. She appeared to be deep in conversation with a handsome, genteelly rounded woman in a soberly purple turban; Pierce knew her to be Sir Henry's wife. Fascinating, this development. Cordelia Blackburn was the widow of the last Duke of Dunbrooke, Richard Blackburn, a bit of a rakehell who had met a shocking but not wholly unexpected end. And yet Richard had been the brother of Roarke Blackburn, and Colonel Pierce had liked young Roarke. He had been a young man of wit and integrity, a skilled, courageous, and clear-eyed soldier, if a bit rash in his decision to join the infantry. Dead at Waterloo, like so many others. Colonel Pierce regretted his loss very much.

Pierce felt his ennui sputtering into something like enthusiasm. Truth be told, he *would* enjoy a chat with Sir Henry. He strode from his spot and planted himself in front of the little group, smiling with pleasure.

"Why, Pierce!" Sir Henry said, looking both relieved and glowingly pleased. "What a delightful surprise. Jolly good it is to see you. You do remember Lady Tremaine? And may I present to you the Duchess of Dunbrooke and my daughter Miss Lorelei Tremaine."

Colonel Pierce bowed deeply as the three ladies dipped

polite curtsies. When they stood and lifted their faces to his, he was momentarily struck dumb by his first glimpse of Lorelei Tremaine.

A man could become a poet, a philosopher, merely by gazing at the expanse of creamy throat and bosom that rose up out of Lorelei's gown; the string of pearls she wore seemed redundant, an obstruction of the view. Her gown was of the palest blue silk, the color of a full moon in winter, and shot through with silver threads. The colors echoed to uncanny perfection the shimmer of her hair and eyes. He sought those eyes to see whether anyone truly occupied the body of this vision, and was intrigued to note the slightest of shadows darkening the luminous blue. Something was troubling Miss Tremaine, and though it might be nothing more than tight shoes, Pierce found this perversely more interesting than the determined empty brightness of the other young women around them. Even more intriguing, perhaps, was the fact Cordelia Blackburn, the *ton's* reigning beauty, was willing to appear at the side of this young swan.

"Take my daughter for a twirl around the floor, won't you, Pierce?" Sir Henry said, rescuing his friend from a riveted silence. "Then bring her back so we may have a good catching up."

As Pierce held out his arm for Lorelei's gloved hand, he was amused to notice the faintest furrowing of Lady Tremaine's forehead; it indicated disapproval. Pierce sympathized entirely; having had the bizarre good fortune to produce such a prodigy, Lady Tremaine would naturally feel a certain amount of pressure to procure a triumphant match for her.

Pierce found himself basking for a moment in the

serene colors of this girl. She fit very neatly into his capable soldier's arms as he steered her in the familiar rhythms of the dance.

"Why are you sad this evening, Miss Tremaine?"

Lorelei's eyes went wide for a startled instant. "I do believe you are supposed to compliment my gown before you say anything else, Colonel," Lorelei replied, in all seriousness, before stopping to consider how she ought to have responded.

"Ah, but then what will be left for all the young bloods to say to you as they escort you about the floor? Let us leave the issue of the gown to them, or by the end of the evening you will have gone mad from hearing about it."

Lorelei smiled up at him uncertainly. The colonel had russet hair touched with gray at the temples and hazel-green eyes that crinkled a bit at the corners when he smiled, which he was doing now. He was not exactly Papa's age, but he was also not a young man, nor did he have a title. Mama would not expect her to marry him, and therefore Lorelei felt she could be a little freer in her conversation with him. She hesitated, and then, because she had been forbidden to so much as utter a word about it to anyone, even to her parents, and because the thought of it was preying upon her, and because his hazel eyes were so kind, she blurted, "I am concerned for my sister Rebecca, sir."

Behind them, a young man steering another young lady across the floor caught his first glimpse of Lorelei. He promptly stumbled over his partner's feet, trod on the hem of her gown, and collapsed on all fours, bringing his partner crashing down after him.

Colonel Pierce deftly maneuvered Lorelei away from

the chaotic little heap. Lorelei's thoughts were elsewhere; she seemed not to have noticed it at all.

"Your sister?" Pierce asked. Good Lord, could there really be another such vision in the Tremaine household?

"She is . . . she is indisposed," Lorelei said, and then clamped her rosy lips firmly shut, as if forcing herself to close the door on the topic, and her blue eyes went wide with alarm. Pierce's imagination wheeled about for a moment, picturing everything from a young woman with a case of the sniffles to a young maiden pregnant and disgraced and confined to the country forever. He tried to keep the intrigued glint from his eye.

"And you are not to speak of it," he said gently, more a statement than a question.

"I am not to speak of it," Lorelei repeated in confirmation.

"You are here to marry a duke or an earl," Colonel Pierce said, another question that he stated as fact.

"Or a viscount," Lorelei added, "if one can be had."

"I will do my utmost to assist you in your quest, my fair Miss Lorelei," Pierce said gravely, but with an unmistakable sparkle in his eye, "if it will ease your worries for the moment. We have a splendid selection of earls and viscounts in London this season."

Lorelei giggled in spite of herself, amusement turning her eyes into great blue lamps, and Pierce was enchanted. It occurred to him, suddenly, that the opportunity to make Lorelei Tremaine's eyes light like lamps this season would more than compensate for the excellent hunting he would be missing.

Chapter Ten

❦

To Connor's satisfaction, Mr. Augustus Meredith's Pawn Brokerage was still conveniently located not more than fifty paces away from the Thorny Rose Tavern, the only place in town a man could lose a month's wages in the space of a card game. In the event of this unhappy occurrence, Mr. Augustus Meredith would happily supply you with more coin in exchange for your wife's best dishes, or your Sunday coat, or perhaps, if the straits were indeed desperate, a horse harness. Connor remembered the villagers surrounding Keighley Park often speaking of Meredith's establishment with both gratitude and resentment.

It was just past sunrise, but the boards of Mr. Meredith's shop window had already been thrown open, revealing a variety of homely and promising objects arranged with a nod to aesthetics: a few china plates and cups surrounded a large cooking kettle, a sturdy chair was stacked with two or three books, a well-worn but quite serviceable-looking musket leaned against the display wall. This was good, if the musket could be had for a reasonable amount; given their dwindling funds, he might need to hunt for their dinner before they arrived in Scotland, and he couldn't do it with pistols. Connor smiled faintly when he peered closer and noticed that one of the books was Dr. Mayall's famous Herbal, a compendium of useful medicinal herbs along with sketches and receipts for simples and salves. He was satisfied he would find precisely what he needed here.

But he hesitated momentarily on the threshold of the place. He had persuaded Rebecca to stay behind for a few more moments of sleep at the Thorny Rose. She had surrendered the locket this morning with surprising reluctance. But Connor gently reminded her of the reason she had stolen the locket to begin with, which was her desire to help supplement their exodus. This was how he finally convinced her that turning the locket over to him was the noble thing to do.

But Connor was still feeling a bit like a scoundrel for a number of reasons, not the least of which was that Marianne Bell was now indirectly helping her "dearest love, Roarke Blackburn," to run off with another girl. Pangs of guilt notwithstanding, he'd rest a good deal more easily once he'd disposed of the locket. He was poised to embark on a new life, and the locket felt oddly like an anchor preventing him from sailing with the tide.

Mr. Augustus Meredith was behind the counter preparing his morning tea. He glanced up sharply as the shop bell rang, his features reflexively settling into an appropriate pawnbroker expression, a piquant blend of welcome and wary condescension. He opened his mouth to issue a greeting, and then he took his first good look at Connor. He instantly straightened his back and puffed out his chest.

"Good morning. And what can I do for you today, good sir?"

Connor was a little taken aback. One was not usually welcomed so warmly in a pawnshop.

"Good morning. Mr. Meredith, I presume?" Connor asked.

"Indeed," Mr. Meredith replied, drawling the word regally.

"Perhaps you can be of some assistance, Mr. Meredith," Connor said, deliberately refraining from introducing himself. "I would like to exchange this"—he opened his palm to display the locket—"for a few supplies. That musket in your window, some cooking pots, and the like. I am on my way to visit my aunt in Scotland, and I promised my nephew a stop for hunting along the way. Unfortunately, I find myself rather short this morning. I was hoping I could select a few items and take the balance in coin."

Mr. Meredith's eyes had goggled in his head at the sight of the locket. He cleared his throat. "It is gold, I suppose?" It sounded like an attempt to speak casually, but his words emerged rather croakily instead.

"Of course," Connor said coolly. "Would you like to inspect it?"

Mr. Meredith eagerly held out his hand for the gleaming thing and expertly ran his thumb along the locket's edge to spring the catch. He gazed down for a moment, a small pleased smile playing about his lips.

"Oh, my. It is a very handsome likeness of the Duchess of Dunbrooke, isn't it, sir?"

Connor gawked at Meredith as though he had suddenly begun babbling in Turkish. *The Duchess of Dunbrooke?*

The last Duchess of Dunbrooke he knew of had been his *mother* . . .

"I . . . I beg your pardon?"

"The Duchess of Dunbrooke," Meredith repeated, cheerily and with growing confidence. "Oh, yes, it is she, all right. Pretty as a fairy princess. She was through town with the duke a year or so ago and we got a look at her, me and the missus did. They were paying a visit to their estate on the border, word was, and high time, too, seeing as how the lands there have been neglected for so long. Right shame about the duke's murder, it is, too. Footpad, they said it was."

Connor's head was spinning unpleasantly. "Mur—I'm sure I do not know what you are—"

"And oh, look here," Meredith continued. "There's an inscription, too. Let me just fetch my spectacles so I can—"

Connor adroitly plucked the locket out of the man's hand and clapped it shut. Meredith looked up, startled. He narrowed his eyes at Connor, who had gone a bit green around the mouth. Noticing, Meredith's jowly face softened.

"Changed your mind, sir? Can't say as I blame you. S'right hard, it is, giving up a family heirloom."

Astounded, Connor attempted a response, but when he opened his mouth all he could manage was an arid little yawp.

"Oh, you've the look of Dunbrooke, lad. Tall and dark like. Jaw sharp as an ax blade. I saw it right off when you came into the shop. Are you a cousin, perhaps? Fallen on a bit of hard times?"

Connor inhaled deeply, exhaled, and then drew himself

up to his entire formidably long and elegant height. "I've changed my mind, Mr. Meredith," he said, his voice successfully under control again. "I'll use coin to pay for the supplies. If you would be so kind to fetch while I point? Starting with a book in the window. The Herbal."

Mr. Meredith looked a bit rattled at how abruptly their cozy chat had become chilly servitude, but he immediately scuttled to do Connor's bidding.

When Connor exited Mr. Augustus Meredith's shop a half hour or so later, his arms were full and his pockets were nearly empty. He paused on the street, unseeing for a moment, and a tiny laugh of near hysteria burbled out of him.

Marianne Bell—*his mistress*—had become the Duchess of Dunbrooke? How could that *be*? And Richard, it seemed, had been murdered. His younger brother, his rival and ally, the innocent little boy who became a young man seemingly hellbent on self-destruction, had been murdered.

He was so absorbed in his thoughts that he never heard the footsteps behind him.

"Well, ye've not improved any wi' age, ye ugly ol' whoreson, but 'tis glad I am to see ye. Ye're supposed to be dead."

Connor spun on his heels. Behind him stood a man with skin the color of a polished walnut, eyes a shade darker than oak leaves, and a majestic potato of a nose. His green eyes were shining with affection and mischief, and a bulging burlap sack dangled from one of his hands.

"Raphael Heron!" Connor was delighted. "Still a blight on the face of mankind, I see."

Raphael Heron gave a whoop of laughter and seized Connor in a crushing hug, the contents of the burlap sack clanking as it shifted. When Raphael released him, Connor placed a testing hand over his ribs, fearing they were all now in splinters. He eyed the burlap sack with wry amusement. Raphael was a Gypsy, the head of a small Gypsy *compania* that had often camped near Dunbrooke land when Connor was a child, and his moral compass pointed in one direction only: just about anything—lying, stealing, and cheating included—was acceptable as long as it contributed to the well-being of the members of his *compania*. Consequently, Raphael and the members of his *compania* were exceedingly cheerful and original liars, thieves, and cheaters. The burlap sack no doubt contained a few purloined candlesticks or some silver plate intended for Mr. Augustus Meredith's perusal and purchase.

In a peculiar way, the simplicity of Raphael Heron's code made him the most honest man Connor had ever known. Raphael gave his loyalty begrudgingly but irrevocably, and had given it to Connor years ago the day Connor caught him poaching hare with two hounds and a net on his father's land. Connor had promised not to alert the authorities in exchange for being shown how on earth one caught hare with two hounds and a net. At first, befriending Raphael had been just another way Connor secretly rebelled against his father. But Connor had soon found Raphael's unique blend of wry wit, arcane wisdom, and unapologetic larceny irresistible, and they had become true if unlikely friends.

"Ye've a story, no doubt," Raphael prompted. "For I've no' heard that ye've been anything but dead."

"I've a story, aye. But only four people alive, myself

and yourself included, know that Roarke Blackburn did not perish at Waterloo, and I'd like it to remain so," Connor said mildly.

Raphael's eyebrows lifted, and he eyed Connor appraisingly for a long moment. At last, as though arriving at some private yet satisfactory conclusion, he shook his head admiringly.

"Roarke Blackburn? I once knew a Roarke Blackburn, but he died at Waterloo, rest his soul." Raphael invariably approved of artful subterfuge, since so much of his livelihood depended on it.

"Aye," Connor agreed, relieved, though he had been certain Raphael could be trusted with his secret. " 'Twas a great loss."

The corner of Raphael's mouth twitched upward. "If ye say so. Tell me, Roarke Blackburn, or whoever ye might be, will ye share yer story over a pint?"

"It's Connor now. And I would love nothing better, but I am traveling with a companion and cannot linger much longer, I'm afraid."

"Very well, then. Another day. I must say, I've never seen ye looking better, despite yer face still resembles a dog's behind."

Connor and Raphael always accepted insults from each other with the amused equanimity of two men utterly confident of their own charms.

"Odd, but you took the words right out of my mouth, Raphael. And . . . well, I've never been happier."

This was true, Connor realized, startled by his own words. And yet how could it possibly be true? He'd been accosted by highwaymen, his former mistress seemed to have married his brother, who had then been murdered, he was running out of money . . .

"Ah, I see," Raphael said sagely. " 'Tis a woman."

"It is *not* a woman," said Connor, irritated.

"And yer travelin' companion—would this be a woman now, or another gent?"

"And *how* does this matter, precisely?"

Raphael merely shrugged and grinned knowingly.

Connor, feeling strangely panicked, changed the subject. "Have you word of any of the Dunbrooke villagers—the Pickerings, the Browns?"

Raphael's demeanor changed almost imperceptibly then: his spine stiffened a little, he averted his eyes; it was almost as if, Connor thought with apprehension, Raphael regretted hearing the question.

"Ah, well, since yer brother's passing—before then, if truth be told—the lands and the people on them have fared . . . poorly . . . as there was no one t' take an interest. Th' youngest Pickering boy was hanged for stealing a pig. The family wanted food, ye see."

Connor flushed. They were delicately chosen words, diplomatic words, and not an accusation, precisely, but they fell on his ears as one nevertheless. And the worst part of it was that Raphael had known how they would sound to Connor, and had averted his eyes to spare Connor's pride. He had *assumed* that Connor should feel ashamed.

Connor stood very still for a moment, his face flaming. The villagers had been kind to him when he had been a lonely young lord, riding through town on a horse that cost more than any of them would see in a lifetime. He had held their babies, eaten their bread, talked with them of sheep and drainage ditches. *It is not my fault*, he told himself vehemently. *It is not my fault that Richard was shiftless; it is not my fault that Richard is dead; it is not my fault that the Pickering boy met a bad end. Soon this will all be a bad memory. Soon I will be on a ship to America . . .*

And yet an image formed in his head: a stately home collapsing into rubble upon the removal of a crucial beam. *But I could never have been so important,* he told himself.

Connor cleared his throat, breaking the awkward silence that had settled over them.

"And what is it you have in the bag, Raphael?" he asked pointedly. It was a childish and petty way, he knew, to attempt to deflect his feelings of guilt, but his pride seemed to have taken over his wits at the moment.

Raphael glanced down at the bag and gave it a little shake to make the contents clank again. "Oh, a bit o' this an' that," he said easily. " 'Twasna nailed down, nor was anyone standin' guard o'er it, so clearly the owner could spare it."

Connor stared at him, wondering what it might be like to never feel even the slightest twinge of conscience.

"You should get a fair price for it all. Mr. Meredith has a good eye for merchandise. Why, just look at this wonderful Herbal he sold to me." He produced the tattered little book with a flourish.

Raphael laughed and folded Connor into another bruising hug by way of farewell.

"If ye've need of anything at all on your journey, Connor, follow the *patrin* to find me—ye ken how, aye? We've marked our path with stones and branches and the like," Raphael said. "We leave for the Cambridge Horse Fair in a day's time. We'll make some blunt selling horses and *dukkering* and healing and the like."

"Thank you, my friend. Godspeed. And try not to feel unhappy about that nose of yours."

Raphael tossed a wry grin over his shoulder as he clanked into the pawnshop, conceding the final point to Connor.

The afternoon sun coaxed a green perfume from the fields and trees and warmed a place between Rebecca's shoulder blades; it felt as though a large benign hand were resting there, guiding her along. In the distance, sheep dotted meadows like whitecaps on an emerald sea, and from a perch in a tree, a bird trilled a giddy string of notes.

Between the sun and the steady clopping of her own and Connor's horses, Rebecca was lulled near to dreaming. Despite the fine coat of grit she seemed to be acquiring (a perfunctory splashing in the washbasin at the tavern had accomplished little), and despite the itch and pull of her bound-up hair and stuffy cap, and despite her overall weariness, Rebecca could not recall ever being more completely happy. June had arrived with a holy, humbling perfection, she was on a lovely brown mare who had a white star between her eyes, a mare who could be forgiven for once belonging to a highwayman, and she was with Connor Riordan.

Connor had returned to the Thorny Rose Tavern from the pawnbroker's with locket still in hand and with a gift for her: a book that contained drawings of herbs and receipts for medicines, draughts, and poultices. He had presented it to her solemnly, a little shyly, but the gold flecks in his eyes were dancing as he watched her face.

Rebecca had been speechless. Connor had remembered her eighteenth birthday. And no one had ever before given to her a gift that acknowledged, even celebrated, precisely who she was. Gifts from Mama and Papa tended to be hopeful and slightly reproachful: embroidery silks, books on comportment, gifts that told all about who *they* wanted her to be.

As she held the book, she felt tears tightening her throat, so she had hugged him, hoping he wouldn't notice. And though she had hugged him before as a child, today she was mindful of the length of him, of the scratchy press of his cheek against hers, the cheek she had traced secretly last night in the dark, and the weight and heat of his hands on her back. His hands had hovered a moment, hesitating, before coming to rest on her—she noticed that, too—and then he had held her, almost gingerly, a tick or two longer than a hug usually lasted.

When Connor had at last pulled away from her, he seemed unable to meet her eyes.

Yes, today, life was as perfect as life could be, and she felt too tired and peaceful to feel even a twinge of guilt about Mama and Papa, who would have happily consigned her to a sort of purgatory with Edelston.

Connor, watching Rebecca's slim straight back centered above her horse, was feeling considerably less peaceful. Acknowledging the sweet warmth of the day, he rode in his shirtsleeves, but this road was sparsely traveled and he was fairly certain his breach of gentleman's etiquette would horrify few, if any, other travelers.

In contrast to the ease of his attire, his new musket lay across his lap half-cocked. They were now officially on Dunbrooke land, and every one of his senses were heightened and wary; he felt as though he were a prisoner strolling nonchalantly through a prison toward an open door, hoping no one would notice. He half expected the trees that lined the road to bow all at once to form a cage, trapping him in his past like a rodent.

Several other disturbing thoughts were simultaneously orbiting his mind competing for attention. In no particular order they were:

If the garrulous Mr. Augustus Meredith had it right, his brother Richard had been murdered and Connor's former mistress was now dowager Duchess of Dunbrooke, which made her sole beneficiary of the Dunbrooke fortune. And a certain *Her Grace* had apparently sent two highwaymen to retrieve the locket—a very incriminating locket, if one was once an actress named Marianne Bell, and one was deeply invested in keeping this little morsel of information from the *ton*. It all now made a terrible sort of sense, though how Marianne Bell had learned that Rebecca Tremaine had absconded with the locket was a mystery. No doubt Edelston was the connection there.

And if Raphael Heron had it right, the villagers near Keighley Park had suffered ever since Marianne Bell had become the Duchess of Dunbrooke. Connor wasn't at all sure what he wanted to do, if anything, about this, but he knew he wasn't at all pleased. It ate at him.

The third thought was that it seemed entirely possible that he and Rebecca were being followed, as two people on horseback had been riding at some distance behind them since shortly after they had left the Thorny Rose Tavern. The two puffs of dust kicked up by their horses on the road were clearly visible. He recalled the greasy ruffians who had eyed them with a certain keen malice as they entered the Thorny Rose Tavern yesterday evening, and wondered if perhaps their malice did indeed have intent.

The fourth thought was that the only thing he really wanted to do at the moment was indulge an appalling impulse to pull Rebecca off her horse, wrap her in his arms, tug off her cap, plunge his fingers up through her hair, and—

"Well, well, we meet again, guv."

Bloody, *bloody* hell. The two wretched highwaymen they had encountered a night earlier were on the road in front of Rebecca, mounted on freshly acquired horses, pointing freshly acquired pistols, a pair each at Connor's chest and at Rebecca's. Their faces were kerchief-free, a nod either to boldness or to the futility of the gesture; Connor had seen them both vividly by the light of the full moon a night ago.

Connor silently cursed himself and glanced wildly about; they had been lying in wait in a thick stand of birches. What Connor could have done about it was exactly nothing, but this realization only enraged him further. His mistake, he knew, was arrogance: he had assumed the highwaymen would not dare to come back for more after being so thoroughly humiliated by him the night before. *I deserve to hang right here and now for allowing anyone to point a pistol at Rebecca's heart.*

"Ned," he said, his voice low, resonant. Rebecca understood: it was a warning to remain absolutely still and silent. She complied, her hands motionless on the pommel of her saddle.

"Pretty mounts ye have under ye," the highwayman named John said, as the two of them rode closer to Connor and Rebecca. A distinct petulance colored his tone. "Ye willna have the pleasure of them much longer. Now if ye aim that musket our way or reach for the pistol in your boot, guv, we'll shoot ye and then the lad. Or maybe we'll shoot the lad first, and then yerself. The way we sees it, Edgar and me here, we owes ye. Now raise yer hands up where we can see them, like, both of ye."

Connor, slowly, with a great show of reluctance, lifted his arms into the air and watched in a seething silence as Rebecca did the same. But his mind was a pulse ahead of the moment: he could now hear a rumble of approaching hoofbeats. It meant that their distant mysterious escorts were now riding toward them at a gallop.

Moments later, the two riders pulled up alongside Connor, horses snorting and stamping. Surprising no one, they were also brandishing pistols. A general expression of puzzlement flashed across the face of each man on the road: suddenly, no one had the foggiest idea at whom to aim.

"And *'oo*," John the highwayman finally said indignantly, "the 'ell are *you*?"

"Them's *our* 'orses," one of the men spat in Connor's direction. He was indeed, Connor noted with resignation, one of the greasy ruffians that had been eyeing Connor and Rebecca back at the Thorny Rose. Face like a sullen slab of dough sprinkled with whiskers, hair hanging in oily hanks to his shoulders. His partner looked eerily similar, if somewhat larger and fleshier. The Brothers Grime, Connor silently christened them.

"Ye stole 'em," the ruffian insisted. "And we've come to take 'em back."

He decisively turned his pistol on Connor, who raised his musket to meet the challenge, which caused John and Edgar the highwaymen to lurch forward a bit in their saddles and point their own pistols at Connor more emphatically, if such a thing was possible. The greasy ruffian's compatriot, feeling left out, took this as a cue to aim his pistol in Rebecca's direction. Rebecca's hands were flat against her thighs, heartbreakingly empty. But then again, she was new at the business of fending off gun-wielding attackers, Connor thought.

It was silent for a moment, until Connor's horse blew air through its nose. It sounded remarkably like a snort of disgust.

An exchange of a sort involving shifting eyes and raised eyebrows was taking place between John and Edgar, the highwaymen. Connor felt a distant sort of amusement; clearly, the two highwaymen had somehow stolen the horses from these two greasy ruffians, and Connor suspected the greasy ruffians had stolen them from someone else before that. Few men would take justice into their own hands unless justice already wanted to hang them for something else.

John, as usual the spokesman for the highwaymen, cleared his throat and began.

"We understand yer plight, gentlemen," he addressed the greasy ruffians, who moved their pistols indecisively away from Connor and Rebecca and pointed them in the general direction of John and Edgar, as though they were loathe to commit their enmity fully just yet. "We'd like to make a little bargain with ye. We've some dealings with these two"—he paused, searching for an adjective that would adequately describe Connor and Rebecca, and failing to find one, continued—"blokes, and it will take but a minute. We'd be much obliged if ye'd aim yer pistols in their general direction while we . . . conduct our business.

An' after *that*, ye can take yer 'orses off, and we'll aim our pistols at these two lads whilst ye do it. Ye've our word on that. Fair enough?"

The greasy ruffians conferred with grunts and mutters, and the first one spoke again.

"Done. Do it fast." With these words, all guns were trained on Connor and Rebecca.

"Keep yer 'ands in the air, there's a good lad," John said to Connor, and smiled, revealing a gap where one of his front teeth should have been. "Remember, guv, one wrong move an' Ned 'ere is dead." Connor gave him a faint smile and complied, watching, his mind planning, sorting.

"Keep an eye on this 'un lads, 'e's a right devil," John remarked to the greasy ruffians.

"Now, Ned," John said, turning his efficient attentions to Rebecca, "come down off that beast ye *stole* and let Edgar 'ave a look inside yer pack. If we find naught in it, then we'll take a look inside yer clothes, eh? Or ye can always jus' show us the locket and be done wi' it."

Rebecca glanced at Connor for guidance, and Connor, mindful of the loaded and cocked guns surrounding them, nodded once. Rebecca scowled at John and slid down off her horse. John tucked one of his pistols into his waistband and then stepped behind her, wrapped a hairy arm tightly around her shoulders, and pointed his other pistol at her temple. Connor's heart began pounding in his ears.

Edgar dismounted from his horse and trudged toward the pack strapped to the back of Rebecca's mare.

But Connor's eyes were on John's hand, which had begun, almost absently, to creep over Rebecca's coat. And he saw it when John's face changed subtly, saw the shock, the wonder, the abstracted, slow-dawning lecherous glee.

It was the expression of a man who has suddenly and accidentally found his hand on a woman's breast.

"Well, 'ere's something, lads," John drawled. Some primal note in his voice caused everyone to pivot alertly in his direction, like wolves catching a hint of deer in a passing breeze. "It seems Ned here has a *bosom*. This *lad* is a *lass*."

His hand moved over her coat again in a crawling caress and then closed decisively, triumphantly, over Rebecca's breast. The hand that held his pistol yanked off her cap with a flourish.

Rebecca's hair came tumbling out, an explosion of color in the afternoon sun.

An odd stillness descended. The expressions of the men shifted as one. Enthralled, ominously focused, they stared at Rebecca.

The greasy ruffian mounted next to Connor cleared his throat. "I'll 'ave a go at 'er," he said to John, politely. "After ye've 'ad yer turn, of course."

A rage so pure burning it approximated bliss almost lifted Connor out of his body. The faces of the men, the leaves on the trees, the barrels of guns, Rebecca's hair tossed by the breeze, his own breath and skin, fractured into minute shards of brilliant clarity. He looked at Rebecca; her face was white and pinched, her eyes glittery slits. She met Connor's eyes; rage met rage and understood.

"Now," John drawled, "ye canna really blame me fer thinkin', guv, that if ye were fibbin' about 'avin a *girl*, ye might be fibbin' about 'avin a *locket*. I think I'll jus' 'ave a peek inside yer shirt now . . . *Ned*." He thrust his hand roughly between the buttons that closed over Rebecca's breasts and froze in true surprise when his fingers met warm metal.

"Well, *hullo*, boys! Could this be a lock—"

Rebecca sagged in John's arms in a staged faint and Connor seized the heartbeat's space of diversion to ram the butt of his musket into the head of the greasy ruffian mounted next to him, who promptly toppled from his horse and dangled by one stirrup, senseless. From her near crouch, Rebecca drove her head up under John's jaw, and when his grip went lax with shock she twisted free from him and hurled her fist into his groin. Connor swung his musket with all the inhuman strength loaned to him by fury, once, twice, the third time succeeding in clubbing the other greasy brute from the back of his horse.

The horse shifted its feet indolently, and its haunches gave a little twitch, as though ridding itself of a fly. For now the man lay still. Connor doubted this happy condition would last.

Immediately lifting the miraculously unharmed musket to his shoulder, Connor trained it on the frustrated Edgar, who for the minute or so of chaos had seemed unable to decide who to shoot.

Rebecca swept John's dropped pistol from the ground and eyed John consideringly; the highwayman was entirely focused on his physical torment, bent double and making ghastly wheezing noises. Rebecca decided to finish the job by delicately hooking her leg around the back of his knees. John tipped over like a neatly felled tree. He lay folded in on himself, his hands bunched between his legs, emitting low horrible moans. Rebecca, her nose wrinkled in distaste, yanked his other pistol from his waistband.

"Shall I kill him?" Connor asked Rebecca politely.

She pretended to mull his question. "Not just at this very moment, I should think," she said thoughtfully.

"*Oh—dear—God—*" John gasped.

"Now, Edgar," Connor said, very reasonably. "You are aware I am an excellent shot, are you not? Lock your pistols, drop them, and kick them over to Ned."

Edgar dropped his pistols and gave each of them a disconsolate kick. Rebecca obediently plucked them off the ground.

"If ye'd only just give over the locket, guv . . ." Edgar said despairingly.

"I told you before, Edgar, we haven't a locket," Connor replied, his consonants spires, his vowels great shining unbridgeable moats. The lord was back.

"Aye, guv, but ye said before ye 'adn't a girl, either, and John 'ere said—"

Connor smiled a smile that held all the warmth and understanding of a scimitar blade, effectively slicing Edgar's sentence in two.

"Tell me who sent you."

Connor feared he knew without a doubt who had sent them, and her name was Marianne Bell, now known as the Duchess of Dunbrooke. Marianne Bell would see him in hell before she would ever get her hands on the very incriminating locket.

Behind them, a saddle creaked; the dangling ruffian seemed to have recovered his senses and was wriggling about, attempting to free himself of the stirrup.

Sweat had created a slick over Edgar's chalky face.

"We told ye all we know, guv, we did. 'Er Grace sent us. By way of 'Utchins. Ye can shoot me now, guv, but I can tell ye no more."

Connor let a moment of silence beat by to allow Edgar to fully enjoy the feeling of having a musket pointed directly at his face.

"And why does *'Er Grace* want to kill me?"

"We wasn't t' kill ye, guv, until ye gave over the locket. Oh, unless ye'd gold specks in yer eyes. I . . . I . . . don't suppose ye'd tell me whether ye've gold specks in yer eyes?" Edgar hazarded weakly. It was a desperate act by a man who meant to earn his pay.

From his position on the ground, John groaned, a sound of pure frustration. Clearly Edgar had said too much.

A chill curled down Connor's spine. He stared at Edgar, stunned. *Sweet Mary Mother of God*, he thought, though he was not at all Catholic. *What kind of farce has my life become?* She *knew*. Marianne Bell knew, somehow she knew, that Roarke Blackburn, currently living as Connor Riordan, was the man traveling with the girl who had stolen the locket. And what were the highwaymen's orders, Connor wondered, once they had retrieved the locket? No doubt it involved his murder. For Connor, alive, was a threat to all that Marianne had fraudulently achieved. He saw that very clearly. He also knew, with an unshakable gut-level certainty, that Richard's murder had been no coincidence.

Behind him, a rustle in the dirt in the road and the squeak of leather told him that the ruffian on the ground was attempting to right himself by grabbing hold of his horse's stirrup.

"To horse, Ned," Connor said. Rebecca shoved one of her new pistols into her waistband and Connor almost smiled when she frowned down quizzically at the other three, wondering where to put them. She glanced up, saw urgency in his eyes, and stuffed her absurd bouquet of pistols quickly into the pack strapped to the brown mare. Almost as an afterthought, Rebecca bent down and retrieved her cap, cramming it down over her head. Her hair fluttered out from underneath it, an incongruously bright and cheerful thing in the aftermath of violence.

"If there is a next time, *gentlemen*," Connor said, in the tone one would use to invite the vicar to tea, "I will kill you in the slowest, most painful imaginable way. I am weary of games. Kindly convey my regards to *'Utchins* and *'Er Grace*, and tell them I recommend they cease their pursuit. Good day."

Connor doffed his hat briefly, while John remained curled on the ground and Edgar continued to sweat from frustration.

But John's awkward position on the ground afforded him a unique view of the aristocratic madman. And when Connor doffed his hat, the afternoon sun struck sparks from very distinctive, quite unmistakable gold specks in Connor's eyes.

Connor nudged his horse to move alongside Rebecca's.

"We are going to *run*," he hissed into her ear. He could see that she still had the unnaturally blanched skin and hot eyes of the righteously furious. He smiled at her, an enveloping smile of tender reassurance, a teasing warmth kindling his eyes. Rebecca returned his smile with one that was full of the sort of joy most inappropriate to the occasion.

"Now," he whispered.

They kicked hard. Their horses wheeled briefly in surprise, then stretched out into a blistering run just as the first greasy ruffian made it to saddle.

Their mounts were swift, but hooves were soon thundering uncomfortably close behind them; Connor glanced back over his shoulder and saw the greasy ruffian riding recklessly, his pistol hand waving free. Sunlight glinted on the barrel of the man's pistol; it seemed their pursuer meant to have blood for his humiliation. Connor swore savagely, slowing his mount just a little to ensure Rebecca remained in front of him. He had no choice but to shoot. He lifted his musket and turned to aim.

It was too late. A sudden blow to his arm was already giving way to numbness. He glanced down, watching as though in a dream as the red of his own blood rose up through his shirt. *Oh, Christ above, oh, God, help us, I've been shot*, he half thought, half prayed. *That bastard has the luck of the devil; he shot me.*

Connor squeezed off a shot, then watched with both a crisp sense of accomplishment and a sense of despair as the ruffian jerked in his saddle, his hand pressed to his chest, his horse stopping, rearing in sudden confusion beneath him. Connor had so hoped to never take another life, and cursed as he felt his own crystal-edged thoughts dimming as the ragged circle of red on his arm darkened and spread. Pain was yet to come, Connor knew. Pain would be fortunate; it would mean he was still alive.

Behind them, far behind them, clouds of dust rose in the road. The rest of the men were now following. But Connor knew this country well, and he knew his destination. As long as he could stay lucid, he knew he could lead Rebecca to safety and these men would never find them.

"*Rebecca!*" he screamed. She glanced over her shoulder and pulled her horse to follow when Connor jerked his horse hard to the right. They galloped off the road, plunging over low fences, through thick stands of trees, the leaves lashing at them, the coats of their gratifyingly game horses blackening with sweat. Connor wove a path from memory, a path that careened through a meadow sprayed in bluebells that gave way to a brief swooping valley that led into a wood that grew more dense and shadowy as the sun slowly dipped lower in the sky. Their hoofbeats were soon muffled by deep layers of soft old leaves.

After what seemed both an eternity and merely an instant, they came upon it: the hunting box, his father's rarely used, discreetly located hunting home in the woods. Connor had been certain it would still be here, relatively untouched; these woods had been part of his family's holdings since Edward III. He pulled his wet horse to a halt and managed to dismount without stumbling too badly. And then he lifted his pack from his horse with his good arm and stared at the hunting box blankly for a moment, as if trying to remember why he was there.

Rebecca pulled her heaving mare up next to him and swung herself to the ground. She bent slightly, breathing hard, before straightening herself to look around. She began to smile, but something in Connor's face stopped her.

"Connor?" she said, puzzled. And then she saw the blood on his arm.

There was a buzzing in his ears. He put his hand against the door of the hunting box and it gave, swinging open. He looked out at Rebecca from the doorway, noticing that the light pouring down through the leaves had turned her hair into a soft molten halo. *She has lost her cap.* "Becca," he thought he said, for he could not hear his own voice, and then the black came in from the sides of his vision like a curtain pulling closed and he fell.

Chapter Eleven

❧

Oh God, Oh God, Oh God," Rebecca murmured like an incantation over Connor's fallen body. His head lolled sickeningly against the boards of the floor. She touched his eyes, his brows, as though searching for him, willing him to reinhabit his face; he was breathing, otherwise he seemed lifeless as an effigy. A haze of panic began to move over her eyes.

Her vast and unseemly knowledge of bullet wounds and amputations clamored in her head, words like *bandages* and *suppurating* and *saws* and *opium* and *Peruvian bark* jigging among all the other learned advice from her father's scientific journals. She gave her head a rough shake to sort it. This did the trick; somehow it all fell into place, the things she needed to do in the order she needed to do them.

She drew in a deep breath to fortify her nerves and pressed two fingers to Connor's throat. A good pulse thumped there, a bit fast, but strong and even. Rebecca closed her eyes against an almost bruising wave of relief; it meant he had not yet lost a dangerous amount of blood.

Her own short sobbing breaths beat in her ears as she considered the chore of unbuttoning his shirt; how ridiculous, how dangerous, even, all those buttons seemed now. She tore it open instead, sending tiny buttons flying like shrapnel across the room.

She only needed to lift him a little to peel the shirt completely away from his body, but she could not. His weight was astonishing; the solidity of his unconscious body as stubborn as gravity itself. It made her absolutely, irrationally furious. She tore at the seams at the shoulder of his shirt, and then lifted the sleeve away from his arm with breathless care. His own blood and sweat matted the hair of his arms, and this made her angrier still; for miles he had bled, leading her to safety. By the time Rebecca confronted her first musket ball wound, a hideous red little crater in the smooth hard muscle of his arm, it had become her mortal enemy, and she would have victory.

The wound was only oozing now; the bleeding had slowed, the blood was congealing. She delicately touched the edge of it; she could feel the ball move. It was close to the surface of the wound, which meant she had a very good chance of retrieving it whole from his arm.

Water. Where was his water flask? She plunged her hands into Connor's pack and began pulling things out of it in a controlled frenzy, a small sheathed knife, needles and thread, a length of rope, a flint, candles, something wrapped in cloth that turned out to be a brush for the horses, something else wrapped in cloth that turned out to be a couple of meat pies from the Thorny Rose Tavern. All the evidence of Connor's careful thought and planning, all things she had taken for granted. But no flask. She found his fine brown coat folded neatly and began tugging it out of the pack, but something heavy hindered its progress. *Please be the water flask*, she thought. *Oh, please.*

Fumbling among the folds of the coat, she found a flask in the inner pocket. When she pulled it out, something tumbled out along with it: a soft copper lock of her own hair.

She went blank for a moment, thrown oddly off balance. The things lined up neatly on the floor in front of her were like words to a sentence in a language she had only begun learning, a sentence punctuated poignantly by a copper curl. They told a story Rebecca sensed she already half knew; she could feel it radiating, increasing in light, on the far reaches of her awareness.

She gave her head another rough shake. Mulling was a luxury she could not indulge at the moment. She sniffed the flask. Whiskey. In the absence of water, it would have to do.

Rebecca spilled a bit of the whiskey in her hands and rubbed them together, creating a little puddle of dirt in her palms, and then she rinsed the puddle away with another prodigal splash. Cleansed as well as she was able, she tugged her shirt out of her pants and, using her teeth and fingers, ripped the hem of it into a length of bandage.

Placing her fingers on either side of the wound she pressed gently, muttering prayers, apologies, vicious imprecations. She felt the ball shift. She pressed again, gritting her teeth, breathing heavily, and this time it surfaced, whole and bloody. With cool antipathy Rebecca held the thing between two fingers and glared at it, then flung it to the floor with an oath, as though concluding an exorcism.

She soaked a bit of the bandage in whiskey and cautiously, in tiny strokes, swabbed the blood away from the hole torn in Connor's flesh. The edges of the wound were thankfully relatively clean, and Rebecca marveled momentarily at how much her life had changed: she had never dreamed that something like a clean-edged musket-ball wound could cause her to give thanks.

She would need to irrigate the wound, she knew, before she bound it up. She took a deep breath before tipping a bit of the whiskey into it.

At this Connor moaned, a long sound that writhed up out of him like a hot wind blowing through the caverns of hell, and he stirred, his legs moving restlessly. The sound frightened Rebecca nearly witless. "Dear God," she whispered, but found herself at a loss for words to include in the prayer; it seemed her vocabulary had abandoned her. Of necessity, for the moment, she had become a creature comprised of instinct and nothing else.

Rebecca bound the wound neatly, with exquisite gentleness, then sat back on her heels and stared down at him. She placed a tentative hand on his chest over his heart to reassure herself of its steady beating, and after a moment, unable to resist, her fingers curled into the crisp hair there.

Lord God, the man was lovely in a way she had never imagined. The join of his neck to his shoulders, the taper of his shoulders to his slim waist, the swell of taut muscle above his rib cage, the wondrous texture and temperature and smell of his skin—this hidden beauty made Connor seem a stranger with powerful secrets, like a whole other country with its own laws. A restless curiosity and delight spiked through her, finding its way even through her fear for him. Beneath her hand, beneath his skin, his heart beat. She put her other hand on her own heart, to compare.

"Was it Robbie Denslowe?"

Rebecca jumped, jerking her hand away.

"Robbie Denslowe?" she repeated numbly.

"Who . . . who taught you just where to hit a man?"

Connor's voice was frayed, dragging, but the sound of it filled Rebecca near to bursting with some nameless emotion.

"Yes," she said, almost a whisper. She sought his eyes. They were dark and glazed with pain, but behind the pain, he was fully there, indomitably amused and warming at the sight of her. Rebecca uncertainly touched his hand, and his fingers closed over hers tightly.

"Robbie Denslowe should be knighted," Connor muttered.

He managed to lift one corner of his mouth in a smile before closing his eyes. His face contracted, the quickening of his breath betrayed his struggle with pain. His thumb began moving in an unconscious stroke across the top of her hand.

"The horses?" he asked, after a moment.

"I will see to them," Rebecca assured him.

"My arm—"

"The bleeding has stopped. I took the ball out, Connor. I took it out whole."

"Did ye now?" He smiled again, eyes still closed. "Oh, but you are a marvel, wee Becca." His voice had begun to sound like a sigh.

"A marvel," Rebecca repeated softly. It was all she could manage. It seemed just the appropriate word for everything at the moment.

"Hmmph," he said, an ambitious attempt at a laugh. "Wee Becca, I think I shall need to get very drunk, very soon. Take . . . take the musket and knife out with you when you see to the horses. There is a stream nearby . . . ye can find it by sound. And put the flask in my hand, if ye will."

He gave her hand a squeeze and released it. His face had retreated from her again, contracting. She folded a blanket in quarters and positioned it under his head, and he accepted her ministrations without a word. With one more glance down at him, she picked up the horse brush and the sheathed knife and took them outside.

The horses were nosing about the front of the hunting box quietly, looking for tender grasses. "Come, my dears," Rebecca said softly. "We are sorry to leave you so long, but we had urgent business inside." She unsaddled both horses, then unwrapped the brush and gave the mare a rubdown, murmuring to her about her bravery, her speed, her beauty.

And then she turned her attention to Connor's horse, the gray, and he was told how handsome he was, how valiant, how swift. The horses' ears twitched forward, enjoying the lilting softness of her voice, the smooth sure strokes of her hands.

"Let us find the stream now, shall we?" She collected the reins of the horses in her hand and shouldered the musket, then stood still, looking up, listening. A breeze shook the dazzling little coin leaves that hung from the aspens; the larger oak leaves waved at her like languid hands, glowing in the lowering sun as if lit from within. Beneath the hushed rustle of the leaves she heard it, a soft melodious rushing. She led the horses toward the sound, stopping every now and then to mark a tree with her knife so she could find her way back to the hunting box.

The stream was a pretty thing, silver and gilt in the sun, winding among large smooth stones, bridged by slim trees thick with leaves. When the horses bent their heads to drink, Rebecca pressed her palms against her weary eyes. They smelled of horses and Connor, musk and salt and blood and whiskey. They spoke of the enormous distance she had come. She did not want to wash them just yet.

Rebecca leaned companionably against her brown mare, then closed her eyes so the remaining warmth of the day could touch her eyelids. After a space of time she let the sobs take her, surrendering to a tangle of emotions that burned and confused and goaded and excited. The day came back at her in a torrent: the gift of an Herbal, Connor's hands warm against her back when she thanked him. Pistols pointed at her. The fetid breath of a highwayman on the back of her neck, his hand crawling over her breast. Connor bleeding, his head lolling against the floor, his dark hair stark against his white face. His heart beating beneath her hand.

A soft copper lock of her own hair.

And through it all, through all the chaos and terrible, wonderful newness, a strange blooming elation had buoyed her, a hot bright thing that swelled and pressed at the very seams of her being. It demanded release, demanded *something* from her. She wasn't sure yet what to call it, but she had her suspicions.

She did know it had everything to do with Connor.

She would happily face a dozen pistols, a dozen highwaymen, without flinching. For Connor.

When the sobs had run their course, Rebecca felt renewed and absurdly, dizzyingly cheerful. She knelt next to the stream and rinsed her hands, then splashed a little cool water on her face, a baptism, in a way, of her new self. Today she had taken a musket ball out of Connor Riordan, and he had gripped her hand, seeking strength from her and finding it. This did not tilt the balance between them, but righted it momentarily: Rebecca had not fully realized until that moment how much she had wanted, *needed*, to give something to Connor. One did not need to pose naked on a chaise to feel powerful and womanly, she now understood. One needed only a musket-ball wound and the feel of a beautiful man stroking the back of one's hand.

The ground felt solid beneath her feet for the first time in days, and Rebecca, relishing her new balance, thrust her arms high into the sky as if trying it on like a coat, and stretched deliciously. Then she turned to lead the horses back to the hunting box, humming a little tune of her own invention.

Chapter Twelve

❦

$\mathcal{S}$he is quite the success, is she not? A diamond of the first water."

Lady Tremaine addressed her remarks to the Duchess of Dunbrooke as they watched Lorelei sail by in the arms of Viscount Grayson, one of a clutch of titled gentlemen in need of a wife this season. He looked besotted, but then again, one of his eyes had a tendency to wander, which could lend a besotted effect to anyone's aspect. Cordelia curved her lips in what she hoped was a fond smile of agreement, one of thousands of smiles of agreement she had been forced to issue over the last several days.

Lady Tremaine, Cordelia thought, was a new form of torture. As the Duchess of Dunbrooke, Cordelia had never been obliged to suffer boredom for any significant length of time; if the vise of tedium began to tighten, she merely moved on to another conversation group, or joined a card game, or visited the buffet table, or took the air. She deployed her movements much the way she deployed her fan—to keep from suffocating.

But she was obliged to suffer Lady Tremaine, and Lady

Tremaine registered on Cordelia's senses like a mediocre soprano hitting and sustaining one high quavery note again and again and again. Lorelei—her beauty, her charm, her success, her suitors, her prospects—was what her song was about. Cordelia's head had begun to throb with it; she half feared it would shatter like a wine goblet in the not too distant future. She wondered if she should plead a headache and go home, retire to her room, mercifully alone, draw the drapes and take to her bed until . . .

Until what? Until the locket was safely in her hands again? Hutchins's assistants had questioned a pawnbroker in Sheep's Haven, the Godforsaken town nearer to Scotland and the cold Dunbrooke estate Keighley Park than Cordelia ever wanted to be again. The shop's fat proprietor had confirmed that yes, a lad with the look of Dunbrooke had tried to sell a locket there, but had changed his mind the moment the proprietor had exclaimed over the splendid miniature of the Duchess of Dunbrooke. The locket scarcely mattered now, or at least paled in significance to the fact that they now knew that the man traveling with the girl did indeed have gold flecks in his eyes.

And oh, what a fool she was, but when Cordelia heard that Roarke had attempted to trade the miniature of her for pots and a musket and an *herbal*, of all things, her heart had twisted savagely. She had thought she was beyond feeling that kind of pain now. Or feeling anything at all so powerfully.

Convincingly portraying a groom for five years would have required cunning and calculation and a great deal of control to keep his refined breeding from poking out of the seams of his duplicity. She should know. She had done precisely the same thing—in reverse—for almost as long.

And then there was the matter of the annuity that Melbers had paid him. Imagine, Melbers, the dear old family retainer, a traitor. Somehow Roarke had contacted Melbers when he arrived in England again from Waterloo. But not her. Not Marianne Bell.

Rebecca Tremaine. Who was she to Roarke Blackburn? Could they be headed for Gretna Green? Did Rebecca know who Roarke really was? Cordelia was stunned by something she rarely felt: jealousy. It tasted like rust in her mouth, turned her palms to ice. Roarke was risking everything for a daughter of a knight, but he had left Marianne Bell without a thought, it seemed. A rage Cordelia had not allowed herself to feel when he had left her, and had forbidden herself to entertain when she thought he had died, caught her now utterly by surprise and nearly made her gasp for breath. She struggled for control, masterfully and inconspicuously, and regained it.

Cordelia glanced up and inadvertently intercepted the sultry gaze of Lord Lanford. The gazes of men tended to do that as they passed her; they heated and melted, as though held to a candle flame. She nodded absently in acknowledgment, and turned her head toward Lady Tremaine once more. Cordelia had begun to take this for granted, the fact that her position meant that her beauty could be used as a shield, a means of intimidation and not just as a means to an end. She had been an orphan and destitute, and at one time her beauty had been her only source of power. She had learned to wield it nimbly, but men were always stronger. A persistent man weary of her sweetly worded dodges could pin her down and take her by force. Before Hutchins entered her life, her beauty had brought her an inordinate amount of grief.

One could not pin down a duchess and take her by force. Or rather, one could not pin down an *unmarried* duchess and take her by force. If she were married, her husband, of course, would have the right. Cordelia intended to remain unmarried, and she intended to remain a duchess.

This aim, however, was now threatened by the fact that the Duke of Dunbrooke had arisen from the dead and was now ricocheting across the English countryside with a red-headed girl in tow. What did Roarke intend to do? Appear, a veritable English Lazarus, at Keighley Park, rally the servants, and undertake a coup to depose her? Was Roarke even aware that she had married his brother? Perhaps he considered the fat old pawnbroker's comments mere blithering. Perhaps he had thought to himself, "The Duchess of Dunbrooke, my left foot. That's just my mistress, you old sod."

Cordelia knew better.

Viscount Grayson returned Lorelei to them with a bow, and almost by magic Colonel Pierce appeared and led Lorelei out onto the floor again. Cordelia wondered if Lady Tremaine noticed how animated Lorelei looked in Pierce's arms, how comfortable and happy. Two balls in two evenings, and Lorelei had danced several dances at each with Pierce.

Ah, it seemed Lady Tremaine *had* noticed; she watched them take the floor together, her mouth opening as if to say something, then closing again immediately in a tight little frown.

Feeling slightly mischievous, Cordelia could not resist a tiny goad disguised as reassurance.

"He has forty thousand pounds a year, you know," she

said to Lady Tremaine, who, mercifully, momentarily, had
gone quiet with dark thoughts. Cordelia gracefully and
subtly gestured with her fan to the "he" in question,
Colonel Pierce.

"Yes, but no title," Lady Tremaine replied. "Lorelei's
father very nearly has forty thousand pounds a year. Quite
fortunate in his investments, you see."

They both donned bright smiles when, as if on cue, Sir
Henry Tremaine rejoined them. He quietly deposited a
minor piece of gossip in his wife's ear, something about the
daughter of a friend of theirs, and left them once more.

Forty thousand pounds. Good heavens, Cordelia
thought. Edelston had known what he was about, then,
when he had ensnared the Tremaine girl. She was fairly
certain Viscount Grayson's fortune didn't even approach
thirty thousand pounds.

The Dunbrooke fortune, on the other hand, exceeded
forty thousand pounds by far. In the capable hands of Melbers, who had been the only person who seemed to care a
fig for the Dunbrooke finances and investments and who
had been given a free rein to do what he liked with it by
Richard, it had grown like a weed, extraordinary expenses
notwithstanding.

Cordelia absently fingered a fold of her gown, one of
those extraordinary expenses. A midnight blue silk over-
laid with gossamer-fine gold tissue, edged in tiny embroi-
dered gold flowers, cut deeply at the neckline. A necklace
featuring an enormous sapphire in the shape of a tear
stopped just short of vanishing into her bodice between her
breasts. It drew male eyes like a magnet, as she had known
it would. Suddenly the very fact of this bored her; she had
a bizarre impulse to tear the thing from her neck and fling

it into the chandelier. It was a far cry from a gold locket. That stupid, stupid gold locket.

After giving his report this afternoon, Hutchins had asked her very simply, very quietly, what she wanted to do. Cordelia usually found the very absence of emotion in Hutchins's delivery reassuring. But this afternoon, this particular "What do you want to do?" had fallen on her ears like a death knell. She could sell the Dunbrooke jewels and steal a good portion of the Dunbrooke fortune and disappear, perhaps to Italy, leaving scandal in her wake. But the continent was a small one; she would be located, she would be known.

In the midst of her reverie, her fingers fluttered up to touch her sapphire, and she was jolted back to the present, a ballroom full of spinning couples and chattering matrons and ogling men. Something about the solidity of the gem, of all it represented, focused Cordelia's careening thoughts.

The Duchess of Dunbrooke was the invention of a lifetime, and Cordelia feared she had no energy left for another invention, and no will to begin again in any other fashion.

"Forgive me, but I need some time to think," she had told Hutchins this afternoon, faintly. "I shall have an answer for you this evening."

And now she did have an answer for him. Passion and sentimentality were foolish indulgences at this point in her life. She must be practical. Which meant she must remove Roarke Blackburn from her life. Permanently.

Cordelia glanced up suddenly, sensing an intent gaze upon her, and saw Edelston across the ballroom. He was leaning against a pillar, and not surprisingly, his fine eyes

were fixed on her sapphire and on the snowy swell of
bosom that cradled it. A rare involuntary smile leaped to
her face, accompanied by a peculiar and unexpected sense
of relief. The greatest luxury in Cordelia's life, greater by
far than gowns and jewels and London townhouses, was
being understood. Edelston understood her and, to her continued bemusement, failed to judge her. He was, she supposed, the closest thing she had to a real friend in the *ton*.
No matter that the now-habitual haunted look on his face
seemed to drain the very light from the room. She was delighted to see him.

Deftly she tapped the arm of Charlotte, Lady Caville, a
beanpole topped in plumes who was drifting by, with her
fan.

"Lady Caville, may I introduce you to my dear friend
Lady Tremaine?" Thus having procured a substitute for her
presence, Cordelia made her way over to Edelston.

"You will make all the young girls swoon from the romance of it all, Tony, if you go about with that look of torment on your face."

"Hello, Cordelia." Edelston bowed low, which Cordelia
knew afforded him a better view of her bosom on the way
down. "I fear the mamas of those young ladies have all
been forewarned about Lord Edelston and his desperate
need of a fortune."

"And of Lord Edelston's engagement."

"And of Lord Edelston's engagement," Edelston repeated, with a touch of bitterness. "It matters not. They are
all boring. They are none of them Rebecca."

"Even that one?" Cordelia gestured to a brunette minx
with enormous dark eyes who was casting a saucy look at

Edelston over the shoulder of her dancing partner. "She has the look of a budding adventuress."

Feature for feature, Edelson was still the most handsome man in the room, Cordelia assessed objectively. He would likely be the recipient of a number of saucy looks before the evening was over.

Edelston's eyes followed the young lovely about the floor for a spell, and he couldn't disguise the speculative interest in his eyes. Still, he repeated, "They are all of them boring." Cordelia had the faintest suspicion that he was attempting to convince himself of this.

"Tell me, Tony," Cordelia said. "Is it Rebecca that you yearn for, or is it the *idea* of Rebecca?"

Edelston stared at her openmouthed for a moment, indignant. "What on earth do you mean?"

"Is it that *Rebecca* is particularly enthralling, or would you be just as enthralled by any young girl who managed to slip your grasp?"

Edelston frowned. "It is Rebecca," he said firmly.

"Say the word, Tony, and I can find you another heiress, despite what all the mamas know about you."

"It is Rebecca," he repeated stubbornly, but the conviction in his voice was, in truth, wavering. Cordelia knew his thoughts: what a relief it would be to not deal with all of his creditors, to spend freely and recklessly again as a young man was meant to do.

Cordelia nodded, her face unreadable, a slight smile playing on her lips.

"How are you faring, Cordelia?" Edelston asked suddenly. "You look . . . very well, indeed. But a trifle pale."

Cordelia gave a start. Imagine Edelston noticing such a detail. A gentleman would never dare suggest a lady might not be in the pink of health, but a friend would. Cordelia was so absurdly touched that, for a moment, she could not find words to answer. She felt her cool, ironic smile, that faithful tool of her disguise, falter.

"I remain somewhat distraught, Tony, but I am well enough, thank you," she managed to say glibly, regaining control of her face. How could she possibly explain Roarke Blackburn to him, even if she wanted to, in the middle of a crowded ballroom? "How do you fare?"

Edelson glanced over his shoulder before responding to determine whether any interested ears were pitched in their direction.

"My creditors are haunting me at every turn. They await me on the doorstep of my house, at the entrance to my club. No doubt one of them is standing outside in the street at this moment, awaiting my emergence. And my fiancée apparently despises me, and is missing." He concluded this recitation with a fatalistic shrug.

Cordelia knew not where the impulse came from, but suddenly she wanted to give to Edelston the thing he wanted most, if only to take the shadow from his face. "Tony, may I ask you a delicate question?"

A wicked half smile touched Edelston's lips. He and Cordelia had struck numerous indelicate poses together in the past; *delicate* was not typically a word they associated with each other.

"Ask away, Cordelia."

"You must promise not to impugn my honor when you answer."

"I promise."

"If Rebecca has, shall we say . . . surrendered her honor

to this Irish groom, this Connor Riordan, would you still want her back?"

Edelston recoiled as though struck.

"She would not do such a thing."

"Still, if perhaps she was expertly seduced . . . we are all of us human, you see . . ."

But this was the rub precisely, and Cordelia knew it; Rebecca had become an icon in Edelston's head, something other than, or more than, human.

"Have you heard anything?" he demanded. "Has she been . . ." He shook his head roughly. "I would still want her," he said stubbornly. "Let us not speak of it further."

Who was this young woman, to inspire such nearly unthinking devotion? Cordelia pushed the fresh twinge of jealousy away; she hated how the feeling weakened her.

"I *have* heard something, Tony," she said slowly. "And I will do what I can to ensure that Rebecca is restored to you shortly, with the help of my assistants."

Edelston turned his head her way. His eyes were still bright with hot emotion, but as they looked at her, taking her in, they softened, and his head cocked with curiosity.

"Cordelia, you would do this for me?" His gentle words surprised her. She had expected him to pounce on her words with enthusiasm, to demand news of Rebecca.

"I—" She sputtered to a stop.

"Even in light of the locket?"

Cordelia felt an inexplicable flush rise in her cheeks. "It is nothing, Tony, really."

Edelston, ascertaining first that the pillar blocked them from the view of the people milling about the ballroom, reached out and drew a finger along the silky skin just above the neckline of her gown, then brushed his hand across her breast as he dropped his hand to his side again. He could feel her nipple stiffen against the silk.

"You look a trifle peaked, Cordelia," he murmured. "Perhaps you should plead a headache, and I can escort you home?"

Cordelia was in the mood to be held by a man who wanted her, and if Rebecca Tremaine and Roarke Blackburn were specters in the room, it mattered little, at least for tonight.

"I will make my excuses to the Tremaines," she said, and it was done.

Connor awoke with a start and lifted his head abruptly, a motion he immediately regretted. The throbbing in his head now rivaled the throbbing in his arm, and when he moved it felt as though a collection of billiard balls were colliding violently in his skull. In some respects this could be considered a good thing, as the pain in his arm was now much less severe, at least in contrast.

A fire was leaping merrily in the grate, and the warmth and gentle light felt wonderful. He slowly, gingerly moved his eyes, mindful of not disturbing the billiard balls, until they lighted upon Rebecca. She was sitting at the oak-plank table near the fire, and she had roped her hair back with what looked like his cravat. Her shirt was filthy, the white now officially a dingy gray, and her left cheek sported a great black smudge roughly the shape of Italy. She had gotten the fire started on her own, but not without some struggle, it seemed. Her head was bent intently over something. Looking at her, Connor was suddenly overcome with a sense of peace so alien he felt oddly disoriented, as though the boundaries that normally surrounded time had dropped and left him floating.

And then he saw what she was reading.

"Oh, no," he blurted before he could stop himself.

Rebecca's head jerked up from her Herbal, and he watched concern and then satisfaction flicker across her face as she ascertained once more that he was not at death's door.

"*Oh, no*, what?" she asked.

"Ye shall not go experimenting with any of those potions on me, wee Becca."

"But your whiskey cannot last forever, Connor, and the woods outside are full of wonderful remedies for pain. Why, if I had a little henbane—"

"You'd likely use a pinch too much and either send me to my reward or turn me into a toad, and then you would be lonely, indeed."

Rebecca gave him such a look of pitying condescension that Connor smiled. Already she seemed more like a doctor.

"The receipts include careful measurements, Connor, and dosages for people of different weights. How do you suppose Dr. Mayall arrived at the receipts if he did not actually use them?"

"He was an Englishman. He experimented on enemy soldiers, no doubt."

Rebecca rolled her eyes. She finally lifted her head up from her beloved new book and gave him a long look.

"Connor, you look dreadful," was her verdict, delivered with some trepidation. "Are you feverish? I will make some tea."

"I likely look worse than I feel, wee Becca. For example, you, my fine lady, look like a chimney sweep at the moment."

She grinned mischievously, showing her dimples, and Connor, inspired to impress the chimney sweep, made a great show of standing up.

Oh, dear God. His stomach heaved and the ground swayed and a cold sweat rained over his body and if he didn't lie down again immediately he would collapse into Rebecca's arms in a very embarrassing faint.

Connor stretched his body back out on the floor as gently as he could and closed his eyes, waiting for the world to still.

When he opened them again he found Rebecca kneeling over him, pale and anxious. He offered her a wan smile. Lord, but she was a sight, lithe and blessedly real in her filthy clothes. He took a breath, and the scent of her rushed into him, sweat and soot and something wild and green and earthy that was Rebecca's alone.

Rebecca reached for his hand to check his pulse.

"Connor, please, do be still for now. You need to rest. You've lost a good deal of blood."

"And gained a good deal of whiskey." Connor closed his eyes. He was enjoying the feel of her fingers pressed against his wrist. What a woman she had become, so fearless. They were silent together a moment; he could feel his heart beating against the press of her fingers.

Those fingers. A secret touch in a dark room in Sheep's Haven, a moment almost excruciatingly erotic. Because of its innocence, perhaps.

No. Because it had been Rebecca.

What the bloody hell was *wrong* with him? Connor moved his feet restlessly.

At last, Rebecca took her hand away. "I will make you some tea. But you need broth, and all we have for food are these meat pies. How can I get some fresh meat to make a broth?"

Connor opened his eyes. "Put a pot outside the door. A wee squirrel will no doubt oblige you by unbuttoning his fur coat and climbing in."

Rebecca scowled at him. Connor felt contrite, but only a little.

"Wee Becca, it is true I am injured, but it is also true that I am still a bit drunk, and it's the whiskey now that's making me more ill than the hole in my arm, this I promise you. Tea is what I need, and more sleep, so we can be on our way in the morning."

"We are going nowhere in the morning," Rebecca said firmly.

"We cannot stay here." He was deadly serious.

"You said no one knew of this place."

"No one would dare come near it, because my fath—" He caught himself in time. "It is legend that the gamekeeper would shoot any trespassers. This is Dunbrooke land. But the land has been neglected for many years now, and there is no longer a gamekeeper."

Connor searched Rebecca's face for signs of suspicion, for something that indicated she had noticed his slip.

She was silent for a moment, a tiny furrow forming between her eyes.

"How is it that you are so familiar with Dunbrooke land, Connor? Isn't the Dunbrooke fortune the largest in all of England?"

"I lived near here as a lad."

"But . . . you're Irish."

"My da worked near here, ye see," he said quickly, after a pause that he hoped was barely discernible. "Still, we cannot be sure that it is safe."

Oh, how deft he was becoming at evasion. Safe, it would have been, had not his former mistress somehow become the Duchess of Dunbrooke and taken it upon herself to have them ambushed at every turn. Safe, they would have been, but he could not be certain that Marianne Bell knew nothing of the hunting box. She had been married to his brother, after all.

"Connor, you are in no condition to move on yet. If you leave, you will have to leave without me, because I refuse to go for a day or so."

"Then I shall drag you with me, Miss Tremaine."

"And then perhaps collapse in the road, leaving me to the whims of fate."

They looked into each other's eyes, stricken silent for a moment.

"I am sorry I am of so little use to you," Connor muttered finally, turning away.

"Connor!" Rebecca was astonished. "How can you say that?"

"I've left ye to deal with the horses, with the fire—"

"Because you went out of your way to get shot?"

He smiled reluctantly.

"They are after the locket, whatever their motives, Connor, and the locket is my fault."

No, the locket is my fault, he wanted to say, *and thus the fault is mine for putting you in harm's way when all I wanted to do was take you away to a place, any place, where no one would try to kill or own your spirit.*

"Let us not think in terms of blame, wee Becca. Let us

just think of now, and of the future. We should be safe for a day or so, I am certain." He was *not* certain, but he wanted to see the tension leave her face, and it did.

"May I look at your wound?" she said almost shyly.

Connor nodded, slowly levered himself up, and shrugged his shoulders until his tattered shirt drooped about his waist.

It was one thing to take in Connor while he was unconscious, another to feel his eyes upon her, feel the warmth of his breath upon her face, while she confronted anew those fascinating slopes and ridges of muscle and the incongruously soft skin stretched over his hard bicep. Rebecca kept her head down and her eyes focused on her work, unwinding the bandage with infinite care, but her fingers trembled a bit when they met his skin. She could feel heat rising in her cheeks.

She paused when the bandage was at last loosened, her breath catching. Oh, his curves simply begged for exploration. Rebecca imagined the route she would take: her fingers would drag softly through the coarse hair of his forearm, her palm would glide up over his hard round shoulder, then slide down to fit itself over the swelling muscle of his chest; her fingers would trail down to explore the seam between his ribs . . .

The blood slowly migrated from her head; it seemed to be pooling, heating, somewhere much farther south, instead.

Do it, said a wicked little voice in her head. *Janet Gilhooly probably did it.*

But what if Connor seized her wrist midway on its journey and demanded to know what on earth she was doing?

She would simply die.

What does he see when he looks at me? A child, a friend, a . . . woman?

Rebecca closed her eyes briefly and took a deep steadying breath, and then reopened them, her sanity regained. She refocused on the task at hand.

The wound looked splendid, if a musket-ball wound could be called splendid; not angry, not even oozing terribly much. All in all, a nice piece of work, she congratulated herself, feeling a little glow of pride through the fog in her head.

"Have I thanked you, wee Becca?" Connor said softly. His voice traveled up her spine; he was so close, the words so resonant, they seemed almost to come from inside her.

It was too much for her raw senses at the moment. She stepped away from him abruptly and released the breath she'd been holding so she could take the breath that would allow her to speak.

"Connor, if *I* said thank you to you every day for the rest of my life, it would still not be enough."

Connor smiled crookedly in answer.

"Well, then, wee Becca, see if ye can do something about the woeful state of my shirt this evening, aye?"

I never noticed before, but his eyes are dangerous. Dark and soft as the hearts of pansies but full of wicked glints. She took another step away from him and then turned and quickly moved to poke at the fire, which didn't need poking.

"Perhaps when you are sober you can go in search of your buttons," she told him.

Connor laughed and lowered his head to the cushion of

folded blanket. "Aye, we can make a contest of it. Whoever finds the most buttons will win."

Rebecca was suddenly delighted by the image of the two of them crawling about the floor, searching for buttons.

"I will win."

"You are wrong," Connor murmured. A moment later he was asleep again, and the cheerfully atrocious sound of his snores filled the room.

Chapter Thirteen

❧

The bath was Connor's idea.

"How well do you swim, wee Becca?" he asked, laughing, when she staggered from her room in the morning, scowling and blinking away her sleep.

The hunting box fortunately had two rooms, the main room featuring two bunks and an actual bed, a hearth, a table and benches, and the rather bedraggled stuffed head of a buck mounted on the wall. The second room was tiny and seemed to be for storage of such useful things as brooms and snares and old powder horns, but it also featured a bed. Apparently the previous Dukes of Dunbrooke had believed in comfort for all members of their hunting parties.

Rebecca had done a cursory bit of dusting and chasing of spiders with the broom while Connor slept the day before, and had given the beds a good smacking with the broom, as well, which had at least rearranged the dust. Fortunately the structure was snugly built, and there was no evidence that rodents had moved into the mattresses.

But it would hardly have mattered if they had. Rebecca

had fallen into bed like a rock shortly after she and Connor had shared one of the meat pies from the Thorny Rose, and slept even through the sound of Connor's impressive snoring in the next room.

Connor had already made tea and sliced the second meat pie into pieces for each of them. Never shy when it came to meals, Rebecca nearly lunged for her half.

"Swim?" she finally asked, through bites. And then she stopped chewing.

"Connor, you divided this pie evenly. You should have given yourself a larger slice."

"Why is that, wee Becca?"

"You need nourishment to heal quickly."

Connor gazed at her for a moment, bemused. It was a sweet and curious feeling to be fussed over.

"My thanks, wee Becca, but I think God favors those who share selflessly, aye?"

Rebecca snorted. She studied him objectively for a moment.

"You really do look much better this morning, Connor. Your eyes are clear and your color is good."

The corner of Connor's mouth quirked.

"Thank you, Dr. Tremaine. Though how you can see my color through my beard is beyond my ken."

"How does it feel?"

"My arm? As though it may fall off." When Rebecca blanched, he quickly amended, "Better, it feels better this morning, truly. I am healing quickly, I promise." He added, unable to resist teasing her, "My eyes are clear and my color is good, you know."

She made a face at him.

Truthfully, the ache in his arm had acquired the rhythm

of a storm tide: rushing in to torment him, then ebbing deceptively, then rushing in again. It was malevolently consistent. He'd experienced worse, however. Favoring his arm seemed to help. Talking about it did not.

"I will snare a hare this afternoon, for supper, wee Becca. I promise I shall eat the better part of it, if that will ease your mind. We can even make a stew, if we can find a few edible mushrooms."

"Poaching?" Rebecca sounded half aghast, half thrilled.

Connor almost laughed. His string of crimes was certainly lengthening. Although it wasn't strictly a crime to snare hares on his own land.

"One hare surely will not be missed, and our supper will be, if we have none."

"Will you show me how to set a snare?"

"Oh, aye, why not? We will turn you into a regular lad, yet, wee Becca, what with the pistol in your boot and the trousers."

Instead of laughing as he had expected, to his astonishment, Rebecca flushed pink and lowered her head.

All at once he was conscious of having made a mistake with his words, but he had no idea of the precise nature of it or how to fix it. He supposed, in a way, that teasing her about turning into a lad was his way of trying to convince *himself* that she did indeed resemble one. In truth, the last thing she resembled was a boy, and that was in no small part the fault of the trousers. It might be preferable to put her back in a dress, where he could not see precisely where her legs began and ended.

Idle observations, nothing more. He tried to push these thoughts away. But fatigue and nearness were making it almost impossible.

He cleared his throat awkwardly. "Aye, swim. I know of a place to bathe, if ye'd like to be a bit cleaner, and perhaps change into fresh clothing."

A look of such longing crossed Rebecca's face that Connor burst into laughter. The embarrassed pink left Rebecca's cheeks in the face of the merry sound, and she laughed, too.

"But before we have a swim, wee Becca—you do swim, aye?"

"Aye," she drawled. "Robbie Denslowe taught me."

"Naturally," Connor said. "I think we should put the locket in a safe place, lest it go floating down the river. Ye're wearing it still?"

By way of answer, Rebecca fished about inside her shirt and plucked out the locket.

"I know a very safe place for it," Connor said, and waggled the fingers of his outstretched hand until Rebecca unfastened the locket and deposited it into them.

The heat of the smooth metal surprised him; he frowned at it, puzzled. And then he comprehended: *It's warm from her skin.* Specifically, the skin between her breasts.

Connor stared dumbly down at the locket.

Dear God, man. It's not as though you're holding an actual breast. But suddenly, the soft heat of the locket seemed searing.

I am weak. I am weary. I am injured. It's weakness, that's all.

The sooner they were in Scotland, the sooner he left for America, the safer they both would be.

He waited a moment before lifting his head, because he could not guarantee what Rebecca would see in his eyes at that moment. He drew in a long, steadying breath before he spoke.

"I have the perfect place for it, wee Becca." He strode over to one of the solid wooden posts that flanked the hearth, untwisted the top of it, dropped the locket in, and twisted it back on again. "A little discovery I made last night," he said to her astonished face. It was a lie. He'd known about the post since he was a boy. All Dunbrooke heirs knew of this particular hiding place. "I defy anyone, particularly a daft highwayman, to find it there."

"Shall I give you my pound note for safekeeping, as well?" Rebecca dug it out of her trousers. Connor, thinking quickly, rolled it into a cylinder and tucked it into the toe of his boot.

"Only the truly brave or truly perverse would think of looking for it there," Connor said with satisfaction.

After breakfast, they wandered out to set the snares for their hoped-for dinner.

"I knew a Gypsy once," Connor said, "who had trained his dogs to help him poach hare with a net. One dog was taught to wait at one end of a field, while t'other dog chased the hare into his net at the field's other end. The hare had no choice of where to go, really. Clever dogs, those."

"Was he ever caught?" Rebecca asked, watching Connor as he deftly laid the snares that had been stored in the hunting box. "The Gypsy, I mean?"

"Aye, but not punished," Connor said, thinking how Rebecca would enjoy knowing Raphael. "Did you know, wee Becca, that if you are very patient, you can catch a fish by tickling its tummy?"

"Tickling it?" She was fascinated.

"You let your hand dangle, just float, in the water near where fish like to linger, so the fish get used to the sight of it there. Ye must be patient. And then when the fish come near, ye rub their tummies, as ye would a hound. They rather like it. When ye've calmed them, ye can grab them out o' the water, and then enjoy your dinner."

"It hardly seems fair to the fish." Rebecca sounded skeptical.

"Ah, but let that be a lesson to you, wee Becca. Never let a stranger tickle your tummy."

After setting their snares, they took the horses, which had spent a comfortable evening in the small stable behind the hunting box, and packed them up with the musket and clean clothes and blankets, and together they rode to the place where the stream widened.

The day was mild, and the trees on either side of the bank formed a graceful arch over the pool, providing shadow and light in equal parts.

"This is how we shall do it, wee Becca," Connor instructed. "Ye can remove your clothes under the blanket and splash on into the water. I shall keep this blanket over my head until you do, and then I shall keep an eye out for predators, wolves and highwaymen and the like, while ye bathe. When ye've finished, it will be my turn."

Rebecca turned crimson, but Connor kept his expression faintly amused and challenging, and held the soap out to her.

"*Wolves*," she said derisively, finally, and took the soap from him. "Cover your head."

He dutifully covered his head and listened to the soft

thump of her clothes hitting the riverbank, and then the patter of her feet and a splashing as she parted the water.

"*Eeeee!*" she shrieked in glee. "Oh, this is wonderful!"

Connor took the blanket from his head.

All thought fled his mind.

"Connor! It's lovely!"

He couldn't breathe.

Her body was just a silvery blur, really, shimmering beneath the surface of the water, but then she lifted her slender white arms and shoulders from the water and pushed her wet hair back from her face and smiled, her eyes glowing. His imagination completed the symmetry of her body for him, and suddenly the blur was torture.

"I have never been happier to have a bath," she declared, and stroked her way into a patch of light in the water.

Connor's will had abdicated. He could only stare helplessly.

"Any wolves?" she called to him.

He opened his mouth. He could not speak.

"Connor?"

"No wolves," he managed finally, hoarsely.

He sat down heavily on the bank and briefly cradled his head in his hands. What the bloody hell was the matter with him? It was hardly as though women were mysteries to him; it was not even as though he'd been deprived of one for any length of time, thanks to Janet Gilhooly. But this was different. For days now, something immense had been creeping up on him; and now it had finally knocked him sideways. He couldn't name it, couldn't even get a grip on it so he could hold it still in the beam of his mind to determine whether it was friend or foe. It had overcome him so completely that he *was* it, and now he could only cower like a boy on the riverbank, feeling exposed and confused and aching with a need so absolute it seemed unconscionable.

This, at last, made him angry, which was a relief; anger was at least familiar. He worked on the anger, gnawed upon it until he was good and irritable.

"Will you be all day, Rebecca?" He heard the petulance in his voice; he didn't care.

Rebecca glided through the water toward him, looking for all the world like a selkie.

"Sorry, Connor! Blanket, please!" she demanded cheerfully.

He took refuge under a blanket while she rustled around on the bank of the river. He identified the sounds to himself as she rustled: now she was rubbing the water from her skin, now she was tossing her head, her wet hair slapping lightly against her bare back, now she was stepping into her dress. He remained motionless and silent; it seemed safest at the moment not to jar himself overmuch in his current peculiar condition. He was painfully, appallingly hard; the fabric of his trousers stretched taut, teasing his sensitive skin.

The water would cool his thoughts. Not to mention his thrumming, bulging, mutinous body.

"Ready!" Rebecca called.

Connor lifted the blanket from his head, caught a split-second glimpse of sleeked-back hair, shining eyes, and brown muslin dress, and immediately dropped the blanket over Rebecca's head. He stripped down in seconds and hit the water to her squeaks of protest.

"You forgot the soap! Mind your arm!"

Connor had forgotten all about his arm. He jerked it from the water just in time to keep from wetting the bandage.

"Throw me the soap, there's a good lass." The bar went hurtling through the air, and miraculously Connor caught it in one hand before it could go bobbing out to sea. Rebecca clapped her hands in appreciation, and Connor gave a little bow in the water. His mood was rapidly improving.

He pushed his body through the water a bit, taking care to keep his wounded arm elevated. It *was* wonderful; the first foot or so of the water warmed by the sun; from his hips down, the water was cool, velvety. He dunked his head and spluttered, rubbed the soap over his grimy face and hair, dunked himself again, as cheerful as a bird in a mud puddle.

"Blanket!" Connor finally called cheerfully; he *was* feeling a good deal more cheerful.

Rebecca dutifully tented her head. Connor waded ashore, shook himself out like a duck hound, ruthlessly rubbed himself dry and rustled into his clothes.

"All right, then!" he announced brightly.

Rebecca dropped the blanket from her head. She smiled at him, her eyes shining, streamers of damp hair floating about her face.

And because it suddenly seemed unthinkable not to, Connor kissed her.

It astounded both of them; he hadn't known he intended to do it until he was committed to the act. He felt strangely disembodied; his head was bending and his lips touching hers, he felt Rebecca go rigid and draw in a little astonished breath, heard the distant, feeble, panicked voice in his mind suggesting he should stop, for pity's sake. But the kiss had a momentum of its own.

He pulled her lower lip between his lips, and the taste of her, the play of textures, was shocking: cool silk, a drugging sweetness and heat, maddening. Undone, Connor groaned softly, and his hand went up to cup her face, as much to steady himself as to touch her skin. He drew closer, until his painfully sensitive arousal just grazed her thighs; he dared not move any closer. His mouth moved over hers softly, savoring the silk of her lips, coaxing her open. And glory of glories, her lips trembled and parted, inviting him in. Tentatively, his tongue stroked into her mouth, and then when her head went back, it stroked deeper still.

"*Rebecca.*" Half moan, half whisper.

He slid his hand from her face to her throat, his fingers finding the tender skin beneath her jaw. Her pulse jumped there. He trailed them over the column of her neck, over the fine bones at the base of it, and then down, down, to just above where her breasts swelled against her bodice. *Oh, God, just another inch or two . . .*

Rebecca sighed, perhaps the sweetest sound he had ever heard. He felt her go boneless against his rigid, fevered body; her astonishment had dissolved into yearning. Her hands rose to touch him.

And suddenly this terrified him.

In perhaps the greatest act of will of his entire life, Connor abruptly stepped away from Rebecca.

Rebecca stumbled forward a little, startled.

And then she slowly, hesitantly, lifted her gaze up to him. Her eyes were clouded with wonder. She touched her fingertips lightly, absently, to her lips.

Connor stared back at her, breathing as though he'd run the length of the river. His hands were curled into fists at his sides.

"I am sorry, Rebecca. It seems I am just a man, after all," he said with a bitter sort of irony.

Rebecca watched Connor gather their things, his motions stiff and almost angry, then stride purposefully to his horse and mount. He stared down at her with a sort of inward-turned wildness in his eyes.

Rebecca stared back at him, still dazed. She'd forgotten how to speak; it seemed an unimportant skill, anyhow, when such kisses were to be had, when a whole world could be made from a kiss. She could not imagine ever moving from where she stood. She would happily stay rooted forever to the spot to commemorate the moment.

Desire. She knew that this was the thing that had burned and pulsed in her for days, the thing that wanted release. Tiny white-hot flames of it licked at her; the remains of a conflagration fanned and then abruptly denied air.

Connor had walked away.

You don't just light a fire and walk away from it.

Connor's stare finally penetrated the haze around her brain; he was looking at her as if she were a stranger who made him wary. She could think of nothing appropriate to say. Her perspective on life had just been dramatically shifted; she felt as though she now understood absolutely everything and yet absolutely nothing, and she was now being pulled like a wishbone between the two poles.

Rebecca shook herself free from her reverie, and then, because it seemed to be what Connor wanted her to do, she trudged over to her brown mare and mounted. Connor nudged his horse into a walk. He did not look at her, he did not speak, and his back was a wall that seemed to forbid conversation. And so they rode back to the hunting box in silence.

Chapter Fourteen

❦

After several days of sleeping in boy's clothing, the soft nightdress felt like the purest form of decadence. But tonight, its very looseness somehow made Rebecca too aware of her body. The gown slid and settled sensually over her skin with every toss and turn, infecting her with a peculiar alertness that had everything to do with a bone-melting, life-changing kiss and the suddenly taciturn man sleeping in the next room.

The snare had done its job and the resulting roasted hare had been a triumph, but Connor had been monosyllabic for most of the evening, and Rebecca's attempts at conversation fell so awkwardly on her own ears she finally abandoned the effort. Once she had glanced up to find him watching her with an intent, somewhat abashed, almost accusing expression on his face. But he would not meet her eyes for any length of time, and this was excruciating, because she wanted to look into them to find answers to questions she did not know how to ask.

Perhaps she had done it incorrectly; perhaps he was disappointed. She'd never before had a proper kiss, after all;

Edelston's midnight surprise notwithstanding. But surely with a little practice . . .

Rebecca listened for the sound of Connor's breathing in the next room, something that would tell her he was asleep. But she heard nothing except the occasional snap of the fire and a stick of wood shifting as it burned down.

Finally she could bear it no longer. She threw off her blanket and padded into the main room.

Connor was sitting at the table, staring into the fire. He started when he saw her, but when she stepped in front of the fire he covered his eyes as though shielding them from the sun.

"Connor . . ."

"Go to bed, Rebecca, please."

"Your arm . . . is it your arm? Is it bothering you?"

He kept his eyes shaded. "No." A single curt syllable.

The fire popped, sending sparks up the flue. It was the only sound in the room for almost longer than Rebecca could endure.

"Connor . . . did I . . . have I . . . done something wrong?"

It was a moment before he answered. "No, Rebecca." That strange, bitter tone again. "*You* have done nothing wrong."

The fire leaped and snapped, marking off more long seconds of silence.

She tried again. "Connor, this afternoon . . . when you . . . when you . . ." Rebecca fumbled, mustering her courage. "When you kissed me . . ."

Connor went utterly still.

". . . well, I thought perhaps I upset you. Or perhaps I

didn't do it correctly. I've very little experience, you see, but—"

"Good *God*, Rebecca. Let me put your mind at ease. You kiss like . . ." His voice broke. ". . . like a dream."

Rebecca's heart began to thud wildly. *I kiss like a dream.*

"Connor, then *please* talk to me. Tell me what is wrong."

The swift belligerence of his answer startled her. "When you stand in front of the fire, I can see your body through your nightdress."

Rebecca went hot to the roots of her hair with embarrassment. But there was a hint of small frightened boy in Connor's tone, she'd heard it. Suddenly she understood that Connor was as much at sea here as she was, and the realization was both frightening and exhilarating.

"Good. Then look at me. It is what you want to do, is it not?"

Connor gave a humorless laugh. "Wee Becca . . . please. Go back to bed. Perhaps we can talk tomorrow."

"It's what I want, as well. I want you to look at me."

Connor was silent. She could see his shoulders rising and falling with his quickening breath.

Rebecca inhaled deeply.

"I should like it if you made love to me, Connor."

Connor gave a short laugh. "And how on earth would you know that, wee Becca?"

The words and the short laugh stung.

"I am eighteen years old, Connor. I am not a child," she said, struggling to keep her voice even. "I am a woman. I see you with a woman's eyes. Perhaps it makes you feel less *afraid* of me to treat me as a child, but I know for certain—I know for *certain*—you do not see me as one. I know what it is to *want*, Connor. And I am not afraid to tell you that I . . . that I want you. And I suspect that you want me, too."

I know what it is to want. Connor looked up at her then, helplessly. The firelight illuminated her through her night-dress, the heart-stopping curve of her breasts and hips, the long shadows of her legs. Something caught in his throat.

"You do not know who I am . . ." He faltered, in torment. He did not know what to say, or how to put his thoughts into words, but now he could not stop looking at her. He had held these feelings at bay for days, but she was ever in his senses, the way she moved, the scent of her, her laughter, the light in her eyes when she was thinking, formulating yet another question, certain to disarm or challenge or delight him. The kiss today . . . it had simply *possessed* him . . . and it had shaken him to the bone. He took her in now, the loveliness of all that she was, and he knew all of his banked longing burned in his eyes. He hoped his expression did not frighten her.

Rebecca took another deep breath, and he watched in tortured fascination as her breasts lifted against the thin fabric of her nightdress.

"Connor, I know you are something other . . . or something more . . . than you claim to be. You are Irish one moment and English as Wellington the next . . . but it matters little. I think I know the man you are, perhaps better than anyone. And you are . . ." She hesitated, sounding unutterably shy suddenly. "You are . . . very dear to me."

Dear to me. Gentle words, but staggering, somehow, in import. Connor felt as though he was teetering on the edge of a precipice, but he still did not understand why. So here he was, retreating into silence and petulance like a callow boy, while Rebecca, with her usual courage, sought out the heart of things with tentative words.

And she was right, Connor realized. Rebecca had always seen the truest him. Perhaps this was what terrified him so completely. He could not merely seduce, or fence, or strategize, or hide.

"Connor?" she said softly.

It was devastating. He closed his eyes again, briefly, against the onslaught of feeling. What kind of man would he be if he made love to this young woman who trusted him, a young virgin who relied on him for safety? A young woman he intended to leave behind in Scotland? What kind of man would let a woman like Rebecca plead with him to make love to her?

If not him, then someday it would be someone else, and this thought, he found, he could not bear.

"Wee Becca, I—" he said, and stopped, when he heard a rustle; Rebecca had moved away from the hearth and was now standing next to him. It was her nearness that allowed the wisdom of his body to finally overcome the flailings of his mind. His arms, as if of their own accord, reached up for her and pulled her across his lap.

For a moment he merely held her, loosely, breathlessly. They were both silent, absorbing the sweet shock of the meeting of their bodies, their quickening breathing, the crackling fire the only sounds. Rebecca looked down at her lap. Her hand was resting there; Connor covered it with his own hand, and the rough warmth of it against her soft skin, and what it now meant to them, stole his breath. Rebecca turned her face up to him, questioning, and Connor met her eyes.

Oh, the terrain was so familiar, and so very dear, the slant of her brows, the dimple in her chin, the arc of her cheekbones. Connor traced them with a single finger, first one brow and then the other, then her cheek, her chin, like a sculptor bringing her into being. Rebecca watched his face, her eyes lulled and soft, fascinated by the fierce tenderness she saw there. He drew his fingertips up the length of her throat and then rubbed his thumb across the plump curve of her lower lip, a mere ghost of a touch, remembering. Rebecca's mouth lifted in a soft smile, and Connor gave a shaky laugh; he felt like a green lad, nearly shivering at the feast before him.

"Aye, I want you, too, Rebecca."

And then Connor took her face between his hands and moved his mouth to cover hers, intending at first a mere brush of a kiss, but her mouth parted for him as though she had known the shape of his mouth all her life, and what could he do but drink her in.

Never before like this, Connor thought. *Never before this endless languorous falling, falling.* Tentatively at first, and then recklessly, his tongue delved deeper into her mouth, testing all the textures within it; he delved deeper still, and yet somehow it never seemed deep enough. He pushed his fingers up through the silky tangle of her hair to tilt her head back, and he moved his mouth beneath her jaw; he found her pulse and pressed his lips against the swift beat of it.

"Tell me to stop, Rebecca, I will stop," he murmured against her neck. He was not at all certain that this was true, but it needed to be said.

She did not reply.

"Rebecca?"

"Please do not think of stopping." Her voice was thick, bemused.

He smiled. Rebecca shifted a little on his lap.

"Oof," Connor said.

"Oh, sorry. Am I heavy?"

"You *are* rather a great girl. Correction, a great *woman*." He slid his hands down over her shoulder blades, hard as two unsprouted little wings beneath her gown.

Rebecca smiled, and put her hands on either side of his face, cupping the strong planes of it. "You are nothing at all like Edelston," she murmured.

"I should hope not," Connor murmured in reply. He covered her smile with another kiss.

Rebecca cupped her hands around the back of his head and opened herself to him instinctively, gave and took with him, matched his searching hunger and urgency, melted against him. And lost in the incomparable sleekness of her mouth, Connor could feel himself spiraling dangerously toward some place where control had no use or meaning, toward an almost unendurable unanchored bliss. He pulled her body tightly against him with one arm; his other hand, trembling, hardly daring, slid down to skim across her breast. Her nipple was stiff beneath his palm; he could feel the heat of her skin beneath the fine fabric of her nightdress. The totality of his desire was almost terrifying; it humbled him, it owned him completely.

It might have been centuries, or moments; at last, Connor pulled away to breathe. He turned his head from her, shaken. Beneath his hands, Rebecca's body rose and fell with ragged breathing.

"What happens next?" she whispered.

Connor turned to her and smiled faintly. Always a question, that was Rebecca.

"There's *more*?" he said in mock wonderment.

Rebecca dimpled.

"You know very well there is more."

"Tell me all about it," he encouraged.

"In Papa's book—"

"Tell me all about it without mentioning your papa."

"I think next we must lie on the bed," she said speculatively.

Once again, for perhaps the hundredth time in her life, Rebecca Tremaine had rendered Connor Riordan speechless.

In truth, Connor could barely remember what happened next; tonight, with Rebecca in his arms, felt entirely new.

"Aye, I think the bed sounds right," he managed to say hoarsely. "Why don't you lead me there?"

She slid from his lap and stood, extending her hand, and he obediently took it. She led him like a child to the bed where he'd slept the evening before, and they knelt on it across from each other, smiling.

"Aye, there's more." Connor tugged at the tie at the throat of Rebecca's nightgown. "An infinity of things." He hoped he could remember at least two or three of them.

Like an archaeologist unearthing a rare treasure, his eyes never leaving her face, Connor slowly, slowly nudged the nightgown away from Rebecca's shoulders, stopping once to place a tender kiss at the base of her throat. Inch by devastating inch, with trembling fingers, he revealed skin that glowed amber and pearl in the firelight, until at last her nightdress pooled at her waist.

Rebecca's forearms came up reflexively, shielding her bareness from his gaze. He could see a question, as well as apprehension, move across her clear gray-green eyes, those eyes that hid nothing. And then, as if gathering her courage, she took a deep breath and slowly lowered her arms.

Connor flinched as though he'd been struck.

For a moment, he felt a strange disconnect, as though the exquisite arcing white-and-rose breasts before him could not possibly belong to the Rebecca he had known for years, the one who could shoot an apple off a fence post at fifty paces and who incessantly peppered him with questions. Mesmerized, he gawked long enough for the moment to become awkward, and then, with some difficulty he slowly lifted his eyes to her face.

The apprehension had left Rebecca's eyes. They were now warm with amusement and a hint of very feminine triumph, for the taut wonder in his face had just given her the first taste of her own power.

With hands gone a little clumsy with nerves and eagerness, Connor drew his fingertips up the length of her rib cage, feeling Rebecca's muscles contract, her breath draw in, at his touch; his own breath caught when he cupped the satiny weight of her breasts in his palms and dragged his thumbs across her nipples. And when Rebecca closed her eyes and said "Oh" very softly he felt like the Emperor of the Universe.

"Connor?" Her voice came to him faintly, as if from a distance. The wanting of her nearly buckled him.

"Aye?"

"I'd like to touch you, too."

"Ye'll get no objection from me."

She opened her eyes and gave him a dreamy smile, and his heart bucked.

"Will you show me how?"

"Aye," he said huskily. "I will show you how."

"Your arm—"

"—I feel only you, wee Becca."

He lowered his head and touched his tongue to one of her rosy nipples; then drew it delicately into his mouth, twined his tongue around it, savoring it as though it were a rare cognac.

"*Oh.*" It was more a breath than a word. Rebecca's fingers combed up through his hair to hold him against her breast.

He needed to feel all of her against him. Now.

Connor pushed her back, gently, gently, against the bed, and his eyes left her no doubt there would be no turning back. Her eyes reflected back to him nothing but desire. Laughing self-consciously, they fumbled with Connor's trouser buttons and struggled to disentangle Rebecca from the voluminous folds of her nightdress. Impatience ultimately got the better of them, and soon the buttons of Connor's shirt once again littered the floor of the hunting box.

Soft amazed relieved laughter, then silence except for the first tentative glide of hands over skin now feverish with need. And as promised, Connor showed her: he placed a hot, gentle kiss in Rebecca's palm and then guided her hand to the thick erection that curved up toward his belly, murmuring to her how he wanted to be touched. She dragged her fist up the length of him, testing; he inhaled sharply and closed his hand around her wrist.

"Connor? Was that—"

"—*too* good, wee Becca," he rasped, on a choked laugh. "We'll return to this later, aye?"

Connor swept her hair back with his hands and then gently, almost chastely, pressed his lips once more against the plush wonder of her mouth. And then his hands, trembling with tenderness and greed, traveled her body, claiming her: they roamed over her breasts and the smooth mound of her belly, skimmed the sharpness of her hip and the fullness of her buttocks, found the astonishingly silky, vulnerable skin hidden between her thighs and beneath her arms. Rebecca rippled under his touch, her breath catching; her eyes fluttered closed to isolate herself with sensation, then fluttered open again to watch his hands move over her. Connor paused a moment and propped himself up on his elbow, his hand fanned over her belly. He stared down at her.

"God, but you're beautiful, wee Becca."

Rebecca smiled shyly up at him. Connor brushed his mouth against hers; her hand rose to cup his face and she parted her lips beneath his. Their tongues twined languidly; Connor stroked the satiny side of her breast with the backs of his fingers, luxuriating in the feel of it. Then he took his mouth from hers and bent his head to her nipple; he wound his tongue around it, teasing the rose velvet into a tight little bead as his palm rubbed over her other breast, glided down over her ribs, skimmed the copper curls below the curve of her belly, lightly stroked, with just the tips of his fingers, the inside of her thigh.

"*Connor . . . oh . . . wonderful . . .*" Rebecca's fingers combed up his neck into his hair, sending little rivers of flame through his limbs.

"What are you trying to say, wee Becca?" he teased.

"*Hush.*" She tried to laugh, but his fingers were dragging back up her thigh, up through the downy hairs there, dipping lightly, lightly into the damp cleft covered in copper curls, and the laugh became a gasp.

"Touch me, wee Becca." A hoarse command. But her hands were already on him. Her palms moved over his chest and over his belly, over his arms and thighs, making the same discoveries, making the same claim on his body as he had made on hers. She gently raked through the hair on his chest with her fingers; with her tongue, she followed the trail of dark curling hair, tasting his flat nipples, tracing the seam between his ribs, drawing it along the swollen curve of his erection as her hands slid down over his thighs. A groan ripped from Connor's throat; he closed his eyes, tortured by the carnal innocence of her exploration.

"What are *you* trying to say, Connor?"

He swore, half laughing, then seized Rebecca's arms and pulled her roughly up over his chest. He took her mouth fiercely; their tongues dueled, and then they writhed together, a tangle of demanding hands and mouths sliding over sweat-sheened bodies. Connor gripped her buttocks and rocked her up against him and softly bit the cord of her neck; her tongue found the whorls of his ears; he gasped her name. Then Connor rolled her over and pinned her. He stared down into Rebecca's eyes, lifted himself up over her, his arms trembling, and tormented both of them by rubbing his aching erection up through the cleft between her legs, slowly, once, twice, again. Rebecca's knees fell open; instinctively, she arched against him.

"*Connor . . . I want . . . please . . .*"

He knew it was time. Connor lowered himself again and, taking her in his arms, turned her and gently lifted one of her legs over his hip. He dipped his fingers into the moist heat between her legs, stroking, circling knowingly, relentlessly. Rebecca murmured incoherently and moved her hips against his hand, clutching at his arms, making a breathless question and plea of his name, trusting him to take her safely to wherever it was she seemed to be hurtling.

At last, a string of soft cries tore from her and her body bowed and bucked, jerked upward by the force of her release. She sank back against Connor, her breathing quick and harsh.

Connor lifted her damp hair away from her face, tucking it behind one of her ears; he brushed his mouth tenderly across her kiss-swollen lips.

"Connor?" Rebecca's voice was thick with awe.

"Aye." He could barely speak through the lump in his throat. "It is like that." Her tremors continued to pulse beneath his hand; he felt a tender triumph. *I did that for her.*

"For you, too?"

Connor's own need clawed at him. He lifted himself up over her again; the smooth muscles on his back quivered, his wounded arm shook. "Soon, wee Becca." He looked down into her eyes; they were still glazed with passion and release. "It may hurt you a bit, but just the once. Are you afraid?"

She reached up and brushed his forelock away from his eyes. "I am the opposite of afraid," she said grandly.

Connor smiled slightly; he could hear the bravado in her voice. "*I* am a little afraid," he confessed.

"But why?"

He could not explain.

"Don't be afraid. I am here with you," she said softly,

folding her arms and legs around him, fitting herself beneath him. And then at last he was filling her, murmuring words of reassurance, and then hoarse syllables of ecstasy, moving inside her slowly, then blindly, toward his own release.

He breathed her name when it came.

They slept a little, an hour or two, still entwined. Connor woke when he felt Rebecca stirring, and she smiled sleepily up at him. He brushed a kiss across the top of her head.

"I love you," she murmured.

The words . . . it was though an entire sun had exploded in his chest.

He'd been ridiculous. His thrashing thoughts, his grand confusion and torment and helplessness—it was only love, had always been love, he supposed. It was no precipice he stood at, or rather precipices have little meaning when one finally acknowledges that one has wings. Connor stepped off.

"I love you, too."

Such grave, inadequate words for what it was he felt.

Rebecca smiled and closed her eyes, and was soon asleep again.

He needed her with him forever. And somehow, through all the previous days, perhaps from the day he had met her, he had known it.

Everything was simple now, highwaymen and lockets and multiple identities notwithstanding. All he was, and all Connor could ever imagine being from that point on, was the man who held Rebecca while she slept.

Chapter Fifteen

❧

"... And in Georgia, great scaly monsters with long snouts full of teeth live in the water. They can snap up a deer with one bite."

"You are lying!"

"God's truth," Connor said solemnly. "They swim about in pools just like this one, only a bit murkier, and crawl out onto the shore every now and again to sun themselves just like we are doing now."

Connor and Rebecca were lying side by side on a blanket at the bathing pool, nude and glaringly white in the afternoon sun, covered in little pearls of water. Rebecca had wanted another swim, and though Connor had at first been reluctant to indulge her impulse, grumbling about how they should at that very moment be on the road, he at least deferred to her argument that it could very well be their last opportunity ever to frolic naked in a pool together. "A very good argument indeed," he had told Rebecca, solemnly.

And now he was regaling her with tales of America.

"Do they eat people?" Rebecca asked after a moment.

"Only on occasion," he said breezily. "They are called 'alligators.' Would you like to see one someday?"

There was a beat of silence.

"Well, of course," Rebecca said weakly.

"Are you quite sure?" Connor's voice quivered with suppressed amusement.

"Of course I should like to see such an interesting creature," she reiterated stoutly.

Still, she couldn't help eyeing the pool with uneasy speculation. Another short silence settled over them.

And then Connor grabbed her thigh and roared.

Rebecca leaped nearly straight into the air with emitting a series of shrieks. "You beast!" She pounced on him and attempted to pound his chest with her fists while Connor laughed helplessly.

"My arm! My arm! Have a care for my arm!" he choked out between laughs, attempting to capture her wrists. She giggled and squirmed out of his grasp, but soon enough he was able to grip both of her arms, and rolled her over.

They were motionless a moment, entranced by the perfect fathomless joy they saw in each other's eyes.

"Hello," Rebecca said softly.

"Hello," Connor replied politely, then licked a pearl of water from her breast. Rebecca watched his eyes go nearly black with desire, and felt a surge of exultation.

Connor lifted her arms over her head and pinned them there, grinning wickedly; Rebecca dragged her feet up the length of his calves in a slow caress and locked her legs around him. He eased into her, one long unhurried thrust, and then they rocked together slowly, slowly, savoring the feel of each other's bodies, cool and slick from the water and warmed from the sun. *Beautiful.* The word filled Rebecca's mind. Her head went back; Connor nipped at her throat, dragged his whiskered cheek against the smooth column of it, sought her lips and lost them again as her head thrashed with desire. She watched him, relishing the primal cadence of his hips as he thrust in and out of her; a white flame lit and snaked through her veins until she was incandescent, frantic with need. *Beautiful. Beautiful. Beautiful.* Rebecca cried out, a thin wild sound, arcing beneath the quickening rhythm of his thrusts, and then her skin dissolved into a thousand brilliant burning stars and she was quaking beneath him.

Connor collapsed against her, shuddering. She cradled his head, stroking that splendidly unruly thick black mop, sweeping his curving forelock away from his brow. They remained that way, in silence, until their breathing became more settled and even.

Connor finally rolled away from her reluctantly, but then immediately reached for her and folded her into his arms.

They lay quietly together until he began to doze, and Rebecca gazed up through the trees. Shards of blue sky glowed between the luminous green of the leaves; it was like lying beneath a ceiling of stained glass. She transferred her gaze to the arm that wrapped her and then delicately traced the faint blue road of the veins there with her finger, grateful beyond words for the life that coursed all through him.

She was awed by the very fact of lovemaking. By how their attempts to assuage their hunger for each other merely created more hunger, by the exhilarating, terrifying moment of utter surrender in the midst of it, when she could no longer say where her body ended and Connor's began and could not imagine ever caring again. She gloried in all of it: in the weight of Connor's body against her, in how her touch could make him bury his face helplessly in the crook of her neck and hoarsely murmur her name, in how his eyes went hot and distant, unseeing even as they never left her face, as he moved in her toward his release. And now her body ached thoroughly, deliciously, as though it had at last been used for the reason it had been invented.

Somehow, it all made learning to play the pianoforte seem that much more pointless.

And oh, God, how she loved him. But there was something she needed to know. As time and distance from the stables eroded Connor's Irish accent, something that seemed more indelible was revealed. She saw the changes in his bearing, his voice, the very way he occupied a space, and she saw how they fit his body more truly. He fought and shot like a gentleman, he spoke like a gentleman, he wore his clothes like a gentleman. But there was something more, something almost intangible; his grace, his wit, the words he had at his disposal, his reflexive ease in commanding a situation. She needed to know.

"Connor?"

Connor opened one eye and cast it in her direction. "Mmm?"

"Will you tell me who you really are?"

The woman did have a talent for asking the most unexpected questions at the most unexpected times. Wide awake now, Connor sat up and pushed a nervous hand through his hair. But he did not speak.

Rebecca continued, faltering a little. "It is just

that . . . you remind me of the time that Papa tripped over something poking up out of the ground in the back garden, after it had rained for days and days, poured down, really. He rubbed at it with his handkerchief, and he saw that it was a little chest, and when he had Tom the gardener dig it up, it turned out to be full of Roman coins. Pretty things, and quite valuable, he found. But it might have stayed buried, and we would never have known about it, if not for the rain."

Connor gave a rueful laugh.

"Ah. So I call to mind something that has been buried for centuries, wee Becca?" he said, quirking one corner of his mouth ironically. "I realize I am in need of a shave, but I am not certain I appreciate the comparison."

But he was looking out across the swimming pond and beyond it, not at her.

Rebecca did not reply. She wrapped her arms tightly around her knees. Connor turned toward her, and his heart constricted at the pale tautness of her face.

"Please forgive me, wee Becca," he said softly. "It's that you are wondering what you will find in the chest when finally we have it all dug up, aye?"

"Aye," she answered softly.

He looked back out across the pond.

"Are you perhaps in trouble with the law, Connor?"

"Not before I met you, wee Becca, upon my honor," he replied promptly. "Now, however, it is a different story."

She smiled a little at that.

"Then are you . . . were you . . . somebody . . . important?"

Connor still did not meet her eyes. He was gazing down the length of the river. Somewhere beyond the reach of his vision it met the sea, and across that sea was America, a new life. If only the tendrils of his old one did not strangle him before he reached it.

"Yes," he said, finally.

The word seemed to land between them with the weight of a monument.

Rebecca drew in a short sharp breath. And then she nodded once, as though in confirmation of something she already knew.

They were both quiet for a moment, pensive, and then Connor stood and began pacing restlessly. He spoke, his words tumbling out in a rush.

"When I was injured in the war, wee Becca, I saw my chance. I hated the life I had led, and the life that awaited me when I returned from the war. Everything proscribed, dictated, stifling. I had, in fact, gone to war to escape it. And so I simply left it behind. I swear to you, there was no scandal. I left no wife or child. Everyone who knew me simply thought I was dead, killed at Waterloo, and so it was easy to begin a new life."

"*I* would have known the truth," she said softly.

"How would you have known, wee Becca?"

"You are my heart, Connor. I would know if my own heart had stopped beating."

It was said so simply, so matter-of-factly. And once again, Rebecca Tremaine had left him speechless.

Connor stopped pacing. *She will do this always*, he thought. *And I need her with me always*. He looked down at her, his eyes tender, pleading.

"Oh, they believed it, wee Becca. If you had been at Waterloo, you would understand how easy a thing it was to believe. I left an immense duty behind, and wealth, too, and I am not proud of it. But I do not want it back. God help me, I am happier now than I have ever been. I pray you do not think less of me for it."

Rebecca looked back at him incredulously.

"For heaven's sake," she said gently.

"Sorry?" Connor said, a little startled.

"I left my duty behind, too, Connor. It was my duty to marry Edelston and play the pianoforte and do embroidery and most likely live miserably alone in the country while my husband went off to the gaming tables in London. And you do not think less of me for forsaking it, do you? I could not bear the life that was meant for me, and so I took another one for myself altogether, with scarcely a second thought. With your help. How can I think less of you, Connor, when, of all the people in my life, you have always cared for me best, in your way? I cannot imagine you would have ever left anyone who truly needed you."

Ah, yes, but *you* did not give up the seat your family has held in Parliament for hundreds of years, wee Becca. You did not give up the land we rest upon at the moment. You did not let your family and friends grieve you for dead. You did not leave a mistress without saying good-bye.

He almost said all of it aloud.

"Rebecca, it is not that simple. Duty is different for men and women—" he began softly.

"Bosh," Rebecca interrupted cheerfully. "We are both of us selfish and I care not a fig. I care not as long as I am with you."

Connor stared down at her in amazement. He wondered if there would ever come a day when Rebecca would cease to amaze him. There wasn't a coy bone in her body; she had taken to lovemaking with relish and a humbling tenderness. Reveling with her in the discovery of her own body had been the greatest pleasure of his life.

But how callous and exclusive new love could be, recognizing nothing outside of its own bubble, Connor thought. They *would* care a fig for other things, in time, he knew. But the version of himself he saw through her eyes was seductive, and he wanted it to feel that simple; he wanted to be selfish, and to not mind being selfish. He thought perhaps, having survived the violence and wars in his life, he was entitled to a bit of selfishness. And included in that selfishness was the fact that he did not want to tell Rebecca the whole truth about himself, not just yet. Not until she was his entirely, legally. Not until it would be extremely difficult indeed for her to walk away from him out of disillusionment and disappointment, if ever she knew the full truth about him.

His palms went clammy. How was it that he had reached the ripe old age of twenty-nine without even considering marriage? It was not as though one aristocratic heiress after another had not been thrust before him from the moment he turned eighteen years old. Balls and soirees had been veritable gauntlets of fluttering eligible females, none of whom had registered for more than a moment on his awareness. He had been angry and self-absorbed, occupied with testing the limits of his freedom and his father's patience. Perpetuating the ancient Dunbrooke bloodline had seemed a distasteful duty belonging to the distant future.

But from the moment he had awoken with Rebecca in his arms, marriage was all he could think about. God help him, what if Rebecca would not marry him? What if he asked, and she hesitated, or needed persuasion? He knew what he would do: for the first time in his life, he would beg. He would threaten, if necessary; frighten her by declaring that even now she could be carrying his child. By God, wedding her was the only true desire he'd ever had in all of his born days. And then he would make it up to her by making her happy for the rest of her life.

"Connor?" Rebecca said quizzically. "Are you quite all right?"

Connor had never heard of anyone proposing in the nude before. Doubtless there was precedent, however, as there was for nearly everything, if one only looked.

"Rebecca . . ." It came out a dry croak. Oh, quite the auspicious start.

"Connor, please sit down beside me. You look unwell. Is it your arm? May I look at it?"

"No!" he barked nervously.

Rebecca flinched.

"I mean . . ."

Perhaps this would go better if he knelt. Resolutely, he knelt next to her, but she scooted back from him an inch in a slight show of wariness. He had to stop himself from burbling a hysterical laugh. How did anybody in love perform this moment gracefully? How did proposals ever get made, when they were such an exquisite form of torture?

"Connor—"

"Hush, Rebecca," he blurted, more irritably than he intended. "I am trying to ask you to marry me."

Her mouth dropped open in astonishment, and she stared at him blankly for a moment. And then she began giggling.

Connor frowned at her darkly.

"Oh, yes, yes, yes," she gasped, still giggling helplessly.

"Of course! I'm sorry, I'm sorry. It's just—'*Hush, Rebecca,*'" she imitated sternly, her voice vibrating. "Oh, my. So romantic."

Connor's frown began to waver and curl up at the edges in the face of her peals of giggles, and then, finally, he opened his mouth and a great whoop of laughter and victory emerged. He supposed it mattered little that he had issued the world's clumsiest marriage proposal, as long as, through all the giggling, he got the response he wanted.

Rebecca flung herself into his arms, and he closed his arms around her as tightly as he could.

"I have so little money, Rebecca, but perhaps I can work for my aunt for a short time and she will no doubt lend us money, and we can be married at Gretna Green tomorrow, but we must leave soon to get there, and you *do* want to go to America, don't you? And perhaps you can be a doctor there . . . ?" He was babbling, from relief, unbridled happiness, panic at the enormity of what he had just done.

"Yes," she murmured against his chest. "Yes to everything. As long as we are together."

Connor held her and buried his face in the sweetness of her hair, breathing her in. But no matter how close he held her, images of Marianne Bell, his brother Richard, his father, the youngest Pickering boy, played at the edge of his consciousness like the remnants of a dream.

Chapter Sixteen

༄

The hunting box had no windows, but there were a few very fine chinks in its walls, and daylight inevitably found them. Rebecca's eyes opened to darkness lifting.

Connor was sitting up in bed next to her, his arms wrapped loosely around his knees; he seemed to be gazing in the general direction of the door. Rebecca sleepily pushed herself into a sitting position and placed a soft kiss on his bare shoulder. He smiled faintly, and her heart gave a little kick. She had felt that same kick often over the past several days; she liked to think it was her heart stretching to receive a fresh rush of joy.

But Connor didn't speak or reach for her; he remained lost in thought, oddly absorbed. She sat up next to him quietly, companionably, gazing in the same direction, as though she could see whatever it was he saw there, too.

It was minutes before he spoke. "Wee Becca, the other day, when I went to the pawnshop . . ."

"When you bought my Herbal?"

He smiled. "Aye. When I bought your Herbal. Well, I met a friend there—"

"You have friends?"

Connor's mouth twitched. "'Tis a bit early for wit, isn't it, wee Becca? *Aye*, I've a friend, an old friend . . . and, well, I think we should . . . visit him today. If we can find him."

"If we can find him?" Rebecca was confused. "But what about Gretna Green? Why haven't you mentioned him until now? Why must we visit him? Does he live near here?"

"After a fashion."

"After a *fashion*? What does that mean, after a fash—"

Connor covered her mouth decisively with his own, interrupting her question. He nipped at her lips gently until they parted to allow in his tongue.

"*Mmmm . . .*" She sighed, and put her hands on either side of his face, surrendering to his sinewy exploration, and doing a little exploration of her own. At last Connor lifted his head, his eyes kiss-drunk and half-mast.

"Did you like that, wee Becca?"

She smiled fuzzily. "Couldn't abide it. Now, your friend—"

"No? How about . . . this?" He dipped his head; his tongue traced a slow, hot filigree over her nipple, teasing it into a tiny rose pucker. And then he took it into his mouth and sucked gently.

Lightning coursed through her veins, fanning out from where his hot mouth joined her flesh. "*Oh . . . God . . . that's . . . simply . . . awful . . .*" she gasped, half laughing. She felt his lips curve into a smile against her breast.

"Oh?" he purred impishly, "then you'll just bloody *hate . . .* this."

His head disappeared under the blanket, and his tongue

dipped once into her navel before it stopped and touched once lightly, and then with a long stroke, the sensitive nub at the crook of her legs. Rebecca jumped. He did it again.

"Oh, God . . ."

"Is it just horrible?" he asked in mock sympathy, stifling a laugh. He tossed the blanket back; his hands gently pushed her thighs farther apart. He applied his tongue again.

"Please . . ."

"Ye taste of heaven, wee Becca," he murmured huskily.

"Stop . . . talking . . ."

Connor laughed a low pleased laugh and complied. And when she began moving her hips against the strokes of his tongue, he lifted her legs up about his waist and guided himself into her, met the movements of her hips with his own. In mere seconds, they shattered together.

Tendrils of mist were winding in and out of the forest foliage, and the rising sun sent dusty columns of light slanting through the trees, striping Connor and Rebecca in light as they rode. Rebecca was uncomfortable; her eyes were still gritty and raw from her interrupted sleep, and her legs hung on either side of her horse like sacks of flour. She would much rather have stayed in bed all day. *There should be a law*, she thought. *A minimum of two hours in bed for every hour of lovemaking.* But no; Connor had been adamant. And now it was all she could do to stay in the saddle.

At Connor's insistence, she rode alongside him, not behind or in front of him, and she was back in the clothes she wore as Ned, which itched her. Connor seemed distracted. He'd said only a few very terse and uninformative things since they'd left the hunting box, and now she could see him scanning the floor of the woods as if hunting desperately for something in particular.

"Connor?"

The look he sent her questioned her temerity in speaking to him when he was so clearly occupied.

Rebecca sighed windily, but refrained from any further questions. But she was growing increasingly nervous. She could see they were riding not north, not toward Scotland as they had planned, not toward Gretna Green where they would be married . . . but back the way they had come.

Connor suddenly pulled his horse to a halt to examine a broken tree branch that seemed to have been purposefully planted in the ground. It was forked, and the longest end of the fork pointed south. He smiled faintly and rubbed his hands on his trousers, as though drying perspiring palms, and the tension visibly left his body. With something approximating cheer, he turned his horse in the direction of the forking branch. Rebecca followed suit.

She thought she'd try again.

"Connor? Where are we going? Where is your friend?"

He gave her a sideways look.

"You will like where we're going, wee Becca, I assure you."

"That was not my question."

"Aye, but that is all the answer I have."

He gave her a smile, the smile that usually lit her world as surely as the sun lit the day. She wanted to kick him.

They rode for another hour or so, Connor periodically becoming fascinated with neat little piles of stones, or more planted branches; each time he turned his horse accordingly.

"I wish you'd tell me where we are going."

" 'Tis a pity, then, that I am not a wish-granting fairy, wee Becca."

Well, she thought. *I suppose sarcasm is better than silence.*

They rode on.

Finally, faintly at first, then growing in strength, she heard sounds that didn't belong to the woods: voices in a strange language, a laugh, a cough. Horses whickering, the jingling of tack. Something savory was cooking; it made her stomach clench in longing.

A moment later they were in a clearing, surrounded by a collection of dark faces and bright eyes, men, women, and children. The voices in the strange language fell silent.

A movement caught Rebecca's eye; a tall man with bright pale eyes stood in the center of the clearing, hands planted on his hips; he was swinging his head from Connor, to Rebecca, then back to Connor again, then back to Rebecca.

And grinning broadly.

"That's quite enough out of you," Connor said to Raphael.

Raphael turned his palms up in a placating "Did I say anything?" gesture. "You followed the *patrin*, I see," he said.

Connor nodded. "Mr. Raphael Heron, this is my friend Miss Rebecca Tre—" Connor stopped himself, thinking better of it. "My friend Rebecca," he concluded. "Rebecca, this is Raphael Heron."

Rebecca, her eyes wide with wonder, nodded to Raphael from atop her horse. Raphael bowed low to her, still grinning broadly.

Connor slid from the saddle and held Rebecca's stirrup so she could dismount.

"Gypsies?" she breathed to him, thrilled. Her mother, quite simply, would clap a hand to her heart and keel over if she saw her now.

"I *told* you you would like it," he whispered smugly, as though it were a special treat he had arranged just for her. "Oh, and they prefer to be known as the Rom."

"And is he the Gypsy who taught you to tickle a fish?"

"Aye. And he'll tell you 'tis true, too, if ye've doubts."

Raphael Heron said something rapidly to Connor in the strange language; it sounded to Rebecca like water tumbling over rough stones, melodic and guttural all at once. To her astonishment, Connor rattled off a reply in the same language. Raphael nodded once, thoughtfully.

Rebecca glanced around the clearing at the silent staring faces. One of them, a young woman, was watching Connor with undisguised avidity.

"Leonora, Martha," Raphael said, and two women turned to him, including the one who was so openly admiring Connor. "Perhaps the young *Gadji* would like to rest in your tent."

"Go with Leonora, Rebecca," Connor said gently. "I need to speak to Raphael."

Rebecca opened her mouth, then closed it again. She wanted something more from him, a touch, some reassurance, some explanation of why they were here. But though his eyes were soft, they were stern with command as well, and his hands remained at his sides.

The woman named Leonora smiled at her and reached out a dark hand. Because she seemed to have no other choice, Rebecca reluctantly took it, and Leonora led her away.

They almost missed the card; it was an innocuous thing amid the numerous other cards and the profusion of bouquets that had been arriving for Lorelei from the moment the Tremaines had descended upon London. Judging from Lady Kirkham's parlor, the greenhouses of England were being picked clean on Lorelei's behalf.

However, only one bouquet truly interested Lorelei: a simple spray of bluebells. Every day, ever since her first evening at Almack's, the little bouquet had arrived at the door shortly after breakfast."For my bluebell," the card always said, and that was all.

Her mother thought the anonymous bluebells sweet and very naive when compared to the extravagant hothouse bouquets sent by the likes of Viscount Grayson and the Earl of Pennyworth's heir. No doubt the bluebells were a sign of regard from someone who had no reason to hope for Lorelei's attention.

The truth, unbeknownst to anyone but Lorelei, was quite to the contrary.

After Lady Tremaine had sorted, clucking and gloating, through Lorelei's invitations, she came across the note. It was addressed, much to her surprise, to Sir Henry, not to herself or Lorelei. Wordlessly, she handed it to him.

Sir Henry's eyebrows shot upward. He preferred to be excluded from social fripperies; a card addressed to him was therefore very likely momentous, and not necessarily pleasantly so.

He opened it, and with mixed feelings recognized the

Duchess of Dunbrooke's stationery. Ironically, the Duchess of Dunbrooke's generosity had put the Tremaines in a delicate position; they had been reluctant to request frequent updates about the search for Rebecca, lest they seem ungrateful or mistrustful. The duchess was, after all, responsible for Lorelei's entry into Almack's, and who knew how useful she might prove in the future? But the days of silence, the hours of not knowing, their inability to do anything at all to find Rebecca, had been excruciating.

Sir Henry read the note, then closed his eyes and exhaled slowly, gustily, as though he'd been holding his breath for days.

"Henry? What is it?" Lady Tremaine's voice was sharp with anxiety.

Silently, Sir Henry gave the note to Lady Tremaine.

She has been seen in Scotland, it said.

Sir Henry looked at his wife. Her lower lip was trembling.

"About bloody time." Sir Henry crushed the note in his fist.

"Scotland? But *how*?"

Sir Henry and Lady Tremaine and Cordelia Blackburn, Duchess of Dunbrooke, sat in Lady Kirkham's parlor, clutching teacups. Lorelei had been dispatched on a series of social calls accompanied by her maid, with instructions to tell her friends that her mother was suffering from the headache and would not be joining them today.

"We are not at all certain at the moment," Cordelia said. "We do know, however, that she is unharmed. There is speculation that perhaps a neighbor assisted in her leaving."

"Robbie Denslowe! That young scoundrel—"

"Now, Henry," Lady Tremaine soothed. "Robbie was not at home when Rebecca disappeared, so he could not possibly have helped her leave. What matters is that Rebecca is safe."

"Sir Henry, I must emphasize that we do not know how she managed to travel to Scotland, so we must not leap to conclusions," Cordelia added. "I know no details other than a young woman meeting Rebecca's description has been seen, and that she seemed well. I have arranged for my assistants to continue their search, and no doubt they will find her soon."

"Was she alone?" Lady Tremaine's voice trembled.

"I know not." Cordelia was apologetic. "I have told you all I know, which is all that my assistants know."

"I will go and help fetch her at once." To Sir Henry, a trip to Scotland in order to bring his never-boring youngest daughter home seemed like the perfect escape from this endless dull round of parties and balls.

"You cannot go now!" Lady Tremaine gasped. "The viscount is on the very brink of proposing to Lorelei, I'm certain of it, and I daresay we cannot afford to compromise Lorelei's future."

"I fail to see how searching for Rebecca will compromise Lorelei's future," Sir Henry replied, with ill-disguised irritation.

"People will wonder where you've got to, Henry. A sudden disappearance—"

"Sir Henry, Lady Tremaine. Please forgive my interruption . . ."

Sir Henry and Lady Tremaine turned heated expressions toward Cordelia.

"I do believe," Cordelia said slowly, "that in this instance, Sir Henry, Lady Tremaine has the right of it. Why take any risk with Lorelei's future, when it is virtually certain that Rebecca will soon be returned home, safely? She has been seen; my assistants will no doubt be able to see her themselves, soon. And Lord Edelston is willing, even eager, to *marry* her, despite her . . . excursion. He has a decent title, and stands to inherit a good deal of land. My assistants will bring her home while making very certain that nothing . . . *untoward* takes place. And think of the triumph: you shall have two daughters wedded in the space of a season." Cordelia concluded her speech with a glowing smile of encouragement.

The Tremaines heard all that was unspoken, or rather spoken in the code that the well bred seemed to be born understanding. "Willing, even eager, to *marry* your daughter"—despite the fact that he was able to very nearly ravish her in the Tremaines' own back garden at midnight. "He has a decent title, and stands to inherit a good deal of land"—they could count themselves lucky that any titled gentleman would be at all interested in Rebecca, in light of this particular escapade. "My assistants will make very certain that nothing . . . *untoward* takes place"—nothing, that is, more untoward than what had already occurred, most of which Rebecca had instigated. The duchess was absolutely correct.

Lady Tremaine sent a beseeching look to Sir Henry, who returned it with a stare of pure frustration. The resistance was token, however, and at last he sighed. It was always so much more soothing to his peace of mind to acquiesce to his wife's wishes. The duchess's assistants, if they were anything like Bow Street Runners, no doubt knew better than he how to locate his daughter, and likely he would simply be underfoot if he went traipsing off to Scotland.

"Very well. I shall stay. And we thank you for all that you've done to help us, Your Grace."

Lady Tremaine heaved a sigh and rolled her eyes heavenward with relief.

"The pleasure is mine, Sir Henry," Cordelia said kindly.

Cordelia was relieved that the Lord and Lady Tremaine had swallowed and digested the Scotland tale. She had been concerned that they would become restive and decide to take matters regarding Rebecca into their own hands if she did not give them some information, however fabricated. In truth, after their last encounter with the highwaymen, both Rebecca Tremaine and Roarke Blackburn seemed to have disappeared somewhere into the godforsaken land near the Scottish border. But she would find them. Or rather her assistants would find them. Hutchins had called back to London the bumbling pair who had been twice thrashed by Roarke Blackburn, and engaged a few others to watch the roads and harbors in that part of the country. But all of the assistants had been promised great monetary rewards if they could bring proof to her of Roarke Blackburn's death.

She just needed a little more time. And she needed the Tremaines to refrain from asking questions. For now, it appeared they would be docilely cooperative.

Once again, a title had proved all the credibility needed. Cordelia intended to protect that title at any cost.

Chapter Seventeen

❦

Rebecca perused her surroundings frankly. Along the walls of Leonora's tent, a number of chests were stacked neatly and a few blankets were rolled into tight cylinders, as though the tent's occupants had either just arrived or were just packing to leave. Most curiously, a long chest against the far wall of the tent supported several rows of jars and boxes, each labeled carefully with a word or two in black ink. Some of the jars were filled with what appeared to be dried herbs and flowers; others were even more intriguing, filled with liquid and dark bobbing objects.

Rebecca's eyes went to her hostesses; she wondered whether they spoke English, whether she could speak to them before they spoke to her. The older woman, who was lean and swarthy and had a head of dark hair threaded with silver, gazed back at her with kind dark eyes. The younger woman, who seemed to be comprised of soft round parts—a blunt little nose, a rosy plump mouth, a full round bosom, a head full of loose dark curls—also stared at Rebecca, with a pair of eyes as round and amber as two harvest moons. But her expression was something other than placid. It was . . . baldly assessing. And definitely disconcerting.

Perhaps she has a blinking disorder, Rebecca thought. Perhaps she had only *appeared* to be staring at Connor earlier.

"I am Leonora Heron, and Martha is my daughter, Rebecca," the older woman said at last. "Would ye like some water? A bit o' something to eat?"

"Leonora?" Rebecca asked, as though she hadn't heard Leonora's polite question. She'd had the most delicious suspicion from the moment she entered the tent. And though she realized she was being hopelessly rude, she couldn't wait another moment for the answer.

"Yes?" Leonora apparently didn't know or didn't care that Rebecca was being hopelessly rude.

"What do you keep in those jars?"

"Herbs, Rebecca," Leonora said. "I am a healer for our *compania.*"

Rebecca's heart skipped a beat. "You are . . . a doctor?"

The Gypsy woman snorted. "I am a *healer*. Which is more than I can say for most *Gorgio* doctors. I am known far and wide among the Rom for healing." The pride and absolute assurance in her voice thrilled Rebecca strangely. She could not imagine her mother sending for this woman in a time of sickness. Though nearly every woman in the English countryside had a receipt or two for special draughts and salves, and though midwives were still called to birthings at least as often as doctors, Rebecca could not imagine any English woman being lauded or admired throughout the land for her skill in healing. Women did not attend physicians' college. Women held the basin that caught the blood of their loved ones while doctors bled them, women cleaned the vomit, fetched the clean linen.

"What are the names of the herbs in your jars?" Rebecca bit her lip, but she could not seem to stop asking questions.

"There is adder's-tongue," Leonora said, "for dressing wounds. And coltsfoot, for troubles of the lungs, and also to hasten the healing of wounds. There is feverfew, for ailments of the digestion, and henbane—"

"—for pain," Rebecca said eagerly.

"Yes, but not too much, just a very weak infusion, or your patient will feel no pain forever."

The two women surprised each other by sharing a dark laugh.

Martha had finally peeled her eyes away from Rebecca, and now her full-moon gaze was idly roaming the tent.

"And?" Rebecca urged Leonora to continue.

Leonora obliged. "Elder bark, for . . ." Like a teacher, she waited for Rebecca to complete her sentence.

"Rheumatism?" Rebecca guessed.

"Yes, and it is good for boils, as well, and many other things," Leonora said approvingly. "And I've bettony . . ."

"Good for . . . bites and stings." Rebecca knew this from her Herbal. "You make a poultice of it."

"Yes, and it is good for the farting, too," Leonora reminded her. "When ye make a draught of it."

Martha's face, Rebecca noted, had taken on a distinctly sour cast.

"You've an interest in healing, little *Gadji*?" Leonora asked.

"Oh," Rebecca said reverently. "Oh, yes. I think it's wonderful." She could hardly believe an adult woman, somebody's *mother*, had asked her that question in all seriousness.

Leonora laughed, pleased with her answer. "What a fine thing, little *Gadji*. I wish Martha cared for it as much. Martha thinks young Gypsy men are more worthy of her time than healing."

I have a feeling she thinks Connor is worthy of her time, too, Rebecca thought, eyeing Martha cagily.

Something on the ceiling of the tent seemed to have captured Martha's attention. Rebecca felt a little twinge of sympathy: ceiling gazing, after all, was a time-honored way to ignore one's mother. Substitute "mucking about in the stables" for "young Gypsy men" and "pianoforte" for "healing" and it was the same conversation she'd had with her own mother dozens of times. Still . . . to be *encouraged* to learn to be a healer, and not to want it! It defied belief.

"Ye must be thirsty and hungry, Rebecca. I'll fetch ye some breakfast. Perhaps we can talk more of healing whilst ye stay wi' us." With a smile, Leonora slipped out of the tent.

Martha's amber eyes were immediately back, unblinkingly, on Rebecca. Bracing herself, Rebecca returned her gaze.

"Your hair is loud," Martha said at last, sadly, as though it pained her to think of someone having hair that was any less beautiful than her own. She twirled one of her loose dusky curls languidly over her finger.

"Yes, I suppose it is," Rebecca said. There seemed to be no point in disputing something that was patently true.

"It is not . . . *Gypsy* hair," Martha said regretfully. To emphasize her point, she gave a head toss that sent her bountiful mane bouncing over one shoulder.

"Perhaps," Rebecca said slowly, struggling to rein in the sarcasm, "it is because I am not a *Gypsy*."

Martha smiled faintly and tilted her head, gazing at Rebecca with eyes brimming with pity.

"The man ye travel with—he is your brother, yes?"

"Er . . . no . . ." Rebecca felt her face grow warm. Would Martha be shocked to learn that she, an unmarried woman, was traveling alone with a young man?

"Because," Martha continued, as though Rebecca had not spoken at all, "he looked at you as one would look at a sister."

It was Rebecca's turn to stare, flabbergasted.

Martha gazed back, her expression almost entirely neutral. Almost. There was a definite gleam of something in the depths of her eyes.

"I . . . he . . ." Rebecca spluttered. She drew herself up proudly. "Connor is my fiancé. We are to be married. And *he* rather likes my hair." Rebecca winced at the childish tone she heard in her own voice. Still, she couldn't seem to help it. Who *was* this creature?

"Oh," Martha said, her expression faintly troubled. "Well, I suppose that could be true."

"You *what*?"

Leonora reentered the tent, carrying a bowl of steaming, heavenly smelling stew and a flagon of water.

"Eat, little *Gadji*, and then rest. We will be leaving camp very soon."

"Where is Connor?" Rebecca asked, her eyes darting to Martha. *Brother*, indeed.

"He is still with Raphael, Rebecca. The two of you will be traveling with us."

Rebecca was silent, wishing she'd heard those words from Connor. Why was the man being so bloody reticent?

"Of course," she said, smiling weakly. "Thank you." She accepted a spoon and the bowl of stew and tucked into it. It tasted as heavenly as it smelled.

"Martha, ye're needed to help break down camp. We shall let the little *Gadji* sleep a bit."

Rebecca was about to protest that she wasn't sleepy, that she would like to help break down camp, too, but on a moment's reflection she decided that would be a lie: her full belly combined with her unexpectedly early morning made her outrageously sleepy; it was growing difficult to keep her eyelids aloft.

Leonora unfurled a blanket for her, and with pleasure Rebecca lay back against it on the floor of the tent and watched her hostesses leave. She had to admit, as she nodded off, that she was very happy to see the back of Martha, at least for now.

Connor told the harrowing tale of the past few days to Raphael in bursts, because Raphael occasionally needed to step away to shout orders or supervise the packing and loading of various Gypsy carts.

"Of course ye can ride wi' us as far as the Cambridge Horse Fair," Raphael said when Connor was finished with the story. "Ride wi' us as long as pleases ye. Ye'll be safer wi' us; the *boro dom engroes*, the highwaymen, will no doubt be seeking two riders alone."

"My thanks, Raphael."

Just then, a Gypsy girl flounced past the two of them, leaving Connor with a general impression of bobbing roundness and a cloud of dark hair.

"And then what will ye do once we've come to the fair . . . ?" Raphael prompted.

"I'll ride to London. Try to arrange a meeting with the 'duchess' through Melbers, I suppose. Frighten her—with any luck, my sudden appearance ought to do the trick, since she's been trying to kill me—and threaten her with exposure and humiliation unless she leaves the continent immediately, that very moment, simply vanishes without a trace. I'll escort her to the docks, if necessary. And then I'll see that Melbers discreetly bestows several thousand pounds on the villagers near Keighley Park. After that, I'll disappear with Rebecca, forever, to America, and no one will be the wiser. With no heirs and no one else to claim it, the Dunbrooke title and fortune will revert to the crown. Good riddance to it, I say. Prinny can do with it what he will."

Raphael nodded once, thoughtfully, as though Connor had just recited his itinerary for a trip to the shore.

The Gypsy girl flounced past again, this time from the opposite direction.

"Ye've thought it through, have ye?" Raphael mused.

"Aye. I've thought it through."

"Does she know?"

"No. Rebecca knows nothing—about the duchess being my mistress, about my being the Dunbrooke heir, about any of it. And I never want her to know—God knows what she'd think of me then."

"But she'll wonder why the two of ye must go to London, aye?"

"That's just it: I cannot take her with me to London. The danger—to our lives, of discovery—is simply too great. I would rather die than expose Rebecca to that kind of risk again. And her family is no doubt in London at this very moment, and we might be seen, and . . . no, I cannot take her. I need to deal with this on my own, as the trouble is all of my own making. I rather hoped she could stay here with you while I am gone."

Raphael shrugged. "'Twould be our pleasure to look after 'er, Connor. But tell me this: what will ye tell 'er when ye go?"

Connor, all of a sudden, felt cornered.

"I . . . well . . . I thought perhaps I would not tell her I was going. She'll ask questions that I simply am not prepared to answer, and I don't want to lie to her if I can avoid it. I'll simply go, and return. No doubt she'll hardly miss me at all."

Raphael nodded thoughtfully, and a little skeptically.

"So, ye're quite certain ye've thought this through?"

Connor nodded again, somewhat warily.

"For, ye see, 'tis no easy thing to think clearly where a woman is concerned."

"Rebecca needn't ever learn anything about my former life, Raphael, if I do this properly," Connor insisted. "I want her to be my wife, but I find my conscience will not let me start a new life with her without first addressing my past."

The Gypsy girl flounced past again.

"Pesky things, consciences," Raphael said.

"And how would you know?"

"I've heard stories."

Connor laughed.

"*Martha.*" Raphael, irritated, interrupted her mid-flounce. "Have ye no work to do? Bring our guest some stew."

Martha twirled away in a graceful flourish of skirts.

"Perhaps you'd like America, too, Raphael."

"A wild country, ain't it? Filled with savages and the like?"

Martha returned with a steaming bowl and held it out to Connor, smiling beatifically, as though bestowing a blessing. Connor took the bowl with barely a glance at her and dipped the spoon in enthusiastically.

Martha's smile dimmed a little, but she remained planted in front of Connor.

"Wild country, yes, but alive with opportunity," Connor said to Raphael, between bites.

"Martha, why are you standing there staring at our guest like a looby?" Raphael made an exasperated shooing gesture. "Go help Leonora."

Martha's brows dove to form an angry "V" between her eyes. She glanced at Connor, who was entirely focused on his stew.

"*Go*," Raphael commanded, and Martha flounced away a final time, muttering something that may well have been a Gypsy curse under her breath. Raphael shook his head and muttered something of his own in Rom that made Connor raise his eyebrows.

Raphael returned to his conversation with Connor. "Aye, but I warrant there's little silver plate to be had in a country as <u>new and</u> wild as that. I dinna mind workin' for my bread, but no 'arder than I needs to, ye ken. I wasna bred to be a farmer." He grinned at Connor unapologetically.

"Aye, well, I'll miss knowing we're on the same continent when it comes to that, Raphael."

"As ye should, 'elpless sod that ye are."

Connor smiled at him. They were silent together for a moment.

"I was right," Raphael said softly. "'*Twas* a woman."

Connor's shoulders went back. "Shouldn't we be moving on soon?"

Raphael laughed and clapped him on the back.

"Oh, dinna take on so! Ye wouldna be the first, my friend. But I've news for ye: ye canna share a tent wi' 'er whilst ye stay wi' us, as ye're not yet wed. 'Tis the way of the Rom, and well ye know."

Connor went still. "Can't we just agree to lie about it?" he asked desperately.

"Aye, that may well 'ave been a good plan, but Rebecca, honest girl that she is, ruined it: she told Martha the pair of ye were engaged, not wed, and Martha told all the women in the camp. And I willna 'ave a scandal, no' even for you, my friend. 'Tis trial enough t' keep the young in line. Ye'll sleep in my tent, and Rebecca can stay wi' Leonora, and we'll . . ."

Raphael stopped talking when he noticed that Connor's attention was concentrated elsewhere. He followed Connor's gaze.

Rebecca was now standing, awake and blinking in the sunlight, at the entrance to Leonora's tent. She was back in her brown muslin dress and wearing a bonnet, which made Connor smile; perhaps Leonora had coaxed her into them in a nod to proprieties. He had become so accustomed to Rebecca bareheaded or covered in a boy's cap that the bonnet seemed faintly silly.

Raphael saw the expression on Connor's face, the wonder and possessiveness.

"Oh, *how* will ye survive?" he said in mock sympathy.

Connor snarled something profane in Rom, and strode away from him toward Rebecca.

"Did you have a good rest?"

It was strange, Rebecca thought, to stand so close to Connor and not touch him. That had been one of the luxuries of the past few days: touching him whenever she pleased, as he had touched her; so casually, so often, it almost seemed as if their hands never left each other. A lock of hair lifted from a cheek, a brush of fingers against an arm, a touch on the thigh, soft kisses freely and extravagantly bestowed, kisses that turned into . . . her face went warm at the thought.

But she took her cues from Connor, and Connor's hands were at his sides, his fingers restlessly drumming his thighs. And now he was asking her, as politely as if he were a stranger, if she'd slept well.

"Good enough, thank you," she replied tersely.

Connor lifted an eyebrow at her tone and lowered his voice. "What is it, wee Becca? Can you not sleep when I am not next to you? I would think it was the first decent rest you'd have had in a day or two." He leered charmingly.

She rolled her eyes, and he stifled a laugh.

"Connor, where are we going? What are we doing here? Did you know Leonora is a healer? Is she married to Raphael?"

"Which question shall I answer first?"

"Answer all of them, in that order, and quickly."

"Very well, then. Wee Becca, I have some final business to conduct before we can go to Scotland. We will be safer traveling with the Gypsies for a few days, much more so than if the two of us went on alone. And yes, I knew Leonora was a healer, which I thought would please you to no end. And no, Leonora and Raphael are not married. Leonora is a widow, and Raphael is a widower. They are cousins."

"Business?" Rebecca said slowly.

"Yes."

"Does this have to do with . . . with your past, Connor?"

"With my past, wee Becca," he said softly. "And with our future."

She fixed him with a penetrating stare. Connor met it valiantly.

"Business where? And how long?"

"Just a few days, wee Becca. We will travel with the Gypsies as far as Cambridgeshire. And then we will go to Scotland straight away to be married."

His eyes were full of promise and entreaty, begging her silently not to ask any more questions.

Rebecca looked away from him for a moment, gazing out across the camp, as though mulling his words.

At last she returned her gaze to him.

"All right," she said reluctantly.

Connor released the breath he'd been holding.

"There is one more thing, wee Becca. While we travel with the Gypsies, we must observe their . . . proprieties. Which are, I'm afraid, much like your own dear mama's proprieties."

"Which means . . ."

"You will ride with Leonora in her cart, and I will ride horseback with the men. And at night, you will stay with Leonora in her tent, and I will stay with Raphael."

Unease prickled the back of Rebecca's neck. Martha's

words echoed in her mind: *He looked at you as one would look at a sister.* It was ridiculous, really, she knew: no brother would look at his sister the way he was looking at her now . . . a look that she could almost feel on her skin, a look almost as hot as his hands. Still, every moment of her adventure had been spent with Connor so far. And though he would be but a few yards away from her at night, she already felt bereft.

"Why can't I ride horseback with you?"

"Are you asking why you canna ride astride alongside me and a pack of strange Gypsy men, wee Becca?" he asked mildly.

She took his point. Still . . .

Connor saw her stricken expression and made a sound, half laugh, half moan.

"*Believe* me, wee Becca, it will be the longest two days of my life."

She gave him a weak smile.

He wanted to touch her, kiss the weak smile from her lips, kiss her senseless. But Gypsy eyes flitted toward the two of them regularly, even as everyone seemed to be bustling about the camp packing the wagons. And he had promised Raphael there would be no scandal.

So Connor smiled, too, a smile she could normally have wrapped around herself like a soft blanket.

But it was clear from her expression that for Rebecca, at the moment, his smile wasn't nearly enough.

The little caravan consisted of five carts brimming with Gypsies and Gypsy belongings, flanked and followed by Gypsy men on horseback, Connor among them on his gray horse. The men shouted to each other in jesting tones, their teeth winking like chests of diamonds in their swarthy faces. The women laughed and called to each other, teasing, instructing, shushing the children, who wiggled and fought boredom by driving their mothers to distraction. Rebecca sat between Martha and Leonora, who had the reins to the wagon. She felt like an island amid an eddy of Gypsy conversation.

A cart was approaching the caravan from the opposite direction on the road. In it sat a man and a woman, farmers possibly, dressed in what was probably their finest clothing. Perhaps, Rebecca thought, they are on their way to visit relatives, or to dinner with the vicar. Rebecca prepared to nod as they passed, a reflex of her breeding, expecting a polite nod from the woman in response, perhaps a doffed cap from the man.

But the woman's eyes remained fixed on the road in front of her, as though the entire caravan of Gypsies was invisible, or as though she wished them so. The man met Rebecca's searching eyes, and a chill unfurled down her spine at the contempt she saw there. His cap remained on his head. He held Rebecca's eyes for a moment, then leaned slowly, pointedly, over the side of his cart and spat as he passed them.

Shaken, Rebecca looked at Leonora, who was gazing contemplatively at the road ahead of her.

"Do you mind it?" Rebecca blurted to her.

"Mind it, *Gadji*?" Leonora asked distantly.

"*Rebecca*," Rebecca corrected. "Do you mind how he looked at you?"

Leonora turned to Rebecca in mild surprise.

"They are . . . what is your word? Jealous," Leonora said. "The *Gorgio* do not understand our way of life. They cannot imagine living where they please, and moving when they please. They prefer the shackles of big houses and land. They do not understand us, and it frightens them, and fear makes them cold."

"Perhaps it is also that Gypsies *steal*," Rebecca said, somewhat defensively, conscious that the "they" to which Leonora referred included her. Immediately regretting her words, she swiftly turned to Leonora to gauge her reaction.

Leonora was grinning broadly.

"Ah, but stealing is wrong to your people, not to ours. If ye've so many things that you canna keep them from being stolen, then surely ye've too *many* things? And is it not right to share? It is merely another difference in . . ."

"Philosophy," Rebecca completed for her.

"Yes," Leonora said triumphantly, pleased with this odd little *Gadji*'s grasp of things Rom.

Rebecca was both appalled and strangely enchanted by this exotic point of view. She imagined repeating Leonora's words to the vicar. The thought made her smile and crane her head for a glimpse of Connor. He was riding behind the cart, and his head was thrown back in laughter, probably at something hopelessly male and profane that Raphael had said.

Hmmph. There he was, she thought, riding in the summer sun, having what looked to be the time of his life, while she was relegated to this jouncing cart and . . .

Well, if she was being *completely* honest about it, she wasn't exactly miserable. In fact, if it weren't for the presence of Leonora's owl-eyed daughter, she would be having the time of *her* life. Leonora had been genuinely enthralled by the story of Connor's musket-ball wound, and she had been full of praise for Rebecca's decision to bind the wound instead of stitching it closed, which could have led to infection. Rebecca was thoroughly enjoying basking in the unfamiliar rays of near motherly approval.

Their conversation then careened between wounds and effluvia and herbs for the rest of the morning. It was about as close to heaven on earth as Rebecca had ever come in her life—with the exception, of course, of the moments spent in Connor Riordan's arms.

None of it, however, seemed to be endearing Rebecca any further to Martha.

As Rebecca and Leonora chatted, Martha was busy with mending; shirts and skirts and trousers were heaped in a basket on the seat next to her in the cart. Despite the rattle and jounce of the cart, her needlework was exemplary— one tiny, even stitch after another. Her lips were pressed tightly together, however, and she drove the needle into the cloth with motions that bore more resemblance to stabbing than sewing.

"You do that very well," Rebecca told Martha, feeling magnanimous in the glow of Leonora's praise.

"Aye," Martha said matter-of-factly. "I sing very well, too. And I can *dukker* best of all."

Clearly modesty was not among the proprieties Gypsy mamas taught their daughters.

"But can you play the pianoforte?" Rebecca found herself blurting. As far as Martha knew, Rebecca could play like Bach himself, and she was suddenly prepared to lie, lie, lie if it would help in any way to stem the flow of Martha's insane self-assurance.

But Martha stopped stitching for a moment and gave her a gently incredulous, pitying look.

"Why would I want to play the pianoforte?"

An excellent question, Rebecca saw now, especially since Gypsies didn't typically have drawing rooms in which to entertain guests with pianoforte tunes. She could feel her face growing warm.

"What does *dukker* mean?" she asked, instead of answering the pianoforte question.

"Yer palm," Martha said. "I can read yer future in yer palm. I will *dukker* for ye later." She said it in a conciliatory manner, as though offering a treat to a feebleminded child.

Rebecca surreptitiously turned her hand over and gazed down at it. Perhaps the lines that hatched across it *were* a sort of Gypsy hieroglyphics. Imagine if everyone was born with a map to their entire life in their hand . . . *Does it say*, Rebecca wondered, *that I will one day be trapped in a Gypsy wagon with an insufferable Gypsy girl*?

"Martha does sing very well," Leonora said, perhaps feeling guilty for showering praise on another young woman within earshot of her daughter. "Perhaps ye'll hear her one day."

"That would be lovely," Rebecca lied. "What kinds of songs do you like to sing?" she asked Martha, hoping, probably in vain, to impose a sort of drawing-room pleasantry on the conversation.

Connor rode up next to the cart just then, his cheeks ruddy with sun and good spirits.

"Songs of love," Martha said, throwing her shoulders back to display her round bosom at its best advantage. "I sing songs of love *very* well."

Connor looked at Martha, startled, and frowned faintly, perplexed. He opened his mouth as if to say something to her, then closed it and nodded politely to her and to Leonora before turning his attention toward Rebecca.

"How are you finding your trip, wee Becca?"

How was she finding her trip? Pity she couldn't think of a word that meant both "wonderful" and "horrible."

"Oh, it's . . . it's lovely," she said lamely. "Not a single highwayman in sight. When will we stop?"

"When we arrive." But then something in her face must have told him that she was *not* in the mood for glib answers, because he gently amended his answer. "We will stop in a few hours more, wee Becca. Just before sundown. Raphael knows of a place to camp. Near a town."

"You need to rest, Connor," she said awkwardly, when what she wanted to say was *I love you.*

"Aye," he agreed softly, "I do. Thank you for looking after me." And when he smiled down at her, his expression said *I love you, too.* For a moment, Leonora and Martha and all the Gypsies dropped away, and they were aware only of each other.

Martha cleared her throat.

"I will *dukker* for you tonight, Rebecca." She stabbed her needle one last time into the trousers.

The town was barely a town at all, a few little houses and storefronts. The caravan rode down the center of it just as the sun was sinking in the sky. Rebecca watched as Raphael rode toward a meadow at the outskirts of the town and motioned to the rest of the caravan with his hand; this was where they would be stopping for the evening.

Swiftly, tents were erected, a fire built, pots and pans extracted from the baggage in preparation for supper. To Rebecca's tired eyes, it was like watching a tightly choreographed dance; each Gypsy seemed to know their role and performed it deftly.

She stepped down from the cart, ecstatic to be on solid ground again. Strangely, riding in a cart for hours was far more grueling than riding a horse, she thought; one almost becomes an extension of a horse, one could adjust to the rhythm of the animal's body. But with a cart . . . well, one merely suffered a cart. Her body was stiff in ways she never felt from riding on horseback.

Across the camp, Connor was sliding from his horse. Whatever envy she may have felt about his day on horseback vanished when he paused and touched his forehead against the saddle briefly, as though waiting for a dizzy spell to pass.

She was next to him in an instant.

He turned to her when she placed a hand to his arm. Even in the rapidly purpling evening light, she could see his face had gone ashen.

"Connor—"

"I'm merely tired, wee Becca."

"You are still somewhat weak. You should—"

"I am NOT weak."

And though Rebecca knew the edge in his voice had been honed by exhaustion and injury and frustration over the events of the past few days, she still flinched.

Connor was instantly the picture of contrition. He drew in a deep breath, and began again.

"Wee Becca, forgive me. I am more weary than weak; please believe me. I merely need to sleep. I am sorry to worry you."

"Will you see Leonora about your arm?"

He sighed. "Oh, aye, if it will make you feel better."

"It will make me feel better," she said firmly.

He smiled crookedly. "Then take me to her, wee Becca, by all means, so we can get it over with and I can spend the rest of the evening sleeping."

Leonora unwound Connor's bandage with a sense of solemn ceremony, as though she were unveiling a public statue.

In a nod to modesty, Connor's shirt, now woefully bloodstained and haphazardly mended, remained draped over his uninjured arm and shoulder. Martha, unsurprisingly, had watched the unbuttoning of his shirt raptly, and was now tracking the progress of the unwinding bandage with the same held-breath fascination. Rebecca had to admit there *was* a certain prurience to the proceedings; even she had felt a certain heightened anticipation as Connor's bare skin came into view, and she already knew exactly what that skin looked—and smelled and tasted—like. But the slow revelation of Connor's gorgeous contours was also like watching someone else unwrap a gift that rightfully belonged to her. A gift certainly not meant for Martha's eyes.

Why was the bloody girl allowed to remain in the tent at all? It seemed unlikely that Rom proprieties were lenient enough to allow unmarried girls to ogle half-dressed male strangers. Perhaps Martha had spent many an hour watching the dressing and undressing of men, young and old alike, while her mother poked and prodded and healed them. Rebecca wondered whether Martha's fascination with Connor had to do with a curiosity about men that remained unfulfilled . . . or one that was all *too* fulfilled.

Leonora grunted appreciatively when the wound was at

last exposed, and motioned for Martha to hold the lamp higher so she could look at it more closely. Martha moved in nearer to Connor, her bosom perhaps a hairsbreadth away from his shoulder, and lifted the lamp. If Connor so much as exhaled, his arm was certain to brush against at least one large round breast.

Rebecca sent Martha a look that could have mowed down Napoleon's front line. Martha ignored her. Connor, happily, seemed oblivious of any bosoms at the moment.

Leonora gently touched the edges of the wound, and Rebecca leaned in for a look. It was still oozing a little, but the edges were pink, not red or angry or swollen, and no streaks radiated from it, which meant no poisoning of the blood. Leonora peered into Connor's eyes, examined his fingernails, felt his pulse, all of which Connor submitted to with a certain stoic amusement.

Rebecca watched Leonora, her heart hammering in anticipation of a verdict.

At last, Leonora turned to her, smiling.

"Well done, Rebecca. We will clean it gently once more, apply a salve of—"

"Saint-John's-wort," Rebecca and Martha said simultaneously, Rebecca sounding eager, Martha sounding bored.

"—yes, Saint-John's-wort, and then we will rebind the wound. Ye're lucky to have such a talented healer for a fiancée," Leonora clucked to Connor.

"I know," Connor said proudly.

But Rebecca hadn't heard him at all.

Healer. Leonora had called her a *healer!* Elation nearly sent her out of her shoes. She felt as if she had just been knighted.

Connor was watching her face, a soft smile playing at his lips.

"Aye," he repeated warmly, "she is very talented."

This time she heard, and she turned to beam at him.

From behind Connor's head, Martha lowered the lamp and scowled.

Leonora swabbed the edges of Connor's wound, applied the salve of Saint-John's-wort, and wound a length of clean bandage around his arm.

"Now, try to use yer other arm, not your injured one, for a few days. And if you feel feverish, come to me."

"He needs to rest," Rebecca said proprietarily.

"He needs to rest," Leonora confirmed, smiling at her.

"And as I need to rest," Connor said, smiling, rebuttoning his shirt, "I will thank you ladies for your attentions, and bid you good night."

He made bows all around. As he backed from the tent, he caught and held Rebecca's eyes in a tenderly smoldering gaze, and then he was gone. It took all of her self-control not to run after him.

"Now, *Gadji*," Leonora said briskly, "I have work to do to prepare my medicines, and I wonder if you would like to help. Supper will be brought to us when it is ready."

Rebecca could scarcely believe her good fortune.

"Oh," she breathed. "Yes, please."

Martha gave a nearly inaudible snort.

Leonora fished about in the trunks and extracted several of the dark bottles Rebecca had seen earlier, which were nestled in a bed of straw to prevent breakage. A little more rooting about in the trunk yielded a mortar and pestle, some folded muslin, several little cloth bags pulled shut with string, and startlingly, a bottle of whiskey.

"Martha, if you would bring the lantern here," Leonora said. Martha did as bid, albeit sluggishly. A soft corona of light pulsed about the trunk.

"So we can see our work," Leonora murmured. She fussed with her things a moment more, lining up the bottles, opening the bags to sniff the contents. Rebecca waited impatiently.

"Now, these herbs have been in their bath of whiskey for one course of the moon—"

"Why whiskey?" Rebecca said.

Martha sighed loudly. Leonora shot her a quelling look.

"The healing power of the herbs is drawn into the whiskey, and then we can use it for medicine for a very long time. These are strong medicines, for strong ailments, when a tea will not do."

"Tinctures," Rebecca and Martha said at the same time, Rebecca eagerly, Martha sounding exasperated that anyone could be so ignorant about healing.

"Tinctures," Leonora repeated, agreeing. "They have been in their bath of whiskey, and they are now ready to become medicines. We must pour them through the muslin to catch the herbs. What is left behind in the pitcher is the medicine, like so."

Leonora settled a square of muslin over the mouth of the pitcher and poked it in the center to tuck it in, then tipped one of the dark bottles over it. A dark broth dotted with shreds of herb gurgled out slowly over the muslin, sending a greenish stain spreading across it. The little shreds of herb were caught as the liquid passed through.

When she had emptied the bottle, Leonora gave the muslin square a hard twist to extract as much liquid as possible. Then she placed the stained muslin aside and poured the contents of the pitcher back into the dark bottle.

"Shepherd's purse," she announced with satisfaction as she stoppered the bottle. It was already labeled; clearly, it was a bottle she had used for shepherd's purse time and again.

"Now, Rebecca, if you would wipe the pitcher with this muslin, then strain each of these bottles as I have done. Use a different piece of muslin for each herb, for it is not good to mix them."

Martha knelt down next to her mother with her own packets of herbs, settling into the work as if it were something that took place every evening.

For several minutes, Rebecca and Leonora and Martha worked side by side in absorbed silence, Leonora shaking herbs from the bags and examining them carefully, measuring them in her palm, sorting them into little piles. Rebecca felt quietly powerful as she pressed the herbs through the muslin and poured the fresh tinctures back into their bottles. Aside from extracting a musket ball from Connor, everything else she knew of healing was theory, information derived from her father's journal and books. But *this* . . . an ailing person would someday taste the medicine she was helping to create, and then they would become, with God's help, healthy again. It was magic, nothing short. It was a vast, humbling responsibility. Still, all things considered, she felt equal to it; it felt right, more profoundly right than the keys of a pianoforte had ever felt beneath her fingers. She was hungry to learn.

But there was a precariousness to it, too; she half expected Leonora to announce that it had all been a terrible mistake, tear the muslin from her hands and force her instead to practice the pianoforte. She was afraid to move too abruptly, or breathe too emphatically, lest the moment dissolve like a dream.

By stark contrast, there was Martha, whose utter indifference to the art of healing was apparent in her every motion, in the slump of her shoulders, in the the stiff, almost angry movement of her fingers as she poked about in the piles of herbs, in the grim set of her plump mouth. In Martha, Rebecca saw herself, hunched glumly over a pianoforte, poking at it apathetically, and she felt an errant twinge of sympathy again. Opportunities to rebel must be few and far between for Martha; her mother was ever-present, and perhaps the Gypsy family group felt suffocatingly insular. Perhaps Martha was simply waiting for someone, anyone, to take her away. And perhaps Connor looked like that someone.

Rebecca stole a sideways glance at Martha, whose skin was glowing a soft gold in the lamplight. Martha was beautiful in an extravagant, very singular way, utterly convinced of her own superiority, and no doubt accustomed to turning any man's head. She probably found Connor's inattention maddening and inexplicable.

Funny how short-lived her twinges of sympathy toward Martha tended to be.

Rebecca forced her own concentration back to the herbs.

"What are you making, Leonora?" she asked, breaking the silence, after she had stoppered her third bottle.

"Tonight I make a special medicine of many herbs. For dropsy," she said, gesturing to a little mound of herbs she had collected. "Tansy leaves, dandelion root, parsley, and—"

The face of an older woman appeared in the opening of the tent, and rattled a few words in anxious-sounding Rom to Leonora, who nodded and gave her a short answer that sounded like an affirmation.

"I will return in an hour or so," Leonora told Rebecca and Martha. She tucked the bottle of shepherd's purse into her apron pocket and ducked out of the tent before Rebecca could say, "Please do not leave me alone with your horrible daughter."

It was quiet in the tent for a moment except for the rustle of dried herbs and the gurgle of tinctures as Rebecca and Martha continued their chores.

She's like a snake, Rebecca thought, tensing. *She'll wait, and then she'll strike. Any minute now . . .*

"Rebecca, shall I *dukker* for ye?"

Aha! There it was, the strike. Still, Rebecca *was* curious to know what her palms had to say about her life. *Good heavens,* she told herself firmly, *if you can handle highwaymen, you can certainly handle Martha Heron.*

"Of course, Martha. I would like that. How do we go about it?"

Martha scooted toward Rebecca on her knees.

"Give me your hands," she said.

Rebecca presented her hands, palms up. Martha grasped them in her own unusually soft hands and smoothed her thumbs over them, spreading them flat. She peered into each one intently for a while, occasionally tracing a line with her forefinger, or tilting one closer to the lamplight.

"First I will ask of you, Rebecca: do ye want me to be honest?"

"What would you be otherwise?"

"The *Gorgio* who pay to hear their futures read in their

palms only want to hear one kind of fortune. But I think you are brave enough to hear the whole truth."

"By all means, tell me the whole truth."

Martha spent a few more moments examining her hands, as if deciding where to begin.

"This line, this long line that curves so, here? It means you will have a long life," Martha mused. "And right here, the fork in this line? It means you will go on a journey, far from your home . . ."

"Ah," Rebecca said politely, unimpressed. It would be abundantly clear to anyone who looked at her that she was on a long journey, far from home.

"It looks as though you have two lovers, one dark and one fair . . ."

"Mmm." This was a little more plausible, given the existence of Edelston.

Martha drew her finger across the line that bisected Rebecca's right palm, as if following a map.

". . . but the dark lover is faithless. He will leave you for another and your life will take yet another turn, one of hardship and confusion."

"And it says that *where*, precisely?" Rebecca didn't bother to keep the skepticism from her voice.

"Oh, here and here." Martha gestured over her hand vaguely. "As I said, the dark lover is faithless, but you will have a happy home with your fair-haired lover when you are . . . when you are . . ." Martha peered closely at Rebecca's left hand. "Oh, many years older. You and your fair-haired lover will be blessed with child after child after child—"

Rebecca snatched her hands away.

"Thank you, Martha," she said slowly, through gritted

teeth. "But I suspect that *dukkering* actually means 'non-sense' in English."

Martha stared at her wonderingly. Then a look of pitying comprehension crossed her face.

"I only tell you this, the truth, because I am concerned for you, Rebecca."

"Concerned," Rebecca repeated flatly.

"Yes. Concerned. You say you are engaged to this *Gadje* Connor Riordan?"

"I *am* engaged to Connor Riordan." It was becoming increasingly difficult not to give Martha a good hard shake.

"But I am confused," Martha continued, her brow wrinkling. "If Connor Riordan meant to marry you, Rebecca, ye'd travel to Gretna Green, would ye not? But Gretna Green is *that* way," she said, gesturing dramatically. "We are going in another direction altogether."

Rebecca was speechless. It was her own most subliminal fear given voice.

And Martha knew it, Rebecca could tell. Martha's features remained composed in a reasonable imitation of sympathy, but she was having difficulty keeping a gleam of triumph out of her eyes.

She gently took one of Rebecca's hands in her own and covered it with her other hand. It was all Rebecca could do not to jerk away from her.

"I hope, Rebecca," she said passionately, "I do hope that you have not . . . *given* yourself to him. For in giving yourself to him you take away his reason to marry you."

Rebecca stared at her, stunned. Slowly, with admirable restraint, she withdrew her hand from between Martha's.

"Thank you for your *concern*, Martha." Her voice was

cool, and only shook a little. "But I assure you that it is unfounded."

Martha shrugged and returned her attention to the herbs.

"Every unwed man in our *compania* would like to be my fiancé," she said casually, poking about in a small pile of chamomile.

"Not exactly spoiled for choice, though, are they?"

Rebecca surprised herself by actually saying the words out loud.

Martha only laughed delightedly. Rebecca realized too late she'd just confirmed for Martha how truly the *dukkering* had hit its mark.

Chapter Eighteen

~∽~

She'd had worse days. For instance, the day she'd caught her hair in the latch of her bedroom window, after Robbie Denslowe had convinced her she could climb out of it down the ivy trellis. She'd been nine years old. She'd spent half the morning twisted at an awkward angle, half in, half out of the window, before her mother found her. They could only free her by snipping off half of her hair. Needless to say, her father had ensured that sitting down had been uncomfortable for days thereafter.

But she'd never had a day that approximated actual purgatory quite as closely as this one had.

For hours and hours, down roads leading God knows where, Rebecca's bones had been shaken atop the Gypsy cart. And though Leonora had taken it upon herself to give Rebecca an ongoing verbal instruction in herbcraft—where to find them, when to pick them, how to grow them, how to harvest them, what they were for—her daughter Martha remained silently bent over her pile of mending. Rebecca had rarely felt a presence as profoundly. She'd glanced at the girl nervously several times throughout, and then forced herself to stop, because she couldn't bear seeing her knowing, pitying, enigmatic half smile one more time. Odious girl.

And she hadn't been able to speak with Connor alone. The morning had been a bustle of packing and leaving, and they'd only been able to exchange looks from across the camp, and absurdly polite greetings when he rode up next to her cart. She was happy to see that he looked well rested. But he also seemed distracted again; he was wearing the inwardly turned expression that was becoming all too familiar. It did nothing to loosen the anxious knot in the pit of her stomach.

When at last Raphael rode ahead of the caravan to the crest of a hill and signaled the group to follow him, she was unbelievably relieved. It meant they would be stopping for the evening. Perhaps she would be able to speak to Connor, share her worries with him, and —

What on *earth* was that noise?

Puzzled, Rebecca scanned the horizon behind and in front of her; the early evening sky was flawlessly clear, which more or less ruled out thunder. But the dull rumbling noise had persisted for several minutes, and now seemed to be increasing in volume. It was more consistent than thunder, too, in that there was no pulse to it. It simply went on and on.

Leonora noticed Rebecca swiveling her head about and frowning, and supplied an answer to her unspoken question.

"Wagons," she said. "And horses."

Rebecca furrowed her brow more deeply. "What—"

And then they crested the rise they had been approaching.

Wagons, indeed.

There were dozens of them, swarms of them. The rumble, Rebecca now understood, was the sound of hundreds of wheels turning over the ground and hundreds of hooves churning the earth, mingled with human voices.

Thus Rebecca heard the Cambridge Horse Fair before she actually saw it.

Soon their own cart was swept into the tide of wagons and horses, and they were immersed in a cacophony of impressions: shouted greetings and laughter and arguments in Rom and coarse English, barking dogs, the jingling of tack, the stamp of boots. Colorful tents and booths pitched in orderly rows, stages for pantomimes and Punch and Judy shows, even for Wombwell's menagerie of exotic animals, red and blue and yellow triangular flags strung between them, flapping gaily in the breeze.

She swiveled her head for a glimpse of Connor, bursting with questions and the need to share, but he was nowhere in sight. Martha saw her looking for him and smiled knowingly. Rebecca jerked her chin upward and ignored her.

"We shall be busy, Rebecca," Leonora said to her, her voice raised over the din. "Every sick Gypsy from miles around will come to see us. I hope you will help."

And despite her worries, Rebecca's heart leaped. *Us*, Leonora had said. They will come to see *us*. Not only was Wombwell rumored to travel with an actual *lion*, which she very much hoped to see, but every sick Gypsy from miles around would come to see them. Rebecca was morbidly delighted at the prospect.

The fire crackling at her feet was making Rebecca feel a little sleepy. Leonora sat closely, her thigh touching

Rebecca's, chatting to a woman seated to her left. Around her, the firelight picked out the white of eyes and teeth as the Gypsies chattered and laughed in Rom, reviewing their plans for the next day. The squeals and giggles of children occasionally pierced through the adult conversations, but most of the children had either nodded off in the arms of their mothers or had been coerced into going to bed. Beyond their campfire, dozens of other campfires blazed, lighting other Gypsy families. The commerce and festivity that was the Cambridge Horse Fair would begin in earnest tomorrow.

She glanced across the fire and caught the eye of Rose Heron. She was feeling particularly proprietary about Rose at the moment, because Rose had cut her hand with a knife while preparing dinner, and Leonora had allowed Rebecca to sew it up.

It had been an odd sensation, but strangely not unlike stitching flowers into a sampler. For one wild moment she had imagined spelling "Bless Our Home" on to the back of Rose's hand in black thread; she wondered what her mother would think of her happily volunteering to stitch anything at all. While Leonora hovered alertly and gripped Rose's other hand in her own, Rebecca, hardly breathing, her universe narrowed to a cut, drew five neat horizontal stitches through the very top layer of Rose's skin, pulling each at just the right tension so as not to pucker the wound or tear it farther. She finished with a tight little knot, and the wound was closed.

Rebecca had looked up to find Leonora beaming at her. "A steady hand, to be sure, Rebecca, and a swift one."

Even Martha, she of the stabbing mending needle and

flawless stitches, had lifted her eyebrows in what seemed perilously close to approval.

So it is not that I have no talent for needlework, Rebecca thought smugly; *it is just that I have no talent for* useless *needlework.*

And then she turned her head from Rose because somehow she knew the moment Connor appeared at the edge of the fire. It was her first glimpse of him since they'd arrived in camp, and to her eyes his shoulders looked rounded from exhaustion. He took a place next to Raphael and pushed his hair wearily out of his eyes, scanning the circle. *For me.* He's *mine*, she thought fiercely, with an ache of love and possession. And something in her, ever since she was a little girl, had always known it.

He saw her and straightened, took a step toward her. But Raphael put a hand on his arm, gesturing toward the far end of the circle, and Connor paused.

A long, slow, rich note, a testing note, welled up out of a fiddle, echoing in the clear night air. One of the Gypsy men had risen to his feet, and a fiddle was tucked under his chin. Next to him stood Martha, her hair and skin burnished in the firelight, her hands folded in front of her. She closed her eyes briefly, as though gathering her thoughts.

And then the song began.

From the very first, it was a wild shameless thing, plaintive and almost cruelly penetrating. It was wholly unlike anything Rebecca had heard in her life, certainly nothing like the pieces played in English country parlors by dutiful young daughters. Her breath caught; she felt each note as though the bow was being drawn across her own heart.

And then suddenly Martha's voice, as pure and powerful as a river, was soaring above the notes, passionate, teasing, pleading. In no time at all, the men in the Gypsy circle were staring at Martha, glassy-eyed, slack-mouthed, and rapt. *Martha must be in heaven.*

But Martha's amber eyes were fixed on a single point across the fire.

The bloody girl was singing to Connor.

Rebecca couldn't bear it any more. Leave she must, or she would throw something at her. Unobtrusively, gingerly, as though taking care not to jar an inner injury, she stood up and carried herself away from the fire to the edge of the encampment.

She paused between two tents and covered her face in her hands, breathing unsteadily.

*You will not cry you will not cry you will **not***, she told herself furiously.

She longed to tell Connor everything Martha had seen in her palm, just so she could hear him refute each and every one of her predictions. But what if he didn't refute them? What if he stumbled over his words, or laughed, or . . . ?

The crunch of footsteps behind her barely registered on her hearing.

"Wee Becca?"

She was muttering to herself.

"I swear I will *kill* that girl if I have to spend another minute of—"

Connor put his hand on her arm, and Rebecca jumped.

"Wee Becca, why are you standing here alone muttering about murder?"

"*Martha*," she spat.

"Ah. And who is Martha?"

She turned to him incredulously.

"Connor! *Martha*. Leonora's daughter. Surely you've noticed her. She has most certainly noticed *you*."

"Now which one is she? And please do not say 'dark hair, dark eyes . . .'"

"She has dark hair, and *light* eyes, and very large . . . very large . . ." she trailed off.

"Eyes? Ears?" he suggested, teasing.

"Breasts," she said flatly. "She has very large breasts."

Well. He should have known that Rebecca would never choose demureness over accuracy.

"Oh. *That* Martha. At the moment, she is singing."

"Singing to *you*, Connor."

"Was she now? Was she singing to me? Perhaps it was rude of me then to wander off."

"Connor, if you tease me, I will murder you, too."

He sighed. "Wee Becca, you best start at the beginning."

"She *dukkered* for me, Connor."

"Free of charge? That seems very unlike a Gypsy."

"Oh," she said bitterly. "It was quite voluntary."

"And what did she see? A tall dark stranger? A journey over water?"

"I am afraid she was a good deal more specific than that."

"Well?"

"You see, Connor, it's just that . . . it's just that . . ." She angled her face away from him, took a deep breath, as though gathering her courage.

"What is it, wee Becca?"

Rebecca sighed. "She said I had two lovers, one dark and one fair."

"Hmm. Well, I suppose if you factor Edelston into the equation—"

"But the dark one is faithless," she continued in a rush. "And will leave me for another."

Silence.

"There is more, Connor."

"I am all ears." His voice was odd. Cold.

"She said . . . I would have much hardship for a time, but that I will eventually find happiness with my fair lover, and we would have child after child after child . . ."

Silence again.

"Fascinating," he drawled the word. "Your palm says all of that?"

"She said more, Connor. And this was not in my palm. She said . . ." Rebecca paused. He could hear her breathing unsteadily.

"Wee Becca?"

She turned away from him, said the words to the ground.

"She said that if you truly meant to marry me, we would have gone to Gretna Green, instead of to the Cambridge Horse Fair."

Silence. Fragments of another song, of Martha's muscular voice, floated toward them from the campfire.

Connor cleared his throat awkwardly.

"Wee Becca, she is merely jealous of you because I am so very handsome."

She said nothing.

"I can hear your eyes rolling from here, wee Becca."

She laughed at that, a brief muffled laugh. But she still would not meet his eyes.

"Rebecca? You cannot possibly think . . ." he said. He

stopped himself and gave a short choked laugh, a sound of disbelief. "Rebecca. Look at me."

She slowly lifted her head up to his. Tears glittered in her eyelashes.

It pierced him clean through.

"Rebecca," he said helplessly, but the words, the right words clogged his throat. He swallowed hard.

She waited.

"Rebecca . . . surely you know you are my heart?" And there was genuine pain and bewilderment in his voice.

She swept a hand across her eyes, knocking the clinging tears from her lashes; she was impatient with herself for crying, he knew. The gesture seemed to capture her precisely, the tender brave spirit she was.

And though he knew he would regret it, because it would be torture to let her go again, he pulled her into his arms and pressed his lips against her temple. He closed his eyes, savoring the feel of her, held her tightly, rested his cheek against her hair.

"Oh, wee Becca, my love, my brave girl," he murmured. "Please do not cry. I am so sorry. I sometimes forget . . . I sometimes take for granted your courage, because it is so much a part of who you are. And here you are far from home, among strangers, in circumstances that would daunt many a full grown man, let alone a young woman, and you've only me to trust. And this hateful Gypsy girl—"

"She *is* hateful," Rebecca agreed, sniffling, her voice muffled against his shoulder.

"—fills your head with false and ugly things."

"Do you think I am foolish, Connor?"

"Foolish? Because a jealous, bored girl played upon your fears?"

"You *do* understand."

"Aye, I am like that. Very understanding."

She laughed a little, her face still buried in his shirt.

"I know it is difficult, wee Becca, but I thank you for your trust. It means everything to me." He said it softly, his hands stroking her back, moving gently in her hair.

"I just want us to be together, Connor."

"We will be. Forever. Soon. One more day, wee Becca, is all I ask."

There was a silence. His hands rose and fell on her back as her breathing became more steady.

"All right," she agreed at last, with a sigh. "Connor, did you know that I sewed Rose Heron up this evening?"

"Rose Heron wanted sewing up?"

"She cut her hand on a knife, and Leonora allowed me to sew it up. It was very peculiar, but very satisfying, too."

"Did you sew your initials into her to honor the occasion?"

Rebecca giggled and lifted her face up to him.

"Speaking of breasts, wee Becca . . ."

"Were we?"

"I have not seen yours for one entire *day*."

She laughed again. Oh, he loved to make her laugh.

"But what of the proprieties?" She whispered it mockingly, then rubbed her lips lightly against the base of his neck. He tensed, shivering.

"Hang the proprieties." And even though he had promised Raphael, and even though he knew he was sunk if he kissed her, he was already lowering his head.

His mouth fell on hers like scorching velvet, supple, intent, and almost painfully demanding; the force of it, of his suppressed longing, bent Rebecca backward. She took fistfuls of his shirt in her hands for balance and opened herself to it, and he lost himself in the sweet heat and taste and scent of her. It astounded him, how new his hunger for her felt every time they touched, how limitless it seemed.

I could drag her into that stand of trees and take her up against one of them, Connor thought with the logic of the love-drugged. *In no time at all.*

But he couldn't make love to her when he planned to leave her tomorrow.

The thought shocked Connor to his senses. He pulled away from Rebecca and held her firmly at arm's length. Which Rebecca found helpful, because her legs had been rendered nearly useless by the kiss.

"Whatever you do, wee Becca, keep your trust in me," Connor said, breathing hard. "We both have need of it."

"All right," Rebecca said after a moment; still a little kiss-befuddled, she probably would have agreed to just about anything.

Voices were moving toward them; the music had ended, and the Gypsies were heading toward their tents.

"Good night, wee Becca. Remember that I do love you."

And then he was walking swiftly away from her toward his own tent, leaving her weak-kneed and dazed and wondering.

"What a lot of pistols."

The groggy voice came from the direction of Raphael's bedroll. He had propped himself up on his elbow to watch Connor in the predawn darkness.

"Yes, but no powder or shot for any of them," Connor said glumly. By the light of a single candle, he was sorting through the numerous firearms he'd managed to collect from the highwaymen. All fired and spent, unfortunately.

Raphael clucked sympathetically.

"I can lend ye a knife. Or perhaps a whip. I've no powder or shot, I am sorry to say."

"A whip?" Connor's head snapped up. "What on earth could I do with a whip?"

"Ye can take a man's legs right ou' from under 'im wi' a whip," Raphael said with some relish. "If ye wield it proper. Or take a gun out of 'is 'and."

"*Now* you tell me," Connor said.

Raphael smiled and lay back down with his hands behind his head.

"My apologies, Raphael. I never meant to wake you. Not until just before I left, anyhow."

"Ye're sure ye want to keep to this plan?"

"You know I must."

There was a beat of silence.

"Aye," Raphael said with resignation. "I know you must."

"I *will* return," Connor said, after a moment's silence. "Perhaps as soon as late this evening. I have to at least try to resolve all of this, Raphael."

"I wasna arguin'," Raphael said mildly.

And then Raphael was quiet for so long Connor thought he must have gone back to sleep.

"She doesna know ye're leaving this morning, does she?"

Apparently Raphael was still awake.

"She knows I have business to take care of before we can head on to Scotland, and that's all," Connor said grimly.

"Ye're sure now, about not tellin' 'er?"

Connor sighed.

"All right: no, I am not sure. But I *am* sure that it's easier this way, however—no questions to answer, no pleas to tear at my resolve. I will go, and return, in the span of a day."

"If all goes according to plan" were the words they both left unspoken.

"Ye ken we'll be at the fair only for two days?"

"I will return," Connor reiterated, emphatically.

Raphael nodded.

"Will you make sure she sees Wombwell's lion?" Connor said.

"I'll see to it."

"And if anything happens . . ."

"We'll take care of 'er," Raphael said gently.

"Thank you for everything, Raphael."

"Ye kept me from the noose years ago, Connor. 'Tis a small price to pay for my life," Raphael said easily.

"Yes, I suppose it is," Connor answered, and Raphael laughed.

Connor did not appear for the morning meal.

Raphael was there, and the other men, too; Rebecca had begun to recognize faces, so she could tell. But the food (the ever-present, mysteriously delicious stew; she was, in fact, growing very tired of it) had been cooked and served and the fire tamped out, and there was still no sign of Connor.

Was he ill? Perhaps his wound . . . ? Rebecca's heart lurched at the thought. But no; Raphael woud have sent for Leonora if Connor was unable to leave his tent.

The strange, almost angry kiss last night. There had been a thoroughness, a finality to it.

Almost like a farewell.

Remember that I do love you, he had said. Why "Remember"? Why not simply "I love you"?

In a mounting panic, Rebecca scanned the horses tethered about the campground. An enormous surge of relief swept through her when she saw both the brown mare and Connor's gray gelding patiently cropping grass.

"He took Raphael's black horse," Martha said, from behind her. "He left before dawn."

The words landed like hot cinders on the back of Rebecca's neck. Of course. The highwaymen would be looking for two riders, one on a gray horse, one on a brown horse. She turned slowly to face Martha.

Martha was shaking her head knowingly. "Dinna worry, Rebecca," she said. "I am sure your *fair*-haired lover will never leave you."

She flounced cheerfully away.

Rebecca stood still for a moment, then saw Raphael, and started toward him. She could hardly feel her legs as she moved; it was as if the bottom had dropped out of her world, and her legs were paddling away in nothingness.

Raphael saw her white face and answered her question before she could ask it.

"He had business, Miss Rebecca," he said gently. "He will return."

Rebecca drew herself up proudly.

"I knew that, of course," she said.

"I can tell ye no more."

"What more is there to tell?" Rebecca said, feigning blitheness.

She still could not feel her limbs. Connor had left without telling her. *Business*, he had said. *I have need of your trust*, he had said. But never once, even as she told him her worries, of Martha's *dukkering*, had he told her he would be leaving. Just silences, and protestations of love.

Her pride prevented her from pelting Raphael with questions. How long will he be gone? Where did he go? Why?

I have need of your trust.

It was beginning to feel like too much to ask of her.

She felt a soft touch on her arm, and turned to find Leonora's gently concerned face.

"Come, Rebecca. I would have yer help today wi' the sick, if ye please."

The day would go more quickly if she was to keep busy.

"Of course, Leonora. I'd be delighted."

Chapter Nineteen

⁓

After seven hours of hard riding from Cambridgeshire, Connor was not, unfortunately, what anyone would consider inconspicuous. He frankly assessed his reflection in the window of Bingham & Sons, a bookshop. No hat, which on Bond Street equated almost to nudity. A very fine coat over a tattered and bloodstained shirt. Good boots, certainly passable gentleman's boots, if a bit smudged; dusty trousers, the fawn going dingy. He brushed at them surreptitiously. Eyes a bit shot with blood, hair mussed. He patted and smoothed his hair; his hair, however, had never been very cooperative. His burgeoning beard could not be helped, and around him faces were scrupulously bare. Perhaps if he kept his collar turned up and his face lowered into his cravat . . .

Ah, well. It simply could not be helped.

Melbers & Green, the sign said. Who on earth was Green? Had Melbers taken on a partner? Connor took a deep breath and turned the knob.

A pale bespectacled chap looked up from a sturdy desk, startled. A few strands of fine graying hair were standing alertly up, as though they, too, were suspicious of the visitor. He'd probably just run his hand through his hair absently as he pored over his work, Connor thought. Melbers had the same habit.

"Good afternoon," the man said pleasantly enough. "Do you have an appointment, er . . . sir?"

Connor smiled faintly at the hesitation before the word "sir." Clearly his appearance made his status difficult to categorize.

And then he noticed the portraits, and almost choked.

There were three of them. A veritable haughty continuum of imposing jaws, beetling brows, and luxuriously waving hair, lined up on the wall behind Mr. Green.

Three Dukes of Dunbrooke.

His grandfather on the left. Richard, sulky-mouthed and handsome, in the middle. And his father glared at him from the end, angry at the world for posterity.

"Mr. Green, I presume?" Connor said finally, recovering. He took great care to make each word sound succulently aristocratic; it was an attempt to put Mr. Green at ease.

As expected, the man's face relaxed a bit.

"Yes, sir. I am he."

"Mr. Green, I am here to see Mr. Melbers. Is he available?"

Mr. Green looked confused.

"I'm sorry, sir, but Mr. Melbers passed away in April of this year."

Sadness swamped Connor. He had half expected this news, and yet it was still a blow. Kind old loyal Melbers, who had quietly protested the brutality of the old duke by secretly sending money every year to the wayward son.

Connor decided he could not afford to confide in Mr. Green; he hadn't the time to determine whether Mr. Green knew, or could be trusted with, his secret—that he had no intention of ever adding his own portrait to the collection on the wall.

Mr. Green watched Connor curiously, a gentle sort of puzzlement furrowing his brow. His was the expression of a man searching for a word just at the tip of his tongue, and who has every confidence his brain will yield it up in just a moment. Connor's eyes flicked involuntarily to the three dukes glowering over Mr. Green's shoulder, three glowering answers to Mr. Green's unspoken question. *Don't turn around, Mr. Green*, he silently entreated.

"I am sorry to disappoint you, sir. Melbers is sorely missed. Were you a friend?"

"A business associate," Connor said quickly, taking a step backward.

"Perhaps I can help you?"

"I think not, Mr. Green."

"But I have a number of clients of high rank who are very happy with my work," Mr. Green said proudly. He turned his back to Connor to gesture to the row of portraits. "Why, I manage the affairs of Her Grace, Cordelia, dowager Duchess of . . ."

His voice trailed off. His gesturing hand froze midair.

But when Mr. Green spun around again, Connor was gone.

Collar up, head down, cravat fluffed up over his chin, Connor strode for two blocks before stopping between two parked hackney coaches to rest and contemplate. Three words rang in his ears as he walked.

Cordelia, dowager Duchess . . .

Cordelia, eh? Well. It was a good deal more aristocratic than "Marianne," he had to admit. A fine choice. A fine name for a murderess.

He stood between the parked hacks and quietly seethed, watching the foot traffic in the street, the tide of men about their business. *I tried*, he told himself. At least I *tried* to make amends. Perhaps everything is as it should be; perhaps I should just leave it all be, concede defeat, return to Rebecca . . .

But no. He knew his past would dog him as long as Marianne—correction, *Cordelia*—suspected he was alive. And he supposed if it came to that, alone he could handle a lifetime of sleeping fitfully at night and always looking over his shoulder during the day. But he would not, could not, subject Rebecca to that kind of life. And he fully intended to live a life with Rebecca.

She deserved a life that was safe and happy, and he deserved a life with her that was free of the encumbrances of the old one.

Oh, God. What, then, were his choices?

His stomach rumbled; he thought he'd think more clearly with a meal inside him. He contemplated ducking into a cheese shop, and scanned the street for a likely one.

And then his breath caught.

Outside the bookshop, a tall, distinguished fellow, his bearing as upright as a ship's mast, was deep in conversation with a small older gentleman. The tall gentleman held a book between gloved hands; it appeared to be the subject of their conversation.

It *couldn't* be, could it?

He watched for another long moment, motionless, his heartbeat accelerating.

When the tall gentleman laughed a familiar booming laugh, Connor knew for certain: it was Colonel William Pierce, looking much the same as he did when Connor had glimpsed him last on the battlefield at Waterloo.

If ever God actually sent a sign to anyone on earth, surely it would manifest just like this, Connor thought. Pierce was a pragmatic and accepting sort, difficult to surprise and not inclined to form an opinion of a man until he'd heard him out. Pierce, who moved in London circles, would help him meet with Cordelia, and Pierce, who knew exactly how Connor felt about everything associated with his father and the Dunbrooke title, would no doubt keep quiet about the Duke of Dunbrooke returning from the dead.

Connor closed his eyes briefly against a tremendous wave of relief, and then opened them quickly again. The last thing he wanted to do was lose sight of Pierce.

But what now? He could not simply walk up to Pierce with a hearty "Hallo! Remember me?" He was supposed to be dead. The best he could hope for was a moment alone with him in a relatively discreet place, where he could approach him cautiously.

Pierce, at that moment, was making his bow to the older gentleman. The two parted, and after a moment's hesitation, as though waiting for his companion to disappear from view, Pierce stepped into a flower shop only a few feet away.

Connor hovered outside the shop, pretending to be absorbed by a handbill plastered to the side of the building. He didn't have to pretend for very long. The shop door opened again shortly, and he heard a man's voice, the shopkeeper's, no doubt, raised in what sounded like despair.

". . . but, Colonel, they are much harder to come by in London than you might think. Hothouses do not like to devote space to them when they can be had by the handful in the country at no expense whatsoever."

"Bluebells, Mr. Gordon," came Pierce's voice, polite but firm, from the doorway. "I have a standing order for bluebells, and well you know. Find them and deliver them as usual, if you please. And I will, as usual, make it well worth your while. I bid you good day."

Bluebells? Connor thought. What could a war hero possibly want with *bluebells*?

Pierce exited the shop and stood in the doorway of it a moment, his face a little thunderous. He paused for a moment, tapping his walking stick against his boot as if mulling over something. And then he strode onward decisively in the direction of the Coach and Six, a tavern known for unwatered ale and good plain food.

Connor fell into step behind Pierce and watched him push open the door of the Coach and Six. Taking a deep breath, Connor fluffed his cravat up over his chin once more, counted to ten, and followed Pierce into the pub.

The pub was teeming with a variety of actual gentlemen, as well as a collection of chaps who stretched the definition of gentlemen rather severely. The wives of the actual gentlemen, Connor knew, would be appalled to see their husbands tipping ale and trading jokes and back slaps with the other sort. This crowd in its entirety would never meet in a ballroom, but at a cockfight or a pub, they would certainly mingle quite happily.

Pierce traded greetings with a number of men that Connor did not recognize, while Connor pushed his way to a corner table.

"What'll it be, guv?"

Connor pretended to be fascinated by his own fingernails as he spoke, not wishing to give the barmaid or anybody else in the vicinity a full-on look at his face.

"A pint of dark, miss, if you would."

"The color of yer money, if *ye* would, sir."

Connor unfurled the pound note that was balled in his fist.

Satisfied, she swished her skirts away toward the bar.

"I say, Pierce, will you be attending Lady Wakefield's do this evening?" called a voice from across the bar.

Connor pitched all his senses toward the conversation. Tempting though it was to crane his head for a look at the speaker, self-preservation forced him to keep his eyes lowered. Lady Wakefield, last he knew, lived in a townhouse in St. James Square. Two doors away from the Dunbrooke townhouse. She had also, rumor had it, been his father's mistress. During a visit at Keighley Park, she had once come upon Connor in the hallway with his hand down the dress of a giggling maid. She never mentioned the incident to his father, which had endeared Lady Wakefield to Connor for eternity.

"Aye, Rutherford, that I am. I am assured it is a social requirement."

Scattered, good-natured laughter greeted Pierce's comment.

"Bloody dull, these social requirements. Save for the presence of a certain fair-haired angel, am I mistaken, Pierce?"

More good-natured laughter, as well as the unmistakable thump of a hand slapping a solid back.

"You might have to make a run for it with the fair Lorelei, Pierce. Her mama is intent on marrying her off to a marquis or some such."

Good God. Connor seriously doubted more than one girl named Lorelei was being shepherded through the *ton* by an ambitious mama this season. He was rocked by the irony that Lorelei Tremaine would be associated with Pierce, and for a brief perverse moment, Connor wished he'd been able to witness the stir that Lorelei had no doubt created among the young bloods and matrons of the *ton*. Rebecca, no doubt, would have enjoyed watching her sister create a sensation, as well. But the Tremaines had not planned a season for their younger daughter. Instead, for the sake of family honor and expediency, they had forced her into an engagement to a dissolute baron. He felt a little surge of anger on Rebecca's behalf. *I hope they are losing sleep over her right now. They deserve to lose sleep over her.*

Colonel Pierce's voice rose up out of the laughter. "Oh, come now, Rutherford, you know I am not in the market for a wife. In fact, let us drink to the success of Lorelei's mama."

Connor smiled faintly at Pierce's tone. He remembered it well, that pleasant timbre shot through with steel. It meant Pierce intended to brook no further discussion of the topic of Lorelei Tremaine.

There was laughter, and the clink of glasses touching as Lady Tremaine was toasted. Then Rutherford cleared his throat and said in a loud inclusive tone, "Well, now, and I heard the king is expected to appear at Lady Wakefield's do, as well. Do we think he'll get his divorce?"

Rutherford had predictably changed the topic to a very popular one. George IV might be a sot, but his wife was a harlot, or so he claimed, and he was doing his best to divest himself of her. Perversely, the entire *ton* had sided with Queen Charlotte. A racket of enthusiastic voices chimed in with opinions.

A pint of dark ale landed with a clunk on the table in front of Connor, and next to it the barmaid slapped down a small pile of coins by way of change. She waltzed off into the crowd once more before he could utter a word of thanks. He lifted the pint to his mouth and tilted, watching with an ache that bordered on the sensual as the thick silky white foam slid toward his lips.

"Tonight, then, Pierce! We'll have a cigar at Lady Wakefield's," Rutherford called.

Blast. Pierce was already weaving his way through the crowd toward the door. Connor took a long draught of the ale and lowered his head as Pierce passed his table.

"That, at least, I shall look forward to, Rutherford," Pierce said, and exited the pub to the sound of friendly laughter.

Connor waited a moment or two, then slid his chair back and discreetly followed Pierce out of the darkness of the Coach and Six. He stood on the threshold of the pub for an instant, blinking to adjust to the daylight, then took a step forward.

And nearly collided with John and Edgar the highwaymen.

Connor recovered first.

He plunged into the Bond Street crowd, making for the thickest part of it, all the while keeping a desperate eye on

Colonel Pierce, who was now moving at a brisk and determined pace. It would be difficult to get off an accurate pistol shot in this throng, Connor knew. But that didn't mean the highwaymen would not try.

Connor walked swiftly, moving as fast as he dared without breaking into a rather more conspicuous and less dignified gallop, and took refuge at the sides of the plumpest men he could find in the hope that it would make him an even more difficult target. But John and Edgar had managed to separate from each other and were now more or less flanking him. Connor caught glimpses of them now and again as the three of them dodged purposefully between men in the street, one man seeking cover and two men seeking a gap in the crowd through which a pistol ball could travel. It was like participating in a deadly sort of reel.

A long, feminine scream followed by a torrent of cockney curse words suddenly captured the attention of the crowd, and the cluster of people that Connor had been moving through halted and massed in the direction of the noise.

And just like that, Connor was exposed.

They stood for a stunned instant, the three of them, within ridiculously clear shooting distance of each other. And then John and Edgar reached into their coats for their pistols.

In the space of a second, sights and sounds raced past Connor like detritus caught in a floodtide, the sun glinting off the barrels of the pistols, Pierce mounting a bay horse, the steady clop of hooves and the grind of the rolling wheels of an approaching hackney coach. Connor made what seemed the most logical choice at the moment.

He threw himself under the hackney coach.

Dive, tuck, roll; from the recesses of his memory of war and pugilism, the sequence of motions returned and served him. Connor remained coiled in a tight ball, watching in a state of suspended reality as the coach wheels rolled to a complete stop inches from his nose, the horses whinnying shrilly and dancing in their harnesses. He became dimly aware of a swelling hubbub surrounding him; it seemed a good portion of the crowd was now captivated by what might well prove to be a gory coaching accident. A crowd meant protection. But a crowd also meant curious eyes on his face. Connor waited, motionless, barely daring to breathe.

A minute or so passed, and then a large face peered underneath the coach. The face stared at him for a moment with deep anxiety, which subtly evolved into astonishment, and then split into an enormous, delighted, gap-toothed grin.

"Why, yer *lordship!*"

It was Chester Sharp.

Little Thomas had the colic. Alice had a nasty cough. Nicholas Heron's gout was plaguing him, and Uncle Louis complained of loose bowels. All day, Leonora peered into eyes and down throats, felt foreheads and examined tongues, poked and prodded and asked questions, and then administered her cures. And all day, Rebecca leaped to do Leonora's bidding; once, without being asked, she handed over the tincture of meadow saffron. Leonora had gifted her with a smile. It was just the thing for Nicholas Heron's gout.

Their last patient, Raphael's Great-uncle Louis, was an

elderly widower, and mostly just wanted someone to listen to his complaints. After ascertaining that he had no fever or other ailments that might cause his bowels to misbehave, Leonora teased him and told him he should count himself lucky, as most men his age could not move their bowels at all. He laughed appreciatively and accepted a concoction of tormentil, and threatened to return to bother all of them if it had no effect.

Throughout the day, Rebecca would occasionally lose herself in a task, or in the knowledge that Leonora imparted, or in gratitude that Martha was absent—no doubt she was off greedily collecting admiring stares from a broader array of Gypsy boys than her own *compania* provided. But eventually the cramp of anxiety in her stomach reminded her: Connor was gone. Connor had left without even saying good-bye.

She'd been patient with him, patient with the secrets, the half-truths, with the unknowns. She was certain that anyone who'd known her from birth would be incredulous if they knew just *how* patient. But because she loved him, and because he seemed to need it, she had given Connor not only patience, but trust, with hardly a question—well, at least, fewer questions than she would normally have asked. And *still* he would not trust her with the truth. What, precisely, was he afraid of? Did he think she would fly into a rage, or burst into tears, like a child?

Evening yawned chasmlike before Rebecca. There would likely be the stew, which she doubted she could choke down again, and possibly more heart-scalding songs sung by bloody Martha Heron. And laughter and chatter in Rom, which Connor could understand and she could not, and he had left her here alone. Because he was afraid to tell her the truth, whatever that truth might be.

Leonora stretched languidly when Uncle Louis finally left the tent. "What would ye like to do this evening, little *Gadji?*"

Throw something very hard at Connor Riordan, and possibly at your daughter, too.

"Ye're welcome to join us at the fire," Leonora added when Rebecca did not answer.

And then Rebecca had an inspiration. "Do you have any herbs you need . . . crushed? With a mortar and pestle?" Crushing something seemed like a very appropriate way to spend the evening.

Leonora looked at her for a long silent while, then the corner of her mouth lifted. "Certainly. Something always needs to be crushed. I'll bring a meal to ye in a bit." She turned to leave, then paused at the threshold of the tent. "Welcome to love, Rebecca," she added wryly.

The tedium was almost like a gas; Connor swore he could feel it pouring out of the huge double doors of Lady Wakefield's London townhouse, much like the noxious fumes that poured off the Thames on sweltering summer days. He'd always loathed balls, throngs of people in finery that was bound to be sweated in and spilled upon packed together like pickles in a jar, nattering about nothing in particular to people they saw virtually every day during the season, hopping about like lamed frogs during ridiculous reels, although waltzes *were* now allowed and were, in Connor's opinion, somewhat more tolerable. On the whole, balls offended Connor's sense of the practical. Normally they were not accounted a total success until some maiden fainted from lack of air and was hauled dramatically out to the garden.

He thanked God once more for the practical redheaded girl waiting for him in Cambridge. Rebecca would much rather snare a hare or swim in the nude than squeeze herself in among the fools at Lady Wakefield's ball. Suddenly a vivid and highly distracting image of Rebecca nude, covered in little pearls of water, filled his mind. Connor took a deep breath and forced himself to refocus on the matter at hand. The sooner he accomplished his mission, the sooner he could return to her.

Mercifully enough, Lady Wakefield seemed to be leaving the doors open to invite in the night air. She had apparently purchased every candle in London. A rectangle of lamplight extended several yards beyond the front steps of the house, nicely illuminating her pair of liveried footman, who were there as much for decoration as to direct the guests to the ballroom. Ironically, the bold light merely enhanced the shadows, and Connor found a perfect vantage point for viewing the arrivals while remaining almost completely hidden, sandwiched between the Wakefield townhouse and the house next door.

Chester Sharp had, no questions asked, taken Connor back to his quarters in Cheapside, loaned him a razor, fed him, and agreed to take him to the ball and return for him again at midnight. He had even liveried the horse Connor had left tethered in Bond Street.

"Think naugh' of it, yer lordship. Things were right dull before ye came along," was Sharp's response when Connor attempted profuse thanks.

Coach after coach rolled up to the townhouse and disgorged groups of women resplendent in silks and turbans and jewels, and men in crisp white shirts and billowing cravats, their somber-colored coats over adventurous waistcoats.

Connor recognized some of the people who disembarked from the carriages, but he did not feel one whit nostalgic; it was like watching a battle from a distance, one that he had retreated from gratefully. Tiny battles would take place tonight inside Lady Wakefield's house, he knew, and the weapons would be silken barbs and insincere compliments in the name of social ambition. Real war, Connor thought, was a good deal more honest.

He could hear Sedgewick, Lady Wakefield's ancient and semidaft butler, announcing guest after guest in his sonorous, deliciously indifferent voice: Sir Gregory Markham. Lord and Lady Bryson. The Earl and Countess of Courtland. Dr. Erasmus Hennessey.

And at last, stepping out of a hackney coach, was Colonel Pierce, dignified and slightly unfashionable in a black coat and gray waistcoat. Connor watched Pierce for a breathless moment, praying. His prayer was answered as the coach Pierce arrived in rolled away. Pierce was alone.

Colonel Pierce hesitated in front of the Wakefield place, an expression of bald dismay on his face as he took in the liveried footmen and heard the buzz of hundreds of voices and the squalling violins. Connor smiled crookedly. He sympathized immensely. Resignedly, Pierce squared his shoulders and took a step forward.

"*Pierce!*" Connor hissed from the shadows.

Colonel Pierce stopped abruptly and his head jerked up. He gazed about him, frowning quizzically, then shrugged to himself and continued up the walk.

Connor cursed softly under his breath. He took a risky step forward, into the light.

"*Colonel Pierce!*" he said, just slightly louder than a whisper, imbuing the words with all the resonance, if not volume, he could muster.

Pierce halted and frowned again, swiveling his head about impatiently.

And then he went rigid.

Recognition, joy, fear, bewilderment, flickered across Pierce's face in rapid succession. He took a hesitant half step forward, then stopped and gave his head a little shake, and stared again. It was clear that he was not convinced that Connor was more than an apparition.

Another coach pulled up before the townhouse, regurgitating a half dozen or so drunken young men who immediately began listing merrily up the walk. One of them collided with Connor, teetered a bit, then clamped both his hands on Connor's arm to keep from falling outright. He gave Connor a bleary, affectionate smile.

"*S'ank* you, old chap. You're myfren for life, you are."

"*Get off me!*" Connor hissed, horrified. He tried in vain to peel the man's fingers from his arms; they were clamped as tight as pincers. The man swayed a bit, gazing up at Connor limpidly and with the faintest sort of surprise, as if he could not recall precisely how he came to be there. He remained clamped.

The rest of his young friends were suddenly upon them in a drunken, noisy, pushing, teasing, jabbing clot, all wriggling arms and legs and swinging walking sticks.

"Come now, Farnsworth, don't tarry, the young ladies await us," one strapping lad bellowed, and they pushed Farnsworth up the walk. And because Farnsworth was loath to relinquish his savior, Connor was dragged along with them, right past the footmen and up into the house.

Pierce gaped after him.

Nearly gagging with alarm, Connor managed to uncurl the young Farnsworth's fingers from his arm and turned to bolt out the door, but the jungle of young men proved nearly impassable. Connor took a deep breath and ruthlessly shoved and squeezed his way through them, ignoring the protesting, "I say, old man, have a care, now," until he found himself on the threshold of the doorway once more.

But the Baron and Baroness Leighton-Hyde were just making their entrance, a limping, leisurely sort of entrance, as the baroness was immense and the baron suffered from the gout. The baron was an old friend of his father's, a bluff friendly sort. Connor was forced to flatten himself against the wall, eyes lowered, chin tucked into his cravat, until they cleared the hallway.

He craned for a view out over the footmen to see if Pierce was still standing on the walkway, but another mass of people were now sauntering up it.

Two of those people were Sir Henry and Lady Tremaine.

Connor looked about wildly, seeking an escape route, and jumped when a familiar set of fingers gripped his arm again.

"Come t' the *ball*, olman," Farnsworth encouraged slurringly. He dragged Connor over to where Sedgewick was dutifully, stoically announcing each of the rowdy young men.

"And you are, sir?" Sedgewick said to Connor.

"He'sh my goo' friend," Farnsworth enthused.

"Lord Goodfriend?" Sedgewick asked.

"No!" Connor blurted, writhing to free himself from Farnsworth's viselike fingers. "God no!"

"Sir Godno?" Sedgewick suggested helpfully.

"Roarke," said a voice softly behind them.

And before he could think to stop himself, Connor turned to the voice. Colonel Pierce stood there, shaking his head wonderingly in confirmation, a small smile of genuine joy playing about his lips.

"He's the Duke of Dunbrooke," Pierce said.

"His Grace, the DUKE OF DUNBROOKE!" Sedgewick bellowed, before he could plumb the recesses of his own mind and recall that the Duke of Dunbrooke had been dead for years. Farnsworth gave Connor an encouraging push into the center ballroom.

The violins playing the reel screeched to a halt, the chattering voices faltered to a dead silence, and finally, as the hundreds of eyes in the ballroom landed on Connor like so many greedy bees, the only sound that could be heard was the soft plop of a woman fainting.

Chapter Twenty

❧

I do not," Connor said slowly, because it seemed as though everyone expected him to say *something*, "feel very much like dancing at the moment, if that is quite all right."

His words, spoken in a conversational tone, nevertheless reverberated in the silent room. No one else moved, breathed, or spoke. The bows of the musicians hovered, frozen, above their instruments. Silence ticked by, while faces, unanimously incredulous, remained fixed upon Connor.

Finally, a tiny woman dressed in gray silk and lace detached herself from the crowd and moved purposefully toward him, the click of her heels echoing throughout the ballroom.

Lady Wakefield stopped before Connor, lifted her quizzing glass, and peered up into his face.

"Why it *is* you, young Roarke," she breathed finally. "I'd know the Blackburn eyes anywhere. You're the spit of your father."

"It is indeed I, Lady Wakefield," Connor admitted.

His words sent a buzzing throughout the ballroom.

". . . looks like my *groom*," came a puzzled voice through the crowd. Good God. *Sir Henry.* Connor resisted yet another urge to bolt.

A movement in the crowd, as subtle as shifting light, caught Connor's eye. He would have known her anywhere; after all, the way she moved was what had first drawn his eyes to her so many years ago.

"Don't go anywhere, Pierce," he murmured to the colonel, who had stepped up to his side.

He was in front of Cordelia in three long strides.

Slowly, as though her head was in danger of toppling from her neck unless she took great care with it, Cordelia lifted her eyes to Connor's face.

"You can either take my arm and come quietly," he hissed under his breath, "or I will drag you with me through the crowd. Choose."

She hesitated a moment, and then her gloved fingers came up and landed, light as a butterfly, on his arm. A smile, slight and quivering, but a smile all the same, found its way to her pale lips, and she lifted her chin.

"Nicely done, *Cordelia*," Connor murmured. His body was nearly rigid with fury. He led her, with deliberate and almost cruel nonchalance, through the silent, staring crowd. He stopped when he reached Lady Wakefield again.

"Lady Wakefield," he said quietly, "perhaps there is a room the duchess and Colonel Pierce and I can retire to momentarily? I must attend to business before I can consider pleasure, you see. We have much to discuss."

"Why, of course," Lady Wakefield said. "The library is up the stairs and to the right."

"Thank you for understanding." He gave her his crooked smile.

"You will share your story with me later, my boy," Lady Wakefield said coquettishly, and tapped his arm with her fan, a triumphant smile playing about her lips. Her place in history was now assured. Not only was the king expected to make an appearance tonight, but Lady Wakefield's soiree would now be forever known as the occasion of the long-dead Duke of Dunbrooke's resurrection.

Connor kicked the library door shut behind him and shook Cordelia's fingers from his arm.

"*Sit.*"

Cordelia, with admirable composure, settled herself on the edge of one of the large library wing chairs, her spine erect, and folded her hands in her lap. Colonel Pierce leaned against the mantel and watched the two of them impassively.

If anything, Marianne Bell was even more beautiful now that the blur of youth had left her face; her bones seemed more finely etched, which made her mouth seem as soft as a pillow. She held herself very still, but Connor thought he detected a slight trembling, like a breeze disturbing the surface of a pool of water. He sincerely hoped she was terrified.

Odd to think that he had once wanted her so badly, pursued her so ardently. He looked at her now. She might have been a vase for how profoundly she moved him. *Rebecca.* He clung to the thought of her like a talisman. And as he looked at Cordelia he felt only purpose.

And rage.

Rage fought for control of his voice. He finally took

refuge in his breeding in order to speak. His words were soft, polite.

"Cordelia, have you by any chance been looking for *this*?"

He extended his closed fist and uncurled his fingers. In his palm lay the gold locket.

Cordelia drew in a sharp little breath through her nose.

Connor sprang the catch and handed the locket to Colonel Pierce. "The *duchess*, here, once upon a time, was my mistress. This locket was meant for me years ago, but I left her before she could present it to me. A recent twist of fate put it in my hands, and when she discovered I had the locket—that I was in fact alive—I do believe she decided to have me killed."

By way of illustration, Connor shook himself out of his coat. Colonel Pierce and Cordelia stared speechlessly at his tattered, bloodstained shirt. Granted, the shirt wasn't bloodstained courtesy of either of the highwaymen sent by Cordelia, but it did help make his point rather eloquently.

"If you read the inscription, Pierce, you'll understand part of her motive."

Pierce studied the locket, then glanced up at Cordelia.

"Ah. An actress, were you? And all the while you had the *ton* believing you were a half-French aristocrat. Very impressive. Yes, I can see how the reappearance of Roarke, not to mention this locket, might rather . . . ruin things for you."

Cordelia ignored Pierce.

"You were living as a groom," she said to Connor, in the soft, low voice he recalled so well. "With the family of Sir Henry Tremaine."

"Yes." Out of the corner of his eye, Connor saw Pierce's eyebrows go up.

"Sir Henry Tremaine was under the impression that you were Irish."

"Yes."

"'Tis a funny thing," Cordelia said, pensively, her eyes traveling about the room, taking in the library's expensive fixtures, the gilt and ormolu, so much like the library in the Dunbrooke townhouse. "Perhaps it is mere laziness, or lack of imagination. But I've found that, on the whole, people prefer to believe exactly what they are told."

"Perhaps it has something to do with the skill of the teller," Connor said.

Their eyes locked; a brief and peculiar understanding sparked between them, then died. Connor almost admired Cordelia's achievement. She had used the skills at her disposal—beauty, acting, and an intimate knowledge of the Dunbrooke world—to marry his brother Richard and become the Duchess of Dunbrooke. He had underestimated her; more accurately, he had never estimated her at all. He had merely partaken of her. What had he ever really known about Cordelia, apart from the topography of her naked body? She had loved him once, or so the locket said. *My dearest love.* And yet . . . he looked at her, at the coronet in her gleaming blue-black hair, the mulberry satin gown corded in gold and scooped low at the neck to show much of her white bosom, the rubies at her throat . . . all of it purchased with Dunbrooke money. And he fully comprehended that regardless of whatever love she might once have felt for him, she would have killed him for all of it. Rebecca's life had been threatened, and Connor had nearly been murdered, for dresses and jewels and a position in society. And his rage nearly choked him.

"Cordelia, tell me—how did my brother die?"

"His throat was slit by a footpad," she said evenly.

Connor nodded once, thoughtfully.

"How tremendously convenient—oh, forgive me, I mean *wrenching*—that must have been for you."

Cordelia stared at him in silence, her dark blue eyes huge and nearly black in her face. He could see her pulse beating in her throat.

"Clearly it was wrenching for *you*," she said finally, ironically.

A devastatingly skillful play on his own guilt. Connor inhaled audibly.

Cordelia smiled slightly at the sound.

"Knowing Richard and his . . . predilections," Connor said slowly, when he was able to speak again, "I can imagine that life with him was not easy. And I can almost understand why you would want to kill me. Perhaps you wanted revenge—I left you without a farewell, which, believe it or not, I am not proud of, and I do regret. And then you must have worked hard for the life you fraudulently won, a life as Richard's wife and the Duchess of Dunbrooke. I can almost understand why you would do anything at all to preserve it. But you sent highwaymen—cutthroats with guns—after *Rebecca*. A highwayman put his *hands* on her. And for that, I would happily see you hang."

It seemed to Connor that Cordelia swayed a little then, but perhaps it was a trick of a light. Only her hands truly betrayed her state of mind: they were twisted into a tight white knot in her lap.

"Could it be that you intend to faint, Cordelia? I expected more originality from you."

Cordelia gave a low scornful laugh.

"You know nothing of me, do you, Roarke? You never did. If you had any idea of what I have survived in my life, any idea of the things that I have lived through, you would know that nothing *you* say or do to me could possibly cause me to faint."

Connor regarded the beautiful woman before him, half awed, half repulsed. She had the pride of an aristocrat, the soul of a criminal, and the heart of . . . ? Possibly she merely had the heart of a woman. It mattered little now. The only thing that truly mattered at the moment was the love of a redheaded girl. As long as Rebecca loved him, he felt he could forgive nearly anything. And all at once, his rage drained away.

"I want you to witness, Pierce, that the duchess denies nothing," Connor said, tearing his eyes from Cordelia. "She very likely had my brother killed, and attempted to kill me."

"So witnessed," Pierce said in a deceptively bored tone. "Although, Roarke, as a price for such, I believe you owe me your entire story. An Irish *groom*? For five *years*?"

"Ah, yes, er . . . that. You'll know my story soon, I promise, but first I must go to the Cambridge Horse Fair. Immediately."

"The Cambridge Horse Fair?" Pierce's brow furrowed. "Why the devil—"

A tap on the library door made all of them jump.

Connor jerked the door open. Lady Wakefield stood there, her face flushed from an excess of excitement.

"You missed him! You missed him!"

"I beg your pardon, Lady Wakefield?"

Lady Wakefield was staring at Cordelia.

"I say, Your Grace, are you quite well? You look—"

"Lady Wakefield," Connor interrupted as Cordelia opened her mouth to speak. "Who did we miss?"

"The king! He was here but a few minutes. But he learned of your return, and he wants to see you. He *demands* to see you. Tomorrow evening for a private dinner."

"*Tomorrow*? No. I simply cannot. Tell him—"

"Roarke," Pierce interjected quietly. "He is the king."

Connor absentmindedly shut the door in Lady Wakefield's very surprised face and turned back to Pierce.

"You do not understand."

"You best explain then, lest I decide you've lost your wits," Pierce said

Connor inhaled deeply. "Rebecca Tremaine," he said. "It's Rebecca. My fiancée. I've left her with an old friend, Raphael Heron, at the Cambridge Horse Fair, and I promised to return for her by morning. I *must* return for her. I originally intended to take her to my aunt in Scotland and then leave for America on my own, and . . . well, my plans changed."

"*Rebecca Tremaine*? The mysterious sister that Lorelei refers to as 'indisposed'?"

"So it's 'Lorelei' is it, Pierce, and not 'Miss Tremaine?' "

Pierce, usually unflappable, looked flustered for a moment, and Connor almost laughed.

"The subject is you and Rebecca Tremaine, so please do not attempt to divert me from it. By 'indisposed,' did *Miss Lorelei Tremaine* by any chance mean 'missing'?"

Connor nodded.

"And did you, when you were a groom to Sir Henry Tremaine, assist Rebecca in becoming 'missing'?"

He nodded again.

"And no one knows?"

"You and the lovely murderous duchess. And one other friend who does not move in the circles of the *ton*."

There was rustle, a restless sound: satin against satin. The heretofore statue-still Cordelia had shifted in her chair. Connor and Pierce swiveled to stare at her.

"Perhaps the *lovely murderess duchess* objects to her new . . . sobriquet," Connor said to Pierce.

"Taunting your captive," Cordelia mused. "How gallant of you, Roarke."

"My apologies, Cordelia," Connor said in mock contrition. "But my finer qualities have never before been challenged by the presence of a murderess, and it seems they are not equal to the test."

"Roarke," Pierce interrupted gently. "Is Rebecca safe with your friends?"

"As safe as if she were with me."

"Then she will be safe for one more day. You're the Duke of Dunbrooke, Roarke. And the King of England has requested your presence tomorrow."

The words sucked the breath out of Connor. He was. He *was* the Duke of Dunbrooke. And it would be deucedly difficult to escape now, given that all of London, not to mention the *king*, knew he had returned.

"Will you help me secure the . . ." Connor almost facetiously called Cordelia "the duchess" again, until he realized that Rebecca would soon be his duchess, and suddenly it was no longer amusing. "Will you help me discreetly secure my brother's widow until I return from Cambridge? I will decide her fate then."

They both looked at Cordelia, who, though white-faced, gazed back at them levelly, her chin high.

"Oh, happily," Pierce said. "House arrest, a few armed Bow Street Runners, a word dropped to Lady Wakefield that the duchess is feeling unwell . . . leave it to me."

Connor's hope for a discreet and hasty retreat from Lady Wakefield's townhouse was quickly dashed: a small crowd had gathered at the foot of the stairs awaiting his exit from the library.

And planted at the very foot of the stairs was the unmistakable, very solid form of Sir Henry Tremaine.

Connor swore so colorfully under his breath that Pierce, who had a firm grip on Cordelia's arm, looked at him askance.

Feeling panicked, Connor contemplated simply barreling past Sir Henry and out of the door of the townhouse. Surely no one expected a duke to be polite *all* the time . . .

Did Sir Henry know his role in Rebecca's escape? But *how* could he know? Guilt did lazy cartwheels in the pit of Connor's stomach.

"I wonder if he'll challenge me to a duel," he muttered. "The man is an excellent shot."

"He certainly is." Pierce sounded amused. Connor slanted him a quelling look.

Finally, with the enthusiasm of one approaching the gallows, Connor took the stairs one at a time, Pierce and Cordelia behind him.

Sir Henry's gaze, unreadable from the top of the stairs,

never moved from him. Connor's gaze never moved from Sir Henry.

At last Connor reached the foot of the stairs and eyed Sir Henry warily.

But Sir Henry didn't look angry. Or even accusatory.

He looked . . . *tickled*.

"Er, good evening, Sir Henry." Connor felt a trifle strangled.

"By God, it is *you*, Riordan," Sir Henry breathed.

"Well, sir . . . I suppose it is."

"Dunbrooke, is it?" Sir Henry sounded delighted to be trying out the name. "The Duke of Dunbrooke? My *groom* is the Duke of Dunbrooke? I *told* Elizabeth when you walked in, I said to her—"

"Yes, Sir Henry, 'tis I. Now, if you'll excuse me, I really must be—"

"But *how*? That is, but how, *Your Grace*?" Sir Henry added. " 'Your Grace,' " he repeated, chuckling and shaking his head.

Feeling like an utter scoundrel, Connor stepped around his former employer. "Sir Henry, I would be pleased if you and your family would join me for dinner in a few days' time. But now I really must be—"

"Don't suppose you'll be returning to the stables, eh, *Your Grace*?" Sir Henry couldn't seem to stop chuckling.

"No, Sir Henry, I'm afraid not. Perhaps you should promote Michael from stable boy. Or persuade Viscount Grayson to take the position."

Sir Henry gave a bark of startled laughter and thwacked Connor heartily on the back.

Connor was so relieved his knees almost buckled.

Thank *God* Rebecca hadn't entered the conversation yet. And she wasn't likely to—as long as he kept moving.

"Very good to see you, Sir Henry. Good evening, Sir Henry." Connor all but bolted toward the townhouse front doors, a grinning Pierce and a glum Cordelia on his heels.

"Best damn groom I ever had," he heard Sir Henry telling someone in the crowd as they left.

Edelston waited a moment just to be very, very sure he was alone again. When at last he was certain, he let out a ragged groan of relief.

It had been no mean feat to remain absolutely still and absolutely silent for the better part of an hour—his right leg was asleep, for heaven's sake, and he was nearly dizzy from taking shallow breaths —but oh, the rewards. Once again, it seemed, fate had intervened on his behalf.

He'd seen Dr. Hennessey downstairs at Lady Wakefield's, or rather Dr. Hennessey had seen him, and one look at the man's face had told Edelston he'd better flee. For some time now, he'd owed Dr. Hennessey an outrageous amount of money, the result of a card game he could barely remember; he'd been rather too deep in his cups at the time to recall exactly how the damage was done. And now that Dr. Hennessey owed somebody else an even more outrageous sum of money, he was dogging Edelston relentlessly.

So Edelston had fled the festivities to the one room in Lady Wakefield's townhouse where no one would ever expect to find him: the library. Safe at last, he thought, and then the damned library door had opened. He'd immediately ducked behind a tall corner chair, closed his eyes like a child trying to make himself invisible, and silently prayed. And then listened, avidly, with a steadily growing glee, to a fascinating conversation between Connor Riordan and Colonel Pierce and Cordelia Blackburn.

An hour later, he was in a philosophical mood. He stood, stretched, and stomped his sleeping leg, which was needling him, and smiled. *Odd*, he thought, *how my gambling debts keep leading me to Rebecca. Clearly, it is all meant to be.* For now he had a plan, a deucedly clever plan, perhaps the first concrete plan of his life. Anthony, Lord Edelston was going to the Cambridge Horse Fair, and he would come home with a bride.

Chapter Twenty-one

❦

The first thing Edelston noticed about the girl standing at the side of the road was her hair. It was sinfully loose and waving like a sable flag in the breeze. His eyes were drawn next to her feet, which were bare, petite, and dusty; she was indolently scratching the ankle of one foot with the toes of the other. Up and down, up and down, up and down. The gesture for some reason communicated directly and immediately with his groin.

Aside from her bare feet, she was attired modestly enough in cotton faded to an indeterminate color, but her skin had an exotic tint to it, milk with a hint of tea. A necklace of reddish stones circled her throat.

A Gypsy, Edelston thought, pulling his horse to a halt. He was still several miles from the Cambridge Horse Fair, where all the Gypsies would be convening. Perhaps the Gypsy girl was lost, had been accidentally left behind, or had met with some accident—from what he knew of Gypsies, they rarely traveled alone, particularly the women. Perhaps she would need a ride to the fair; he imagined, with some pleasure, those slender arms around his waist as he rode. Perhaps she would not be adverse to a ride of another sort, he thought, eyeing the stand of trees she stood near. He gave himself a shake. It was becoming increasingly difficult to curb such thoughts; he was, in fact, a trifle resentful at the self-imposed need to do so. It would be an immense relief to finally have Rebecca Tremaine in his arms and in his bed.

"I can *dukker* proper, brother," the Gypsy girl called to him, voice low and inviting. "If you've the blunt."

Edelston swallowed hard. What on earth was *dukker*? It certainly didn't *sound* proper. It sounded as though it was something one did quickly in a stand of trees, skirts lifted and trousers dropped. Could this be a test of his moral fiber? Did he even *want* to pass it? He eyed the stand of trees she stood before speculatively.

"*D-d-ukker*?" he stuttered.

She laughed, showing pretty white teeth, and turned her tiny palms up to him. "I can read your future in your palm, brother. Just give your hand to me, and I will tell it. But first I must see your coin." Up and down, up and down, went her foot against her ankle.

Although he knew his immediate future included triumphantly returning with his wayward fiancée, he would enjoy standing close to the little Gypsy, admiring her sable hair and dusky skin, allowing her to hold his great hand in her tiny one. His heartbeat accelerated a little, as it always did when he contemplated a sensual adventure.

"If you will accept a sixpence, miss, I will be happy to hear my future," he said gallantly. He dismounted and led his horse over to her.

"Aye, brother, I will accept a sixpence. Come closer,

please." She smiled, and tucked a bit of hair behind her delicate little ear.

Edelston moved until he stood about two paces from her, close enough to see the downy hairs on her cheek, the tiny freckle next to her mouth. He held out his hands, palms up.

There was a soft rustling, a mere hint of a sound, really, and a motion from behind a tree. Edelston idly lifted his head. *Squirrel*, he thought. But then he froze, dumbstruck: two men, faces swarthy and grimly intent, stepped forward, toward him. One of them raised an arm high.

It was the last thing Edelston remembered.

He regained consciousness an hour or so later, stripped of everything save his shirt and trousers, pain playing his head like a drum and reverberating through every limb. When he opened his eyes, two dark faces were floating over him—two men, but not the men who had beaten him. Their eyes were gentle and concerned. But then their mouths moved, and to Edelston's horror, gibberish emerged. *My wits have been beaten from me*, he thought, terrified. But among the gibberish he thought he heard a word, a woman's name. It sounded like *Leonora. Perhaps I should try to speak to them,* he thought distantly, but when they touched him to lift him, consciousness drifted away again.

Cool competent hands were touching him, a cup of something was held to his lips; he drank, thankful to be told what to do. Cool cloths were applied to his head. He answered "yes" and "no" to the dark-faced woman who asked "Hurts here?" and pressed her knowing hands in various places on his ribs and arms. Someone else hovered on the periphery of his vision; a woman with red hair; she had Rebecca's eyes. The eyes widened in shock as recognition set in, and the woman reared away from him. The rearing motion made Edelston woozy.

"I've . . . I've come to rescue you," he pronounced as gallantly as he was able. And then he was sick all over Rebecca's skirt.

Rebecca was surreptitiously divested of her dress and installed in another one. Leonora continued the ministrations while Rebecca stared in disbelief.

Dear God. *Edelston.* Not in all her dreams or nightmares had Rebecca imagined she'd ever be confronted again with Edelston, not to mention a semi-nude Edelston, prone and pale and helpless as a freshly caught fish.

His presence could mean nothing good.

"You came to *rescue* me," Rebecca repeated flatly.

"Um . . . yes?" Edelston said weakly.

"How is it," Rebecca said slowly, as though addressing a three-year-old child, "that you knew where to *find* me?"

Edelston opened his mouth, then closed it again, then opened it and closed it again, as if trying to decide what to say. He resembled a freshly caught fish more than ever.

"Love, Rebecca. Love was my compass. I would follow you to the ends of the—"

"Try again, Lord Edelston."

Edelston fell silent, his handsome face a study in petulance.

"Well?" Rebecca demanded.

"Does that *matter* so very much? I'm *injured*."

Rebecca looked at Edelston's pale body, which was well enough formed and not displeasing, though his chest was nearly as hairless as a boy's, and his arms were slim, with just a hint of muscle. He was a rainbow of bruises. He was not Connor, and that was his gravest crime.

"Didn't you have a *pistol*?" Rebecca said crossly.

"Yes, well—" Edelston was startled.

"Then why didn't you use it? Did you even *try* to fight?"

Edelston gave an indignant squeak.

"I will return in a moment, *Gadji*," Leonora said to Rebecca. "I would like Raphael to meet our . . . visitor." She slipped out of the tent.

"Where is Connor?" Rebecca demanded, an ambush.

"Connor?" Edelston spluttered. "Who is Connor? Why should I know where this *Connor* is?"

"How else," Rebecca explained through gritted teeth, "would you know I was here, *Lord Edelston*?"

Edelston sighed gustily.

"Oh, very well. If you must know, Connor sent me for you."

Rebecca stared at him. "You are mad."

"Am I, Rebecca? Well, you see, Connor, your father's groom, the one who was so *helpful* to you, has really been the Duke of Dunbrooke all along, and—or perhaps you knew?" he added, in a mockery of solicitousness.

Rebecca stared at him, dumbstruck. Her heart began pounding sickeningly.

"The . . . the *Duke of Dunbrooke*? How—I mean—"

"Oh, yes, the Duke of Dunbrooke. Seems he lost his memory in the war, regained it recently, and returned to London. He is due to wed his brother's widow, a very beautiful woman, before summer's end. And this is why I've come for you, Rebecca—to rescue you from a hope-

lessly ruined reputation. A little gratitude would not be inappropriate, you know. The duke himself—*Connor*, as you
call him—swore me to secrecy and told me where to find
you, and wished me felicitations in our marriage. He has
changed his mind about you, for now he cannot possibly
marry the daughter of a mere *knight*."

Rebecca reared back from him as though he had
slapped her.

"The . . . the *Duke of Dunbrooke*?" Somehow it was all
beginning to make a hideous sort of sense.

"Oh, yes, it was quite the talk of the *ton* when I left. His
real name is Roarke Blackburn, or did you know that?"

"Roarke Blackburn. The locket . . . the locket said . . ."
An icy hand clawed her heart. Rebecca stared at Edelston,
unseeing, disbelieving.

"The damned locket," Edelston agreed morosely. "I
wish I'd never seen the bloody thing."

"Who is Hutchins?" Rebecca was prompted by a sudden foreboding.

"The duchess's footman?" Edelston was confused by
the question.

"The duchess? *Her Grace*," Rebecca whispered to herself, remembering. "*Her Grace* sent the highwaymen."

A horrible suspicion crept into her mind. She remembered the look on Connor's face, how still his body had
gone when he'd opened the locket. *The dark lover is faithless . . .*

"Marianne Bell," Rebecca said. "Is the duchess the
woman in the locket?"

Edelston's silence drove through Rebecca like a bayonet. It said all she needed to know.

There were questions she should have asked Connor,

specific questions, but she had feared the answers would taint her perfect happiness. She now knew her happiness had been illusory. She went still for a moment, testing: Connor still thrummed inside her, as essential as her own blood. Would this be true, she wondered, if he had decided to sever her from his life? *God help me, I am happier now than I have ever been,* he had said to her, right before he had asked her to be his wife.

Perhaps it was true; perhaps he had lost his memory and had regained it only recently only to discover that his past exerted a sort of gravity, one that pulled irrevocably on him. Perhaps it was easier for him to surrender to it than to fight it. Perhaps he thought it wiser to leave her behind than to struggle onward to a new life.

But she did not believe it. She could not.

"It was *she*," she spat suddenly, sitting bolt upright.

Edelston winced. Apparently sudden movements were visually unwelcome.

"The duchess. She sent *highwaymen* after us. Because she wanted Connor for herself. And she was an *actress*."

"Even if she did send *highwaymen* after you," Edelston said, as though the very idea was absurd, "he does not seem to mind it overmuch at the moment. She *is* a duchess now, you know. In fact, he seems overjoyed to be reunited with her. It appears he is enjoying being a duke very much."

"Has he . . . did he say anything else about me?" She hated herself for asking the question, but perhaps, if there was a chance . . .

Edelston merely shook his head regretfully.

"But my father—surely he has questioned Con—I mean, the duke . . ."

"As your mama has been preoccupied with securing a titled gentleman for your sister this season, your parents left the finding of you in the hands of the duchess, who has been all that is solicitous in this manner." Edelston said this without a shred of irony. "As far as they know, the duke— er, Connor—had nothing to do with your disappearance at all. But none of this will matter, of course, once we are married. And we should be married straightaway. If you gather your things, we can leave for Gretna Green in the morning."

Rebecca stared at him, numb and incredulous.

Edelston's face softened somewhat.

"Perhaps . . . perhaps you shall enjoy being married to me."

Unfortunately, it was the worst thing he could have said. Rebecca's face spasmed in revulsion.

Leonora pushed into the tent, Raphael on her heels.

"I am Raphael Heron," he said to Edelston.

"Ah," Edelston replied awkwardly.

Raphael raised his eyebrows in a prompting manner.

"Oh! And I am Anthony, Lord Edelston," Edelston said, finally remembering his manners. "I have come to . . . to . . . ah . . . rescue . . . to rescue . . ." He trailed off, as though he had at last been struck by the absurdity of it all.

Just then, Martha poked her very unwelcome head into the tent.

"He says Connor is actually the Duke of Dunbrooke," Rebecca said to Raphael.

Raphael went utterly still.

"And why would 'e say a thing like that?" he said at

last. To his credit, he delivered the words with convincing indignation.

"Oh, perhaps because it's *true*," Edelston said irritably. "Perhaps that's why."

Resignedly, Raphael met Rebecca's accusing stare.

"It *is* true," she said slowly. "And you knew it, as well."

Raphael shot a helpless look at Leonora, who shook her head; he would get no help from her.

Behind Leonora, from the opening in the tent, Martha was also shaking her head, but although her sorrow was masterfully feigned, her brown eyes were simply luminous with glee. Rebecca growled and took a quick step toward her. Martha gave a surprised little yip and ducked out of the tent.

"Ye best wait to talk wi' Connor, little *Gadji*," Leonora said gently. "We can tell ye no more."

"Lord Edelston claims Connor is not returning." Rebecca's own voice sounded distant to her over the buzzing that had started up in her ears. "He says Connor will marry his brother's widow, and that I am to marry Edelston, with Connor's blessings." She could hardly believe she was saying such words; each one hurt her physically, as though they were sharp little stones called up from her depths.

"Nonsense," Raphael said firmly, but Rebecca noticed the glance he exchanged with Leonora. Though his tone was entirely confident, Raphael was not.

Rebecca took a deep breath and squared her shoulders.

"He *will* return," she said, cursing the wobbly sound of her voice; how naive she sounded.

The weight of Raphael's and Leonora's sympathetic gazes on her was almost a tangible thing; she wanted to shrug both of them off violently. Nobody said anything for a long uncomfortable moment.

"I think I shall leave Lord Edelston to rest now," she said stiffly. "If you will excuse me?"

Raphael and Leonora stood aside so she could leave the tent. She refused to meet their eyes as she passed, because she knew she would find nothing there but pity.

Didn't you have a pistol?

Dear God. What manner of woman *was* she?

Edelston waited for some emotion to stir in him, some celestial joy that would transcend his physical pain. It seemed he'd waited so long to see Rebecca again.

Nothing came.

The thought of Rebecca had consumed most of his waking moments, except for perhaps the moments that had included bedding Cordelia . . . good heavens, Cordelia did make the most amazing noises in the throes of passion . . . and then there was the Gypsy girl who was indirectly responsible for the godawful throbbing in his head and ankle and ribs . . . well, perhaps, he *was* partially to blame for that . . .

Still nothing.

Oh, wait, here was something: *humiliation.*

Rebecca had seen him lying helpless and nearly nude. He'd cast his accounts all over her skirt. He'd gotten himself beaten to a near pulp more or less on her behalf, and from the looks of things, she was perfectly content as she was, consorting with Gypsies. In love with a groom who was really a duke. She wasn't the least bit pleased to see him. *And is she in love with you?* Cordelia had asked him the day of Rebecca's disappearance. Cordelia had tried to warn him.

Edelston recalled the look on Rebecca's face when she'd taken in all of his lies, and a foreign little burst of compassion for her straggled up out of the depths of his own bitterness and self-pity. Still, as he saw it, he had only two choices: marriage to Rebecca or debtor's prison.

But she was a stranger. He did not love her, and she certainly did not love him.

Edelston, at last, realized he'd been an utter cake all along.

Chapter Twenty-two

❧

The king seemed to have changed little since Connor had last seen him, except to have grown much fatter. George IV was eager to spend the evening with his aging mistress, and not at all eager for her to get a look at the handsome returned duke, so he had kept the audience short, and made noises about hoping Connor would vote with him in Parliament . . . though his father and brother never had. And Connor had made polite noncommittal noises in response, thinking, *Fat chance, Your Majesty.*

He could now see the Cambridge Horse Fair on the horizon; the colorful tents and flags were disappearing, little by little, as workers tucked them away for next year's festivities. His heart leaped. In mere minutes, he would be with Rebecca again.

Before his audience with the king, he had spent the morning going over the Dunbrooke accounts with Mr. Matthew Green. If Mr. Green recalled his fleeting (or, rather, fleeing) visitor, he was diplomatic enough not to mention it. He had instructed Mr. Green to suspend the rents of the tenants at Keighley Park effective immediately, and to send a number of experts on building, landscaping, and farming to the area to prepare a detailed report on the conditions of the home and surrounding lands. Since the corn crop had been too good in recent years to bring decent prices, Connor was interested in suggestions on how the tenant farmers could find other sources of income.

Weston himself had been personally pleased to set two teams of his Bond Street tailors on the urgent project of creating two new suits for him, shirts, trousers, waistcoats and all.

And thanks to Colonel Pierce, Cordelia was being discreetly and securely held at another of the Blackburn properties in London. Bow Street Runners lounged about the place, their big boots up on the fine furniture, their huge rough hands clutching Dunbrooke china and downing Dunbrooke tea, their shrewd eyes glued to Cordelia with nothing more than professional curiosity. Bless them. The little footman that had hovered about Cordelia like a crow, however, had simply vanished.

And the Tremaines—well, he'd successfully dodged Sir Henry so far. He would bring Rebecca to them the moment he returned to London with her.

All in all, Connor had to admit being a duke had felt quite delicious for the past day or so.

He had the intelligence and wherewithal to do real good with his money and position, he realized. With the promise of Rebecca by his side, and without the specter of his father looming over him, his birthright had begun—as much as he hated to admit it—to look more like freedom, like an opportunity, like a blessing, than a trap.

Perhaps he could forge a new Dunbrooke legacy. With

Rebecca at his side, anything seemed possible. He could hardly wait for their future to begin.

He kneed his horse into a run.

While Leonora rolled bedding, Rebecca knelt before the trunk and tucked their herbs and tinctures lovingly into a bed of straw and muslin to cushion them against the jostle of the rough roads.

"What will you do with Lord Edelston?" she asked Leonora.

Edelston had been consigned to his own small tent. The Gypsy men had quickly perceived that he posed no threat whatsoever, unless one felt threatened by incessant grousing.

"I suppose he will travel with us for a few days at least. He is not yet fit enough to travel on his own. Raphael has decided the lord must work to make up for the cost of his keeping. And then, if the lord is . . ." She paused, searching for the right English word.

"Childish? Unpleasant? Ridiculous?" Rebecca suggested.

"Cooperative. If the lord is cooperative, Raphael may give him an old horse to carry him back to London, or perhaps some money for a coach."

Rebecca stopped packing for a moment, pondering this. The prospect of watching Edelston work for his keep held an undeniable appeal.

Rebecca finished packing the trunk, and looked around nervously for something else to do. She had slept only briefly and fitfully last night, and her dreams had been short and raw. She had jerked awake at the conclusion of each one, and yet she couldn't really recall any of them completely. She had awoken this morning with a bitter, metallic feel in her mouth, as though she could taste her own heart bleeding. Even Martha had lost the power to rattle her.

And I dukker best of all, Martha had said. How ironic if that was indeed true. They were leaving the Cambridge Horse Fair, and yet there was no sign of Connor.

"Take these outside to the wagon, Rebecca, if you would," Leonora asked, sensing Rebecca's need to keep moving. She pointed to the bedrolls; Rebecca scooped them up and pushed the tent flap aside.

The Gypsy camp was bustling cheerfully; men were loading the wagons with tents and chests and lifting children up to sit beside their mothers. Rebecca found Leonora's wagon, her placid white horse already hitched to it, and tossed the bedrolls in.

The sound of hoofbeats coming at a gallop made her turn. She searched the periphery of the camp with her eyes until she found the source: a lone rider was approaching, obscured in a puff of dust. Immediately wary, the Gypsy men paused in their work and shaded their eyes from the lowering afternoon sun. A gallop signified urgency, and so far there was nothing at all about the day that required urgency.

But Rebecca knew who it was. Knowing that her hair glowed like a beacon among all the dark heads of the Gypsies, she stood in place and waited for him to find her.

Which he did in moments. Connor pulled his horse to a halt before her and lowered himself to the ground stiffly, and because his own legs weren't quite ready to hold him up after the long ride, he swayed a little on his feet. He was breathing heavily, and drenched; his shirt had gone transparent with sweat, and sweat made little gullies in the dust caked on his face and beaded in his eyelashes and eyebrows. When he reached up a hand to push his hair out of his eyes, his hair stayed where he'd pushed it. He left fingerprints in the dust on his forehead, Rebecca thought distantly.

How is it, she wondered, *that he always seems more real than anything else?* It was as though the world were a painted backdrop against which he stood in stark relief.

Her eyes went to his sweat-soaked shirt. It was new, made of fine linen; new, not filthy and patched by her own clumsy hand. Made for him.

Made for a duke.

"Oh, God. Rebecca." Connor's voice was a joyful rasp, tattered from the hard ride. "I thought . . . I thought I'd never get here . . ."

"Hello, Connor." Icy politeness.

Connor looked troubled for a moment. Then his face cleared, as though he'd decided she was teasing him.

"Hello, Miss Tremaine," he said with mock formality, and bowed.

She remained silent and stared back at him with something akin to impassiveness.

Connor's brows drew down in confusion. He cleared his throat nervously, then reached out a hand to touch her. "I've so much to tell you—"

Rebecca stepped back from him, and his hand dropped like a bird shot out of the sky.

"That's a fine new shirt, *Your Grace.*" Her voice was low, almost contemptuous.

The realization dawning on Connor's face was a thing to behold.

"The name's *Roarke*, is it not? Is that what she calls you, Connor, when you . . . when you . . . *lie* with her?"

"Lie with—lie with—wee Becca, what are you talking about?"

She couldn't help herself; the words kept welling up involuntarily, like the blood of someone who has been stabbed in the heart. "And where is the duchess this afternoon, *Your Grace*? At a fitting for her wedding gown? You are just in time for *my* wedding, Your Grace. Edelston arrived yesterday evening, bearing the glad tidings of your nuptials—"

"Of my *what*? He is lying. He is—"

"—to your mistress, Marianne Bell. And what choice have I, a ruined woman, but to take him to *my* bed?"

It was a lie, designed specifically to hurt him.

And, oh, it did. His expression then almost gave her pause . . . his eyes huge and black, like new bruises.

His voice shook. "Rebecca, I do not know what he told you, but he had no right—I *will* kill him—"

"No *right?* No *right?* You speak of *rights?* You . . . *you* . . . lied to me, Connor. Or should I call you *Roarke*? And how am I to know whether you speak truth now? Whether you've *ever* spoken the truth?" She said this with wonderment, and shook her head, as though she could still scarcely believe it. "But perhaps I am to blame, because I was oh, *so* easy to lie to, wasn't I? I was foolish: I would have believed it if you'd said you were the one who'd arranged for the sun to rise each day. I wore that locket with *her* picture in it around my *neck*. You *knew*. Did you laugh at me, at my naiveté, did you think it was *funny*?"

"I did not so much lie, wee Becca, as . . . omit parts of the truth."

"Are you *amused* by this?"

Connor pushed his hand through his hair again, nervously; it was clear, Rebecca thought with some relish, that she was coming at places he had not expected to need to defend. "Rebecca, I tried to tell you, that morning by the river. Perhaps I did not give you names and places and dates, but I tried to convey to you, somehow, all that I had left behind. You deserved that much, I knew. None of it would have mattered, none of this would have happened, if we had been able to leave then for America. And you asked for nothing more than what I told you. You said . . . you said that it did not matter as long as we were together."

"I think you did not tell me all, Connor, did not give me *names and places and dates*, as you say, because you knew that it *would* matter, that it did matter. You guessed, correctly, that I would be too naive to question you further. You took the coward's way out."

He froze and stared at her; his entire body tensed like a bunched fist before her eyes. Almost unconsciously, Rebecca took another step back.

"Rebecca, you are a *child*." The words were etched in derision.

Rebecca's spine went rigid with outrage; she could feel hot color flooding into her cheeks.

Connor smiled a small, sardonic smile. "Yes, you are in so many ways a *child*. Are you capable of comprehending, I wonder, what I have risked for you? I gave up a peaceful life for you, and now I have my old life back, the one I never wanted, and I did it for *you*. And it was you, not I, who made me into a hero, Rebecca; *me*, the keeper of your father's horses, a hero. Laughable, when you think about it," he added cruelly. "And now you are gravely disappointed to learn that I am just a *man*. Not a god, not a hero. Just a man. I do not always do the noble and right thing; I do not always even know what the right thing *is*. I have lived a whole life, Rebecca. I had a mistress named Marianne Bell, and yes she was beautiful, and yes I made love to her, because that is what one does with mistresses. But I never *loved* her. Is that what you wanted to know, Rebecca? Does that soothe your pride? Need I remind you precisely who brought the locket on our journey?"

"I—"

"I've been to war, Rebecca. I've seen men die horrible deaths right in front of me. I've killed men without knowing their names. But nothing has ever frightened me so much as the thought that I might lose you if you knew the truth about me. And perhaps what I did amounted to lying. I had no experience of love to call upon, you see, to tell me what to do. I did what was easiest, and simply stayed silent about my past, and hoped it would come right, for I wanted none of it, none of my legacy. Perhaps it was not the right decision; perhaps I should have trusted you to understand. But you have not lived as I have lived, Rebecca, and you have not been required to make the choices I have made. You have not earned the right to call me a coward. Do not ever—*ever*—call me a coward."

They stared at each other in righteous, furious silence for a moment.

When she spoke, her voice was subdued. But it was steady, and she was proud that it was.

"Connor, of everyone I've known, I thought I knew you

best. I trusted you with . . . that is to say, I . . . I . . . made love with you." She stammered, blushing, over the words; they still did not spill off her tongue lightly. And suddenly the fact that this should make her blush made her freshly angry. "I gave you my trust freely, but you did not honor me with your own—you chose instead to harbor secrets. And you acted as everyone else always has—my father, my mother, Edelston—you assumed I would do just exactly what I was told, simply because it was *you* doing the telling. And what choice did you give me? You left me here, and I was forced to wait for you, because it was my only choice. That's not choice, Connor. That's . . . that's *captivity*."

Connor lifted an eyebrow. "Captivity, was it, wee Becca? So helping Leonora was much, much worse, was it, than, for instance, staying at home and playing pianoforte?"

She was silent.

"You have to believe me, Rebecca. Please . . . *please* listen to me. Marianne is nothing to me now. *Nothing*. Rebecca, she was trying to have me *killed*. Edelston lied to you for his own gain. And . . . I cannot tell you everything now, it would take so long, but I *will* tell you all, I promise. Just come away with me."

Rebecca stared at him, her eyes brimming with unshed tears.

"It seems everyone is lying to me for their own gain."

"*Please*. I will make it up to you for the rest of my life, Rebecca. Won't it be amusing to have something to hold over me for the rest of your life?" A desperate attempt at humor.

"I am not going anywhere, Connor."

His face seemed to cave in upon itself then, as if the words had punched the breath from him.

"What . . . what do you mean?"

"I am staying here. I certainly cannot go home to my family, *disgraced* as I am. And I am needed here; I am learning to be a healer. No one here pretends to be something other than what they are, you see."

As intended, she had found her mark.

"Yes, I do see," he said softly. "What of Edelston?"

"Edelston will be gone from here in a few days." An admission, of sorts, and yet when Connor turned soft eyes on her, looking for softness in her, he found none.

"Come away with me, Rebecca. You will not regret it," he tried again.

"No."

"Rebecca—"

"How, Connor, can I ever trust you again? It's all very simple. I can only stay here."

"I will not force you to come." A warning.

"I know."

"I can stay with the Gypsies, too."

"I cannot stop you. I strongly prefer, however, that you do not."

Connor was silent for a moment.

"What of your parents, Rebecca?"

"What of them? I will be gone with the Gypsies by the time they arrive, if your plan is to tell them."

Neither of them spoke for another long moment.

"I love you," Connor said quietly.

She turned her head away from him.

"Shall I leave then, Rebecca?"

She nodded.

"And you're very certain it's not just your pride saying that, Rebecca?" Bitterness had crept into his voice.

"You should go," she said softly. "Just go."

She would not look at him.

Connor reached for the reins of his horse.

"What . . . what will you do now?" Rebecca asked hesitantly.

"It matters not," he said.

And as she did not reply, Connor nodded curtly to her, and led the horse away.

Rebecca watched, dully, as Connor approached Raphael, to whom he spoke a few words. And then she could not watch any further. She heard, though, after a space of time, the hoofbeats of a horse cantering away from the camp.

When Rebecca turned, finally, she found Martha watching her, her expression absolutely captivated and ablaze with jealousy, and Leonora, who saw everything, the truth of it, in Rebecca's face.

"You are welcome to stay with us, little *Gadji*, of course," Leonora told her gently. "I have need of you. But I will say one thing: sometimes the wisest, bravest thing we can do is follow our hearts and forgive the thing that seems unforgivable."

Rebecca said nothing. Her eyes were on the place on the horizon where a horse and rider had vanished a few moments before.

Chapter Twenty-three

～

*N*o," Lady Tremaine said. "No, no, no, no *no*."

The note of hysteria in her voice escalated in pitch with each "no." The last "no" was, in fact, delivered with tremolo. A nice touch, Sir Henry had to concede.

Still, he was unmoved. Sir Henry merely eyed his wife with resolve. He had decided that for once he would not be cajoled from his position, not by tears, nor hysteria, or by cold silence. For once, he would simply wait out whatever strategy his wife decided to employ in an attempt to sway him, the way one waited out a spell of inclement weather. It would not be comfortable in his home for some time, he speculated, and yet he rather relished the idea of the challenge it would present. Perhaps his mild rebellion was long overdue.

He could hear the muffled sobs of Lorelei, who was upstairs behind closed doors. Her mother had dealt with her rather harshly for conducting a courtship in secret. A courtship with someone other than a viscount, that is.

"She can be a *countess*, Henry. She can marry an *earl*. She is the greatest success the *ton* has seen in years. What in heaven's name are you *thinking*? She should not be given your blessing. She should be given a *beating*."

"All right, Elizabeth," Sir Henry said, gently but firmly. "That is quite enough. You will sit down and be quiet while I speak."

Lady Tremaine gaped at her husband for a moment, surprised. They were about at the point in the conversation where he normally capitulated.

"Henry —"

"Sit *down*, Elizabeth."

She sat, albeit reluctantly.

"I think," he began slowly, "we have lost sight of something important. I think we agree that it has been our goal as parents to see our children well married. And if we manage to secure a fine match for our child and feel certain they will also be happy in that match, then our joy should be twofold, is that not true?"

"I do not see how this —"

"If Lorelei had decided that her happiness lay with a . . . a . . . *wastrel* of low breeding, Elizabeth, I would certainly interfere. But Lorelei has managed to fall in love with a very wealthy gentleman whom I esteem greatly, a fine man who will treat her well and will be a credit to our family, and who has asked for her hand in a very dignified and proper manner. And because I am certain that she will be happier with him than with any viscount or earl, I have given my consent. And I shall brook no argument from you."

Speechless, Lady Tremaine merely stared at him, her mouth parted slightly.

"Elizabeth, we are missing one daughter, or have you forgotten? We made a mistake, I think, in insisting upon her marriage to Lord Edelston. Perhaps Rebecca would have been happier living out her days as a spinster with a Reputation, poking about in my library or working as a schoolteacher. I tell you, I prefer that be the case to not knowing where she is now. I think that we have failed Rebecca. And mark my words, I will not force another marriage upon any of my daughters, especially since Lorelei has managed to choose so well for herself."

Astounded by her husband's vehemence, tears began to gather in Lady Tremaine's eyes.

"Elizabeth," Sir Henry said, his tone softening, "you have done a fine job raising two—and I do mean *two*— wonderful daughters. You should be proud of Lorelei. She is an unusually beautiful girl, and the fact of this has, quite understandably, excited your ambitions, as it would any devoted mama. But she has proved to be a sensible girl, as well, in her choice of husband, and in this we are very fortunate."

"Oh, Henry," said a decidedly more subdued Lady Tremaine, in a voice gone quavery with tears. "You are quite right, you know. About Lorelei. And about Rebecca. I see that."

Sir Henry was more relieved than he could say.

"I am so glad, Elizabeth."

"But is it not still remarkable that our Lorelei could have married a viscount?"

"I suppose so. But she will marry a colonel instead, and we shall all be happier for it," he said gently. "Now, I think she will enjoy hearing of your change of heart from you. Go to her."

Lady Tremaine nodded briefly and dabbed at her eyes with her handkerchief, then turned to bustle up the stairs to

Lorelei. There was already more cheer in her gait, Sir Henry noted wryly. There was nothing like the prospect of spending money on a wedding to cheer a mama.

"Elizabeth?" he asked suddenly.

Lady Tremaine paused on the stairs. "Yes, Henry?"

"Perhaps we can ask the Duke of Dunbrooke to assist us in finding Rebecca. He seemed fond enough of her when he was my groom."

"A *fine* idea, Henry." She continued merrily up the stairs.

The horse Raphael had loaned him for the trip back to London was a handsome beast, but its gait was so jarring Connor feared it would make him ill. He slowed the animal to a walk, and uncorked a flask of water, wishing he'd had the foresight to bring along whiskey. Whiskey would numb him. Keighley Park, his title, Cordelia, Edelston, Rebecca—they could all go hang. He would forget them all. From London he would sail to America. And from there he cared not. He would finally be able to lose himself in the vast wildness of that country; he would let something greater than himself take the pain out of him.

You will turn into a pillar of salt. But the temptation was too great, and so he did it: he glanced behind him.

Something was moving in the road. Whatever it was, it was still too far away to tell if it was another horse and rider, or perhaps a dog, or a person on foot. He turned his horse to watch.

When he knew for sure, he didn't move to meet her. He wanted, needed, her to come all the way to him. He slid from his saddle and waited.

And then she vaulted from her horse and ran, crashing

into him, heaving from the run. He closed his arms around her. He lifted her up, kissed her hair, her face, her neck, breathing her in, and she clung to him, too weary to stand upright.

"I love you, Connor."

"I love you, too."

"I am so sorry. I wanted to hurt you."

"Well, and you succeeded. Hush now, wee Becca. I am sorry, too."

"I meant none of it."

"Yes you did, but it's quite all right. I deserved it. I was wrong."

"You love me?"

"I love you. I am sorry, wee Becca. For everything. You are my life, you know."

"Shhh . . ." she said, placing a finger against his lips, and then she placed her lips there. He took her face in his hands with a soft groan and kissed her deeply, with gratitude.

"Where shall we go?" she asked, when he lifted his head.

"Anywhere you want. America. India. Brighton."

"All three, then."

He placed gentle kisses on her eyebrows, first one, then the other, and she closed her eyes and smiled. And then they stood in the road and held each other quietly, for a long time, their hands moving softly over each other's bodies, as if to reassure each other they were really there and together.

"We must go back for Edelston, first, I fear," Rebecca said finally.

"*Why?*" Connor pulled away from her.

"He was beaten and robbed on the road, and that is why he is in the camp. He is recovering."

"How did he get himself beaten and robbed?"

"By being Edelston, no doubt."

Connor sighed.

Chapter Twenty-four

⌒

Dear Aunt, the note read. *I hope this letter finds you in good health and humor. Forgive me for intruding yet again upon your peaceful life in Scotland—*

Peaceful? Lady Montgomery thought, amused, as she listened to Miss Honeywell torture another one of the classics with her trumpet.

—but I write to reverse my plans, or rather to extend an invitation to you. I will not be in Scotland as planned initially, but my wife and I would be delighted if you would honor us with a visit to London a week hence. As you can see, much has happened in the weeks since I last wrote to you. All is well, and I assure you, a happier man than I cannot be found in all of England. We shall eagerly await your response, and will tell you our story when we see you.

Yours affectionately,
Roarke Edward Connor Riordan Blackburn
Duke of Dunbrooke

Lady Montgomery stared for a while longer at the bold signature at the bottom of the letter and then touched it gently, once. So young Roarke would claim his birthright; it had not conquered him, after all. She hoped he was indeed happy. There was only one way to find out.

"Miss Honeywell?"

Miss Honeywell pulled her lips away from the trumpet. "Yes, Lady Montgomery?"

"I apologize, but I find that I am needed in London, and I must make arrangements immediately. Will you excuse me? We can resume our lessons upon my return."

Miss Honeywell, wide-eyed at the thought of anyone she knew traveling to glamorous London, nodded silently, and obediently took herself and her trumpet from the room.

Who could be knocking at this hour? The day had just lost the blush of sunrise. Janet Gilhooly smoothed her hair, and bustled to the door.

"Package for ye, mum," a young man said.

A package? From her sister in Ireland, perhaps? It didn't seem likely. None of her relatives had managed to marry anybody who had enough money to send surprise packages.

"Who sent ye, lad? I've no coin t' give ye fer yer trouble."

"Dinna fret, mum, I've been paid. An' I'm to give ye a message." The boy stepped back, cleared his throat, and looked skyward, as though the words he was to speak were written there.

"*Ye'll know who sent this when ye see wot's inside.*"

Janet glowered at him. "Ye best tell me who really sent ye, lad. I'll box yer ears if ye be pullin' a prank."

"Open the box, mum."

With another dark frown in his direction, Janet took the box inside and laid it on the table, then pulled the string from it and lifted the lid. There was a layer of paper; she pawed through it until she saw the fine dark brown coat. Beneath it was a waistcoat striped in gold.

She lifted them out, one by one, with shaking hands. Connor Riordan's things. Why had Connor sent her these things? The coat was torn at the sleeve. Both garments had seen rough use, clearly. Where was Connor?

She heard a soft thud as she lifted the waistcoat out of the box; something had fallen from it. She peered into the box to investigate. And saw a sheaf of pound notes.

Many many pound notes.

Five hundred pounds, all in all.

More money than she had seen in a lifetime. More than enough money to buy a lifetime of comfort.

The boy was watching her face, interested. The woman had gone white, then pink, then white again, and her mouth had dropped open, and her eyes were blank with astonishment. She looked a bit like a looby, he thought.

He decided it was time to deliver the rest of his message.

"The Duke o' Dunbrooke, who ye know as Connor Riordan, sends these things t' remember 'im by, wi' deepest thanks, and he and his wife Rebecca will pay ye a visit by and by."

Janet merely gaped at him, holding her new fortune in her hands. A full minute went by. And finally she found her voice.

"I *knew* the man wasn't Irish!"

The boy shrugged, gave a little bow, and left.

London was shrinking.

Or rather, London was getting farther away.

A cooperative wind snapped cheerfully in the sails of *The Standard*, pushing it inexorably away from the *ton*, away from England itself, away from . . . everything.

He clutched the rail and watched London disappear as the deck pitched subtly beneath his feet, and glanced down so he could watch the ship seam through the cloudy blue-green water. It left great curls of foam in its wake, a trail of sorts that closed again as they moved on from it. He liked the idea of a trail that closed behind them, leaving no trace of their passage. Fine spray was tossed up into his face. Much to his surprise, he found the sensation agreeable.

He transferred his gaze to his palm, where a beautiful woman gazed back at him from a gleaming gold locket. He ran his thumb over her face just once, thoughtfully, and then snapped the locket shut. He closed his hand over it tightly, for a moment, as though committing the feel of it to memory. And then he pulled his arm back and hurled the locket out to sea.

It arced through the air, winked brilliantly for a fleeting moment in the sun, then dropped into the ship's wake and vanished.

"Dramatic, but hardly necessary, Tony," Cordelia said. "We could have pawned the gold."

Truthfully, however, she had enjoyed watching the ocean swallow up the locket more than she could say. She had felt something in her soar along with it when it flew through the air, and now that it was gone, she felt . . . liberated. *I should thank him.*

But Edelston seemed to know what she was thinking.

"Now you can be anyone you like, Cordelia," he said. "Marianne, Cordelia, Queen Elizabeth. We've no reminders. How will the Americans know? Ignorant lot, so I've heard."

He smiled at her. She smiled back. Sometimes, Cordelia thought, Edelston's very simplicity made him sound like a sage.

The Duke of Dunbrooke had given each of them a thousand pounds, the locket, and passage to America, where they were to use whatever resourcefulness they had at their disposal to make a life for themselves. They were not to return to England. Ever. That was the condition of the gift. The duke had also disposed of Edelston's debt. Then again, when one possessed one of the largest fortunes in all of England, one could afford to be generous in the act of ridding oneself of a pair of nuisances.

The shame of it had been scalding: in Lady Wakefield's library, Cordelia had watched as the face of the only man she had ever loved, a man she perhaps still loved (though she had forbidden herself to entertain this possibility), reflected in swift succession awareness of her beauty, and then contempt, and then . . . nothing. Roarke Blackburn, as vibrant and beautiful as the day he had left her, considered her a murderess. And it was clear that beyond a certain dispassionate appreciation for her face, and a certain amount of rage and contempt, he felt nothing at all for her. Nothing at all.

Standing on English shores, Cordelia had found it difficult to imagine ever feeling anything other than heartbreak and shame and wounded pride. Standing on the deck of *The Standard*, however, Cordelia began to think it possible to reinvent herself yet again.

Cordelia looked at Edelston, whose eyes were bright and whose face was pointed directly into a sea breeze, and wondered whether fate meant to tie them together. They had made no promises to each other. They had made no plans. But here they stood, side by side, with a shared history and shared secrets, and they had been given an opportunity to leave the past behind. She would try not to think past this moment.

And Edelston actually looked . . . *happy*. Then again, being relieved of crippling debt was bound to animate anyone.

"And you, Tony," she said. "Now you can be anyone *you* like."

He smiled at her and lifted her hand to his lips.

"I'd like to be someone who is not inclined to be seasick," he said.

She laughed. Edelston hesitated an almost undetectable moment, and then companionably put his arm around her waist. And Cordelia allowed him to do it, a little surprised that she actually found the gesture comforting. Together, they silently said good-bye to London.

He had been working in the office upstairs, going over his father's papers and books and wondering whether they should remove to Keighley Park immediately, when the restless feeling had struck. It seemed he couldn't go an hour or more, these past few days, without seeing or touching his wife.

He found her exactly where he'd suspected he might:

curled up in the great chair next to the fire in the library. With the instinct of the terminally curious, she had discovered his father's library almost instantly, and had found a book on God knows what to immerse herself in. Very likely there were gory pictures. Her hair gleamed softly in the firelight, copper and gold and bronze and chestnut and a dozen shades in between. She had made a half-hearted attempt to tie it back with a ribbon, but a good deal of it had escaped and was spiraling cheerfully about her cheeks and forehead.

She hadn't noticed him standing in the doorway of the library yet, and he contemplated indulging in the shocking extravagance of just walking away from her, perhaps even wandering outside to the club, just to prove to himself that she would be there when he returned, that she would always be there.

He was beside her before he even finished the thought. She glanced up startled, and then her eyes lit, the way they always did when they landed on him after he'd been away from her for a moment or two. He felt his heart squeeze in his chest. He hoped he would always put that light in her eyes.

He dropped to his knees next to her.

"Good book?"

"Excellent. Wonderful diagrams of the best way to treat a head wound. Would you like to see?"

"Thank you all the same, but no."

Rebecca laughed. "How is your arm?"

"Almost healed." He extended it and waved it about, by way of proof.

Smiling, she reached down to stroke his wavy forelock away from his eyes. "I rather like it," she pronounced.

"What's that, wee Becca?"

"Your forelock."

"Mmmm. Bit of a nuisance, it is."

"Makes you look like Byron."

"Oh, yes, and that's exactly how I want to look, just like Byron."

She laughed again. "Perhaps you should give poetry a go. You might wish to start with an ode to my nose or something along those lines. Give Edelston a little competition."

"The world has more than its share of poets and those that fancy themselves poets, as far as I'm concerned. I have my hands full, being a duke and being your husband. And furthermore, I would choose another of your body parts as the subject of my ode."

Rebecca laughed, and he captured her stroking hand and kissed the palm of it gently, so he could watch her eyes kindle.

"Connor?"

"Mmm?"

"Will it be all right? Being a duke?"

"Well, I must admit it's been amusing to shock the *ton* over and over. First my resurrection, and then my sudden marriage by special license. They can hardly wait to see what I'll do next. I've begun to feel a certain social responsibility, you see, to keep the *ton* supplied with gossip."

He was joking, but not entirely.

"Connor. Will it *really* be all right?"

He sighed. So she was not going to allow him to laugh it away.

"The tenants at Keighley Park, they need me," he said slowly. "And perhaps I can do some good in Parliament."

"You long to see America."

"And you long to take musket balls out of people and sew them up, neither of which is among the usual duties of a duchess. Will you be happy, wee Becca?"

"Now that I've delighted my mother beyond all reason by marrying a duke, and now that Lorelei will marry a colonel and be happy, I suppose I shall be."

Connor smiled.

"Perhaps we can find a way to do all we wish to do," she added softly.

"Perhaps," he replied, just as softly. "Perhaps we should hire Chester Sharp as our coachman and have him drive us to Keighley Park. Doubtless someone in the village there will need stitching up or a poultice or what have you. Something grisly enough to satisfy your habit of healing."

She smiled mischievously, and his heart squeezed again.

"I love you, Rebecca."

She slid down from her chair to kneel next to him and hooked her arms around his neck. "I love you, Connor. You needn't wonder about anything. We will be very happy, you know."

"I know."

He kissed her gently, but the kiss quickly turned fierce, as most of their kisses did these days, and the past and the future and everything but the feel of each other ceased to matter.

About the Author

JULIE ANNE LONG originally set out to be a rock star when she grew up, and she has the guitars and the questionable wardrobe stuffed in the back of her closet to prove it. But writing was her first love. When playing to indifferent crowds at midnight in dank clubs finally lost its, ahem, *charm*, Julie realized she could incorporate all the best things about being in a band—drama, passion and men with unruly hair—into novels, while also indulging her love of history and research. So she made the move from guitar to keyboard (the computer variety) and embarked on a considerably more civilized, if not much more peaceful, career as a novelist.

Julie lives in the San Francisco Bay Area with two big fat orange cats, brothers and rivals. (Little known fact: they issue you a cat the moment you become a romance novelist.) Visit her website at www.julieannelong.com, or write to her at Julie@julieannelong.com.

More

Julie Anne Long!

Please turn this page

for a preview of

TO LOVE A THIEF

available in

mass market April 2005.

Chapter One

❦

If Lily were pressed to descibe what she did every day on the streets of London, she would have called it an art. It required a delicate touch and exquisite timing, faultless vision and near-flawless judgment. Yes: an art, that's what it was.

A profoundly dangerous, entirely illegal, unfortunately necessary art.

Lily was good at it.

But she'd discovered recently that she . . . well, she actually *enjoyed* it.

She supposed she should feel more ashamed at this realization. Though it wasn't as if shame had abandoned her completely; even now, Lily could sense its weak, distant little voice *ahem*-ing away in a vain attempt to distract her from her objective. But it was the firm, cold voice of pragmatism Lily listened to as she scanned the men on Bond Street for likely quarry. Pragmatism, not shame, kept her and her younger sister fed and a roof, such as it was, over their heads.

She eyed the flow of men on the street expertly. Like a magpie, her gaze darted and swooped toward things that glittered about their persons, coins between fingers, gold buttons on coats, watch fobs. The cut and color and fabric of their coats and trousers, the polish of their boots, their facial expressions and the way they held themselves, their walking sticks, their companions—the choices men made about these things helped her make her own choices about them.

Her eyes were suddenly arrested by a flash of color. A young man, taller by several inches than most of the crowd, had lifted his hat to push his hand agitatedly through his hair. His hair wanted cutting—it was a bit longer than fashionable gentlemen typically wore theirs—and it was this fact that had enabled a breeze to lift it up into the sun. The sunlight had found the deep red hidden in the glossy black strands, and his hair briefly glowed like a fire burned almost all the way down to ashes.

The man clamped his hat back down on to this head a moment later, but it was too late; his hair had drawn Lily's attention, and she studied him a little more closely.

His shoulders were very broad atop a long, lean body, and he radiated a sort of restless, distracted energy; she saw it in the shifting of his feet in their fine boots and the gestures of his hands as he spoke to his companion, a man only a little shorter than he. His chestnut-colored wool coat was beautifully cut; it skimmed his contours as though he had been sewn into it. An expensive coat, clearly, courtesy of an expensive tailor.

Suddenly the young man thrust his hands into his trouser pockets and the expensive coat bunched out behind him, the pocket of it gaping invitingly. Lily's sharp eyes picked out the gleam of gold in that pocket. A watch, most likely. She considered what that gleam might mean to her and her sister. *Dinner for days. A new blanket for our bed. A bottle of gin for McBride.*

The man's companion was just as beautifully dressed, and he had the pale, open face of someone who has known much of comfort and little of worry or care. He was listening, with an expression of exaggerated patience, while his friend appeared to expound passionately about something. They were utterly absorbed in their conversation.

Perfect, Lily thought with satisfaction. The pair of them will be oblivious.

She had found her quarry.

"Don't go, Gideon, it's as simple as that. You know very well your uncle isn't *actually* dying. And you simply cannot afford to leave the ton again now that Jarvis seems to be making a run for Constance. Have you seen the—"

"Hullo, Cole! Oh, and hullo there, Kilmartin."

Gideon Cole and his friend Lawrence Mowbry, Lord Kilmartin, paused in their heated conversation to bow and smile politely as the marquis of such-and-such strolled by—Gideon had met him only recently at some soiree or other and had forgotten his name.

"Notice how I was a sort of afterthought?" Kilmartin's mouth lifted ruefully. "It's 'Hullo, Cole!' with great enthusiasm, and then, 'Oh, hullo Kilmartin.' And I *introduced* the two of you."

"Sorry, Laurie." But Gideon sounded more amused than apologetic. It was indefinable, really: a charm that was just shy of roguish, a face that was pleasing at first look and riveting on the second. Gideon, much like the sun, often eclipsed lesser lights simply by virtue of being. His friends eventually became accustomed to this. Some of them even eventually ceased minding. Laurie was of this variety, fortunately.

But being popular was often exhausting and distracting, Gideon thought; people forever *hullo*-ing you when you were trying to have an important conversation or read a paper in peace at White's. Given a choice, he thought irritably, he would much rather be rich than be popular. Being rich often seemed to negate any need to be popular.

And furthermore, if he were rich—and it was his own bloody fault he wasn't yet rich—he would very likely not be in his current, absurd predicament.

"As I was saying," Kilmartin continued, "you know

very well your uncle merely wants you to dance atten-
dance upon him again. And you cannot afford to leave
the ton now that Jarvis is making a run for Lady Constance Clary. Jarvis *already* has a title and a fortune."

"Thank you, Laurie," Gideon said through gritted
teeth. "I am painfully aware that Jarvis *already* has a
title and a fortune. But what if this time Uncle Edward
genuinely *is* dying? I *am* fond of the man."

No one knew for certain the precise nature of the
Lord Lindsey's condition, only that it seemed to re-
quire him to be bedridden and waited on hand and foot
at all hours of the day and night. It had also created
handsome dowries for each of the parish doctor's five
daughters. Uncle Edward, in fact, was the most jovial
sick person Gideon had ever seen. And because
Gideon stood to inherit the baronetcy, all the money,
and his extraordinary estate, Aster Park, Edward sent
for him every time he felt a twinge.

Gideon had received another of the notes this morning. "Come at once," it said. "Uncle Edward very ill."

Uncle Edward was forever feeling twinges.

"Allow me to paint a picture for you, Gideon." Kilmartin was growing exasperated. "Let's just say that
your uncle Edward *isn't* actually dying this time. But
once again you rush away from London to Aster Park,
and Constance at last makes up her fickle mind to
marry Jarvis instead of you because he showered attention upon her at Lady Gilchrist's ball and you did
not."

"That possible outcome is the *point* of this discussion, Laurie. You're supposed to be helping me decide what to do." Gideon was growing testy.

Kilmartin sighed heavily. "Look at it this way, old man. Even if Constance is taken off the marriage mart, you would still have your pick of young ladies."

This sentiment brought a smile to Gideon's face. And Gideon's smile, the slow, sultry curve of it, could crack the heart of any female between the ages of twelve and eighty.

"Yes," he acknowledged, without a trace of conceit. For it was true, and he hadn't the strength for false modesty today. "But I want Constance."

Kilmartin sighed. "Bloody hell, Gideon. You and your Master Plan. You could wed any number of wealthy females with the blessings of their mamas and papas, and you choose the most difficult of them all."

"Oh, come now, Laurie. How long have you known me? You should know by now that, no matter what, I *always* choose the most difficult of them all." Actually, it sometimes seemed the difficulty had chosen *Gideon,* but regardless, he'd grown to welcome challenge the way a racehorse welcomes room to run. He grinned to make his friend grin back. Kilmartin gave a short laugh and shook his head.

Gideon knew Kilmartin humored him. He was a good friend, Laurie was, but he was heir to a viscount; he would follow in the well-trodden path of centuries of his ancestors. Wealth and property and a triumphant marriage were merely stops along the way for him. But Gideon had come from nothing, and as a boy he had lost nearly everything. He'd decided long ago he would have all he wanted if it killed him: property, wealth, status, and a spectacular marriage. Whatever order they happened to occur in. And he rather hoped to do it all before the age of thirty.

This, in short, was his Master Plan.

Oh, he was so close, so tantalizingly close. And it was evidence of his stock in the ton that it was not considered a miracle that Gideon Cole, former soldier and current near-penniless barrister (though this bit was more or less a secret), was very nearly engaged to Lady Constance Clary. Glowing, golden, Constance, the uncontested jewel of the season. And Gideon had accomplished this the way he had accomplished everything else in his life: through a steady application of hard work and charm, propelled by his consuming ambition. And a goodly amount of secret regret and guilt.

And he supposed his looks didn't hurt matters, either.

Constance was astounding, really. She set fashions and ended them; she effortlessly won card games and archery contests and most other competitions simply because she wanted to very badly. She associated only with the finest people, dressed only in the finest clothing and rode only in the finest carriages. Constance, quite simply, would brook no rival. She in fact trounced potential rivals with the sheer vigor of her personality.

Gideon fully intended to marry Constance. He *needed* to marry Constance and her lovely large fortune. She represented the very pinnacle of his Master Plan.

Gideon was fond enough of her. And Constance seemed fond of him, as well. Even her father, Marquis Shawcross, was fond of him; he was convinced Gideon Cole would enjoy a bright political future, and was only too happy to assist Gideon along the way. Such were the fruits of Gideon's hard work and charm to date.

But Gideon sometimes suspected that in place of a heart Constance possessed a sort of scale, and on that scale his looks and charm and popularity were evenly offset by his lack of title and fortune. He could hardly blame her, really; Constance was a beauty, but his own motives for wooing her were not precisely rooted in passion.

"Laurie, I have very nearly enough saved to purchase a townhouse on Grosvenor Square. Perhaps that will help to sway her."

"Well, you'd best come up with *something* to sway her. Have you seen the betting books at White's?"

Gideon felt a little prickle of foreboding. "Tell me."

"There are now wagers—not insignificant sums—on the possibility that Lord Jarvis will be engaged to Constance Clary before the end of the season."

Bloody hell. "All the wagers used to be about me."

Kilmartin nodded sympathetically. "Used to be."

Gideon lifted his hat again and pushed his fingers agitatedly through his hair, and then clamped it back down over his head.

"Just do it, Gideon. Propose," Kilmartin urged.

"I can't, Laurie." Gideon's voice was taut with frustration. "Not until I'm certain her answer will be yes."

In truth, Gideon had too much pride to risk a sweetly regretful rejection. Not to mention having to withstand the aftermath of such a rejection. The ton would offer soft condolences to him, and then savor the news like candied fruit behind his back. It was simply the way of their world. *He's just a barrister,* they would mutter half in sympathy, half in relish. *Why on earth would she say yes?*

Kilmartin sighed again. "Well, isn't Constance off to visit her cousins in the country soon? Perhaps you can persuade your uncle to die *then*. And by the time she returns for the Braxton Ball, she will find you a baron and the master of Aster Park."

In spite of himself, Gideon laughed. "Uncle Edward would never be so obliging. He would—"

Gideon could not have told anyone what made him spin around at just that moment. Perhaps it was the same instinct that had enabled him to dodge musket balls at Waterloo and come home with limbs and senses intact.

But spin he did.

And that's how he saw the girl just as she was dipping her slim white hand into his coat pocket.

Gideon seized her wrist. Frozen in shock, breathing hard, they glared at each other.

The impressions came at him swiftly. Her wrist, thin as a child's, her skin shockingly silky, her pulse speeding with terror beneath his thumb. A high pale forehead, luminous in the afternoon sun, a pink mouth nearly the shape of a heart, a pair of extraordinary aquamarine eyes ablaze with panic and outrage. And freckles, a collection of tiny asymmetrical splashes of gold, across her nose. Almost unconsciously, he began to count them. One, two, three, four—

"Oof!"

Gideon dropped to his knees, gagging for breath. While he had been counting her freckles, her knee had come up between his legs with brutal accuracy.

And she was gone, absorbed into the crowd as though she had never been anything more than a shadow.

THE EDITOR'S DIARY

Dear Reader,

Like spin-the-bottle, love can be a complete game of chance. So pucker up—you never know when the bottle will stop and your Prince Charming will reveal himself. Just ask Analise Abbott and Rebecca Tremaine in our two Warner Forever titles this August.

Karen Robards raves "**Susan Crandall** is an up-and-coming star". Prepare to be dazzled for her latest, **MAGNOLIA SKY**, is going to sweep you off your feet. Luke Boudreau has been agonizing for five months over what to say to the mother of his best army buddy Calvin Abbott. After all, how do you express your regret and sorrow that someone died while saving your life? Now, finally at the door of Calvin's Mississippi home, the moment is upon him. Praying to forgive himself for surviving and find a moment's peace, Luke never expected the truth to explode like a bomb. In all the time they were together in the service, Calvin never even hinted that he was married. He certainly didn't behave that way either. Yet Analise Abbott stands before him like an angel, her green eyes full of life, her sweet smile full of warmth and the promise of something more. Torn between loyalty and temptation, can Luke open himself up to love with Analise?

Journeying from the sweet aroma of magnolia in Mississippi to the hint of desperation as a woman bolts from her wedding, we present **Julie Anne Long's THE RUNAWAY DUKE**. Mary Balogh calls this "a delightful debut novel—brimful of wit, action, passion, and romance" and she couldn't be more right. Get comfy—you're never going to want this to end. Rebecca Tremaine isn't the genteel lady her mother dreamt she'd be. She's wretched at embroidery and pitiful at the pianoforte. But when she's caught in a compromising position with a dandy, her parents have had enough. Arranging a hasty marriage, they never suspected she'd find an ally to thwart their plan. Connor Riordan has no idea how this happened. His life as a groom on the Tremaine estate was peaceful and isolated—just what this Duke of Dunbrooke "killed" in action at Waterloo needs to keep his cover. But a true gentleman never turns away a damsel in distress. As Rebecca and Connor race through the countryside, escaping Rebecca's parents, her fiancé and the highwaymen out to get them, can love catch them?

To find out more about Warner Forever, these August titles, and the author, visit us at www.warnerforever.com.

With warmest wishes,

Karen Kosztolnyik

Karen Kosztolnyik, Senior Editor

P.S. September is right around the corner, but don't put away those tank tops yet. Indian summer is about to begin with these two hot reasons to keep your A.C. plugged in: **Sue-Ellen Welfonder** pens a sensual Scottish medieval about an aloof warrior who must marry for money but never expected to lose his heart to his spirited young bride and her searing kisses in **WEDDING FOR A KNIGHT**; and **Toni Blake** delivers the sexy and heartwarming erotic romance about a man determined to get revenge, the woman he falls in love with, and her diary—his weapon of choice—in **THE RED DIARY**.

Look for
RULES OF ENGAGEMENT

by Kathryn Caskie
(0-446-61423-8)

When two elderly aunts mistakenly use the
military strategy handbook Rules of Engagement
to secure their headstrong niece a fiancé, London's
ballrooms become battlefields in a war of wits,
matchmaking, and mayhem.

"Pamela Britton is well on her way to stardom."
—*Romantic Times BOOKclub Magazine*

Don't miss these unforgettable
romances from Pamela Britton.

Seduced
0-446-61129-8

~

Tempted
0-446-61130-1

~

Scandal
0-446-61131-X